CHRISTMAS AT TUPPENNY CORNER

by

Katie Flynn

Magna Large Print Books
Leicestershire

British Libarary Cataloguing in Publication Data.

A catalogue record of this book is
available from the British Library

ISBN   978-0-7505-4755-0

First published in Great Britain by Century in 2018, part of the
Random House Group

Published in Large Print 2019 by arrangement with
Random House Group Ltd.

Magna Large Print is an imprint of Library Magna Books Ltd.

Printed and bound in Great Britain by
T. J. (International) Ltd., Padstow, Cornwall, PL28 8RW

CHRISTMAS AT
TUPPENNY CORNER

Prologue

Rosie O'Leary sat on the side of the towpath, her bare feet dangling just above the surface of the canal whilst her horse Daisy grazed peacefully beside her. Watching the sun sparkling on the water, Rosie knew that this should be one of the happiest days of her life, but try though she might she could not get into the spirit of the occasion. In an hour her mother — Maggie — would be marrying her fiancé Ken Donahue, and Rosie's life would start afresh, or at least Rosie hoped that that was the way things would pan out. But in her heart she knew that the likelihood was that nothing would change for the better. Things would continue the way they were, or, if she were really unlucky, get even worse.

Rosie's father, Jack O'Leary, had died when she had been little more than a toddler, leaving Maggie to take over his role as the *Wild Swan*'s Number One — the bargee equivalent to a ship's captain — as well as single-handedly raising their daughter on the Leeds and Liverpool Canal. Ever since that fateful day, Maggie had forbidden anyone to discuss the circumstances surrounding her husband's death, only ever referring to it as 'that day' or 'what happened'. Rosie herself had not known the events of her father's untimely demise until her mother accidentally blurted it out one day as they queued to go through one of the many locks on the canal.

1

Neville Partington, the old lock keeper, had come out of his cottage apologising profusely to the assembled bargees for his tardiness. 'Sorry, folks, but when nature calls . . . ' he said as he inserted the key into the slot. He had started the arduous task of winding the great gates open when he stopped in mid-turn, his face contorted as he yelped in pain.

'Bloody hell — me back. Someone help me — it's gone again. I can't move!'

Rosie, who had been combing Daisy's mane as they stood waiting, heard the old man's cries and without hesitation left Daisy and ran along the side of the lock, calling out reassuringly as she approached, 'Don't worry Mr Partington, I'll give you a hand — ' She was interrupted by a furious shriek.

'Rosie O'Leary! You stop where you are this minute, do you hear? How *dare* you run off like that? You know how dangerous locks are, and yet there's you runnin' around like a headless chicken, with no thought for anyone other than yourself.'

Rosie stopped short of Neville, her face crimson with embarrassment, as the other bargees craned their necks in an effort to see the cause of all the commotion. Doubled up in agony and unable to move, Neville winced in pain as he dismissed Rosie. 'Go back to your mam, queen. I'll be all right — one of the other . . . ' He broke off as someone came up behind Rosie. 'Oh, Tim, thank goodness. Give us a hand, there's a good lad.'

Tim Bradley, who worked aboard the *Sally Anne* with his parents, cast Rosie a sympathetic glance. 'You'd best go, before your mam blows her lid.'

Rosie, feeling the hot tears of humiliation trickle down her blazing cheeks, lowered her head to hide her embarrassment as she turned on her heel and ran back down the path towards her mother, who stood tapping her toe impatiently, a scowl etched on her face. Apologising, Rosie stepped on board the *Wild Swan*, but not before Maggie's hand had struck the back of her head. 'How many times do I have to remind you that canals are dangerous places; too dangerous for a young chit of a girl like you? I tell you now, Rosie O'Leary, if I could manage without you . . .'

Rosie, eager to protest her innocence, turned. 'I was only trying to help,' she mumbled.

Folding her arms, Maggie shook her head. 'And a great help you'd be to me if you got crushed to death by a lock gate like your father. He ran same as you when . . .' Her voice trailed off.

Without thinking, and louder than she intended Rosie muttered under her breath, 'Probably to get away from you.'

Even though the comment had not been intended for Maggie's ears she heard it all the same, and this time the slap connected with Rosie's hot cheek. As her hand flew to her face, Rosie opened her mouth to apologise, to take back the words that had been spoken without thought, but it was too late. Fists clenched to her sides, shoulders shaking in anger, Maggie bawled, 'How *dare* you? You ungrateful little bitch! Get out of my sight, and don't come back until I tell you.'

Rosie was aware of several onlookers as she ran into the main cabin and flung herself on to her bed, where she buried her face in her pillow in an attempt to drown out her sobs. Why did her mother persist in treating her like some kind of idiotic, clumsy, useless child, who knew little and was capable of even less? She was fifteen years old, and in all the time she had worked the canals she had never once so much as tripped over a pebble, let alone fallen into the water. Clenching her fists, she thumped her mattress at the unjustness of it all. She knew herself to be above average in reading and sums, especially compared to the other youngsters who lived on the canals. She supposed it was fortunate that she was naturally bright; she just wished her mother would recognise that fact instead of treating her like a simpleton who could not be trusted to leave the barge for fear that she would get into trouble through her own naivety.

Rosie remembered how she had once been foolish enough to ask Maggie if she might be allowed to join Tim Bradley and some of his mates on an expedition into the city of Liverpool. 'I know you better'n you know yerself,' Maggie had said, wagging a reproving finger. 'You'd trip over your own feet you would, and if I were stupid enough to give you any money you'd likely come back with a handful of beans, like that Jack in the Beanstalk.'

Rosie had heard the giggles from the assembled youngsters and rather than face them she had gone to Daisy and hidden her face in the mare's thick fluffy winter coat.

If anyone else's mother behaved the way Maggie did, Rosie would have put it down to being overprotective, or concern for their child's welfare; but not when it came to Maggie. Her mother cared only for the running of the *Wild Swan* and believed her daughter to be incapable of functioning without guidance; and with no one to tell her otherwise Rosie would have believed her mother's words had it not been for the fact that Maggie trusted her to look after Daisy.

The large dapple mare stood at nearly sixteen hands high, and was quite capable of causing a lot of damage if not handled properly. But under Rosie's care Daisy was a gentle giant who obeyed her mistress's every command, and never fell lame or ill through neglect.

If I'm that useless, why on earth am I allowed to look after an animal who could quite easily trample me into the ground, throw me from her back, or kick me senseless when I pick out her hooves? If I can't be trusted to put one foot in front of the other without falling into the canal, how can I be placed in charge of someone as important as Daisy? After all, without her the *Wild Swan* would be unable to move, Rosie thought bitterly now, feeling tears of frustration starting to trickle down her cheeks.

Hearing the sound of approaching footsteps, she looked up from the canal surface and saw her mother in an ivory-coloured two-piece suit, her hair curled into waves around her face. It should have been a picture of beauty, but instead Maggie's brow was furrowed in an angry frown. 'Rosie O'Leary, have you not put that bloomin' beast back in her field yet? Stop day-dreaming and get away from the side of the canal. Last thing I need is to start off my new life one crew member down — although I dare say Ken'll make up for more than ten of you. And for goodness' sakes, stop your snivelling! This is meant to be a happy occasion, and I'll not have you ruining everyone's pleasure by blubbing like a spoiled brat.'

Getting to her feet, Rosie apologised resignedly to her mother and began to lead Daisy up the towpath towards the field where she would be grazing overnight. Running her fingers through the mare's mane she whispered, 'You don't think I'm useless, do you? As far as you're concerned I'm your friend, the one who keeps you safe and happy. Gawd only knows, if I can look after you I can be trusted to sit on a towpath.' Plodding along the path, Daisy half closed her eyes under Rosie's gentle caress. 'When me mam and Ken announced their intention to wed, I did hope that mebbe Ken could make me mam see that I'm not as stupid as she believes, but now I'm worried she might persuade *him* to think I'm as thick as she does. I don't think I could bear it if there were two people on board who treated me like a child.' Her bottom lip began to tremble as she stroked the silky hair on Daisy's neck. 'Thank goodness for you, Daisy O'Leary. You're the only one round here who sees me for who I am. Without you I don't think I'd have anyone on my side. I'd like to think that if my father'd still been alive he'd have stuck up for me, only I'll never know, will I, because I'm not allowed to ask any questions, not even supposed to speak his name . . . '

Reaching the gate to the meadow, Rosie pulled it open, led Daisy through and took the halter from round her head. Knowing the routine, Daisy turned to face her and awaited the titbit that was due. Rosie obligingly produced half a carrot and handed it over. As the large mare crunched the treat down she continued, 'I think it's because she knows he was a much better person than she is, kinder, more understanding and caring. Not cold and judgemental like her. I bet if he were alive he wouldn't make me call him Jack. He'd want me to call him Dad, not like Maggie, who insists on Maggie or even Number One — she thinks it ensures the tight running of the barge. I *wish* he was still alive, I *wish* she was more like him.'

Maggie's voice called out impatiently. 'Rosie! For goodness' sakes get a move on, and leave that great lump be!' She placed her hands on her hips and stamped her foot angrily. 'I won't tell you again. Get down here *now*.'

Rosie kissed Daisy's velvety muzzle. 'At least I'll always have you. That's summat they can never take away from me.' Making her way down to the towpath, trying to imagine the look on her mother's face if Daisy were ever to fall lame. She'd soon realise how useful we both were, she thought decidedly. I'd like to see her and Ken try to tow a big old barge like the *Wild Swan* without our help. Smiling at the very thought of it, Rosie joined her mother, and the pair of them made their way to the church.

1

Summer 1939

Rosie did not know what had interrupted her sleep. Annoyed at the disturbance, she fumbled for her bed-covers, but try as she might it seemed the blankets were beyond her reach. Sitting up, she realised that instead of being in her cosy little bed aboard the *Wild Swan* she actually appeared to have been lying in what smelt and felt like a pile of hay. Puzzled, Rosie peered into the gloom, trying to make sense of the situation, while the memories of the previous day came flooding back.

Early that morning, her mother and her new husband had been discussing the possibility of giving up their rented barge, the *Wild Swan*, in favour of one with an engine.

'It'd make sense all round,' Ken had explained to Maggie. 'Everybody's changing over nowadays. You know as well as I do that a mechanised barge can run twenty-four hours a day if need be, not like a horse that needs to be rested, fed, watered and shod, not to mention if the bugger goes lame. It'd be easier on us, too . . . '

Rosie knew that eavesdropping was wrong, but she could not help herself. If they got a mechanised barge then it would mean that Daisy would no longer be needed.

Fearing that she was going to lose her only friend, she had spoken out, causing her mother and Ken to jump six inches.

'You can't get rid of Daisy,' she had said, her voice high with emotion. 'Like Ken said, everybody's changing over to engine power, so who'll want Daisy, and what will happen to her?'

Maggie had glowered at her daughter as she took a step in Rosie's direction. 'Where the devil did you spring from? You know better than to go sneakin' up on folk, and how dare you listen to a private conversation! That's eavesdroppin', that is . . . '

Pulling Maggie back, Ken had tried to defuse the situation. 'I'm sure she didn't mean to eavesdrop. And besides, the girl's gorra point. She's rare fond of that horse, and it's only natural she should be concerned as to where the beast ends up . . . '

Maggie had glanced sideways at Ken; then, holding up her hands, she had addressed her daughter. 'Sorry. You just startled me is all . . . ' and in a rare moment of softness she had placed an arm round Rosie's shoulders. 'If we do change over — and nowt's been confirmed yet — we'll find Daisy a good home, probably on one of the farms next to the canal. Farmers are always after a good reliable horse to pull the plough, and if you're lucky you should be able to see her two or three times a month. But you must realise, Rosie, that with Ken aboard as well as myself and you, it makes good sense to modernise.' The explanation would have been satisfactory had Maggie not added: 'So quit your snivelling and start thinking of others beside yourself.'

Rosie had thought the accusation of snivelling unfair, yet typical of her mother, who never seemed to be able to make pleasant conversation with her daughter without adding a snide remark at some point. Rosie would have liked to argue Daisy's case further, but found it difficult because she knew that her mother and Ken were right about one thing: all the bargees, except for some of the old folk, were converting to engine power. It was favoured when it came to delivering shipments as the barges were able to go faster, further and with fewer stops, which of course was more efficient. As a result, the *Wild Swan* and barges like her were getting less work.

Later that day they had moored at Tuppenny Corner — so called because it led to Tuppenny Lane, which was the shortcut to the small town of Bishopswood — and after a supper of cheese and pickles Rosie had taken Daisy to the field that they rented from the Panks so she could graze there overnight. On her return, she had bidden Maggie and Ken goodnight before snuggling into her bed in the tiny cabin — more like a storage cupboard than a place to sleep, she thought — to which she had been consigned since her mother's marriage. She had tried to rid her mind of thoughts of losing Daisy, but this had proved impossible, and in a rare moment of defiance — for Maggie had strictly forbidden her daughter to go ashore after dark — she had pushed her bed sheets to one side and tiptoed out of the small cabin. Stepping quietly on to the towpath, she had walked towards the front of the barge, smiling to herself as she heard the

11

mingled snores coming from the main cabin, indicating that both her mother and Ken were fast asleep.

It was late summer and the towpath was lit by the large round silver moon which hung low in the ink-dark sky, its bright reflection shining on the surface of the canal. On warm nights like this, when the air was still and all the bargees were tucked up in their beds fast asleep, Rosie would often sit on the deck of the *Wild Swan*, listening to the symphony of nightlife that surrounded her. Owls hooting their presence while badgers shuffled their way through the copses and, occasionally, a brown trout broke the surface of the canal with a small plopping noise, all of them unaware of their secret audience.

Thankful that the moon was shining so brightly, Rosie had walked the short distance along the towpath to Daisy's field. As she climbed the gate a soft nicker of welcome had come from the big mare, causing Rosie's heart to give a small leap of joy. 'Were you waiting for me, you daft old thing?' she had said as Daisy lumbered forward, her outstretched nose nuzzling hopefully at Rosie's pockets. Knowing better than to come unprepared, Rosie had fished out a couple of sugar lumps, and as the mare crunched them down she had walked towards the old shelter in the corner of the field, calling as she went, 'Come with me and I'll run a comb through your mane and get some of those knots out.'

In the shelter, Rosie had started the lengthy task of combing Daisy's long thick mane, taking extra care to remove any knots as gently as she could, while telling the big mare all about Ken and Maggie's plans for a mechanised barge. She assured her friend that if that were to happen, they would find Daisy a good home, with caring owners and plenty of grazing. At last, standing back to admire her work, Rosie had reached forward and run her fingers freely through the untangled mane. Pleased with her efforts, she had returned the comb to the shelf — which was really part of a supporting beam — only to turn back and see that Daisy had sunk to her knees and started rolling energetically, making sure that she rubbed her neck and mane into the soft earth of the floor so that they became well and truly coated in the thick loose dirt. Rosie had given a groan of dismay as she walked back to the mare, who was now settling down next to a large pile of last year's hay. Resignedly, she had plumped up the hay and lain down next to her friend. She knew it was a waste of time to reprimand Daisy for mucking up her mane — all horses preferred to be dirty — and had started to tell her about the new life she might be leading when a thought occurred to her. Perhaps the mare would prefer being on a farm where she would have the companionship of her own kind. Maybe being a canal horse was not so marvellous after all. She had never considered it before, but Daisy's life was probably as lonely as her own, for the mare never had company of other horses. Rosie had felt a pang of guilt. She had always turned to Daisy to grumble about how she had no real pals, apart from Tim

Bradley, who, before Ken had joined the *Wild Swan*, had helped Rosie and Maggie when their cargo was too much for them to manage alone. Now she realised that Daisy, too, had been living a life of solitude, and much as Rosie hated the idea of losing her friend she began to think that her reasons for wanting to keep Daisy were selfish.

She had smoothed her hand over her companion's newly dirty neck. She would miss Daisy, of course she would, but now that Ken had moved on to the *Wild Swan*, maybe her mother would allow her more freedom to make some other friends.

Up until now Maggie had always made sure that when Rosie's chores aboard the barge were complete the girl would be assigned some other task to do, whether it be fetching produce from the local shop or earning a couple of pennies by helping on the farms. Intentionally or not, she had given her daughter little opportunity to get to know the other youngsters on the canal. Rosie chewed her lip thoughtfully. Perhaps if she suggested that her mother and Ken might like to spend some quiet time together they would jump at the chance, leaving Rosie free to make some real friends of her own.

Cuddled in the hay in the peace and quiet of the shelter, Rosie was aware that her head had begun to feel heavy. Telling herself that she would only rest her eyes for a moment or two, she placed her hand on Daisy's side and listened to the sound of the mare's gentle breathing as she slept. Before long, she too had drifted off to sleep.

Now, Rosie chastised herself for doing so. As she sat upright next to Daisy, she knew that she should get back to the *Wild Swan* before she was missed. It was still dark outside, and she was relieved that she had woken before Ken and Maggie were likely to stir. The mere thought of her mother's reaction to finding her daughter missing was more than she dared contemplate. She was halfway to her feet when the sound of voices from outside stopped her in her tracks. What if Ken or Maggie had woken prematurely and come looking for her? Her heart plummeted. She strained to see if she could pick out their tones in the mixture of voices, and gave a sigh of relief when she realised that, from what she could hear, neither of them were present. Continuing to listen intently, she tried to make out the gist of the conversation.

'So, what do you think?' It was a young voice, not that of a child, yet not quite grown up either; he sounded unsure of himself, Rosie thought. Someone from one of the barges? It had to be at this hour. No one in their senses would leave their warm and comfortable bed in the village to come out here for a chat in the middle of the night. Yet Rosie did not recognise the voice. There was something odd about the way he sounded, though she could not think what it was, and while she was still wondering another male voice cut in. This was a deep gruff tone; the sort that was used to giving commands and having them obeyed.

'Aye, lad, I'll give you that; you've chosen well. It ain't too far from the canal, and in daylight the view must take in just about everything we need. But more important, no one can see us all the way up here, tucked up out of sight in this crumblin' old . . . what did you call it?'

The young, hesitant voice said, 'Stable. Well, it was once, but the door's fell off so it's more of a shelter nowadays. Farmer Pank owns the field, but only the bargees use it — they come up here to graze the horses and tack them up — so no fear of any snoopers . . . '

Rosie frowned. There it was again. Something was odd about the way the man spoke. As she tried to think what it was, the older man broke in impatiently. 'You say only the bargees use this field, but I thought that all the barges were engine-run nowadays. You tellin' me there's still some using horses?'

'A few of the old timers still got horses, but most of them graze 'em by the towpath. As far as I know there's only the *Wild Swan* what still uses this field, though from what I've 'eard they'll be gettin' rid of theirs soon an' all.'

Rosie was baffled. Whoever this was knew not only the *Wild Swan* but their plans to sell Daisy, which must mean that he knew either Ken or Maggie, or both. Rosie concentrated as she tried to place the speaker, but the gruffer voice cut in once more. 'That's good. We don't want people walkin' round willy-nilly, 'cos when war comes — '

'You mean *if* war comes. There's no guarantee . . . ' a third, grumpy voice cut in.

There was a grumble of protest, which apparently amused another member of the party

16

who gave a short bark of laughter. 'It isn't 'if', it's 'when'. Maybe not this year, but come it will, and when it does we shall be ready.'

There was a murmur of agreement.

Rosie leaned in further. Judging by the way they were talking it was as if they would welcome war! She did not know a lot about men, but in her understanding they were a far more bloodthirsty lot than women. Craning her neck, she was trying to see if she could take a sneaky peek at any of the speakers when a sharp voice caused her to freeze.

'What was that? I thought you said no one was up here?'

There was a stirring among the group and Rosie was sure she was about to be discovered when another man gave an impatient snort. 'If you're goin' to jump at every shadow you won't be much use to us,' he sneered. 'He told you this place is used by the bargees; I seen the *Wild Swan* down by the towpath so I reckon that big ol' mare o' theirs is probably in there.'

To Rosie's horror, and before she could duck down completely out of sight, one of the men produced a lamp, which he held aloft in the doorway, causing not only his face to be illuminated but also the contents of the shelter. Rosie, who had been curled up behind Daisy when she fell asleep, held her breath as she waited to be revealed, and could not believe her luck when the lamp was lowered and the man continued, 'There, see? Just that big ol' mare. Satisfied?'

Slowly, Rosie breathed out. She had been able

to see the face of the man holding the lamp aloft quite clearly; broad across the cheekbones, with piercing blue eyes set beneath a thatch of thick, black hair and a black beard speckled with lines of grey. She had not been able to see his clothing, but his expression resembled that of a Number One, although she could not recall ever seeing him before. In fact, she could not imagine which of the boats anchored below could support such an authoritative person without her knowledge. As she carefully lay back down, Rosie continued to listen and speculated that there were probably four or five men on the other side of the thin wooden partition. Having spent her lifetime on the canals, she thought she had encountered nearly every single person amongst the motley collection of barges, yet she could not put a name or a face to any of these.

As the men continued to talk, they dropped their voices once more. Despite not wanting to be accused of eavesdropping a second time in less than twenty-four hours, Rosie found herself straining to hear what else was being discussed. Tim had once said that if you closed your eyes your hearing got better, so Rosie tried it. Promising herself that she would not fall asleep this time, she concentrated on what was being said.

But the small snippets of conversation that she did manage to hear did not make sense to her, and despite her best intentions she found herself drifting into a strange dream of drunken nuns floating out of the sky, carrying treasures and trinkets that were hidden down their jackboots.

When Rosie next awoke, bright sunshine was pouring through the slats of the shelter. Scolding herself for being silly enough to fall asleep in the wrong place twice, she ran through the dew-wet grass, calling a greeting to Daisy who was now grazing peacefully under the boughs of a large oak tree. When she reached the gate, she swung herself over the top and continued to run until she reached the *Wild Swan*. She gingerly trod the path towards the barge and climbing cautiously aboard she found, much to her relief, that she could still hear the gentle snores coming from the main cabin. Telling herself how lucky she was to have reached the barge before Ken and Maggie woke up, Rosie hurriedly began her tasks as she did every day, by making a cup of tea for the newlyweds. She stood the stove on the towpath, pumped up the primus, and lit it, then placed the tin kettle on the ring, taking care not to spill a drop of the clean water with which she had filled it the previous evening.

Feeling secure in the knowledge that her disappearance had gone undiscovered, Rosie turned her thoughts to the previous night. Something had happened, something weird and quite out of the ordinary. She sat down on a small three-legged stool beside the stove and waited for the kettle to boil, and let her memories of the previous night take over.

She remembered going to tell Daisy her woes, that was real enough, but then she had fallen asleep. Rosie frowned. *Had* she dreamed it? It was perfectly possible, and yet . . . the kettle hopped on the primus and Rosie began to make the tea. She usually had a cup herself, but this morning her thoughts had been so full of the odd conversation that she had filled only two of the tin mugs before recalling that she, too, was thirsty. She stirred sugar into the two mugs and picked them up, then hesitated. She couldn't very well tell Maggie that she had abandoned the boat while her mother and Ken slept because she was not supposed to set foot off the *Wild Swan* once darkness came. Anyway, what would she tell them? That a group of men *may* have been having a meeting outside Daisy's shelter? There was no law against it, and her mother would say it was Rosie who was in the wrong, first for sneaking off and second for listening to a private conversation, something which she had already been reprimanded for the previous day. Besides, she had not heard much, after all, and it might have been a dream; no, telling Maggie would simply bring her mother's wrath down upon her head. Sighing, she put the mugs down on the decking, and knocked perfunctorily on the cabin doors before swinging them open and picking up the mugs once more. Maggie and Ken were already sitting up, hands held out to receive their drinks, and at that moment Rosie knew that she had made the right decision. Her mother would probably use her story as an excuse to get rid of Daisy as soon as possible, so that Rosie would have no reason to go wandering off again. So she simply smiled, said 'Good morning', and handed over the mugs and left, closing the doors behind her.

It occurred to Rosie that she might ask Tim Bradley whether there was a Number One with a short, thick black beard and sharp blue eyes among the people on the boats anchored nearby, then chided herself with an inward laugh. Even if it had not been a dream, the men had done nothing wrong by gathering for a private conversation. If anyone was in the wrong, it was her for not announcing her presence. Instead, she had listened like some sort of spy. That's *if* she hadn't dreamed up the whole episode, which was quite probable. Rosie shook her head. Best forget it ever happened and go about her tasks as she did every day.

After they had breakfasted, the crew of the *Wild Swan* set off for Liverpool. When they arrived, they moored by the canal offices, where Ken would be told what their next cargo was before it was loaded up. Before he had joined the *Wild Swan*, it was always Maggie who had negotiated the fees for cargo, but Ken was far better at negotiating than she was, so it was he who now handled the paperwork and payments for their various deliveries, while Maggie and Rosie cleaned down, making sure that every single item, including the barge itself, was scrubbed until it sparkled, ready for their new load, whether it be cotton or coal.

When Ken returned he reported that their next cargo was going to be sugar from the Tate and Lyle factory. With the workers standing by ready to load, Ken stored the money and papers in the log book before they started the heavy task. Rosie listened whilst the men passed the sacks to each other with apparent ease as they transferred the sugar from the loading area into the hold of the *Wild Swan*. They were chatting excitedly about horse racing, for they were anxious to get out to Aintree and put their money on what somebody had described as a dead cert.

'It'll be getting out there in time that's the problem, not choosing which horse to back. I reckon we should get a runner to place our bets.'

Someone laughed. 'We'll have to choose a feller who we trust to give us our winnings; my nephew'd do it, but I can't get word to 'im before we've finished this lot,' he said, heaving a sack on to his shoulder. 'So come on, youse lot, get shiftin' if you want to see your fancy beat the field.'

Rosie could not stop her thoughts straying back to the previous evening. She scolded herself. Why on earth was she so interested in a few bargees who'd wandered up to Daisy's field? She could not explain how, but to her mind they had been acting suspiciously, and not just because they had been meeting in the dead of night by what they had believed to be an abandoned shelter. It was more than that. But perhaps she was wrong, and anyone else would say she was being silly.

A voice called out, bringing Rosie back to the present. 'That's it, Tim, there's no more to come.'

Upon hearing Tim's name Rosie looked round to see where her friend was, only to realise that the worker was talking to someone else, but all the same she made a lightning decision. If she were to confide in anyone, it would be Tim Bradley. Out of all the canal folk it was Tim whom Rosie trusted the most. It was Tim who had persuaded Maggie to let him teach Rosie to swim in the Scaldy when she had been much younger.

'I promise you, Mrs O, I'll have her back home and safe before you can say knife, but my mam has allus insisted us kids learn to swim, livin' on the canals an' all. It only takes one slip — '

He had got no further, as Maggie had reached a decision. 'You make sure no harm comes to her, Tim Bradley, or it'll be you I hold responsible.' Her face had been set in a warning grimace and as she spoke she had been wagging her finger at him. 'I agree with your ma, a kid should be able to swim — whether they live on the canals or not — but I'm not sure I'm happy for the two of you to go off on your own . . . '

Tim had shrugged. 'You're more than welcome to come too if you want, only you know what the kids are like . . . '

Maggie had shaken her head dismissively. She was not a natural mother by any means, and she found children to be a nuisance, always getting in the way of work, or being infuriatingly cheeky or rude. She would much rather Tim took Rosie off for an hour by herself than have to tolerate a bunch of unsupervised, and to her mind uncivilised, children.

Rosie had fond memories of that day, the one and only time she had been allowed to stray from the barge without her mother. Tim had assured

Maggie that Rosie would be fine in her vest and pants, which was more than some of the children wore to go swimming in the Scaldy, and before Rosie knew it she was tentatively dipping a toe into the warm waters which were pumped out from the sugar factory, while Tim began to demonstrate the doggy paddle. He had been a good teacher and Rosie had made an excellent pupil, learning how to keep afloat in just an hour. Tim had admired her abilities, causing her cheeks to blush pink under such unfamiliar praise. Maggie had been anxiously awaiting their return, and even though her face was stern, Rosie knew that her mother was grateful for Tim's attention. After that Rosie looked forward to loading up days, because once Tim had finished his work aboard the *Sally Anne* he would come over and ask if they needed a hand.

Rosie remembered one particular time when they had been loading some crates of strawberry jam, which were heavy yet fragile, so one had to be particularly careful when handling them. Tim had strolled along the towpath towards the *Wild Swan*, sweeping his corn-coloured hair back as it flopped over his hazel eyes and whistling a soft tune. Rosie's heart had given a hopeful leap, as she was sure he must be on his way to help. 'Dad says you're loading Robertson's jam, so I've come to see if I can give you a hand,' Tim had said, his white teeth gleaming against his deeply tanned skin.

Rosie had started to nod eagerly, and was about to speak when Maggie cut across her. 'Nearly done, thanks all the same,' she had said, as she guided a large crate down on to the barge.

Tim had shrugged. 'Ah well, the *Sally Anne's* not moving off for another hour or so, so I may as well give a hand as I'm here.' And as he stepped aboard the *Wild Swan* he had winked at Rosie, who felt a blush invade her neck as she looked up into his handsome, tanned face.

Tim's parents and grandparents were familiar figures on the Leeds and Liverpool Canal and Rosie had known the Bradleys for as long as she could remember. They were a kind, hard-working family, and Tim was regarded as quite the catch amongst the other bargee girls whom Rosie had often seen gathered in small giggling groups, admiring him as he strolled casually along the towpath.

One time, Maggie had watched the girls as well, scornfully making loud tutting noises as she observed them tossing their hair and waving at Tim. 'Little tarts!' she had sneered nastily. 'No shame whatsoever, and where are their mothers, that's what I'd like to know.' She had wagged her finger at Rosie. 'Don't ever let me catch you fawning over a boy like that. Bloomin' disgraceful. They're actin' like a bunch of alley cats if you ask me.'

Rosie had sighed. She wouldn't dream of fawning over any boy, let alone someone as popular as Tim. She knew that she was not attractive; what with her underdeveloped figure and short dark hair she had been mistaken for a boy on more than one occasion. She thought of herself as a plain Jane, with a nose too big for her face. Her mother, on the other hand, was a real beauty, with thick, curly raven hair, large sky-blue eyes and plump rosy lips. Rosie knew the story about the ugly duckling turning into a beautiful swan and could only hope that one day a similar miracle would happen to her. Having no memory of her father, who had died when she had been barely four years old, Rosie could not say whether she resembled him more than her mother, for even though she had seen an old wedding photograph of her parents it had been badly faded, and her father's features were all but lost. Yet she supposed he must have been quite handsome to attract a beauty such as Maggie. Rosie sighed. She was no fool, and she knew that it didn't matter how nice a feller Tim was, he had too many girls to choose from to end up with an ugly duckling such as she.

Now, standing on the deck of the *Wild Swan*, she tucked her short hair behind her ears. She knew that Tim would not dismiss her previous night's encounter, but she had no desire to admit to him that she had sneaked off during the middle of the night to talk to a horse! He might think her silly and too young to bother with. No, she wanted Tim to see her as an equal and not some little kid who talked to animals. He was, after all, nearly sixteen years old, and was given a lot of freedom not just because of his age, but because he was a boy, and all boys on the canals were expected to work alongside the men as equals from an early age, maturing them beyond their years. No, it seemed that her adventure from the previous night would have to go unspoken.

A few weeks later, Rosie awoke at five minutes to six to find that another sunny day had arrived. She scrambled out of her bedding, folded everything away neatly and jumped on to the towpath to go through her usual routine of setting up the primus stove and boiling the kettle before briefly knocking on the main cabin doors and presenting Maggie and Ken with the first brew of the day.

By the time they had drunk their tea Rosie had got their breakfast of bread, cheese and pickles plated up, and the three of them sat around the small table enjoying the late summer sunshine as they broke their fast. The decision had been made to exchange the *Wild Swan* for a mechanised barge, and as they ate Maggie reminded Rosie that today she and Ken were going to be starting their course in engine management. 'We'll need a few days to learn all the ins and outs of working a boat with an engine,' she said, casting Rosie a fleeting smile. 'Ken was remarkin' the other day as to how you're norra bad girl, allus doin' as you're told with never a grumble, and how you've made him feel right welcome aboard the *Wild Swan.*' Her mother glanced at Ken and cleared her throat before continuing. 'Ken was also sayin' as how the *Sally Anne*'s havin' some minor repairs done and is goin' to be moored up for about the same length of time as we are, and seein' as there ain't goin' to be nothin' for you to do while me and Ken learn the engine, he thought that you and that Tim Bradley could go for a wander around the city.'

Rosie sat, transfixed, a chunk of Red Leicester half-way to her gaping mouth. She was about to speak when her mother continued. 'Anyway, I spoke to the Bradleys and they said that it was okay by them and Tim said as how he'd be happy to look after you. I'll admit I weren't too sure I wanted you on the loose in Liverpool, or any other city for that matter, but Ken reckons you'll be fine with Tim around. So you've him to thank, and it's him I'll blame if you gerrin any trouble. Remember that and do as young Tim tells you, like you did that time he taught you to swim, and you won't go far wrong.' She raised her brows expectantly.

Rosie was flabbergasted. Yesterday her mother would not have dreamed of letting her daughter stray further than the local shop unless someone accompanied her, yet today she was allowed to go into the city. Not knowing how to respond, she looked from Ken to Maggie and back again, still holding the chunk of cheese halfway to her mouth. Was Maggie actually beginning to treat her daughter the way other parents did?

Clearly annoyed at Rosie's lack of response, Maggie spoke sharply. 'Of course, if you don't want to . . . ' she began, but before she could renege on her suggestion, Rosie dropped the piece of cheese back on to her plate, leaned over the narrow table, and gave her mother an impulsive hug. 'Thank you, Mam. I won't let you down, and Tim's ever such a nice feller. Can I go to the picture house with him? I must be the

28

only bargee on the Leeds and Liverpool who's never seen one of these movin' pictures they talk of.'

Maggie smiled, obviously pleased at her daughter's reaction. 'That's more like it,' she said. 'And I s'pose if it's all right by Tim then I don't see why you shouldn't both go and see a fillum together, and you don't need to worry about money neither. Ken reckons you should've been paid a wage years back, so we'll give you enough to get by for the day, including a trip to the picture house and wharrever else you may need. If you make some sandwiches that'll be one meal that you won't have to worry about spendin' your cash on, leavin' you free to spend it on summat else. You can make some sarnies for Tim too, as a way of thanking him for taking you about the city — although I'll give you extra for a chip supper.'

Rosie beamed with delight, though her smile soon faded when her mother's voice took on a more serious tone. 'But before you go rushin' off, I thought you should know that I've had a word with Mr Pank, what owns the grazing field on Tuppenny Corner.'

Rosie, who had been feeling on top of the world, was pretty sure that this next piece of news wasn't going to be as welcome as the last.

Maggie continued. 'You must have realised that Daisy would be going, what with us getting the new boat an' all. So I suppose it's no real surprise, but like I was saying, I've spoke to Mr Pank and he said that Daisy would be a welcome addition to his stock.'

'But she's never pulled a plough, and it's completely different from a barge, you know, 'cos ploughs move off as soon as the horse starts pullin' . . . ' Rosie began.

Maggie pulled a face. 'She's the best, and even though she's never drawn a plough or a wagon in her life, I've no doubt she'll soon get used to it.'

'Did you ask Mr Pank if I could visit her whenever the barge moored close by?' Rosie asked hopefully.

'Course I did, and he said you'd be very welcome and he'd treat Daisy like his own daughter,' Maggie said, clearly relieved that her daughter had not made a fuss.

As her mind conjured up a picture of Daisy in a sun bonnet and little white socks, Rosie giggled briefly before straightening her face. 'Of course I'll miss her very much, but she'll have the companionship of other horses, which I'm sure she'll enjoy. Will they use the same old field, the one with the shelter in the corner? I do hope so, because it's close enough to the canal to make a visit easy.'

Maggie shrugged. 'I can't say for certain, but you won't mind a bit of a walk if she's on the far side of Pank's land, I'm sure. I know he has other horses, so he'll probably put her in with them. It'll be good for Daisy to have company.' She frowned thoughtfully. 'It must be a good few years since I been up that field. I'm surprised that shelter's still standin'.'

A thought struck Rosie. 'She's not goin' to be leavin' today, is she?'

Maggie shook her head. 'She'll be leavin'

30

towards the end of our stay, so don't worry, girl, you've plenty of time for goodbyes as yet. Just you enjoy your day around Liverpool.'

Rosie smiled with relief. With all the talk about Daisy she had almost forgotten the promised trip to the city. Her mother had suggested Rosie fixed a packed lunch, so she dug out some ham and tomatoes and cut thick slices of bread to make sandwiches, adding a couple of apples and then turning her attention to preparing a flask of cold tea. With everything complete, she fished out the satchel which she used on her rare trips to school and placed the packed lunch inside, nodding with satisfaction. She had been about to change out of her work clothes when Maggie called her over and pressed some silver coins into her palm.

'That's to buy your tea and anything else you might need,' Maggie said, though she rather spoiled the effect by wagging her finger in Rosie's face as the girl tried to give her a kiss. 'I'm only givin' you what you've earned,' she said gruffly. 'Ken'll give you a bob or two an' all so's you can get some new clobber. He said a girl of your age needed all sorts, but you were too proud to ask. Well, from today everything will be different.' She gave Rosie a tight little smile. 'Like Ken said, you're norra bad kid. I'm aware that I can be hard on you, Rosie, but you know as well as I do that it's a tough world out there, specially for women. You can't afford to be soft, not nowadays. I may not allus show it, but I do care for you.'

Rosie stared. What a peculiar thing to say to your own daughter. But before she could find her tongue Maggie had left the barge, making way for Ken as he jumped on to the deck. He eyed Rosie thoughtfully; the stained dungarees, the shirt with three buttons missing, her bare feet in a pair of ancient plimsolls.

'You ain't goin' into the city like that, are you? You gotta wear summat decent; hows about that blue dress with all the little squares . . . can't remember what they're called . . . that the Reverend give you for Sundays? And get young Tim to take you to Paddy's Market, so's you can buy yourself wharrever you young'uns wear.' He delved into his pocket and produced a handful of loose change, and picking out four shiny half-crowns he pressed them into Rosie's startled hand. 'Maggie told me young Tim was callin' for you at ten o'clock, so you'd best get yerself changed and ready.' He looked at her with approval. 'You're clean as a new whistle already; in fact you've always kept yerself nice, and that ain't easy livin' on a barge.'

Rosie thanked him and rushed off to get changed. A few moments later she emerged on to the deck of the *Wild Swan*, clad as suggested in her Sunday best with her short dark hair brushed until it gleamed, and was just in time to see her friend approaching. Tim's eyes widened with surprise and he gave a wolf whistle. 'Well I never!' he said. 'You're pretty as a picture, Miss O'Leary! I'll be right proud to take you about.'

Rosie laughed and eyed him shyly from top to toe. 'Well, as today's a sort of holiday I spruced myself up a bit.'

Tim smiled approvingly. 'I thought we could

go to the cinema. Ken said you've never seen a moving picture, lerralone a talkie, so you're in for a treat.' He gave her a mock bow. 'And I'm the feller to introduce Cinderella to her first sight of the fillum world, so ain't I the lucky one? Are you ready? Then let's go. Where would you like to start?' he asked, as they left the canal and headed towards the Vauxhall Bridge, where they looked down on the barges being loaded with various cargoes.

Rosie did not hesitate. 'Liver Birds first, please,' she said eagerly. 'I'd like to climb right up to the very top and look out and see America!'

Tim laughed. He was wearing a short-sleeved stripy shirt, long trousers and a cap tilted at a jaunty angle. 'First disappointment coming up,' he said. 'The Liver Building is owned by insurance companies — don't know which ones — and unless you've business there you can't even get in the ground floor, lerralone up to the birds themselves.' He twinkled down at her and it struck Rosie how lucky she was to have Tim as her companion. She knew that there were at least half a dozen girls longing for his attention, but today she was the fortunate one. The fact that her mother had chosen him as a suitable person to introduce her daughter to the city of Liverpool was just chance, for Maggie would not have considered looks a recommendation. As Rosie continued to stare at the older boy, she realised that he had stopped talking and was looking at her expectantly.

Aware that she had not answered, she spoke

quickly. 'That's a shame. I've often wondered what it would be like to be a great golden statue looking down on humans, scurrying round like mice . . . I'm afraid I'm always daydreaming; I'm sure you must've heard Maggie bawling me out for not paying proper attention.'

Tim raised his brows. 'I should think the Liver Birds themselves have heard Maggie shouting at you for one reason or another over the years.' He placed a comforting arm around her shoulders, which sent a shiver of pleasure through Rosie's body, and as he guided her across the bridge she hoped he had not noticed her secret delight and was relieved when he continued to talk. 'According to my dad all the kids on the canals are daydreamers, so don't think you're alone. And even though we can't go into the building, we'll get as near to the Liver Birds as we can, then take in Paddy's Market. Ken said something about getting you some clothes? Us fellers don't see the appeal of all that but he said you could do with some new ones and if we saw summat suitable we were to buy it.'

'Yes, he did,' Rosie said. 'Only I don't know much about what such things cost and Mam'll get cross if I make a mistake and buy summat what's been overpriced.'

Tim chuckled. 'Well, I don't think you'll find the market clothing too costly. It's all second-hand, you know, just like a huge jumble sale. If you wanted new clothes, you'd have to go somewhere like Blacklers. I like to go in there from time to time just to look at all the fancy stuff, but it's way too pricey for the likes of us.'

He smiled kindly at Rosie. 'So we're agreed. First the Liver Birds, then Paddy's Market, then a spot of lunch and the cinema. After we've seen the movie we can see how much time we've got left before we decide what to do next.'

Rosie nodded happily. It seemed that today was going to be even better than she had imagined. As they reached the base of the Liver Building, she squinted up at the great golden statues, using her hand to shade her eyes from the sun. 'They're huge,' she breathed. 'How on earth did they get them up there?'

Tim shrugged. 'Don't know, but I'm sure they didn't fly up themselves.'

Rosie nudged him with her elbow. 'I'm not a complete idiot, you know!' She glanced around. 'So is the market nearby?'

Tim nodded. 'This way, ma'am,' he said, offering his arm, which Rosie shyly accepted, lowering her gaze to the paving in front of them to hide her blushes.

As they stood in one of the entrances to Paddy's Market, Rosie's jaw dropped. She had never seen a market of this size. There must have been a hundred tables, all covered in clothes. Tim, who had been watching her expression, laughed. 'I'm guessing we won't get out of here before lunch time, am I right?'

Rosie nodded as she walked up to the first stall, which was strewn with dresses of every size and colour. She picked up the most beautiful pink gingham dress, with short puffed sleeves and a neat little bow at the back.

A plump, cheery-looking woman approached

her from behind the stall. 'Like it, do you, queen?' she enquired, a broad smile dimpling her large pink cheeks.

'I was just looking,' Rosie said as she quickly placed the dress back on the table, fearing that the woman might try to insist she buy it.

'No law against that as far as I know, dearie,' the stall-holder said kindly. 'You after anythin' in particular?'

Rosie shook her head, then nodded. 'I've been told to buy a new dress, what fits me better than this 'un,' she said, running a finger round the tight neckline of her own dress. 'Nothing too expensive mind,' she added hastily. 'Summat practical what you can wear for Sunday best'll do.'

The woman stood back and eyed Rosie critically. 'How old are you? Thirteen? Fourteen?'

Rosie shook her head. 'Fifteen. I'm a bit small for my age.' She felt the dreaded blush begin to creep up her neck and looked hastily round to see if Tim was watching, but he had wandered over to a stall a little further up and was inspecting a pair of stout lace-up boots.

The woman nodded and beckoned Rosie to follow her to the other end of the stall. 'Got plenty here that should fit you, and reasonably priced too, if I do say so meself.'

It was an hour later when they finally emerged from Paddy's Market, Rosie having finally decided on a pink gingham dress similar to the one she had first spotted, only without the bow and the puffy sleeves, and a pair of dungarees

36

which reached down to her ankles, unlike her old ones.

'Sorry it took so long, Tim,' she apologised. 'I suppose sometimes you can have too much choice.'

Tim gave her a wink. 'I'm just glad we got out of there before tea time,' he said teasingly. 'Now let's go and eat those lovely sarnies you've made us; all that shoppin's given me a real appetite.'

He led them to a pleasant garden with well-kept flower beds and beautifully manicured lawns. A sweeping path separated the lawns from an impressive flight of elephant steps which led to an enormous building. As they passed between the two stone pillars to gain entrance to the gardens, she clutched Tim's arm and drew him to a halt, asking rather apprehensively whether whoever lived in the big house might object to their presence.

Tim laughed. 'You really don't know anything, do you?' he said, though not unkindly. 'That's nobody's house; it's St George's Hall and anyone can go into St John's garden to eat their sandwiches, provided they behave themselves.'

As they walked towards the building, Rosie admired the stone statues that were placed about the garden. 'They're beautiful, Tim; so grand. I can't believe just anybody can walk in here.'

Tim smiled. 'Well they can, and when we've finished eating I'll take you round the other side and you can pat the lions on their heads and tell them what good boys they are.'

Rosie laughed. After a whole morning in his company she was quick to realise when he was teasing, so she retorted that she was glad that they were eating their sandwiches first as she did not wish to share them with a couple of lions.

Tim chose a suitable bench to have their lunch on, and as they ate, Rosie realised that she had not stopped smiling since they had visited the Liver Birds. She could not think of a single time — apart from when she rode Daisy along the towpaths — when she had been this happy; she was even smiling as she ate. She glanced sideways at her companion to see whether he was just as happy as she, and saw to her embarrassment that he was staring at her, a broad grin etched across his face. Worrying that she might have a tomato seed on her chin, Rosie quickly wiped a hand across it. Glancing back at Tim she saw, thankfully, that he had averted his gaze to the beautiful beds of red and white roses.

After they had finished their lunch, they placed their rubbish in the bins before visiting the lions. Tim then led Rosie to the Palais De Luxe, a cinema on Lime Street, and pointed at the large poster on the front of the building. 'Robin Hood! That's supposed to be a brilliant film; bit of everything for everyone. Fighting, good versus bad, swords, bows, arrows . . . ' he winked at Rosie, 'and even a little bit of romance for the ladies.' He raised his eyebrows. 'Wanna see it?'

Rosie nodded eagerly. 'How much will it be, though, Tim? Will I have enough?' she said hastily, fishing in her pocket and bringing out a handful of loose change.

Tim frowned at her. 'I don't take a lady to the

flicks and expect her to pay her own entrance fee,' he said. 'Put your money away, queen, it'll be my treat.'

Rosie could not hide her pleasure at Tim's last remark; this day just seemed to get better and better. Not only was Tim treating her like an equal, he was referring to her as a lady, and that was how he made her feel. Like a woman, not some silly little girl who talked to horses and couldn't be trusted to wander more than twenty yards away from her mother, but a real woman, capable of looking after herself and being treated as a grown-up.

Tim bought two tickets, and when he handed them over to the usherette she guided them across the darkened auditorium, using her torch to light the way as she showed them to their seats. Sitting down in the dark Rosie could hear voices whispering around her as the other cinemagoers waited for the film to begin.

They sat in the dark for what seemed to Rosie like quite a long time, and she was just about to ask Tim whether something had gone wrong when the beautiful velvet curtain ascended. Behind it the dull screen sprang into life as the bright lights flickered and danced. Rosie sat in awe; she had not realised that the figures on the screen would be so big, or their voices so clear. She watched in amazement as the various characters brought the story to life before her eyes and the heroic Robin Hood braved the wicked sheriff to save his belle, the beautiful Maid Marian.

When the film had finished, and they had

emerged from the darkened cinema into the brightness and bustle of Lime Street, Rosie shaded her eyes and assured Tim that she had enjoyed every moment, every one of the thrills, even the wicked sheriff's attempts to slay poor Robin when his beloved Marian was not around.

'I don't know about you, but I'm famished,' Tim said as he stretched his arms and legs. 'We've got time to go and get us a fish supper and eat it on the overhead railway, if you'd like? That way you can have a look at all the docks an' that.'

Rosie nodded her approval. After watching *Robin Hood*, it was easy to compare Tim to that heroic figure, for he had taken her away from the controlling clutches of her mother and shown her a life she had never known existed. Maggie had mentioned something about the *Sally Anne's* being moored for the same length of time as the *Wild Swan*. After today, Rosie hoped fervently that she and Tim might be allowed to come on more trips into the city and that this was not just a one-off.

As they queued for their fish supper, Tim spotted a few of his mates from the canals further up the line in front of them. 'Hang on here a mo,' he instructed Rosie, 'I'll go an' give Lenny the money and he can get our fish and chips for us; that way we won't have to wait as long.'

Rosie nodded happily, but as Tim disappeared she heard a loud disapproving sniff from the woman in front of her. 'That's queue-jumpin', that is,' the woman muttered. 'Not fair on us what's waited a while, but that's gypsies for you.'

Rosie furrowed her brow indignantly. We're not gypsies, she thought angrily; not that there was anything wrong with gypsies as far as Rosie knew, but the woman in front of her obviously thought there was.

When Tim returned he wore a satisfied grin, but it soon faded when he saw Rosie's glum expression. 'What's up, queen? Don't say you've changed your mind?'

Rosie shook her head. Pulling Tim by the arm, she turned towards the shop door, and as she left the queue the unpleasant woman muttered under her breath: 'Good riddance, thievin' little toerags.'

Tim stopped so abruptly that Rosie lost her grip on his elbow. 'Sorry, is there a problem?' he said to the woman, his tone polite and calm. 'Has someone in this queue stolen from you?'

The woman pretended not to hear him, so Rosie whispered in his ear. 'She thinks we're gypsies,' she said, trying to keep her voice low so that others in the queue would not hear her.

Tim arched his brows in surprise and turned to face the woman. 'Does she really? Well, I'm afraid you've been misinformed. We aren't gypsies, we're bargees; I think you'll find there's a difference, though there's nothing wrong with being either. And we're certainly not thieves.' He smiled fleetingly at the woman, who was still pretending that she could hear neither Tim nor Rosie. When no response was forthcoming they turned away, but just as they walked through the shop door Rosie heard the woman mutter, 'Same difference.'

Rosie looked uneasily at Tim, but although he had obviously heard the remark he continued to walk, a grin beginning to form. 'There's nowt as ignorant as folk,' he called loudly over his shoulder, 'and they don't come more ignorant than that.' He jerked his head in the direction of the woman.

Rosie, however, was not smiling. 'She spoke as if we were terrible people, Tim, as if being bargees was something dirty, that we should be ashamed of . . .'

Tim laid his hand on Rosie's shoulder, then lifted her chin to face him. 'That, my dear Rosie, is because she's ignorant. She's never been on a barge or worked the canal in her life, yet she's happy to put coal on her fire, take sugar in her tea, and knit scarves in the winter.'

Rosie frowned. 'I don't understand. What's knittin' a scarf or havin' sugar in your tea got to do with bargees?'

'What I'm trying to say, queen, is that she's happy to take the goods that we deliver across the country to her door, yet she doesn't appreciate that if it weren't for us she wouldn't have any of the things that she takes for granted.'

'Ohh,' Rosie was beginning, a small smile appearing on her lips, when they were interrupted by Lenny, who dutifully handed over their fish and chip supper. Thanking him, they made their way to the overhead railway.

'You, er, you don't have much to do with the rest of the bargee kids, do you?' Tim said, his voice hesitant.

Rosie shook her head. She hoped that Tim

would not think it was because she thought herself better than the others, because nothing could have been further from the truth. As they settled on one of the seats in a carriage on the overhead railway, she voiced her thoughts. 'It's not because I don't want to, Tim, because I do. It's Maggie's fault. She's the one who doesn't approve of me hanging around with them. I don't know why, but every time I bring it up there's a huge row, so rather than rock the boat I just keep shtum.'

Tim unwrapped his supper, and as the aroma of salt and vinegar filled the carriage he nodded. 'I guessed it must be something like that,' he said. 'But why do you call her Maggie instead of Mam? You don't do it all the time, but you do seem to say Maggie a lot.'

Rosie began to relax. This was an easy one. 'I'm supposed to call her Maggie when we're actually workin' on the canal because she's the Number One, and she says we have to keep our boundaries and know our place. I suppose over the years I've got used to callin' her Maggie, and to be honest she is more like my boss than me mam.' She broke off a large piece of battered fish and blew on it. 'What do you call your parents when you're workin' the barge?'

She half hoped for an answer similar to her own, but Tim shrugged. 'They're me mam and dad whether workin', eatin', sleepin', whatever,' he said matter-of-factly. 'But things are obviously changin' aboard the *Wild Swan*. Ken's a grand chap and he don't like any unfair treatment. I bet a quid to a penny that it was his idea to let

43

you off your tether for a wander round the city with me; am I right?'

Rosie chuckled. 'Yes, you are . . . Oh, Tim, look at the ships! Where are they from?' Rosie was pointing at the ships docked below them.

Tim shrugged. 'Could be anywhere. Liverpool is a very busy port; ships come here from all over the world. But you know that — you've transported their cargoes up and down the canal all your life.'

The train drew to a halt and they finished their supper before joining the queue of people descending to ground level. Rosie handed over her ticket rather regretfully; she would have liked it as a keepsake to remind her of her lovely day.

'Your mam said you have no plans for tomorrow either,' Tim said as they made their way towards the barges. 'We always go to church on a Sunday when we moor up and I know you do too, so if you make some more of those delicious sandwiches how about I pop round about mid-morning and we can go along to Seaforth and have ourselves a little picnic and a paddle in the sea. Would you like that?'

Rosie drew in an ecstatic breath; would she like it? She would like just being with Tim, but to share a day at the seaside with him would be heavenly, *and* he said her sandwiches were delicious! Smiling at her companion, she found it almost impossible to hide the bubble of happiness that his suggestion had caused. She opened her mouth to say something cool, calm and collected but instead her voice came out in an excited squeak. 'Oh, Tim, I've never been to the seaside. I'll see you straight after church is over.'

Chuckling, Tim tucked Rosie's hand in his arm and smiled down at her. 'That'd be grand. Soon be home now. Have you enjoyed your first day of freedom?'

'Oh yes,' Rosie breathed. 'I've always wanted to explore the city. It's everythin' I dreamed of and more besides.' She sighed happily. 'I can't *wait* for tomorrow.'

2

Rosie woke early on Sunday morning, a knot of excitement in her stomach at the thought of her day ahead with Tim. Normally on a Sunday the crew of the *Wild Swan* had a lie-in and Rosie got the breakfast no earlier than eight o'clock, but today, to her surprise, both Maggie and Ken were awake, and instead of having to make the breakfast herself she found Maggie had pipped her to the post.

As her mother handed her a bacon sandwich and a mug of tea Rosie concluded that the adults must be going on a trip of their own, though a quick glance at Ken's face told her that he did not look as though he anticipated the day ahead with pleasure.

As it was another sunny day, the three of them ate their breakfast on the towpath while Rosie described in great detail the wonderful time she had had the previous day.

'That Tim's a good lad.' Ken nodded approvingly. 'You'd best make the most of it, because . . .'

Maggie cut across him impatiently. 'No point in worrying before we've heard anythin' worth worrying about.' She shot a disapproving glance at Ken, then turned to Rosie. 'Eat up, Roseanna, then we'll go along to St Anthony's.'

Rosie glanced from Maggie to Ken and back again. Her mother only ever called her by her full name when she was feeling particularly stressed, but as no one appeared to be volunteering any further conversation Rosie had no choice but to continue with her breakfast.

On the way to church, Rosie saw that Ken looked serious but Maggie was downright grim; so much so that Rosie spent the walk searching her conscience. She must have done something wrong, for every time Maggie's eyes met her own their glance grew colder, or so she imagined. By the time they reached St Anthony's she was in a fret of guilt, and hoped desperately that whatever she had done was not bad enough to spoil her plans with Tim.

After the service, instead of going into the church-yard, everyone gathered round the wireless set in the vestry, where they stood chattering in hushed tones until the Reverend John Brown gained his congregation's attention by rapping his knuckles on the table. As silence fell, he twiddled the knobs on the small box, then raised his voice so that they might all hear what he was about to say.

'As most of you know, Mr Chamberlain had hoped to secure a promise from Germany that they would not invade Poland.' His tone was solemn. 'He is about to make an announcement . . . ' Several people hushed him as the wireless set began to emit the strange noises that usually preceded the start of a programme. Rosie's heart plummeted. She had been so excited the previous day that she had completely forgotten that today they would hear whether there would be war with Germany or not. She looked at the faces around her. All grave, all knowing. Even the children stood silently waiting.

The prime minister's voice broke the silence.

This morning the British Ambassador in Berlin handed the German Government a final note stating that, unless we heard from them by eleven o'clock that they were prepared at once to withdraw their troops from Poland, a state of war would exist between us. I have to tell you now that no such undertaking has been received, and that consequently this country is at war with Germany.

Rosie heard gasps and groans from the people around her. Scouring the crowd, she spied Tim in the opposite corner of the room. A thought struck her and she clutched at Ken's arm. 'Will the boys all have to go off to war like they did in the last lot?' she asked, trying to keep her tone even.

Ken laid a comforting hand on her shoulder. 'One thing at a time, queen. War's only just been declared.' He drew a deep breath. 'Though you can be sure that this will affect all our lives, no matter how old or young we are.'

Mr Chamberlain was going on at some length, talking of the rationing of food and clothing which would have to come, and of the need for everyone to tighten their belts and put their country first, but Rosie scarcely heard a word for the disappointment that filled her. War was a terrible thing and though she had never seen any of the newsreels, she had heard of the horrors happening across the continent. Now, all around her, people were talking in hushed tones, and Rosie could hear the fear in their voices. They spoke of how the overhead railway would not be running and most of the buses and trams would not be taking passengers anywhere near the docks, so her anticipated outing with Tim would come to nothing. For the first time it occurred to Rosie that her newfound freedom might die before it had ever really lived.

As the group began to break up, Rosie spotted Tim making his way towards the vestry door. Now was as good a time as any to go over and face the fact that their days of exploration had come to an end. Following, she soon caught him up and _____ly tapped his shoulder. 'Bang goes our ___ at the seaside,' she said, trying to keep the disappointment out of her voice as he turned to face her. 'I suppose you'll want to talk over what Mr Chamberlain said with your pals. I'm afraid I don't know much about war, except that it's horrid, so I'll say t.t.f.n.'

She started to walk past him, lowering her head to hide the tears as she did so, but Tim grabbed her arm. Shaking his head reprovingly, he steered her out of the church and in the direction of the quayside. 'I agree we can't go to the beach, and somebody said all places of entertainment are being closed until further notice, but that doesn't mean we can't explore the streets of Liverpool. If I promise a lady a day out, then that's what she'll get, war or no war, so how about starting right now? It may be our last chance before all sorts of further restrictions come into play.' He smiled at her. 'I know it sounds dull compared with a visit to the seaside, but I'll do my best to take you to the more interesting parts of the city. Or is there something else you'd rather do?'

Rosie blinked the tears back as enormous happiness filled her. He was not going to use the war as an excuse to drop her, and though he had not actually said so he must have been looking forward to the seaside trip as much as she was. And with this realisation came another; that Tim genuinely liked spending time with her. She was about to nod her approval when a thought occurred to her. 'Oh, Tim, I forgot our snap. I'll have to go back and get it . . . '

He raised his brows. 'Don't you ███ about that. I've got the money I was goin' to ███ the trip to Seaforth; that should be enough ██ a couple of sarnies . . . unless you'd prefer ██e ones you make?'

Rosie shook her head and beamed at him, though her smile soon faded when she remembered the question that had been uppermost in her thoughts. 'Will you be going off to join the war, Tim?'

For the first time Tim looked awkward. Drawing a deep breath, he looked in the direction of the *Sally Anne* before turning his eyes back to Rosie. 'I've applied for the RAF, queen. I had to lie about my age, but I did it a couple of weeks ago.' He ran his fingers through his hair, then placed both hands in his pockets. 'Dad reckons it's best to pick the services before they pick you and besides, I've always dreamed of working on those aeroplanes, or better yet flying one of them.'

Rosie's heart dropped into the pit of her stomach, but she was not about to let her disappointment show. 'Oh. I . . . ' she was beginning, when he gave an exclamation and pointed further up the quayside to where a couple of boys and a girl were in earnest conversation.

'I wondered where Frog, Taddy and Patsy had got to. You must've seen them around, though I don't suppose you've ever had a chance to chat. Frog and Taddy are on the *Reedcutter*, and Patsy's on the *Marsh Harrier* . . . '

The sudden change of subject had caught Rosie off gentard, and rather than continue with the day mious conversation she looked over to where the small group of youngsters stood. 'I've seen them before, of course, and while I didn't know their names I do know which boats they come from. I'm assuming the older boy is Frog and Taddy's his little brother? Why do they call him Frog?' Tim opened his mouth to reply, but Rosie continued. 'Look, he's waving to you. Had you better go over?'

'Might as well,' Tim said. 'Isn't it absurd? You've been on the same canal as them all your life yet you've never exchanged a word. They're grand fellers . . . well, not Patsy of course, although she's as good as any bloke when it comes to helping her parents run the *Marsh Harrier*. You'll like them and they'll like you, but don't worry that they'll want to come round the city with us. That wouldn't be their style at all; they'd start squabbling over trifles. They may be real fond of one another, but when Frog tries to boss Patsy about . . . well, let's just say she won't put up with any of his nonsense.'

Looking at the smile on Tim's face, Rosie realised that the change of subject had been just as welcome to Tim, who had also been grateful to talk of other things than the war. As they walked towards the small group a dark-haired, dark-eyed cherub with an enchanting smile ran up to them and grabbed Tim's hand, words bubbling out of his mouth. 'Tim! Oh, Timmy, we was wonderin' where you were. I thought you was probably in a plane already, swoopin' among the clouds, but know-all Froggy said it were too soon.' He released Tim's hand and spun round to point at Rosie. 'What's she doin' 'ere?' he enquired rudely. 'She's 'Miss Never Smiles', that's what Frog calls her. I call her 'Crosspatch', because that's what she is.'

Tim pretended to clout him, saying reprovingly: 'Don't be so damned rude, you horrid brat. Just because Rosie's quiet and obeys her Number One, that doesn't make her bad-tempered!'

The little boy laughed and put out his tongue. 'Timmy's got a girlfriend,' he chanted. 'Now he'll be sittin' in the back row of the pictures cuddlin' and cooin' an' kissin' . . . yuck!'

Patsy, who had yet to speak, aimed a swipe towards Taddy's curly mop, but luckily for him she failed to connect, so he continued. 'When I grow up I'll be a Number One on me own barge and I won't let no women come on board; and if they try I'll chuck 'em in the drink.'

Rosie smiled into Taddy's rosy little face. 'I take it, then, that you'll cook the meals, do the washin', hang it on the line and iron your Sunday best?' she said seriously. 'As well as steerin' the barge, loadin', unloadin' . . . my, you will be a busy little bee.'

Frog smothered a chuckle and winked at Rosie before addressing his little brother. 'Well, Mr Clever Clogs? I disremember the last time you boiled so much as a pan o' water. I do admit you're grand at eating, but I don't fancy tryin' to live on the sort of things you could cook. And before you say another word I think it would be nice if you apologised to this lady for all the rude things you said.'

Taddy pulled a face. 'Don't know who she is,' he muttered. 'Don't know what 'pologise means.'

Frog laughed. 'You should do, you're allus havin' to say you're sorry for one thing or another — '

'It means you're sorry,' Rosie cut in. 'But you needn't apologise, because you didn't really mean it, did you?'

Taddy gave her a grin that was so broad it nearly split his face in half. 'I've changed me mind! You's nice; I like you,' he said. 'Where's our Tim takin' you? I want to come an' all.'

'Well you can't,' Tim said firmly. 'We're goin' to walk miles and miles and your legs are too short to keep up. No, don't start arguing or it's you who'll be chucked in the drink.' He turned to Rosie. 'Where're my manners? Rosie, meet Patsy Topham, and Frog, and of course the oh so quiet Taddy.'

Rosie smiled warmly at the other youngsters, and though they all smiled back she noticed that Patsy's smile was fleeting. The other girl turned to Tim. 'So how come you two are off on your own? I know Taddy can be a nuisance, but I don't see why me and Frog couldn't come along.'

Tim eyed Patsy shrewdly. 'You two know the city like the back of your hands, but Rosie here is still getting to know it. Besides, I've only money for a couple of sarnies, so perhaps it'd be best if we all went together on some other day.'

Patsy, who had been eyeing Rosie suspiciously, shrugged her shoulders. 'Please yourself. I've other fish to fry anyway. I'm sure you and your new friend will have fun.'

Taddy giggled. 'Ooo, somebody's jealous.' He ducked as Patsy aimed another swipe at his head. 'Tim and Rosie, sittin' in a tree . . . ' he started to chant, the words getting lost as he started to run away from an infuriated Patsy.

'I am *not* jealous!' she yelled as she chased after the little boy. 'Get back here so I can give you a good walloping!'

Frog grinned at Rosie and Tim. 'I'd better go and save Taddy before Patsy gets her hands on him.' He nodded at Rosie. 'Nice to have met you. Cheerio.'

Tim, who was watching Taddy's delight at being chased, laughed. 'He's gettin' awful hot with Patsy runnin' after him. If he keeps goin' at that rate he'll probably welcome a dip in the drink.'

Rosie looked anxious. 'Oh dear, I hope I

haven't caused any trouble.' She glanced in Patsy's direction. 'I don't think Patsy likes me very much.'

Tim started to walk along the towpath. 'Nah, they're always like that, those two. And as for Patsy not liking you, I'm sure you're wrong. Patsy gets on with everyone. She's a grand lass, full of life. Mebbe it's just because she doesn't know you.'

Following behind, Rosie looked doubtful. The look the other girl had given her was not a friendly one; unlike Frog and Taddy, who were full of smiles, Patsy had looked at Rosie as though she had smelt something unpleasant. Rosie had also noticed that when Patsy had looked in Tim's direction she wore the same gooey expression as all the other canal girls whenever Tim was around, making it plain, to Rosie at least, that she was clearly smitten with him. Rosie tried to think why Patsy had taken a dislike to her, but could find no reason other than the fact that Tim had chosen to spend his time with her rather than with Patsy herself. Rosie frowned. Surely the other girl couldn't be jealous of her? Surely she must realise that Tim was only taking Rosie about as a friend, doing her mother a favour by getting her out from under the adults' feet whilst they learned the mechanics of the new barge? She shook her head. If Tim was after a girlfriend, someone like Patsy, with her sleek blonde curls and large blue eyes surrounded by a fringe of thick lashes, made a much more obvious choice than Rosie with her mousy brown hair and boyish looks. She gave a mirthless chuckle. No, if Tim was going to be attracted to either of them, surely Patsy must realise she had nothing to worry about.

★   ★   ★

When Rosie returned with Tim to the *Wild Swan* after their tour of the streets of Liverpool, she had scarcely set foot on the decking before Ken's curly mop of dark hair popped out of the cabin, and he placed a finger to his lips. 'Your mam's been in quite a state, wondering where you'd got to,' he said in a low voice. 'She guessed the trip to the seaside was off, because no one will be allowed near the coast now that war has been declared, so when you didn't come back, she began to worry that something bad might have happened.' He glanced apologetically at Tim. 'I told her you were probably tryin' to see a bit more of Liverpool than you had managed yesterday . . . '

A sharp voice from inside the cabin cut across his words. 'Rosie O'Leary, just you come down into the cabin and help me dish up. I got some best of neck off the butcher for half price 'cos he said it wouldn't go another day, so I made a good thick stew to line our stomachs and then what happens? You bobby off with that Tim Bradley, without a word to me — or Ken for that matter — and you needn't think I'm goin' to feed him as well as you, 'cos it's your fault you forgot your snap — '

'Sorry, Maggie,' Rosie said quickly, in a bid to cut her mother's words off before she had

56

chance to say anything else. She glanced to where Tim stood on the towpath, hoping he had not heard, but guessing he had done so when she saw a blush creep up his neck. 'Tim was kind enough to see me back safe, but he's not intending to stop, so your stew for us three is safe.'

Maggie grunted and poked her head out of the cabin. Rosie was pleased to see that when her mother saw Tim a similar blush to his own mantled her cheeks. 'You might've warned me,' she said, scowling at Ken. She looked at Tim, and seeing that he was about to leave put out a detaining hand. 'I reckon you heard what I said,' she muttered. She fished a handkerchief out of her apron pocket, blew her nose and rubbed at her eyes with the back of her weathered hand. 'If I knew where she was going — '

Tim cut across her. 'No need for explanations,' he said apologetically. 'We should have told you that we were heading into the city; I'm sorry, it was wrong of me. Please don't let me keep you.' He turned to Rosie. 'If you're free again tomorrow, we might as well continue to explore the city' — he raised his voice to gain Maggie's attention — 'if your mother agrees, that is?'

'Oh,' Rosie said doubtfully. 'But I don't think I'll be allowed now, not after today at any rate . . . '

Maggie opened her mouth to respond, but Ken cut her off. 'You may as well be out with Tim as stuck on the barge on your own,' he said baldly. 'You go off, queen, and have as much fun as you can while you've got time.'

Tim grinned at Rosie. 'That's settled, then. I'll be here at nine o'clock on the dot.'

He turned away on the words and Rosie glanced apprehensively towards where Maggie still stood framed by the cabin doors. She expected an angry outburst, but for once she misjudged her mother. Maggie was looking defeated. 'Come down and eat your dinner,' she muttered. 'As you forgot to take the snap you'd made for your lunch today, you can take it tomorrow instead. But don't you forget, I want you home before dusk.'

★   ★   ★

They were nearly a week into their stay and so far Rosie had spent each day with Tim, either going into Liverpool or wandering along the canal, talking to the other bargees and relaxing in the early autumn sun. It was on the fifth day that Maggie announced over breakfast that today was the day when Rosie would have to take Daisy to her new home.

'You can ride her to the farm,' Maggie told her daughter. 'Mr Pank said he'd give you a ride back, and he'll give me the money for her then, as well as pickin' up her harness. Perhaps that Tim feller would like to go with you? You could always ride two up, or walk — it's up to you.'

Whether Maggie had intended this suggestion to ease the blow of Daisy's leaving, Rosie could not be sure, but the thought of Tim's going with her did make the prospect less daunting. She bolted down the last of her breakfast and hurried off to the *Sally Anne*, where to her delight she found Tim still in the middle of eating.

'Morning, queen. Where're you off to?' he said, stepping off the barge and on to the towpath.

Rosie told him about Maggie's suggestion that the two of them might like to take Daisy to Pank's farm together, but instead of the enthusiastic response she was hoping for Tim told her that though it would be fun, he had other duties to attend to. 'Today's the day I go to the RAF offices for my medical, so much as I'd like to I'm afraid I can't,' he said regretfully.

Rosie's stomach lurched unpleasantly. She hadn't broached the subject of Tim's going into the RAF since the day war had been declared. Trying to put it out of her mind altogether, she supposed that she had hoped that Tim would think better of his decision to join the RAF and stay on the canals with her, but this was obviously not the case. 'Well, now that I know where Lime Street station is, how about I come and meet you off your train when you come back?' she suggested.

Tim raised his brows. 'You sure your mother won't mind you comin' into the city on your own?'

Rosie shrugged her shoulders. 'To be honest, I rather think Maggie has given up on the idea of me being tied to the barge.' She gave a chuckle. 'I get the feeling that she's enjoying the time alone with Ken.' She smiled at her friend. 'Anyway, good luck with your medical. I'm sure you'll smash it, but I suppose I'd really better get a move on, especially if I'm goin' to meet you later on.'

Setting off towards the field where Daisy grazed, Rosie felt a lump forming in her throat. As she neared the paddock she could see the big mare standing expectantly by the gate. Blinking back her tears, Rosie placed the rope bridle over the mare's head.

Daisy was a big horse, and Rosie had to use the field gate to get on to the mare's back. Clicking her tongue, she ordered Daisy to walk on. 'You're going to be so happy at the farm,' she said, as they ambled along the towpath. 'There'll be big fields full of grass, and Mr Pank has a couple of horses which he uses to pull his plough, so you'll have some new friends . . . ' She fished a hanky from her pocket and blew her nose noisily. 'Truth be known, it's not you who'll miss me at all, but me that'll miss you.'

As Daisy plodded along the path Rosie used the time to think over her past few days of freedom. She could not for the life of her imagine what had changed her mother's mind about letting her go off with only Tim beside her, but she was jolly glad that her mother had at last begun to release the tight hold that she had always had over her daughter. Maybe it was because she had married Ken, Rosie mused; perhaps having a partner had mellowed Maggie's approach to parenting.

Maggie had been on her own ever since Jack O'Leary's tragic accident, almost eleven years ago. Most of the men who worked the canals did not look kindly on women running a barge, and despite the tragic circumstances Rosie knew that they had not made an exception in her mother's case. As far as the men were concerned, the *Wild Swan* was competition that they did not need. Rosie had even overheard one of the bargees calling out to Maggie that she should go back to where she came from. When Rosie had asked her mother what the man had meant, Maggie had explained that she had met Jack O'Leary on the Shropshire Union Canal, when she had been on holiday there with one of her cousins.

'Before I met your father I used to work in one of the pubs in Liverpool, and I ain't goin' to go back to a life surrounded by leerin', lechin' drunks for no man,' she had said, her voice full of determination. 'And I sure as anythin' ain't goin' to bring up no kid in a pub!'

Rosie shook her head at the recollection. Maggie, it seemed, could not be content with either life. She did not approve of public houses, but neither did she approve of canal folk. It occurred to Rosie that it was probably due to her mother's surly nature that she had been on her own for so long.

Her mother's meeting with Ken had been purely accidental. Maggie had been having an argument over a lock key that she had foolishly lent to one of the other bargees at the Bingley locks. The bargee concerned denied having borrowed the key and said that it was Maggie who had stolen it from him some time ago, and that he was just taking back what was rightfully his. Ken had been waiting aboard his rented

61

barge at the top of the locks and had come down to see what the hold-up was.

The man had been swinging the key round in one ham-like fist. 'Women don't belong on barges, especially thievin' ones.' He had grimaced, revealing a set of crooked yellow teeth. 'Why don't you sod off back down the canal? All you're doin' is holdin' up everyone else what wants to make a livin'.'

Rosie had watched anxiously as her mother tried to gain possession of their key. But trying to grab a rotating lump of metal was no easy task, and the man who was swinging it more like a weapon than a key, guffawed at Maggie's failed attempts.

Maggie had tried to reason with him. 'Look at the handle, it's got *WS* written on it, that stands for the *Wild Swan*. If you look you'll see that it's not your key.'

The man had continued to swing the key round, and not taking his steely grey eyes from Maggie's he had sneered: 'I can't see no writin'. I'm guessin' you must be mistaken. Oi!'

This last remark had been addressed to Ken, who had approached the unknowing man from the back and snatched the key mid-rotation from the aggressor's hand. Ken swung the key within inches of the man's nose. 'Think you should look harder then, Phil Gaspot. If you look carefully you can quite clearly see that she's right, the letters *WS* are written on the handle, so it looks like you're the one who's mistaken, not the young lady here.'

Ken had swung the key so close to Phil's eyes the other man had to jerk his head back so as not to get struck by the handle. 'See?' Ken repeated.

Rosie had smothered a chuckle as the bully had tried to focus on the key handle, going cross-eyed in the attempt. He pushed the key down from his face and turned his back on Ken, muttering that it was still his key, and that they must have painted WS on it, although when Ken asked him to speak up the man fell silent and kept on walking.

Now, Rosie smiled to herself as she listened to the rhythmic thump of Daisy's hooves on the dry earth of the towpath. She had never seen her mother smile as much as she had on the day Ken had come to their rescue, and, thinking back, she supposed that the attraction between them must have been obvious, although Rosie had possibly been too young to see it at the time.

As they started to wend their way through the small copse of trees that led to Pank's farm, Rosie saw to her delight that the woodland floor was carpeted with mushrooms ripe for picking. Sliding off Daisy's back, she pulled a small net bag from the pocket of her dungarees and began to fill it. Once it was full to bursting, she led Daisy the short distance from the fringe of the wood to the Panks' stable yard and tied her up outside one of the stables before knocking politely on the farmhouse kitchen door.

Mrs Pank must have seen them arrive through the kitchen window, for she called out to Rosie to come on in and have a cuppa and a fresh-baked scone; a command that Rosie was happy to obey, for boat people are always curious about the lives of landlubbers and Rosie was no exception. She entered the house and looked around at what to her seemed to be an enormous kitchen, with a sideboard crammed full of beautiful china, a stout pinewood table and half a dozen chairs. A fire burned brightly in the grate and Mrs Pank was standing next to a cooling rack full of scones.

'Sit yourself down, dearie,' she said cheerfully. 'That's a grand mare you've got there. My hubby told me you were rare fond of her, but I need not tell you we'll treat her well because you wouldn't have sold her to us if you hadn't known that.'

Rosie nodded. 'I do. And I know Daisy will be very happy here with the other horses.'

Mrs Pank settled Rosie in a chair by the table and placed a mug of tea in front of her. Then the older woman took two of the scones from the tray and proceeded to slice and butter each one before placing them on two plates and handing one to Rosie. 'Gosh, thank you,' Rosie said, taking a bite.

'Well now, what do you think of this here war?' Mrs Pank asked, settling down on a chair opposite her guest. 'We knew it were comin', of course, same as you must have done. I've been busy makin' blackout curtains so's the enemy can't look out of their spyin' sneaky aircraft and start a-droppin' their bombs at any light which shows a target, though my hubby says the dockyards and shippin' will be their first objective and I dare say he's right. He's a knowin' one, my hubby.' She looked sympathetically at Rosie. 'The canal's right near the docks, isn't it?'

Rosie nodded and wiped her mouth. 'Yes, and I believe they've shut the docks to civilians,' she said, trying not to spray any crumbs.

'Well, mind you keep safe, and make sure you've no lights showin' at night.' The older woman appeared to consider. 'Do you have some young feller in the forces, m'dear?'

Rosie shook her head. 'My friend Tim's joined the RAF, but he's not my feller. I expect he'll be off any time now; in fact, he's having his medical as we speak.'

Mrs Pank sighed thoughtfully. 'He'll be off with the RAF before you can say knife, then. I dare say you'd like to join one of the services yourself, but you're too young as yet, and I hope your time will never come, although I don't suppose this war is going to be over in five minutes.' She reached across the table and patted Rosie's hand. 'I've two sons in the Navy, but I try not to think of the danger and just tell myself that they'll be doin' their bit for our dear old England. Hubby and me do our bit by growin' good food crops and rearin' fine stock, which I dare say will be needed.'

By the time Rosie left Mrs Pank in the kitchen she had been invited to 'pop in' whenever she came to visit Daisy, or indeed simply found herself in the vicinity of Pank's farm. She had also been handed a brown paper bag with three warm scones inside it: one each, Mrs Pank had said instructively. In return, Rosie had offered her hostess half her bag of mushrooms, with which Mrs Pank was delighted. Once outside, Rosie found Mr Pank feeding Daisy a handful of pony nuts, which Daisy was noisily crunching down.

'She likes you,' Rosie said. 'And I'm not going to insult you by asking you to take care of her, because I know you will. Mrs Pank said it would be all right for me to drop by and see Daisy whenever I've the time, so is that okay with you too?'

'Of course it is!' Mr Pank exclaimed. 'You're always welcome, child, you know that.'

Smiling, Rosie ruffled Daisy's mane. 'You be a good girl, Daisy O'Leary, and don't go givin' the Panks here no grief, you understand?'

Mr Pank gave a small chuckle. 'She'll be all right. Now, let's get you back to the canal.' As he spoke he walked over to where his small truck stood and opened the passenger door for Rosie, who obligingly climbed in.

'Mr Pank,' she said shyly, 'would it be okay if you dropped me off in the city before you go to see me mam? Only I'm goin' to meet a friend at Lime Street station . . .'

Nodding, Mr Pank climbed into the driver's seat. 'I've got veggies to deliver to one of the caffs just off Lime Street, so I can drop you there if that'll suit?'

Rosie nodded eagerly. 'That'd be just grand.' As the small truck trundled slowly out of the farmyard, Rosie looked back to where a farmhand was untying Daisy and leading her towards one of the fields. She turned back to Mr Pank. 'Will you ever graze Daisy in the field by Tuppenny Corner? You know, the one that we used to rent off you?' she asked hopefully.

Mr Pank shook his head. 'Sorry, queen. That field's goin' to be rented by some feller for his niece's pony, and he's made it quite plain he don't want no other horses in there with it 'cos he reckons it can be a bit of a nasty bugger wi' other beasts. Nippin' and kickin' — you know the sort of thing.' He chuckled. 'Typical little pony, I s'pose.'

Rosie grimaced. The new pony sounded perfectly horrid, and she couldn't help wondering who would let a child own something so nasty. But instead of voicing her thoughts she turned her attention to the beauty of the high hedgerow, already full of plump blackberries, elderberries and rosehips. She sighed wistfully as they slowly wound their way along the country lanes. If she had more time she would have asked Mr Pank to stop so that she might walk the rest of the way, collecting the luscious fruits as she went.

When they reached the small café Mr Pank had business with, Rosie thanked the farmer for the lift and stepped out of the truck. At the station, she waited patiently on the platform as two trains pulled in and out again, neither of which had Tim on them. They were, however, brimming with servicemen and women, and as she watched Rosie decided that if she were ever to join one of the forces it would be the WAAF, because their uniform seemed to be the smartest and the women who wore them looked the most attractive, the smart blue suits with their brass buttons, belted waists and matching hats making the overall appearance very appealing.

Thinking that she must have missed Tim, Rosie was just about to give up and go home when a third train pulled alongside the busy platform, and Tim hailed her as he stepped down from a carriage. He was wearing his Sunday suit, and Rosie guessed from his enormous smile that he must have passed his medical.

'I'm in, dear Rosie; I'll be off as soon as my rail passes and so on come through. Gosh, my heart was in my mouth, because several of the fellers were turned down, so even though I know I'm pretty fit it was still a real relief when the officer in charge came over to me and gave me my papers. I asked him how long it would be before I started my basic training, but he could only say within the next few weeks.' He gave Rosie's shoulders a squeeze. 'Let's go and tell my dad. He'll be made up, same as I am. Mam still says I'm too young, but I know Dad thinks I'm doing the right thing.'

3

It had been over a week since Ken and Maggie had begun their course on engine maintenance, and, happy in the knowledge that they could cope should things go awry, Ken, Maggie and Rosie loaded up their new barge, the *Kingfisher*, with all their old possessions before collecting their latest cargo. When they were ready to leave, Ken encouraged Maggie to crank the engine into life, but instead of descending to the engine room, Maggie merely scowled at him.

'You know I hate that part. It nearly pulled me arm off the other day; left me with a right bruise it did. Why, even Mr Allenby said it'd be better if you was in charge.' She glanced in the direction of her daughter. 'I've already told Ken: new barge, new Number One. Ken's in charge from here on in. Any objections?'

Rosie was stunned. Until this point she hadn't heard a word about Maggie's disliking the engine, and certainly not of the fact that Ken might be taking over as Number One. But Maggie was staring at her, an expectant look on her face as she waited for a response, so she just shook her head and glanced at Ken, who said cheerfully, 'Come on, queen, I'll show you how to start the engine. I'm sure your mam'll get used to it over time.'

They descended the ladder into the engine room, but before Ken could speak again Rosie voiced her thoughts. 'When the man from the Allenby boatyard left I assumed Maggie was happy with the engine. But she says that you're now the Number One, which implies that she's content to play second fiddle, and I find that hard to believe. So what happened?'

Ken smiled. 'Your mam is scared stiff of the engine,' he said frankly. 'I don't mean she don't understand the changes, I mean she's genuinely frightened. It was pretty plain to both Mr Allenby and meself that she couldn't come to terms with the mechanics, but when he suggested that Maggie and I change roles I thought she'd give him a right ol' tongue-lashin'. But instead of gettin' angry she looked downright relieved. I s'pose when all's said and done it was your pa who was the Number One of the *Wild Swan* before his death, so it's not as if it's the first time your mother's had a man running things.'

Rosie's mother had been Number One of the *Wild Swan* ever since Rosie could remember, but she supposed that Ken was right. 'I don't remember my father at all, Ken, and 'cos I've grown up wi' Maggie bein' Number One I can't imagine her being anything else.' A small smile appeared on her lips. 'Bet she's sorry she gave Daisy up now, 'cos I'm sure the last thing on her mind, back then, was having someone else give the orders.'

Ken nodded, then handed her the starting handle. Pointing to where it slotted in, he instructed her to give it a few strong turns. She did so, and to her delight the engine roared into life. She looked eagerly at Ken, who gave her a satisfied smile and patted her on the shoulder. 'Now *that's* how you start an engine.' He climbed the short ladder back to the deck and waited for Rosie to join him.

As she ascended the ladder, Rosie could see the look of disgust on her mother's face as the older woman peered into the depths of the engine room. Ken took his place by the tiller. 'Come on, I'll show you how to control her. It's pretty easy really.'

As they slowly chugged their way along the canal, Ken demonstrated the lever that controlled the speed of the engine. 'Push it forwards to go forwards, and if you want to reverse just push it back.' He gave the lever a gentle push forward to demonstrate. 'It's easy; the further you push it the faster you go.'

Rosie frowned. 'What does reverse mean? I've never heard of that.'

Ken grinned broadly. 'It means to go backwards, summat you couldn't do easily with a horse, but with an engine . . . ' He slowed the barge down as he spoke and then, checking behind him, he pushed the lever back.

Rosie was impressed. No matter how much she loved Daisy, this was a function that was invaluable to a bargee. 'So you can turn around any time you like, and very easily too.'

Ken nodded triumphantly. 'Easier all round.' Standing aside from the controls, he indicated that Rosie should take over. 'Come on, queen, let's see how you handle her.'

Rosie was thrilled to be trusted with such a

powerful force. Keeping one hand on the tiller and the other on the lever, she gave the latter a gentle push and to her delight she heard the engine pick up speed. When Maggie opened her mouth to object, Ken wagged an admonitory finger at her. 'The girl's doin' a good job, so just you leave her be . . . unless you've changed your mind and fancy havin' a turn yourself?'

Maggie scowled, her lips tightly pursed, as she disappeared into the depths of the main cabin, slamming the doors shut behind her. Realising that it must be hard for her to see her daughter controlling the barge, Rosie lowered her voice. 'Poor Mam! I'm sure that once she gets used to the idea she'll be happier not having the responsibility. We'll all go on better when orders are given quietly . . . Mam never did learn that the way to get the best out of people isn't by the crack of a whip.'

As Rosie continued to steer the *Kingfisher* along the canal she wished that Tim could see her, but the *Sally Anne* was taking a delivery of coal up to Leeds, so was not going to make as many stops as the *Kingfisher*, which was making local deliveries to the village shops along the canal line. Rosie had enjoyed seeing him every day while Ken and Maggie were on their course and would have liked to demonstrate her prowess, but for the time being the two barges were several miles apart, so the opportunity was denied her.

After making their final delivery, the *Kingfisher* was bound once more for Liverpool. As dusk began to fall, they moored a short distance from Pank's farm and, seizing her opportunity, Rosie asked whether she could go and visit Daisy.

Maggie shrugged her shoulders. 'I can't imagine why you would want to go off in the dark just to visit a horse that doesn't belong to us any more, but if the Number One can spare you, that's fine by me.'

Rosie turned to Ken, who had just taken a large bite out of a meat and potato pie. Nodding, he made a hand gesture towards the main cabin doors, his voice muffled by the pie as he spoke. 'Best you take the torch; don't go shinin' it willy-nilly though, else you'll get into trouble.'

As she set off along the towpath, Rosie took care to point the torch just in front of her feet while shading the beam with her other hand, so as not to draw the attention of any patrolling wardens. When she reached the point where she must leave the towpath she gave a little skip. It was lovely to be out of the *Kingfisher's* stuffy cabin; she only wished Tim could be with her, for she was missing him more with every day that passed. Now that Ken was in charge of her freedom, she decided that she would ask him whether she might be allowed to visit Frog and Taddy the next time the two barges moored close to each other. She considered going to see Patsy, but the other girl had only appeared interested in her when Tim was around. Tim had said that he thought it was Rosie's imagination, but there was something in the way Patsy looked at her . . . she had seen the same expression on Maggie's face whenever she thought her daughter was getting under her feet.

Rosie, Tim and Patsy had spent the afternoon together the day before Ken and Maggie had taken over the *Kingfisher*, and Tim had taken the girls to a river not far from the canal. 'We can tickle the brown trout here. C'mon, I'll show you. If you're lucky you might even catch one. That'd be somethin', wouldn't it? Imagine takin' one of them home for your tea,' he had said, and even though Patsy had sighed and rolled her eyes she had still joined Tim and Rosie on their fishing expedition.

When they reached the river, Tim had led the girls to a tight bend where a small pool had gathered in the angle of the bank. Lying down on his stomach, he indicated that Rosie and Patsy should do the same. Rosie eagerly followed suit, but Patsy folded her arms defensively. 'I ain't lyin' down on no muddy riverbank to catch a smelly fish, not in me new dungarees anyway. When you invited me out for the afternoon, Tim Bradley, I thought you had somewhere better in mind than this, and I didn't realise you'd be bringin' a friend along neither.'

Rosie felt her cheeks grow hot at this obvious dig, but Tim appeared not to notice. Instead he just laughed. 'Patsy Topham, you used to love fishin' for brown trout! Don't tell me you're too grown up.'

Patsy scowled at Rosie as she knelt down beside Tim. 'I just wanted to spend a bit of time alone with me oldest friend before he went off to war, that's all.' She gave Rosie a look of distaste over the top of Tim's head. 'No offence.'

Rosie felt very much offended, but rather than say so she gave a small shrug. 'None taken. I s'pose everyone wants to spend time with their friends before they go off. Would you rather I left, Tim?'

Tim shook his head disbelievingly. 'Blimey, what's got into you two? Don't either of you want to catch a trout today?' Before Rosie could answer, he added, 'And of course I don't want you to leave, Rosie. Neither does Patsy, do you?'

Rosie glanced at the other girl, who was staring hard at the back of Tim's head while she sought a suitable answer. Unfolding her arms, she looked at Rosie and Rosie could see that for now, at any rate, Patsy was giving up on spending the afternoon alone with Tim. 'Of course I don't want her to go. Ignore me, Rosie. I suppose I'm just havin' a bad day.'

The rest of that afternoon had passed quite pleasantly, although Rosie still felt an icy air coming from the other girl. Rosie even managed to catch two trout, although one had jumped back into the water — much to her relief — before Tim could stop it.

Now, as she started to cross the field where Daisy used to graze, she concentrated on where she was walking, for she knew there were several rabbit burrows around and she had no desire to catch her foot in one and end up in hospital with a broken leg. As she went carefully forward she saw something moving ahead of her. It was too small to be Daisy or either of the Panks' other horses, and peering into the dusk she remembered what Mr Pank had said about some feller putting a pony in the field. She also recalled that he had mentioned kicking and biting. Forgetting her fear of retribution, Rosie shone her torch wildly around the field. She was too far away from the gate to go back, so she decided to seek safety in the small gap between the shelter and the boundary hedge until the vicious creature went away.

Rosie ran towards the dilapidated building, all thoughts of rabbit holes forgotten. As she neared the shelter she saw, to her relief, that the pony's owners had replaced the stable door. I can shut myself in there, she thought defiantly, only to find to her dismay that the door was padlocked. Squeezing into the small gap between the shelter and the hedge, Rosie cursed whoever had locked the stable. Why on earth would anyone go to the trouble of putting a new door on a field shelter just to padlock it shut so that the pony couldn't use it, she thought crossly. Her heart skipped a beat as the animal merged into view, its small nose — and no doubt its small but vicious teeth — reaching out towards her.

'Shoo!' Rosie commanded. 'Go away. I've got nothin' you'd be interested in . . . ' She suddenly remembered that she had put a handful of sugar lumps in her pocket, intending to give them to Daisy, so she took one out and offered it on the palm of her hand to the curious pony, who snuffled it up as daintily as Daisy herself would have done. Believing it to be her only chance of escape, Rosie dropped all the sugar lumps at the pony's feet, then squeezed out of the other end of the gap and ran with all her might back towards the gate. Once safely out of the field, she turned to see if she had been pursued, but it appeared that the pony was only interested in its treat. Panting, Rosie regained her breath. She would have to cross one of the other fields to visit her old friend in future, but she would come in day-light so that she could find her way.

She was just about to leave when she heard hooves trotting towards her. She looked curiously at the pony, who was stretching his neck towards her, gently breathing through his nose. It was his way of trying to find out whether he liked Rosie or not. Guardedly, Rosie placed her nose next to his muzzle, and awaited a response. To her surprise, the pony blew gently into her face.

'So, you want to be friends?' Rosie said as she rubbed the pony's cheek with her fingers. 'You've got a fearsome reputation, you know, but now I don't think it's true. I think you're a softy — at least with people, perhaps not with horses.' She climbed gingerly over the gate. Stepping slightly forward, the pony began to rub his head roughly against her chest, causing her to stumble backwards. She started to laugh. 'You may be little but you're strong, and a real sweetie,' she said. 'I wonder why they've locked you out of your stable? Where are you meant to go if it rains?'

For the first time in quite a while she remembered the bargees who had come to the shelter when she had been asleep next to Daisy. She wondered if the pony belonged to one of the men who had stood outside talking that night. Rosie grimaced as she conjured up the image of the one whose features had been illumined by the lamp. He hadn't looked the sort to have a pony, certainly not a nice one like this. He had seemed more like a man who owned vicious dogs; the sort that were used for fighting.

Shaking the unpleasant image out of her mind, Rosie remembered some of the things the men had talked about — if indeed it had not been a dream. They were a couple of weeks into the war now, and she had heard no mention of anyone — let alone jackbooted nuns — parachuting into the country. She knew that if that did turn out to be true they would be coming over in planes, and with Tim about to go into the RAF Rosie decided that no matter how silly it sounded, he had a right to know what she may or may not have overheard. What he chose to do with the information would then be up to him.

★   ★   ★

It was another week before the *Sally Anne* and the *Kingfisher* moored close to each other again, and Rosie was able to tell Tim all about the night when she had heard the men talking outside the old shelter. To her relief he neither teased nor laughed at her; in fact he took her seriously.

'A group of men meeting in the middle of a field late at night does seem odd,' he agreed. 'And even though all sorts of false rumours go around in times of war you can't dismiss anything, although I must say I think this particular one is what they call scaremongering.' Seeing

Rosie's puzzled frown, he explained, 'That's when people make up stories that aren't true just to scare other people. Which of the men mentioned the floating nuns?'

Rosie frowned. 'I *told* you,' she said rather pettishly. 'I only saw one of them; I think he was the leader, but I couldn't say for sure.'

'Hmm,' Tim said thoughtfully. 'Well, you were right to tell me, dream or not. I'll ask about, see if any of the lads have heard owt similar.'

Rosie looked surprised. 'Won't they laugh at you?'

Tim shook his head. 'War's no laughing matter, and I wouldn't put anything past some evil beggars.'

'Do you know where you're going to be stationed yet?' she asked.

Tim shook his head. 'No, but as soon I have an address I'll be sure to write to you, so you can write back and tell me all about what's going on on the canal.'

'Gosh, Tim, I quite forgot! I haven't told you about the new Number One on the *King-fisher* — '

Laughing, Tim cut across her. 'Rosie O'Leary, you know as well as I do that gossip is rife on the canals! I knew that Ken was Number One before you left on your maiden voyage.' He smiled at the disappointment etched on her face. 'Sorry, I didn't mean to take the wind out of your sails, so I'll let you tell me all about how you're managing with the engine . . . ' He dodged as Rosie made a playful swipe at his arm.

'I don't care if you do already know,' she said

primly, ''cos I'm gonna tell you all about it again anyway . . .'

* * *

The winter of 1939–40 had been a hard one. The ice on the canal had been so thick that no matter how tempting it was to try to earn some money, the bargees knew better than to attempt to force their way through ice hard enough to penetrate the hulls of their boats, especially when, on occasion, even the icebreaker barge had been frozen to its moorings.

The drifts of snow on the roads were so high that even the farmers' tractors could not get through. Servicemen and women on leave found themselves stranded far from loved ones, while those who remained at their postings spent many laborious hours clearing the snow and ice from runways and roads, only to see it all back again within an hour or so, until with the coming of spring came the big thaw, melting the ice and drifts and allowing the country's transport network to operate fully once more.

Tim had gone into the RAF just before Christmas, but due to the terrible weather it was some time after his initial training had finished before he was able to return home, and Rosie — who was aware that he was due home that day — couldn't have been more excited.

As she stood on the canal path, making the customary first cup of the day, she heard the sound of an approaching engine. Looking up from the primus she saw a motorbike bobbing and weaving its way precariously towards her, its engine giving loud spurts as it hit the many lumps and bumps of the canal path.

Maggie, who was still in the process of getting up, shoved her head out of the main cabin doors, and, seeing the motorbike, yelled out: 'Get off the path, you ruddy idiot! It's not meant for motor vehicles. If you fall into the canal it'll serve you right, and you can forget us comin' to your aid, 'cos we shan't.'

'And a good mornin' to you too, Mrs Donahue,' the rider called out cheerfully, while swerving around a particularly large hump in the path, causing Rosie to jump from the towpath on to the deck of the *Kingfisher* in a bid to get out of his way.

The rider came to a halt, and with a broad grin pulled the goggles off his head. 'Tim!' Rosie shrieked. 'What on earth?' She jumped back on to the towpath in one bound and enveloped him in her arms before hastily stepping back, her cheeks pink with embarrassment at her impulsive reaction.

'Idiot,' Maggie snapped, before disappearing back into the main cabin, slamming the doors closed behind her.

Still sitting astride the bike, Tim grinned at Rosie. 'What d'you reckon? Do you like it? It's not mine, it's a mate of mine's, but I helped him get it runnin' so he said I could borrow it for my leave as a kind of thank you for all my help.'

In all the time she had known him, Tim had tinkered with engines and was known among the boat people as someone who could help out when things went wrong, but right now the motorbike was the last thing on her mind. It had been at least four months since she had last seen him, and in that short amount of time Tim's appearance had changed considerably. His corn-coloured hair was now tamed in the traditional service haircut of 'short back and sides'. His face had filled out, and his shoulders appeared broader, although she supposed that could have been the cut of the uniform. She looked into his eyes and smiled; everything else may have changed but the twinkle in those hazel eyes remained the same. Aware that he was still waiting for a response, she spoke quickly. 'I think it's fantastic, Tim, but perhaps not suitable for towpaths.' She giggled. 'Do you fancy a cuppa? Only I was just brewin' up.'

Tim nodded enthusiastically. 'Sure would, and while it's brewin' I can bring you up to speed with everything that's happened since I last wrote.'

Rosie produced a couple of stools for her and Tim to sit on while they waited for the water to boil, and placed them beside the canal. As they watched the ripples of fish with sunlight glinting off their backs as they broke the surface, Tim told Rosie how they had been taken into a large hall and left to their own devices. At the top of the room there had been three tables, each with a line of men and women snaking up in front of it, so with no one to advise him Tim had taken his place in the shortest queue. After half an hour he had just reached the head of the line when his sergeant pulled him away from the table and shepherded him to the queue on the left.

'This is the one for you, son,' the sergeant had said, tapping the side of his nose knowingly. 'I've seen the work you did on that motorbike of Jimmy's. We all thought he'd bought a right lemon, but you got it better'n new in no time.' He nodded to the procession of people in front of Tim. 'This queue's for engineers and the like. It'll suit you down to the ground. Can't have a talented lad like you peelin' spuds, now can we?'

Tim explained to Rosie how there had been no way of telling which queue was for which trade, and that if the sergeant hadn't redirected him just in time he could have found himself sweeping runways clear of snow, emptying the latrines or making parachutes.

Rosie gave a low whistle. 'What a stroke of luck, Tim! Just goes to show, you're a whizz with mechanical stuff, you always have been. You must've really impressed that sergeant.'

Tim blushed under the praise, then jerked his head towards the *Kingfisher*. 'How's Ken — and your mam? She still bossin' you around and treatin' you like a skivvy?'

Rosie's face glowed with pride, and she began to fill Tim in on the events that she hadn't had the time to include in her letters. 'You're not the only one who's joined the forces. Ken has been accepted by the army and is on an ack-ack battery down south. He was absolutely over the moon when his papers came, which is more than I can say for Maggie. You see, because I'm the only one who can run the engine I had to be instantly promoted to Number One, which was just about the last straw for me mam, who was positively spitting feathers when Ken announced his decision to leave us. But what could she do? She's terrified of anything mechanical.' She smiled mischievously at her old friend. 'Not only that, but because a lot of the bargees have left the canals to go and work in the factories or the forces — the pay's much better, as you know — I've been asked to train a couple of girls up to run one of the empty barges.' She grinned at Tim, who was looking suitably impressed. 'Maggie will instruct them in a good many things including what you might call 'household tasks', but it'll be me who teaches them all about the engine and getting the barge through the locks safely.' She chuckled. 'I bet Mam'll want to interfere, but she won't be able to 'cos she hasn't got the knowledge *or* the authority.'

Tim gave her a mock salute. 'So now you're the Number One, I s'pose I'd best mind my p's and q's.'

Even though he was teasing, Rosie knew that he was genuinely impressed. 'Too right, else you'll find yourself in the drink.' She laughed. 'Poor Maggie's had to put up with an awful lot with me bein' in charge. She can't tell me what to do or where I can or can't go any more.' She looked curiously at Tim. 'Have I told you that Daisy's old field has been taken over by a new pony?'

Frowning, Tim shook his head. 'Why, what's that got to do with the price of fish?'

Rosie shrugged. 'Nothing, 'cept it reminded

me about that story I told you, the one about the men outside the old shelter that night.'

Tim nodded his head slowly. 'I remember. And have I told you that I'm going on a course to learn all about aero engines?'

'Only about a hundred times,' she said, making an elaborate pretence of yawning.

Tim gave her a playful punch on the shoulder. 'Just because you're Number One of the *Kingfisher* doesn't mean you can be cheeky to me,' he said. 'Once I've passed the course I'm going to apply for air crew, and if I get accepted I'll be sure to look out for your nuns.'

Rosie looked hurt. 'Now you're teasing me,' she said, her cheeks turning pink with embarrassment.

Tim repented. 'Sorry, queen, I didn't mean to. Look, if it's any help, I asked around and no one's heard anythin', so I reckon you must've dreamed it, either that or it was just a rumour which came to nowt, thank God. So don't let it worry you, and don't think I was makin' fun, 'cos I wasn't.'

Rosie smiled brightly at him. 'I know, so let's forget all about those silly nuns and you can tell me where you're going to be stationed and what you're going to be doing when you're there.'

Tim shrugged. 'The plain truth is that I don't know myself where I'll be going after I've done the course. I gather from those who've already taken it that it's pretty tough, but you come out at the end of it knowing the dos and don'ts of all sorts of conditions. There's an air force station in — dash it, I can't tell you where, not that it'd mean much to you anyway — who've been losing aircraft at a fair rate of knots; that was until some bright aero mechanic spotted the fact that sand had blown into the engines, sand so fine that it was almost impossible to see. Once they knew what the problem was they worked out how to solve it at almost no expense, so you see they do go into things in depth, and when I come out, with a bit of luck, I'll be a really useful member of whatever team I join — *if* I pass the course, that is.'

'Oh, Tim, of course you'll pass, but they'll probably send you to the north of Scotland or somewhere and we shan't see each other again until the war is over,' Rosie said dejectedly. 'Oh dear, I used to tell my problems to Daisy, but I can't do that any more.' She gave Tim a small smile. 'Having you back, even for a miserable little week, will only make me miss you more. I know we can write, but I wish we could talk . . . '

Tim patted her shoulder. 'We can talk, goose. I'm not saying we can have long conversations, because there's always a queue to use the telephone, and the standard call length is only three minutes. But I'll give you the number and you can ring each day, if you like' — he tapped her playfully on the nose — 'but I shall still expect to receive nice long letters.'

'Or at least long until the censor has his way with them,' Rosie said miserably.

Tim snapped his fingers. 'You've just reminded me. I might be sent abroad, so we shall need a code so we can exchange information which the censors won't cut out. For instance, if I said I

86

was going to have rice for supper that would mean I was going east. Get the idea?'

'Of course I do, though we'll have to think of a few more codewords than that . . . ' Rosie said, chuckling. She sobered almost immediately. 'Oh, I do hope you stay in Britain so that we can meet occasionally. Still, as everyone keeps reminding me, there is a war on, so if you are sent abroad there's not a lot we can do about it.'

Tim got to his feet and held out his hands to help Rosie up. 'Let's not get ahead of ourselves,' he said, pulling her to her feet. He glanced at his wristwatch. 'Good heavens, look at the time! I've got to meet up with Tinker — he's a mate of mine from basic training — did I mention he was doing the course as well?'

Rosie nodded. 'I wish I had lots of friends like you. It's just typical, isn't it? I've got as much freedom as I need now that I'm Number One, but because of the shortage of bargees we're run off our feet most of the time, so I don't get the chance to go anywhere.' She looked shyly at Tim. 'You will be sure to come back and see me before you leave, won't you?'

Tim ruffled the top of her hair. 'Of course I'll come back and see you. I couldn't say t.t.f.n. without seeing you first!'

Rosie smiled. 'Good job too, or I'd have your guts for garters.'

* * *

Tim's week of leave was soon over and Rosie could not hide her disappointment when she waved goodbye to him as he rode his friend's motorcycle back up the towpath — much to Maggie's annoyance.

Turning back to the *Kingfisher*, Rosie had a hollow feeling in the pit of her stomach. Goodness knows when she'd see Tim again, and even though they had agreed to keep in touch through letters and phone calls, it wasn't the same as being able to see someone in person.

Boarding the barge, she called out to Maggie to release the moorings as she ducked down into the engine room. Pushing the crank into its slot, she gave a couple of hefty heaves and the engine juddered into life. She let out a deep sigh as she leaned against the ladder. Keep busy, she thought to herself, and Tim's absence won't seem so bad. Climbing out of the engine room, she took up her position by the tiller and gave Maggie a nod.

Untying the ropes, Maggie jumped aboard the barge to pick up the pole and push it into the bank. She turned to Rosie. 'We pickin' up these city folk what want to be bargees in Liverpool?' she asked, pulling a disapproving face.

Rosie nodded. 'Treat 'em nice, Mam. It's all to help with the war effort, and you'll only have to suffer 'em for a month, just till they get the hang of things, then they'll be off on a barge of their own.'

Maggie folded her arms. 'Yeah, and they'll be takin' the best jobs out from under us noses! We'll be left haulin' unwashed coal while they'll be gettin' all the nice, light, clean work.' She sneered. 'I agrees with the men. It's not fair these people comin' in and takin' the work from under us . . . '

Rosie arched her brows. Her mother was sounding exactly like the bargees who had treated her so badly, yet all that seemed forgotten since Pete in the canal offices had announced the arrival of new trainees. No matter how hard she tried, Rosie could not get her mother to understand that without more running barges to transport essential cargo, the country would come to a standstill. She looked over wistfully as they passed the *Sally Anne*, which was also getting ready to set off with deliveries of her own. Tim had only been gone for ten minutes, yet it seemed like weeks already.

★　★　★

It was May 1940, and a month had passed since Tim's trip home. The *Kingfisher* had played host to several young women who thought that joining the canals was going to be easy money, with a generous shipman's ration to boot. The reality, of course, was completely different. Opening and closing lock gates was hard, heavy work. The demand for goods meant that the *Kingfisher* often carried on into the small hours of the morning, and unloading and loading each cargo required a good deal of stamina.

Some of the women, after a week or less working the canals, would simply up and leave without so much as a goodbye, leaving Rosie frustrated and, worse still, having to face Maggie's insufferable pleasure at seeing yet another trainee go.

'Can't stomach hard work, that's their problem,' she would say with a satisfied smile. 'Told you havin' newcomers to the canal was a bad idea, and I was right, weren't I?'

Rosie could not argue with her mother, for at the end of the month not one of the girls had stayed. Often turning up without any food of their own, they would start taking Rosie's and Maggie's supplies. 'We're not one of the bloody services!' Maggie had snapped, the first time she had snatched the breakfast porridge that she had made for herself and Rosie from one of the new girls' hands. 'You have to buy your own supplies. I'm not sayin' that we won't muck everything in together, but you have to bring your own food to the table, as they say.'

This conversation had taken place on day three of their maiden voyage as instructors. The girl in question — Valerie Duncan — had brought no clothes other than the ones she stood up in, and when she had asked Maggie where her uniform was, Rosie had thought her mother's head was going to explode. 'Uniform? Uniform?' Maggie had shrieked. 'Never mind a uniform! Where's your clothes, wash kit and sleeping stuff? And let me guess; you've no money neither?'

Personally, Rosie was surprised that Valerie had stuck it as long as she had, though she had disappeared as soon as her wages had been placed in her hand at the end of her first week. 'Thanks, luv,' she had said, giving Rosie a hearty smile. 'I'll just nip down the shops so I can buy summat for us teas, you know, to mek up for eatin' your stuff like . . . ' It had been nine o'clock that evening before Rosie had to reluctantly agree with her mother that Valerie was not coming back.

With the evacuation of Dunkirk, soldiers in their thousands poured into Britain's ports, some badly injured, others too traumatised to speak, though all were fraught with hunger, thirst and fatigue. They had been given no orders except to go home and await further instructions.

Fearing invasion was imminent, the government fortified the canal network, believing that this was the way the enemy would infiltrate the country. Anti-tank trenches were dug along the towpaths, and every bridge was packed with explosives, while a large trail of barbed wire, seven feet high, cut straight across farming land in a bid to prevent the enemy from getting through.

Rosie's latest recruits, a couple of girls from Liverpool, had found the defences intimidating, especially the pillboxes that were used by members of the Home Guard. 'There's men in them pillboxes with machine guns,' Sally Woking had said, her face pale with fear. 'Half them Home Guard fellers is granddads! What if they falls asleep and pulls the trigger by accident when we's goin' past? I bet half of 'em can't even see straight! They might think we's the enemy and start shootin'! Friendly fire, they calls that. Well I ain't gettin' shot for nobody.'

This conversation had taken place at the canal offices in Liverpool, when Pete was explaining to the girls what the plan of action was when it came to defending the canals.

'And what about these bridges with explosives all over 'em?' That was Maggie, who, Rosie thought bitterly, was enjoying seeing yet another couple of trainees about to abandon the *Kingfisher*.

Bonnie — Sally's sister — had looked sternly at Maggie, then at Sally. 'She's right, you know. We'd be takin' us life into us hands every time we went under a bridge!' She shook her head decisively. 'Bugger this for a game of soldiers. I'd rather be pickin' sprouts in winter; at least no bugger 'ud be tryin' to shoot you or blow you up, even if it is by accident.'

Rosie heaved a sigh as the two girls left the office, muttering excuses as they went. Maggie shrugged her shoulders. 'Easy come, easy go!' She addressed the manager. 'Got any more for us, Pete?'

Pete shook his head. 'Not for a couple of months. It seems word's gettin' out that canal life ain't an easy one.' He handed Rosie a ticket. 'Here's your next job: a load of grain to go to the mills.'

Rosie looked hopefully at Pete as she took the ticket. 'Make sure you let us know the moment you've got someone suitable; there's just got to be someone out there who's up for a challenge. I don't know how much longer we can keep goin' without help.' She glanced in the direction of the canal. 'Even the men must realise that life would be easier all round with more bargees to share the workload!'

Pete shook his head morosely. 'They're not bothered about too much work; they reckon the more the better. They're more worried about some stranger comin' in and stealin' it out from under their noses.'

Rosie glanced at her mother, who was standing in the doorway, ready to leave. Because she was the only one who could run the engine, it had been left to her to work into the small hours while her mother slept. She rather supposed that this was Maggie's revenge for no longer being the Number One. The sooner Rosie could persuade someone to stick to life aboard the canals the better.

★ ★ ★

As the autumn of 1940 drew to a close, Rosie resigned herself to the fact that it was highly unlikely she would get any new recruits until spring at the earliest. The string of trainees had seemed endless, all unsuitable and all with misplaced conceptions of life on the canals. The days were growing shorter, and pretty soon life was going to get a lot tougher, especially if they had a winter like the last one.

Because the war had taken so many of the workers, the burden of transporting essential goods across the country had increased, and Rosie found herself with very little time to do anything other than run the boat, manage shipments, and sleep. Her hopes for remaining in contact with Tim via the telephone had proved to be futile; with the ever-increasing work-load she simply didn't have time to stand in long queues, so letter-writing had been their main form of communication.

Tim's letters were always short and full of what he thought of as an obvious code, but it quite often left Rosie with more questions than answers.

Hotpot's my favourite thing, and I'm glad to say that my dreams have come true, although I've still got both feet on the ground!

This had been in Tim's most recent letter, and Rosie felt sure it must mean that he was working on aero engines — because he had said that that was his dream — but he hadn't managed to make aircrew yet. The reference to hotpot, she guessed, probably meant that he was in one of the many airfields in Lancashire.

She thought that Tim must find her letters positively boring, as she had no exciting news to impart. Instead, her letters were filled with talk about the weather and whom she had seen that Tim would know. Frog and Taddy were brilliant names as she had no fear of giving away their true identity should her letters fall into enemy hands. Like Rosie, Patsy too had taken over a new barge, but according to Frog and Taddy she was making plans to join the WAAF.

'Dunno what as,' Taddy had said cheekily. 'I reckon she's only joinin' 'cos she wants to be near Tim . . . ' he said, clutching his pudgy hands together in a theatrical manner and fluttering his eyelashes.

Rosie had giggled, but deep down inside the mere thought of Patsy going into the WAAF had filled her with misery. It seemed so unfair that Tim and Patsy might get to spend the war together while she stayed on the same old canal, doing the same boring job, whereas the other girl would be living an exciting life much the same as Tim. They may even end up on the same station together, or even getting married! Despite Rosie's own reservations she knew Tim was fond of Patsy. She tried to shake the image from her mind. It was silly to go jumping ahead when, for all she knew, Patsy might not even get accepted into the WAAF.

★   ★   ★

All references to the phoney war ceased when German bombers targeted Liverpool just before Christmas 1940. Rosie remembered that first night all too well. Ken was home on a rare bit of leave and they had been coming back from Leeds with a cargo of cotton, and Rosie — who by now was well practised in operating the barge — had told Maggie and Ken that she would continue working while they ate a late supper.

Truth be told, Rosie enjoyed the chilly nights on deck. She would wrap herself up in her thickest clothing and revel in the peace and quiet of the canal. At this time of year all the wild animals were tucked up in their burrows or dens, so the only sign of life was the occasional passing barge. With the blackout in force there were no street lamps or shop lights to drown out the beauty of the star-studded sky, and the silver moon, high above her head, lit the night as if it were dawn. Rosie stood with one hand on the tiller, listening to the quiet chug chug chug of the engine.

When Ken had first come home she had half expected him to try to take command of the barge, and was pleased when he had held up a hand and said that it was Rosie who was the Number One of the *Kingfisher*, at least until the war was over. That night, as she heard the air raid sirens start to wail in the distance, he popped his head out of the main cabin. 'See anything?' he asked, his voice muffled by a chunk of bread.

Rosie shook her head, and watched as he disappeared behind the cabin doors. She was aware of a low humming that was nothing to do with her engine and scanned the night sky nervously, but there was nothing to see but the moon and stars. A bright light caused her stomach to lurch unpleasantly, until she realised that it was just the searchlights of the ack-ack guns. As they criss-crossed the night sky Rosie found herself paying more attention to them than to where she was going, and glanced briefly to the front before turning her gaze skywards once more, where she saw half a dozen planes flying away from them. She was wiping the palms of her hands on her thick woollen scarf when suddenly, from out of nowhere, there was an almighty explosion, one so powerful that it caused the *Kingfisher* to rock violently.

Ken burst angrily out of the main cabin. 'What the hell did you hit?' he bellowed. Rosie — who had nearly fallen into the canal from the force of the explosion — stared at him, her face white with fear; she held on to the tiller and pointed towards the bridge, where several barges had been blown out of the water.

'It was a b-b-bomb . . . ' she stammered, but stopped as she heard the sound of running water, and realised what must have happened.

'Bloody hell! They've breached the canal!' Ken cried. He leapt off the barge and began to run along the towpath.

Rosie slammed the *Kingfisher* into reverse and called out to Ken, 'I'll take her back up to safety, then I'll come back and help.'

Ken gave her the thumbs up over his shoulder just as Maggie emerged from the doorway of the main cabin looking bewildered. 'What's all the shoutin'? Where's Ken goin' — and why're we goin' backwards?' she demanded.

When Rosie explained what was going on, Maggie also jumped on to the towpath and raced off after her husband, calling back to Rosie as she went, 'I've lost one husband, but I'll be damned if I'm gonna lose another. You stay with the barge, my gal. I'll be back when I can.'

Rosie had no intention of staying with the barge. People were almost certainly hurt, and she was not going to sit idly by. After backing up to what she hoped was a safe distance, she quickly moored up and set off after the rest of her crew.

Nearing the bridge, she stared in horror at the carnage before her. At least three barges lay wrecked in a large crater in the dry bed of the waterway, while a few others were reared up against the banks. The canal water was flooding into a nearby rail yard, and Ken, Maggie, and a few others were trying to stem the flow.

'Get them railway sleepers and use 'em to block the breaches in the canal.' It was Ken's voice. 'There're fires all over; we need the water to put 'em out.'

Rosie looked closely at the barges that were reared up against the side of the canal. One of them had been torn in two by the impact; the beautiful hand-crafted ornaments that the bargees had prized lay smashed on the muddy canal bed, and the hand-painted board which bore the name of the barge was in pieces. Rosie's heart plummeted as she made sense of the broken words. It was the Reedcutter, Frog and Taddy's boat. Running forward, she shouted their names, but her voice was drowned out by the shouts of others and the sound of rushing water.

As she was looking for a safe way on to the snapped and broken remains of the Reedcutter, she saw that the metal hull had been twisted beyond recognition. Rosie felt a sob begin to rise in her throat. If the blast could do that to metal, what could it do to the likes of the Madisons? She was still shouting out to Frog and Taddy when a small voice called out from behind her.

'Hello, Rosie. Did you see the big boom? Wasn't we lucky? We'd all gone into the city for a fish supper. Dad reckons it were one of them delayed action bombs . . . '

Rosie spun round and flung her arms around Taddy, squeezing him tightly. 'Thank goodness you're all right,' she said, as she wiped the tears from her eyes. 'But what about the others? You can't have all gone for a fish supper?'

Taddy nodded. 'Yes, we did. It's old Ma Higgert's birthday, and Pa Higgert said it could be her last, so we should all go and never mind the ol' boat.'

Despite the severity of the situation, laughter escaped Rosie's lips. 'Well, looks like your fish supper saved you from a right nasty mess,' she said, ruffling Taddy's dark curls.

Taddy, who had been looking down at the barges that had exploded under the impact, nodded thoughtfully. 'Reckon we'd have been dead as dodos, though I don't know what we'll do now,' he said, picking up a piece of wood; the letters *Ree* were just visible beneath the mud.

A thought struck Rosie. 'You can all sleep on the *Kingfisher* tonight. We're carrying cotton, which is nice and soft, so you'll all be comfy and warm.'

Taddy grinned at her. 'It'll be fun with all of us together. Can I go and tell me mam and dad?'

Rosie nodded. 'And all the others,' she said. 'Good job you've had your tea though, as I don't think we've enough food to feed you all. But there's sufficient bread for toast in the morning and hopefully plenty of porridge too. Then we can set off for the canal offices.'

It took some time to repair the breaches in the canal, but once satisfied that they could do no more Rosie, Ken, Maggie and about ten bargees headed back to the *Kingfisher*, Ken was muttering underneath his breath. He couldn't understand why the ack-ack battery hadn't spotted the enemy. If he had been on duty, he said, he would have shot the buggers down.

Frog nodded grimly. 'First thing in the mornin' I'm off to sign up,' he said decidedly, waving a dismissive hand at his mother as he continued, 'I know I'm only fifteen, Ma, but I look older an' I ain't gonna sit idly by while those Nazis try and blow us all to kingdom come.'

Mrs Madison looked pleadingly at her husband. 'Eric, tell the boy . . . ' she began, but instead of arguing with his son Eric Madison gave her shoulders a reassuring squeeze.

'If we'd been on the *Reedcutter* tonight we could all have been killed. At least with our Kenneth watching out for us we'll all be a lot safer in us beds.'

'And me, and me,' Taddy shouted, waving the piece of wood that he had retrieved from the wreck of the *Reedcutter* above his head.

Mr Madison laid a calming hand on his son's shoulder and spoke firmly. 'Not you, Taddy, 'cos you're goin' to have to look after your ma. You'll be the man of the barge.' Taking care not to look into his wife's eyes, he continued, 'You see, I'm with Kenneth on this one. I've been thinkin' about joinin' up for a while, but what with the shortage of canal workers and the like I'd been putting it off. Not any longer . . . '

Mrs Madison gave a wail of despair. 'Not both of you,' she said, looking pleadingly into her husband's eyes.

But Eric Madison shook his head. 'It's no use, love, I've made me mind up.'

100

Taddy tugged at his mother's elbow. 'Don't you worry, Mam, I'll look after you — but I won't be cookin' nothin', else we'll both starve . . . '

A ripple of laughter ran through the group of bargees, and for the second time that night, Rosie called down silent blessings on Taddy's curly young head.

4

Several months had passed since the bombing of the canal. Frog and his father had both joined the army and were off doing their training, while Taddy and his mother were renting a new barge. And although Taddy was doing as much as he could, he was too small to be of any real use, so Patsy had offered to quit her parents' barge and step in until they got themselves sorted.

Rosie, who had been helping them load up, took the opportunity to ask Patsy whether she really did intend to join one of the services. The older girl had sniffed haughtily. 'Too right; I'll be gettin' the dirt of this canal out from under me fingernails just as soon as the Madisons get some permanent help,' she had said.

Rosie had half expected Patsy to deny the rumour that she intended to join the WAAF, but instead the other girl confirmed the gossip. 'I'm surprised you don't want to join up yerself,' Patsy had said. She glanced sidelong at Rosie. 'Have you spoken to Tim?'

Her tone had been disinterested, but she was fooling no one, especially not Rosie. Not wishing the other girl to know too much about her feelings for Tim, Rosie had simply nodded. 'You?'

Patsy, who had clearly been annoyed that Rosie had not gone into more detail, tried to hide her feelings with a false smile before replying. 'All the time. To be honest, I speak to Tim more than I do me own parents. He says he can't wait for me to join the WAAF and hopes we'll be stationed together.' She glanced sideways at Rosie again, a victorious smile on her lips. 'I'll be *sure* to let you know if we are.'

Rosie simply nodded, fearing her voice might betray her true feelings. She was sure that Patsy was lying, but as she had also told an untruth about talking to Tim, she could not in fairness accuse the other girl. If she could join the WAAF herself she'd be in before you could say knife, but with no real education to speak of and no skills to offer she feared she would not be accepted into any of the services and would simply make a fool of herself by trying. Feeling tears of resentment beginning to well up, she was thoroughly relieved when Pete came down from the canal office to inform her that two new recruits might be available in a couple of weeks, should she want them. She gave him a watery smile. 'Oh, Pete, I'd almost given up hope.'

Pete looked into her face, then glanced quickly at Patsy before turning his attention back to Rosie. 'You want to talk about this on the *Kingfisher*?' he asked diplomatically.

Rosie nodded. As they walked away, Pete looked back in the direction of the Madisons' new barge before asking, 'Is, er, everything okay? Not had bad news, I trust?'

Rosie pulled herself together. 'We're just missing Tim Bradley. It's been an awful long time since either of us has seen him,' she said, and saw the relief in Pete's face. He had clearly feared that an argument between her and Patsy could cause even more problems on the canal.

But that had been over a fortnight ago and now, as she stood on the deck of the *Kingfisher*, soaking up the sunshine, she re-read the letter she had just received from Tim as she nervously awaited the arrival of her newest crew members.

Dear Rosie, God how I miss the peace and tranquillity of the canals! I love my new life in the RAF but it seems you never get a minute to yourself. As you know I live in a hut with twenty other fellers, and we all eat, sleep, wash and work together, so there's never any time to be on your tod. I'm so glad that Pete's finally found you some new recruits. Let's just hope that this lot are keepers. I know you're going to be pretty cramped all living in the Kingfisher, but at least you can get off and go for a walk on your own. As for Maggie giving them a hard time, tell her that if she doesn't toe the line you'll give her the sack. That ought to sort her out.

Rosie also hoped that the new recruits would stay. She knew that both were older than she was, and while neither had extensive knowledge of canal boats, both had at some stage of their lives been aboard leisure boats and were not entirely ignorant when it came to nautical matters, or at least that's what their paperwork suggested.

Maggie, who was sulking in the main cabin,

cocked an ear to see if she could hear voices outside. Why on earth Rosie had insisted on volunteering to train up new recruits was beyond her comprehension. As if canal work wasn't hard enough without a couple of imbeciles getting under your feet and ramming the barge into the locks! All that trouble of teaching them not to hit everything in sight and what would they do? Leave because the work was too hard or the pay too poor, or they were missing their homes too much. Well, she was going to have no part in it, as she had told her daughter the previous day. 'You needn't think I'm teachin' 'em,' she had said sullenly. 'Got enough to do wi'out babysittin' a bunch of ingrates what don't know port from starboard.'

Rosie had raised her brows. 'I don't care if they don't know their gaskets from their pistons, as long as they know their front from their back,' she had said, grinning.

Maggie was perplexed. How could Rosie just pass it off like that, as if knowledge was irrelevant? Barges were dangerous enough as it was without a bunch of halfwits running around causing all sorts of chaos. She heaved a sigh. It was all irrelevant — this lot would last no longer than the previous ones, especially if Maggie had anything to do with it. No, she would wait for them to run home with a broken fingernail, or a stubbed toe, and try to persuade her daughter in the meantime that this recruitment business was a bad idea. She sat up suddenly. Was that approaching footsteps she heard?

'Morning, chaps!' Rosie jumped as a voice

boomed from behind her. 'Harriet Swires at your service, but everyone calls me Harri.'

As Rosie turned, she was surprised to see a very tall woman — she must have been nearly six feet, Rosie thought — with a large bosom and an almost equally large waist. Her hair was hidden by a flowery headscarf tied up like a turban, though a few wisps of dark brown hair had escaped around her ears, and large grey-blue eyes made a startling contrast with her lips, which she had painted bright red. Rosie screwed up her eyes to see what the woman had clenched between her teeth, and was alarmed to see that it was a tobacco pipe.

'Morning,' Harri repeated, hand outstretched as she leaned towards Rosie.

'Good morning,' Rosie said, quickly adding, 'I'm afraid you can't come aboard while you're smoking. We often carry highly flammable goods; one spark and . . . ' Rosie stretched her arms wide, 'boom! Will that be a problem?'

Harriet stood blinking at her for a moment or two, then pulled the pipe out of her mouth and waved it upside down. 'Empty, see?' she said cheerfully. 'Damned nasty habit which I gave up a while ago, but I can't seem to manage without sucking a pipe — albeit an empty one. I assume that's okay?'

Rosie nodded. 'Perfectly.' She stepped off the deck of the *Kingfisher* and held out her hand, which the other girl shook with enthusiasm. 'I'm Rosie O'Leary, Number One of the *Kingfisher* — that means I'm the captain — and this is Maggie Donahue.'

She turned to beckon to Maggie, but found

106

herself waving at an empty space. Blushing, she turned back to Harri. 'I'll introduce you later. Have you seen the other girl who's meant to be joining us?'

Harri nodded. 'Babs. She's just getting the birdseed from the bus — well, I hope she is — I left it there by accident. Can't have Pepè going hungry.'

As she spoke she stepped to one side to reveal a bulky brass cage on the towpath behind her. Rosie's jaw almost hit the floor as she locked eyes with a large and colourful parrot.

'What are you going to do with him?' Rosie breathed, although she was fairly certain she knew the answer.

'Well, I'm not going to be serving him up for lunch,' Harri said with a raucous laugh. 'Pepè'll be our fifth crew member. He's as good as any guard dog and he hates men. So he'll fit in with us girls nicely.'

'But where will you put him? The cabin's tiny — barely enough room to swing a cat . . . ' Rosie began.

'Don't worry, I won't be swinging him anywhere, and besides, he's not fussy. You can park him wherever, as long as he's got his seed and his night-time blanky, he'll be grand.'

Rosie looked doubtful, but with help not being easy to find she knew that her choices were limited. She hadn't had a single recruit since the bombing. Most women wanted to be in the WAAF or the Wrens, not least because of the uniforms, while even the Land Army seemed preferable to working in a cramped environment with few breaks and long hours.

Obviously sensing Rosie's doubt, Harri spoke up. 'He can go on the roof in good weather, or in with the load when it's the middle of winter, and like I said he's a good guard dog — or should that be bird? Anyone comes near the boat and he'll sing like a canary.' Making up her mind, Rosie held out a welcoming arm, indicating for Harri to step aboard. Harri grinned. 'Don't worry, You'll not know he's here.'

A loud squawk from Pepè told Rosie differently, and she noticed Harri's brow furrow as she reprimanded Pepè for his outburst. 'He'll be fine once he gets used to the boat, and the crew . . . ' Harri said, her voice trailing off as she heaved the cage on to the cabin roof. 'Give it a month or two, three at the most, and you'll barely notice him.'

Maggie's head appeared from inside. 'What in God's name — ' she began, but Rosie cut her off.

'Harri, this is Maggie, Maggie, Harri.' She smothered a smile at her mother's rounding eyes when she saw Pepè. 'Oh, and this is Pepè. He's our new guard bird.'

Maggie opened and closed her mouth like a gaping fish in an effort to find adequate words, but Rosie wasn't going to give her a chance. 'He stays.' She glanced at Harri, who was holding out a hand to Maggie. 'I like him,' Rosie finished, raising one eyebrow while waiting for the torrent of objections, but instead the cabin doors slammed firmly behind Maggie as she descended into its depths.

Rosie smiled at Harri. 'Don't mind Maggie. She doesn't like change, and what with one thing and another she's had more than her fair share of it the last couple of years.' Feeling that a further explanation was called for, she continued, 'You see, Maggie's me mam, and it's she who rents the *Kingfisher*. On the last boat she was the Number One, but since we got the engine — which she hates — her husband's joined the army and it's me who's now in charge.'

Harri let out a low whistle. 'Bit tough taking orders from your daughter, I imagine, but not to worry. She'll soon get used to us.'

A jubilant cry from the towpath interrupted her. 'Got it!' It was the long-awaited Babs, and she was holding out a bag of what Rosie guessed must be Pepè's birdseed. 'Driver give me a right dirty look when I said what I was lookin' for. He reckons birds shouldn't be allowed to travel on a bus, war or no war, but like I told him, Pepè's doin' his bit for Britain, just like the rest of us.' She grinned down at Rosie and Harri. 'Oops, sorry, forgot. I'm Babs, or Barbara Wilcox, if we're bein' formal. You I know,' she said as she thrust the bag of birdseed into Harri's grateful hands. 'And I'm guessing you're one of us,' she said to Rosie. 'So where's Blackbeard? Is he a looker or have I signed up for a boat run by Peg Leg?'

Rosie raised her eyebrows and checked her reflection in the water. 'Well, I've not got a beard — black or otherwise — and . . . ' she looked down at her feet, 'these are definitely my own

109

legs.' She grinned up at Babs, who was looking like a rabbit caught in headlights.

'Oh my word, I'm ever so sorry. I was just havin' a bit of fun, you know, break the ice kinda thing,' she said nervously, taking Rosie's outstretched hand and giving it a feeble shake before stepping down to join them. 'It's just that you're so young and, well, clean!'

Rosie smiled. 'I'll take that as a compliment. Don't worry, Babs — I expect a lot of people are surprised to see a clean young Number One.'

'That's what they call the captains of these canal boats,' Harri put in with a satisfied smile. 'I'm learnin' the lingo already, even though my doubting parents thought I'd not last more than two minutes on a working boat.' She rolled her eyes dramatically. 'When I said I was going to join the war effort, Mummy and Daddy tried to insist that I go into the WAAF, but I told them no go, I'm not going anywhere without Pepè, and especially not with a bunch of public schoolboys flying their kites. When I said I was joining the canals I thought Daddy was going to have a coronary.' She smiled wistfully. 'Bet you a pound to a penny he still tells his friends I'm in the WAAF.'

Babs raised a brow at Rosie. Harriet was clearly from an upper class family, although on first sight you would never have believed it. Babs on the other hand was a short, buxom woman, with wide brown eyes and bleached blonde hair, and she spoke with a broad Liverpool accent. 'I don't like heights, so that was the WAAF out; I don't like the sea, so that was the Wrens out;

I've not got the best eyesight, so no ack-ack battery for me; and I doesn't like cows nor chickens, so no Land Army.' She paused. 'And I ain't workin' in no factory and comin' out lookin' like a daffodil. I'd look a right sight with my hair!'

Rosie laughed at Babs's honesty. 'Well, let's hope you'll like life on the canals. It's not easy by any stretch, but I believe you've had some experience on boats?'

Babs looked doubtful. 'I went on me cousin Bessie's dad's mate's sailin' boat when I were twelve for a couple of days durin' the school hols ... I don't know whether you could call it experience as such.' She chewed her bottom lip ruefully. 'It were on Lake Windermere, and when it were my turn to steer I nearly capsized us.' She gave Rosie an apologetic smile. 'But it's better than never having set foot on a boat, I suppose?'

Rosie tried her best to look on the positive side of things as she surveyed her motley crew. It looked as though she was going to be doing a lot of teaching from scratch over the next few months, and despite Maggie's insistence that she would not lift a finger Rosie knew that her mother would not see the *Kingfisher* suffer through the newcomers' inexperience. With enough badgering her mother would help, albeit complaining and tutting loudly, while muttering 'For God's sake' under her breath at every given opportunity.

Realising she had not answered Babs, Rosie placed a reassuring hand on the other girl's shoulders, then nodded. 'You're right, it's better than nothing, and don't worry, Babs. You

111

couldn't possibly capsize a canal boat, no matter how hard you tried.'

★ ★ ★

Two weeks into their roles as crew members of the *Kingfisher*, Babs and Harri were coming along nicely, and Rosie had decided that they were ready to take on their first load. Harri in particular had taken to life on board a canal boat surprisingly well, considering she was used to a grand house with large gardens and maids. To begin with Rosie had thought that Harri's parents would soon be patting themselves on the backs when their daughter returned home with her tail between her legs, but instead she revelled in her new role. Her uncle owned a pleasure boat with an engine, and Harri — much like Tim — loved all things mechanical. She was already familiar with that side of things; it was just the steering of the boat — being done with a tiller rather than a wheel — that took some getting used to.

'Pushing the opposite way to where you want to go, that's the tricky part,' Rosie said, as she hastily pushed the tiller back towards Harri. 'Left to go right, and vice versa.'

Harri, pipe clenched firmly between her teeth, had given the thumbs up. Whenever it was her turn at the tiller, the barge would bump its way along the canal banks as she fought to keep it in a straight line, while Pepè's cage spent more time on its side than it did upright, with Babs and Rosie rushing to pick it up before it rolled into the canal. One of them would try to soothe Pepè's frantic squawking as the other scooped the birdseed back into his bowl, trying to avoid his hooked beak as he sought to take his revenge for such cavalier treatment. Harri, on the other hand, would remain completely unruffled at the tiller, calling out: 'Don't worry, Pepè, Mummy'll soon get the hang of it.'

Babs, however, was more like Maggie. She jumped whenever she managed to start the engine, which would splutter and choke before roaring into life, and she found it difficult to keep the boat at an even speed, although steering came naturally to her.

'Bloody useless, the pair of 'em,' Maggie said one night, as the two new crew members went off to fetch supplies from the village shop. 'That bloody parrot ought to have his neck wrung if you ask me, bleedin' screechin' for no reason. And once Harri gets her backside into the cabin there's barely room to breathe!'

Rosie suppressed a chuckle. Her mother had been determined to dislike the new crew members before she'd even met them, and the fact that Harri was a bit of a character gave her even more cause to moan.

'Bet she'll be off down the pub every night gettin' drunk,' she had said with disapproval. 'Probably spreadin' all sorts of rumours, that one. Loose cannon, that's what she is . . . '

Rosie had looked at her mother incredulously. 'Well, people must be pretty hard up for gossip if they want to hear all about life on the *Kingfisher*. The most exciting part of my day at

113

the moment is when I save Pepè from the drink.'

Her mother had pursed her lips and muttered under her breath, but Rosie would not listen to any poison about Harri or Babs. As far as she was concerned her life had got far more pleasant since their arrival.

'You're just jealous because Harri's good with the engine, and even Babs can start it, and keep the boat moving, in spite of being frightened of it. At least she gives it a go, whereas you won't even try any more.' She had given her mother a warning look. 'Don't go criticisin' others over jobs you won't do yourself.'

In all these altercations, whenever Maggie didn't like the sound of something she would retire to the depths of the main cabin, closing the doors firmly behind her. Why couldn't the dratted child see that she was just trying to help? It was hardly Maggie's fault if the girls didn't do things the way she was used to having them done. It had never been her idea to bring them on board in the first place, yet she was the one who was always apparently in the wrong. She tutted under her breath. Maybe she was jealous, but who wouldn't be? First her position aboard the *Kingfisher* had changed, then Ken left, and if that wasn't bad enough, to top it all other women had been brought in, who Rosie claimed were doing a better job than she!

On deck, Rosie shook her head. What on earth did her mother think Harri could say about the crew of the *Kingfisher* that was so bad? They never did anything that other bargees didn't do themselves. And besides, Rosie was grateful for the company. Since Daisy and Tim had gone, she barely had anyone to talk to. She conjured up an image of the big mare in her mind. She knew Daisy was happy in her new role as a farm horse, but it didn't stop her missing her oldest friend. With thoughts of Daisy in her mind, she decided that the next time they moored near Pank's farm she would take Harri and Babs along to meet her.

Today, however, the *Kingfisher* was fully laden and setting off to make her first deliveries with her new crew. Rosie had asked Babs if she wanted to have a go at taking the boat through the first lock, but one look at the small pale face had given Rosie her answer, so now, standing at the rear of the *Kingfisher*, she handed control of the tiller over to Harri. 'Keep her steady as she goes, and don't take your eyes off the cill.' She turned to her mother and Babs. 'Maggie, you and Babs can do the gates.' The two women jumped on to the towpath, and as they did so the lock keeper walked towards them.

'Wotcher, Maggie,' he said with a broad smile. 'Ernie Broad said you wasn't far behind 'im, and with this bein' your new crew's first lock I thought I'd come down and make sure you didn't do no damage — to the lock, that is, not the *Kingfisher*,' he said with a wink.

Maggie shot him a withering look. 'Very funny, Arnie, but I think I've been doin' this long enough not to damage me own vessel.' She turned to show Babs where to put the key. 'Don't turn it till they tell you to, and then I'll give you a hand, else we'll be here all day. And no matter what, don't let no bugger borrow it!'

Down on the barge, Harri addressed Rosie. 'What's the cill?'

'It's a sort of ledge that they use when they want to do repairs,' Rosie explained. 'When the water level sinks, if you're too far back, you'll catch the rudder on the cill.' She pointed to where a large lump of wood was now looming into view. 'That's it, that's the cill. Once we're clear of it, we can move back so's they can open the gates. Now, take her slowly forward.'

Harri did as she was told, and as the boat moved slightly forward Rosie held out a hand, Harri laid off the throttle, and after a moment or so Arnie shouted down, 'Righto, ladies, back a bit so's we can get these gates open.'

Rosie nodded to Harri. 'You know what to do. The gates'll swing inwards, which is why we have to go back, but don't worry about the cill, we're clear of it now.'

Nodding, Harri eased the boat back, and Maggie and Babs successfully opened the gates. Rosie nodded to Harri. 'Well done! First lock done and dusted. Forwards now, then wait for the girls to close the lock gates behind us, and once they're back on board we can move off.'

Harri was beaming with delight. 'That was fun. Quite exciting, in fact, and once you know what the cill is and where it is, it's really quite easy.' She waved enthusiastically at the lock keeper as they slowly chugged away from the gates. 'Thank you, Mr Arnie. See you on the way back.'

Smiling, Arnie removed his hat and scratched

his head. 'Is that a parrot?' he said, pointing at Pepè.

Rosie laughed and nodded. 'Sure is, and a real beauty too.'

The man shook his head. 'Blimey, you see it all on the canals.' He turned and made his way back along the path, calling over his shoulder as he went, 'Cheerio, ladies. Safe journey.'

★   ★   ★

It had been a few weeks since the girls had negotiated their first lock, and Liverpool had become prey to heavy bombing. Standing on the deck of the *Kingfisher*, the women watched in horror as the bombs of the German Luftwaffe rained down on their beloved city. It was the fourth night of raids and the enemy had shown no mercy in their attack on the people of Liverpool. The previous night the SS *Malakand*, which was loaded with munitions, had been hit while she was berthed in Huskisson Dock. Onlookers had compared the explosion to that of a burning barrage balloon, and despite the fact that the firefighters had quickly extinguished the initial flames they had been unable to prevent fires from the dockyard sheds from reaching the ship, causing over a thousand tons of bombs to explode. The dock and several surrounding quays had been destroyed while the *Kingfisher* had been on her way back from Leeds, where she had unloaded her cargo of grain.

Babs covered her face with her hands and sobbed. 'Those poor, poor people. They aren't army folk, just regular folk of Liverpool, like us. No danger to anyone . . . '

Rosie put her arm round Babs's shoulders and, giving them a squeeze, shook her head sadly. 'They don't care, queen. They've been given their orders and that's that as far as they're concerned.'

Harri, her pipe clenched tightly between her teeth, also placed a comforting arm round Babs's shoulder. 'I wish we could be down there helping, but at times like these you have to be practical, and us turning up close to the docks would just give them more to worry about.'

Babs fished a handkerchief out of her sleeve and blew her nose noisily. 'We must go down first thing in the mornin' though, when we're loadin' up, and see if there's owt we can do,' she said, her voice a mixture of statement and enquiry.

Rosie nodded her head decidedly. 'Course we will. The lads from the loadin' bays should know which direction to point us in. We've made good time so far on all our runs, so a day's work helpin' the good folk of Liverpool won't set our deliveries back by much. Anyway, we can travel the canal by night, especially if the moon's as bright as it is tonight.'

Babs gave out a wail of despair. 'Oh, I do hope there's not another bombers' moon tomorrer. Haven't they suffered enough?'

Rosie grimaced. Babs was right. A clear night sky worked both ways. It provided the barge with enough light to traverse the canals safely, but it also meant the Luftwaffe could see their way across the Channel and hit their targets with precision. Looking towards the city, the women could see incendiary bombs falling out of the night sky, while the sound of fire engines' bells rang furiously across the city as their crews fought desperately to control the flames the firewatchers had not managed to get to in time.

Maggie, who had been down in the main cabin preparing their evening meal, poked her head through the doors and called out, 'Supper's ready, if you want it. Best come an' get it while it's still hot.'

Babs, who normally avoided confrontation, or any kind of arguing, turned a tear-stained face to her, a look of sheer disbelief in her eyes. 'Supper? Who cares about supper? There are people down there dying . . . '

Maggie shrugged her shoulders indifferently. 'Please yerself, but if I heard my daughter correctly you want to go and help out tomorrow?'

Babs wiped her nose on the back of her hand. 'And? What's wrong with that?' she snapped, her usual friendly demeanour hidden under her frustration.

'Nothin' wrong wi' it,' Maggie said, her tone calm and even. 'But you'll be a damn sight more use to them folks if you've eaten properly and have a bit o' strength in yer bones.'

Babs placed the back of her hand against her forehead. 'Oh, Maggie, I'm sorry. I didn't mean to snap — ' she began, but the older woman cut her off.

'No need for apologies. These is stressful times

we're livin' in.' Rosie noticed that Maggie was not making eye contact with any of the crew as she spoke, and suspected that her mother — who though she might have been a hard taskmaster, was no monster — was holding herself together by the skin of her teeth.

She smiled at her. 'Thanks, Mam, and you're right. We'll be of no use to anyone without a decent meal in us and a good night's kip. I'll get up real early and have us in Liverpool before the milk carts arrive.' Turning to the two women, she gestured for them to go ahead of her into the main cabin. 'It'll be hard to sleep with all that goin' on, but like I said, me mam's right.'

★   ★   ★

The next day Maggie offered to stay with the *Kingfisher* to supervise the loading, while Rosie, Babs and Harri went into the city to help clear up after the previous night's bombing raid. The three women encountered several volunteers who directed them to a WVS van on Great George Street, where the Belgian Seaman's Hotel had been hit by a high explosive bomb.

'I don't see how anyone can be left alive in the rubble what's left,' one of the men had informed Rosie. 'But you have to do your best, don't you? An' you gals turning up to give a hand is three more pairs of hands to help wi' the workload.'

As they made their way to Great George Street, they passed several buildings where fire crews were still trying to douse the flames. Dust and smoke still clouded the air, and men and women formed human chains as they called out to strangers, friends and family who they feared were trapped beneath the rubble. Every now and then someone would call for quiet and everyone — even the birds themselves, it seemed — would fall silent, straining their ears as they listened for sounds of life.

The three women helped clear bomb debris late into the afternoon, and as they headed back to the barge Babs's cheery demeanour seemed to return. 'We did well, didn't we, girls? We helped find people, and even though some of them didn't make it at least their families will be able to give them a decent burial. And as for those we did dig out, safe and sound, well, the looks on their faces . . . ' and despite her best efforts to remain upbeat, Babs's voice began to quiver.

Rosie took the other girl's hand in hers. 'We did do good, Babs, and every time we have the chance to come and help out we will. We might not be able to do fire watchin' and the like, but we can lend a hand the next day, and as you saw for yourself, that's just as important.'

Babs wiped a tear off the tip of her nose. 'I know you're right, I just wish we could prevent things like this from happening in the first place.'

Harri, who had been walking in silent thought, spoke up. 'That's what our chaps are doin' overseas. Trying to stop Hitler in his tracks. If you ask me, they must be having some sort of effect on him, and that's why we're getting the rough end of the stick, as it were.'

Dropping down into the canal basin, they walked towards the *Kingfisher*, now laden and covered ready for the journey ahead. As they approached the barge, Pepè gave a loud squawk, and the doors to the main cabin opened as Maggie came out on to the deck.

'Ah, so you're back then,' she said. 'I've plated up a tea of ham, eggs and cold pie for you all, so you can get on the outside of that before we set off.' She turned to Harri. 'By the way, that bloody bird of yours needs tellin'.'

Harri looked dismayed. 'What's he done now? He's been in his cage all day, so he's probably got a little bit grumpy, and I dare say he's raised his voice once or twice . . . '

Maggie glared at her. 'Raised his voice? Raised his voice? He's done that all right, and it's you I blame.' Seeing the look of bewilderment on Harri's face, she carried on, 'You need to mind your tongue, my woman, 'cos that there parrot can talk. And when one of the lads made a mistake and dropped the coal from up high instead of down low, he' — she pointed an accusing finger in the direction of the offender — 'come out with some real cuss words, like what you used when them bombs was goin' off the other night.' She scowled at the trio of women, who were trying to hide their amusement. 'And what's more,' Maggie continued, 'the blokes in the loadin' bay accused me of teachin' him swear words! As if I'd ever do summat like that. They thought it were right funny, and I dare say half the docks know about your Pepè by now.'

Rosie watched as Harri tried to apologise while keeping a straight face. 'I didn't know he

122

could talk,' Harri explained. 'He's never done it in my hearing, or I'd have watched what I said in front of him. Don't worry, Maggie — from now on I'll mind my p's and q's.'

The apology seemed to do the trick and Maggie grudgingly accepted it, muttering to herself that the bird was obviously more intelligent than its owner. She sank back into the main cabin, calling out to remind them that their tea was ready. One by one the three women descended, to find that Maggie had laid the plated food on the small table and placed Pepè in his usual spot, just inside the cabin doors. Sitting down, they told Maggie about their day in the city and the devastation they had found there. When they had finished, Rosie announced that she would take the first shift on their route up the canal. 'Harri, you can take over from me, and then Babs will take over from you. Fair?'

The question was destined to remain unanswered. At that moment, Maggie, who had been clearing the table, tripped. As she struggled to regain her balance, the pile of dirty plates she was carrying slipped from her grasp and fell to the floor with a resounding crash.

Pepè said a bad word, so did Maggie.

★ ★ ★

The May blitz had been relentless, and when the break came for the first time in seven nights, the city of Liverpool breathed a sigh of relief. According to the newsreels, Hitler had moved his attention to the Soviet Union. The docks became busy once more and Rosie decided that they all needed a night off.

'The Panks' farm — that's where our old horse Daisy lives — isn't too far from Tuppenny Corner. Let's go and visit her and then walk down Tuppenny Lane into Bishopswood for some fish and chips and maybe catch one of the newsreels. What do you reckern?'

While Babs and Harri jumped at the idea, Maggie pulled a face. 'What on earth would I want to go and see that silly old mare for? She's the reason why I was stripped of my role as Number One — '

Rosie interrupted her. 'No, Mam, it's your fault you lost the position of Number One. It were your idea to get rid of her, not mine. Lord only knows I didn't want her to go.'

Maggie grimaced. 'Well either way, I'm not stoppin' 'ere with that bloomin' thing squawking all night. I'll go for a wander up the towpath and see if the Sally Anne's moored up nearby. If she is, I'll visit the Bradleys for an hour or so while you go off and enjoy yerselves.'

Accordingly, later that evening all four women left the barge. Pepè had had his night blanket thrown over his cage and was happily sleeping on his perch. As they reached the gate that led into Daisy's old field, the girls bade Maggie goodbye and climbed over.

'The pony in here is a bit cheeky, but he's lovely really,' Rosie informed her friends. 'I trust neither of you are scared of horses? Ah, here he comes. Oh, dear . . . ' As the pony approached it was plain to see that he was very lame, and when he drew nearer Rosie looked down at his feet. 'Well! Look at the state of your hooves you poor thing, nobody's trimmed your hooves for ever such a long time.'

Harri ran her hand over the pony's enormous tummy. 'Are you sure it's a he? Only he does look rather like my old mare when she was in foal . . .'

Rosie shook her head in dismay. 'Positive. I'm afraid the man who owns him isn't giving him any exercise or caring for him at all. If you don't mind, ladies, I'd like to call in on the Panks and have a word with them about this poor dear.'

Harri raised her brow. 'They may not take kindly to you criticising someone they rent to,' she said. 'A lot of landowners see it as none of their business what their tenants get up to.'

Rosie shook her head. 'Not the Panks. They're good people, and I'm sure they can't realise what state he's in.' She pushed her fingers into the pony's mane. 'No one's combed your mane or your tail, and yet I thought you were some little girl's pride and joy.'

Babs glanced at her wristwatch. 'I don't mind the pony, but I'm not sure about meeting Daisy. I seem to remember you said summat about her being really big. Besides, if we're to see Daisy *and* visit the Panks we'll have to get a move on else we won't catch the newsreel in time.'

They crossed Tuppenny Lane and Rosie opened the gate into the Panks' stable yard, where, to her delight, she saw that Daisy was being groomed outside one of the stables by Mr Pank himself, who turned to greet his visitors.

'Ladies! And I see that one of you used to own this here fine mare. Come on over and say hello.' He leaned forward and shook Babs and Harri warmly by the hand. Turning back to Rosie, he patted Daisy's flank. 'Notice anything?' he said, a wide grin almost splitting his face in two.

Rosie's eyes lit up. 'She's in foal! Oh, Mr Pank, when's she due?'

Mr Pank was glowing with pride. 'Any day now; that's why we've got her out, so's we can check on her progress.' He pointed to the mare's udder. 'She's swelling, so we know the foal's on its way pretty soon.'

Babs leaned forward to touch Daisy's nose, then changed her mind. Rosie laughed. 'Give her a stroke. It's okay — she's not a cow, and she's certainly not a chicken.'

Babs giggled. 'Bloomin' big chicken.' She stretched out her arm and gingerly stroked Daisy's long nose with the tips of her fingers. 'I wonder whether she'll have a boy or a girl?'

Rosie smiled. 'You mean a colt or a filly! Well I'm guessing Daisy won't be bothered, but what would you prefer, Mr Pank?'

The farmer removed his flat cap and scratched thoughtfully at his balding head. 'The stallion we put Daisy to was a fine chap. Outstanding temperament, plenty of feathers and excellent conformation; he was knocking on for seventeen hands high. On the other hand, mares is easier, 'cos you don't have to worry about 'em escapin' the field in order to sire.'

Rosie giggled as she looked at Babs's blank expression, but before she could open her mouth to speak Harri said kindly, 'He's saying the father has plenty of long hair on his legs and that he's well shaped.'

'Ah ... righty-ho,' Babs said, nodding, although Rosie didn't quite believe that the other girl was any the clearer.

She looked shyly at Mr Pank. 'Talking of mares in foal, we've just come up through Daisy's old field, the one with the new pony in — new since Daisy, I mean — and, well, I hope you don't mind my sayin', Mr Pank, but it looks as though that pony is bein' neglected. His hooves are so long he's lame, and his belly's so big I wouldn't be surprised if he was laminitic.'

Mr Pank shifted awkwardly. 'I know, queen, and I've been in touch with the owner — Mr Farland — and he's assured me he's goin' to come and see the pony sometime durin' the next week, and that he'll bring a farrier with him.' He smoothed a hand over Daisy's bulging belly. 'One of the farmhands reported it to me last week, and I must say Mr Farland didn't take kindly to the news at first, reckoned what with him rentin' the field we didn't have the right to go in there. But when I explained that we hadn't gone in, just that the pony had wandered over to look at the lads replacing some fencin', he eased off a bit.'

Rosie furrowed her brow. Why on earth would someone mind people going into the field the pony was in . . . or maybe he simply didn't take too well to being criticised. She wondered if Mr Pank would tell her not to walk across the field in future, but it appeared that the notion had not

127

even entered the farmer's head.

Feeling better now that she knew the pony was going to receive some care and attention, she decided to let the matter drop. In any case, Daisy was nuzzling her pockets. 'Same old Daisy, always thinking of your stomach,' she laughed. As she pulled out a treacle sandwich from its greaseproof wrapping, a thought occurred to her. 'It is okay to feed her a treat, isn't it?' she asked Mr Pank hopefully.

Mr Pank smiled kindly. 'My life wouldn't be worth living if I stopped you giving Daisy here a treacle sandwich. She'd have my guts for garters.'

Rosie smiled at Babs, who was looking hopeful. 'Would you like to feed her?'

Babs nodded eagerly, although when Rosie handed over the sandwich she sensed her friend's hesitance. Taking Babs's hand, Rosie straightened the fingers, then told her to keep her palm flat and still while Daisy took the sandwich.

Screwing her eyes up, Babs let out an 'Oohh' before opening one eye again and smiling at Rosie. 'She was so soft, I barely felt her take it!'

Rosie patted the big mare's neck. 'A gentle giant, that's what Daisy is, as well as being my oldest and dearest friend.' She turned to Harri. 'I've just remembered. When we were in the pony's field you said something about your old mare?'

Harri nodded. 'Had her since I was knee high to a grasshopper. Father owns a stud in Ireland, and whenever we went over on a visit I used to ride Bramble.' She smiled wistfully. 'She was a strawberry roan, no more than fourteen hands high, and she used to get sweet itch in the summer. Poor thing used to scratch her mane clear off, and the top of her tail. I used to ride her bareback into the sea, because Father said the salt water was good for it, and I'm pretty sure he was right; at least, it always seemed to get better after a nice long swim.'

Rosie eyed Harri with envy. How she would have loved to ride Daisy on a sandy beach, leaving hoof-prints behind for the incoming tide to sweep away. Not for the first time, Rosie wondered why on earth Harri had given up what seemed to be a charmed life to work a barge. If Rosie had the sort of parents Harri had, with plenty of money, land and horses, she was pretty sure she wouldn't want to be on the canals. Still, she supposed it took all sorts.

Babs was nudging Rosie with her elbow and when Rosie turned she saw the other girl making eyes at her wristwatch. 'Sorry, Babs,' she said. 'I think we'd better be off, Mr Pank, 'cos we're headin' into town to catch a newsreel, and then we're goin' for fish and chips.'

Mr Pank licked his lips and rubbed his stomach. 'Cor, I wish I were goin' for fish and chips. Can I come too?'

'Girls only, I'm afraid.' Rosie winked. 'Better luck next time.'

The farmer pretended to wail with despair before giving them a cheery wave goodbye. 'Off you go, then, and have a good time. Who knows, next time I see you, Daisy may have had the foal!'

The girls were heading for the lane that led to the main road, but Rosie stopped short and turned back to face Mr Pank. 'Gosh, I almost forgot! We're in a good routine now, so I should be able to call in next week if that's okay?'

He gave a mock salute. 'Aye aye, Miss Rosie, we'll expect to see you soon.'

Rosie was smiling as she caught the others up. Mr Pank was a dear, and she could not wait to see the new foal.

On their way back from their trip to town, Rosie chose a different route. 'There's rabbit holes in the pony's field, and I don't fancy my foot slipping down one of them in the dark,' she explained to Babs and Harri. 'And to be honest it's quicker this way if you're going home straight from town.'

The *Kingfisher* appeared to be in complete darkness as they approached, for the shutters that covered the small round windows were more than adequate to keep the lantern light from escaping. Rosie gave a perfunctory knock to give Maggie time to shade the light before she opened the doors to the main cabin. Maggie complied, but when the girls were safely in and the doors closed once more, Rosie noticed that her mother appeared to be deep in thought. She looked curiously at her. 'Everything okay?'

Maggie shrugged her shoulders. 'I think so, but I can't be sure.'

'How do you mean?' There was something about her demeanour that made Rosie feel uneasy.

Maggie grimaced. 'When I came back to the

barge, it felt like someone had been aboard. I thought it was you three at first, but of course, you were nowhere to be seen.'

Rosie glanced quickly round the cabin. When Ken had left to join the army she had returned to her old bunk alongside her mother, and now all four women 'mucked in together', as Maggie resentfully phrased it, although when offered the use of the engine room instead she had indignantly refused. 'Is there anything missing? Not that we've much to take, mind you . . . ' She reached up to where they kept their documents and found, to her relief, that all their identity papers, ration books and union cards were still in the cubbyhole. Quickly, she fished under her bed and felt the small collection of letters that Tim had written to her. Satisfied that all was well, she looked enquiringly at her mother. 'Everything's here, so what made you think someone had been on board?'

Maggie shrugged. 'I can't place my finger on it, but it looked like there was something different about the *Kingfisher* when I were walking home. I've been racking me brains all evenin', but I just can't think what's out of place.'

Harri looked puzzled. 'You thought someone had been on the barge before you'd even boarded?'

Maggie waved a dismissive hand. 'Forget I said anythin'. I'm just bein' silly.'

But Rosie knew her mother would not have mentioned it if she hadn't thought it was significant. Glancing around the cabin once more, and still seeing nothing untoward, Rosie was about to make ready for bed when Babs leaned across and gently lifted the corner of Pepè's blanket. An indignant squawk caused everyone to jump. Maggie pursed her lips. 'For God's sake, girl, that's the first thing I checked. Parrots is worth a lorra money to the right people.'

Apologising, Babs hastily dropped the corner of the blanket. 'Well, I reckon if someone did try and get on board, Pepè would've gone off like an air raid siren.'

Despite her anxiety, the older woman started laughing. 'I reckon you're right there, damned bird.'

With good humour restored, the crew of the *Kingfisher* bedded down for the night.

5

Rosie looked at the letter in front of her with dismay. It was from Tim.

24 March 1942

My dearest Rosie,

I'm afraid all leave has been cancelled. It seems we're needed here. Can't say why, obviously, but no matter what the reason, the fact still remains that as far as coming to see you is concerned, it's a 'no go'. I've also got some news on the second part of my dream. I've been told that I'm my own worst enemy as I'm so good with the engines that I can't be spared to go any higher — if you get my meaning — so I'm to remain grounded for the time being at least!

I heard from Patsy the other day. It seems she's leaving the canals. Don't know where she'll be going, but she's following the same route as me. Who knows, with a bit of luck she might be sent here.

Rosie felt her stomach clench. She always looked forward to Tim's epistles, but this one she could have done without. She wondered if she might go and see him, but without knowing where he was it would be impossible, of course. It had been a long time since they had spoken over the phone, but if she were to ring him, maybe they could arrange something. Even if it were only for an hour or so it would be worth it, she thought. Making up her mind, she folded the thin sheets of paper and tucked them beneath the pink ribbon that she used to keep all his letters tied neatly together. She would write to Tim, asking him when would be a convenient time for her to telephone him.

★ ★ ★

'Tim? Is that you?'

The voice that answered sounded tinny and far away. 'Of course it is, you dope. Who else do you think it would be?'

A smile spread over Rosie's lips. He hadn't changed; he was the same old Tim, quick to tease, but always kind. 'You sound so different. Is everything okay? Have you seen Patsy yet?' Rosie crossed her fingers and screwed up her eyes as she waited for his response.

'No, and I don't expect to either. The chances of her coming here after basic training are pretty slim, as there're hundreds of places she could be sent to, that's if she passes . . . '

Rosie let out a sigh of relief and opened her eyes once more. Not intending to spend the entire three minutes talking about Patsy, she cut him short. 'I know you can't say where you are, but you know where I am, so how about we get together when it's convenient for you and have a pub lunch somewhere? Would you be allowed?'

She could hear the amusement in Tim's voice. 'They're not complete monsters, you know. I'm sure they'd allow me out for lunch. I'll ask the sarge and send you a telegram to let you know where and when . . . is there any time you can't do?'

Rosie shook her head before remembering she was on the telephone and adding quickly, 'No, any time's fine by me.'

'*Caller, your time is up, please replace the receiver.*'

'Goodbye — ' Rosie heard the disconnecting click before Tim could get any more words out. Replacing the receiver, she held the door of the telephone box open so that the old man who was next in line might enter. Inside she felt euphoric. She was actually going to see Tim! It may not be for long and it might be an awful drag to get there, but none of that mattered. She was going to spend some time with her dearest friend.

★ ★ ★

Having only ever been on the overhead railway, Rosie was unprepared for the cramped conditions of wartime travel. Sitting in a small compartment with at least ten other passengers, she wondered how on earth they were all going to manage the arduous journey from Liverpool to Derbyshire. She glanced at the young woman sitting opposite her, who had two small children with her. The little girl — Rosie thought she looked about three — was settled firmly on her lap, while her brother, who couldn't have been more than five, had squeezed into the small gap left between his mother and the passenger to her right. As the woman caught Rosie's eye, the two smiled at one another. Rosie thought that if she was dreading the journey ahead, the young mother must be equally anxious, if not more.

Eyeing the rest of the passengers, Rosie saw that military personnel outnumbered civilians. There was a young man in RAF uniform, probably about the same age as Tim. Rosie longed to ask if he knew her friend, but realised that it would be a silly question. The RAF was a huge sector of the armed forces, and the likelihood of this young man having met her Tim was remote to say the least. She chided herself inwardly. Her Tim indeed; she was setting herself up for a fall if she thought of her friend in such a way. She tried to remember the last time she had seen Tim and realised, to her surprise, that it had been almost two years ago. Eyeing the young man, with his short crisp hair and athletic body evident through his uniform, Rosie wondered if this was how Tim looked now. In some respects, two years wasn't very long, but Tim was eighteen now, and considered a man.

Looking out of the compartment window as the train's whistle blew and the engine gathered momentum, Rosie saw her reflection in the glass. In the past she had been mistaken for a boy because of her short haircut and lack of curves, but this was no longer the case. She was seventeen years old and her hair fell past her shoulders, although she always wore it in a ponytail for ease, and her once boyish figure had now revealed a small waist and curves in all the right places. She cast her eyes up at the luggage rack above the young mother's head as she recalled her 'first bra' shopping expedition with Maggie. The woman in the shop had taken Rosie's measurements and informed Maggie that the 'young lady' really should have been bought a bra before.

Maggie's gaze had fallen to Rosie's bust before reverting to the shop assistant, and she had given a contemptuous sniff. 'No point wasting good money on bras while she were still growin', but I reckon she's all done now.'

Rosie had felt the blush race up her neck and face and straight into her hair line. She had felt self-conscious about the shopping trip before they had even set off and had wanted to go on her own, but Maggie had insisted she would not know how to go about it. With no experience of bra-buying, Rosie had believed her mother to be right, but at that moment she had known that nothing she could have said or done would have been more excruciating than that.

Now, as she sat crammed into her seat, she thought that while she had changed it was highly unlikely that Tim would look any different. Boys just got bigger; there were no bras to worry about — or waists — just height and girth.

One of her travelling companions was a young WAAF. Looking at her smart uniform, Rosie tried to envisage how she herself would look in air force blue. And before she could stop it, a picture of Patsy in full WAAF uniform flashed before her eyes. She scowled; why did she have to think of Patsy! There was no way she could try and conjure up an image of herself in that neat uniform now, not after a picture of the platinum blonde, with her slim body and neat curves filling out the uniform, had entered her thoughts. Rosie had no need to see an image of Patsy in WAAF uniform to know that the other girl would be a far more striking image than Rosie herself.

Soothed by the rhythm of the wheels on the track, Rosie leaned her head against the glass window and closed her eyes. A few years ago this journey would have been too much for the naive girl she had been, but now, as Number One of the *Kingfisher*, she knew that, however uncomfortable it might be, she would cope. Knowing that she had a good hour at least before it was 'All change', she snuggled her bag into the crook of her arm, and within moments the rhythmic clickety-clack of the wheels on the tracks and the rocking motion of the carriage lulled her into a deep sleep.

She dreamed of Daisy and the new foal, which she and the girls had visited when the colt was barely a week old. If it had still been up to Rosie she would have kept Daisy in her old field so that she could keep an eye on her, but she knew that that was impossible now. Nevertheless, in her dream state she walked up the pony's field and made for the shelter. If she could get the door open, then the pony could go in for some respite from the heat of summer or the cold of winter. But Rosie could not get a firm grasp on the padlock. She frowned at it; what on earth had they got in that stable that warranted a lock? She supposed it was the pony's tack, or maybe a small cart and harness, but Rosie had kept Daisy's tack in the shelter and no one had ever taken it for their own. Moving round to the side of the shelter, she put an eye close to one of the cracks in the wooden wall and peered inside. In the far corner she could just make out some sort of light; it seemed to be glinting off something. Standing on tiptoe, she spied through a bigger gap, but she was no better off. The stable appeared to be empty apart from the glittery thing in the far corner.

Feeling annoyed, Rosie stood back from the shelter and looked around for a better peephole, but when she put her eye to a larger gap she let out a piercing scream: an eye of sharp blue was staring back at her from the inside. As Rosie staggered backwards someone bumped into her, but when she turned to see who her assailant was she realised it was just the pony. Before she could gather her thoughts the stable door burst open and a man started yelling at her to get out of his field and not come back. She tore down the field and headed for the *Kingfisher*, her heart pounding as she ran. She had recognised him. It was the man from that night when she had fallen asleep in the shelter with Daisy. He was calling after her. 'Miss, miss . . . '

'Miss, miss, wake up. You're havin' a nightmare.'

Rosie opened her eyes and peered round the small carriage. People averted their gaze as her eyes met theirs, but the young man who had been gently shaking her arm gave her a warm smile. 'Sorry to disturb you, miss, but we thought you might end up on the floor, what with the way you was jumpin' about in your seat.'

Rosie felt a familiar blush invade her cheeks. 'Sorry. I hope I didn't upset anybody,' she said as brightly as she could. 'It must be the motion of the train what sent me to sleep.'

The young man held up his hand. 'No need for explanations. As long as you're all right.' He tilted his head to one side and looked at her enquiringly. 'Pardon me for askin', but aren't you off the canals?'

Rosie looked at him more closely. She didn't think she recognised him, but he seemed to know her. He was around the same age as Tim, but not as handsome. His hair was a similar colour to Rosie's, and it was wavy, which gave it a rather unkempt appearance. From his clothing he could have been one of the men who loaded the barges, but she could not place him. Realising she had not yet answered, she nodded her head. 'I'm Rosie O'Leary from the *Kingfisher*,' she said, hoping that he would reveal his identity in turn.

He clicked his fingers. 'That's it, you're the Number One! I knew I'd seen you somewhere before.'

Rosie nodded, smiled, then raised an enquiring brow at him.

'Oh, sorry. I'm Danny Doyle. I'm just learnin' to operate the cranes so you haven't met me yet, but I've seen you and your crew a few times.'

Rosie shifted to a more comfortable position. 'Do you like operating the crane?'

140

Danny shrugged his shoulders. 'It's a job. I'd rather have been in the forces' — his gaze fell enviously on the men in service uniform — 'but it's my asthma; they reckon I'd be more of a hindrance than a help.'

Rosie smiled at him sympathetically. She knew being refused entry was a concern for every man who wished to join up; no matter how fit they were, they all dreaded being turned down. 'Well, as I'm sure you've been told, the work you're doing is essential to the war effort, especially with the shortage of bargees now . . .'

He nodded impatiently, but then smiled. 'Sorry. I know you're right, but I must have heard that a hundred times at least.'

The train began to slow down. Relieved to be able to change the subject, Rosie peered out of the window. 'Are we stopping for something?'

Danny laughed. 'I should hope so. This is where we all get off.' All around them people were hefting bags off luggage racks, or sliding cases out from under their seats.

Rosie blinked at him. 'But we've hardly started . . . how long was I asleep for?'

The young mother opposite smiled wistfully at her. 'I wish *I* could've slept the entire journey.'

As they left the compartment, Danny held out a hand to Rosie. 'It was nice to meet you, Miss O'Leary.'

Accepting his proffered hand, she allowed herself to be helped down on to the platform. 'You too, Danny. And please call me Rosie.' She smiled brightly at him. 'Next time I'm loading up I'll keep my eye out for you.'

He held two fingers to his temple and gave her a small salute. 'Mind you do, and if I've the time I'll come and say hello.'

* * *

Tim approached the small café where he had arranged to meet Rosie. He looked hopefully through the glass frontage, but to his disappointment there was no sign of his friend. It had been a long time since he had seen anyone from the canals, and he couldn't wait to hear all the gossip — there was always plenty of gossip along the Leeds and Liverpool — and to impart all his own news, which he was prevented from doing in his letters. As he entered the café, the bell above the door rang out. Several diners looked up, none of whom were Rosie. He chose a table near the window and took out the newspaper that he had been carrying folded up under his arm. His eyes flicked over the front page, but he did not take in any of the headlines. All he could think about was Rosie. His thoughts were interrupted by someone giving a small cough to announce their presence. Tim looked up hopefully, but only an elderly waitress stood in front of him, her pencil poised over her small pad. 'Oh, I'm waiting for a friend,' he said.

The waitress raised her eyebrows. 'Are you indeed? Well, while you're waitin' for your friend, you're also takin' up a table, so you'll need to order somethin'.' As Tim held up a small menu that had been placed in the centre of the table she continued, 'Lunch menu's not on for another fifteen minutes, but you're welcome to have a drink while you wait — that's if you're havin' lunch here, of course.'

Tim nodded. 'I'll have a cup of tea, please. That should tide me over till my friend arrives.'

The woman started to write down his order then appeared to change her mind. 'A cup of tea it is then,' she muttered as she made her way to the counter.

An impish grin appeared on Tim's countenance; she obviously thought such a small order did not warrant being written down. Settling back behind his paper once more, he continued to scan the page in front of him. War, war and more war. He could not wait for the day when the papers published news which was not war-related. He heard another small cough and folded his paper to one side in order that the waitress might have room to place his tea on the table. However, when a cup failed to appear, he looked up to see what her objection was and found himself looking into the face of a young woman with long dark hair that had been scraped back into a ponytail ... 'Rosie!' he exclaimed. 'Where'd you spring from?'

Rosie pointed to a door at the far end of the room. 'Had to spend a penny,' she said. 'The station was crowded ... '

Tim placed his paper down on the table and pushed the chair opposite him out with his feet so that Rosie could sit down.

'Your tea, sir, and I take it this is the friend you were waiting for? What would you like to drink?' she enquired, although looking into her eyes Tim could see that she was daring Rosie to say that she was not thirsty.

'I'll have the same as Tim, please,' Rosie said, giving the waitress a bright smile.

The older woman gave a disapproving sniff as she pushed her pad and pencil — unused — back into the pocket of her pinny.

Rosie chuckled. 'You should have seen her face when I asked her where the lavvy was. She made sure I were stayin' for a cuppa before she told me.'

Tim's eyes twinkled as he looked at his old friend, but before he could answer Rosie leaned forward and squinted at his face. 'So tell me,' she said, her voice just above a whisper, 'is that a caterpillar on your top lip, or is it a moustache?'

Tim smoothed his attempt at a moustache down with his thumb and index finger. 'Cheeky mare!' he said with a chuckle. 'I think it makes me look rather suave.'

Rosie eyed him teasingly. 'Very sophisticated indeed, and just when I thought you couldn't possibly get any more handsome!'

Tim aimed a playful punch in her direction. 'You haven't changed one bit, I'm glad to see.'

Rosie smiled affectionately at him. 'Nope, and I dare say I never will. So tell me, have you spied any of those sneaky floating nuns yet?'

★   ★   ★

Rosie's time with Tim had been brief but memorable. After they had finished their cup of tea, he insisted on buying some sandwiches and

144

cake to take to the Pavilion Gardens, which were just a short walk from the café. Rosie thought she had never been anywhere quite so beautiful. The pavilion itself was Victorian, and she felt that she had never seen so much glass in one building. While the gardens were yet to acquire the lushness of full summer, the Pavilion housed the most beautiful array of flowers.

Tim explained that it was because of all the windows. 'I suppose it's like a huge greenhouse,' he had informed her as they looked for somewhere to eat their sandwiches. They had ended up on a bench not far from a bridge that crossed a large pool which was home to a considerable number of ducks and geese. Rosie watched the water as it spouted a couple of feet into the air from a fountain that had been placed in the middle of the pool.

'I can see why you come here,' she said, taking a small bite out of a cheese and pickle sandwich. 'It's hard to believe there's a world at war when we can sit in these gardens, watching the birds swimming along, as if it was a regular Sunday afternoon.'

Tim nodded. 'It's good to get away. And even though we know we have to go back, it makes it easier, because it reminds us of what we're fighting for, if that makes sense?'

After they had finished their lunch, he told her that he really should be heading back. Reluctantly, Rosie agreed, and as they approached the train station she saw that a motorbike was parked outside. She pointed towards it. 'Is that yours?'

'Yes. Or at least it's the same one I borrowed

to come and visit you on the canal that time.' He reached out and clasped Rosie's hand in his, sending a shiver through her spine just as it had all that time ago when they had explored Liverpool together.

Rosie looked down at his hand, and when she looked up she was aware of a sense of awkwardness about him. She raised her brows hopefully. 'Yes?'

Tim gave her fingers a squeeze before releasing his hold. 'Nothing. It's just that it's such a shame we couldn't have had more time together.'

Rosie's heart sank. She had been hoping for a kiss. To think she had actually imagined he had romantic feelings for her! She scolded herself. He was just being friendly. He had said that he had forgotten all about the war while he was with her, and that must have been what had caused him to take her hand. He had just wanted some time away from his duties, that was all. And besides, she had seen the way other women had stared at him as they walked towards the pavilion. They were all more attractive than herself, and he must have noticed they would look far better on his arm than she did. Feeling rather silly, she opened her hand and let her fingers slide out from his; then, taking a deep breath, she turned to address him. 'I can see myself off from here, but thanks for a wonderful day, Tim. I had a great time.' She cast her eyes downwards. 'Still no sign of Patsy?'

Tim clapped his hand to his forehead. 'How could I forget to tell you! Of course I've seen Patsy — she's on the same station as me. I'll tell her I've seen you when I get back, and then the two of you can start exchanging letters — or do you already do that?'

Rosie shook her head, not trusting her voice to hide the disappointment that lay within. A large cloud of steam was approaching the station, and looking up she used this as an excuse to say her goodbyes and leave quickly before he realised that anything was wrong. 'Got to go!' she said brightly, clearing her throat. 'I'll write as soon as I get back, and I hope you'll do the same.' Tim held his arms out and leaned forward. She supposed he intended to hug her goodbye, but that would have been too much for her to cope with, so she grabbed one of his hands and shook it vigorously. 'Take care on that thing on your way home.' She jerked her head in the direction of the motorbike, then released his hand and trotted off into the station.

Glancing back, she saw a bewildered-looking Tim standing exactly where she'd left him. She rolled her eyes. It must have appeared rude the way she dismissed his embrace, but having once dared to believe his intentions could have been romantic she was not going to let herself down again. After all, he had the beautiful Patsy to comfort him when he returned to his station. She pictured the blonde beauty exiting an office on the RAF station, a large amount of paperwork slipping through her fingers, and Tim rushing forward to help her pick them up. Rosie's bottom lip wobbled miserably. The thought of that woman smarming up to Tim was more than she could bear.

She showed her ticket and waited for the nearest carriage to empty before climbing aboard and plonking herself down in a window seat. Hot tears of misery and frustration were coursing down her cheeks, and as she pulled her handkerchief out of her pocket she heard the door to the compartment open. Hiding her tear-stained face from the incoming passenger, Rosie pretended to blow her nose.

'Goodbyes is always hard.' Rosie looked up. The voice belonged to a rather plump, elderly lady in a smart tweed suit and a stout pair of brown brogues, who was making herself comfortable in the opposite seat. 'I see your feller's in the RAF; I suppose he's stationed not far from here. How about you? Where are you from? I see you're not in the services yerself.'

Rosie glanced up at a sign on the carriage door. *Careless talk costs lives.*

The woman followed her gaze and nodded approvingly. 'Quite right too.'

Rosie shrugged. 'I don't know where he's stationed. And he's not my feller, he's just a friend.'

The woman raised her brows. 'Really? Well, I admit I've been wrong about these things before, but I think he may see things differently, m'dear.'

Rosie gave a rather strained smile. 'No, we're just good friends. I take it you got a good look at him? Because if you did you'll have seen how handsome he is.'

The woman nodded, and then clutched the arm of her seat as the train jerked forward. 'I did indeed, and you're right, he's very handsome.

But I also saw the way he was lookin' at you.'

Rosie shook her head impatiently. If there was one thing more annoying than having mistaken Tim's intentions, it was listening to a complete stranger poking her nose in. Rather than say so, however, she reassured the woman that any look of affection from the young man concerned was born out of friendship and nothing else.

Leaning down, the woman drew a ball of wool out of her bag and handed it to Rosie. 'Here, chuck. D'you mind windin' this wool up if I carry on unpickin' this 'ere cardy?' Without waiting for a reply, she started working on the brown cardigan in her hands. 'Make do and mend is the motto, as I'm sure you know, so I thought I'd turn me hubby's old cardy into a jumper. It's got too many holes in to bother mendin', so may as well start anew.'

Rosie started winding the wool as her companion continued. 'Sorry if I spoke out of turn; I s'pose I'm just an old romantic at heart.' She glanced up from her work and smiled at Rosie. 'You two reminded me of when me and me hubby were courtin'. He were in the first lot, you know, in the RAF too. Well, the RFC, as it were called when he joined.'

The elderly woman proceeded to tell Rosie her life history. Under any other circumstances Rosie might have been bored by such a detailed description of a stranger's life, but today it was a welcome relief as it prevented her from thinking about Tim and Patsy.

★ ★ ★

By the time Rosie finally got back to the barge, everyone else was asleep. Stealing quietly aboard, she changed into her night things before slipping beneath her blankets. She looked across to where Harri and Babs were both fast asleep, eyes tight shut, mouths formed in little o shapes, allowing soft snoring to escape. Neither of them had a feller that Rosie knew about. What I need, she thought, is someone who can take my mind off Tim and stop me dreaming about things that will never be. But where would she find such a chap on the canals? She knew that several villages held frequent dances; perhaps she and the girls could go to one of those. Unlike her mother, Rosie had nothing against canal folk, but she knew most of the people who worked on the barges, and none of them came across as desirable to her. She turned her thoughts to the day ahead. She would get up betimes, and while Maggie started breakfast she would go to the offices and see what their next load was. Pulling her blankets up around her ears, Rosie tried to put Tim out of her mind. She thought of dances where she would attract the attention of several beaux, and conjuring images of herself in a beautiful pink satin dress and matching shoes she drifted off to sleep.

★   ★   ★

When Tim returned to his barracks after seeing Rosie it was to find that his pals had already gone off to the cookhouse. Never one to miss a meal, Tim headed after them. When Rosie had spurned his embrace at the railway station, he

150

had been left feeling somewhat deflated, as well as slightly bewildered. He considered her to be a good friend and had been surprised by her reaction. Perhaps, he thought, she had misread his intentions; maybe she had really thought he meant to shake her by the hand. As he entered the cookhouse he saw that his pal Jimmy was already seated, a tray of food in front of him. Tim made his presence known before heading to the counter.

'I'll have a cuppa tea, and mebbe one of those lovely-looking Spam sandwiches, please,' he said as he picked up a tray from the stack.

The girl behind the counter gave an exclamation. 'Tim! Jimmy said you'd gone off to meet a pal. Anyone I know?'

Tim looked up at the young woman who had addressed him. 'Sorry, Patsy, I was miles away. And yes, as it happens — it was Rosie O'Leary.'

Patsy raised her eyebrows as if the name were unfamiliar. 'Rosie O'Leary? Can't say it rings — Oh, I know! Maggie Donahue's kid; looks a bit like a boy. Gosh, I've not seen her for ages; how is she?'

Tim shrugged. 'She's doing well. Got her own barge and crew now.'

Patsy placed the tea and sandwich on Tim's tray. 'There you go.' She smiled brightly at him. 'I've only got ten minutes left before I finish my shift. How's about I come over and join you and Jimmy, then you can tell me all about it? I'll bring Sheila along, too. She's always been rare fond of your Jimmy, although you mustn't tell her I told you.'

151

Tim smiled absent-mindedly. 'Sure, although there's probably not much to tell.'

Taking his tray, he joined Jimmy at the long table. 'Why the glum face?' Jimmy said, his mouth muffled by the large bite of sandwich he had just taken. 'I'd have thought you'd be cockahoop after seeing your pal . . . is the bike okay?'

Tim nodded. 'Don't worry, the bike's fine. Got me there and back with no bother.' He told Jimmy about his day with Rosie, and ended with how he felt she had shunned him at the railway station, surprised to find that the memory still troubled him.

Jimmy pulled a face as he sprinkled some salt on his stew. 'Perhaps she ain't into public displays of affection. You told me her mam ain't like no mother you've ever known before. Mebbe she just didn't know how to react.'

Patsy, who had walked over to join them as Jimmy was speaking, cleared her throat. 'What's this about displays of affection?' she asked as she pulled out the chair next to Tim.

Tim started to wave his hand dismissively, but Jimmy had other ideas. 'Our Tim here wanted to give his Rosie a hug goodbye and she shook his hand instead. Tim thinks he's been shunned.'

Patsy glanced sideways at her friend Sheila, who had come over to join them, and looking back at Tim she raised her brows. 'Of course, I'm not one to interfere, but if it'll help I think I may know why she did it . . . although I could be wrong, of course.'

Tim, who was eager for any explanation,

looked at her hopefully. 'So what do you think?'

Patsy appeared sympathetic. 'The last time I spoke to Rosie O'Leary she was talking a lot about Frog. Seemed real fond of him, she did. Mebbe they're together, or perhaps she's holdin' out for him?'

Tim was baffled. Frog? It was something he had never even considered before. He knew that the two of them got on well together, but he had never imagined it was anything more than friendship. He had opened his mouth to voice his thoughts when Patsy continued.

'Tell you what, I'll write to her and ask a few questions, but I'll do it real discreet so she won't think nothin' of it. Then you'll know whether she deliberately snubbed you, or if it were a mistake.' Seeing the concern in Tim's face, she quickly added, 'I won't mention you at all, so no need to go worryin' that I'm gonna drop you in it.'

Tim placed an arm around Patsy's shoulders and gave them a squeeze. 'You know what, Patsy, you're a real pal, that's what you are. Thanks ever so much. I'll rest easier once I know.'

Patsy leaned her head on his shoulder. 'I'll soon find out what's what, don't you worry. It's probably just a misunderstanding.'

Jimmy clicked his fingers. 'What you need is a bit of thinkin' time. Personally, I always go fishin' when I've a lot on my mind. I've heard you say you're a dab hand when it comes to the trout, so how about me and you go down the Witham and do a spot of fishin'?'

Tim looked quizzically at his friend. 'What with? I'm not about to lean over the banks of the

153

Witham and try to tickle trout, and I've not had a rod for years.'

He remembered the day he had lost his father's fishing rod. It was midsummer's eve and the Bradleys had moored for the night when Tim's father had announced, 'Me and your mam are goin' to go for a drink down the King's Head. You comin'?'

Tim shook his head. 'I thought I'd do a bit of night fishin', see if I can catch summat decent.' Tim knew that this was the stretch of water where a huge pike known as the Colonel was said to reside. He had never seen the pike himself but a few of the bargees had laid claim to seeing it, even to having him on the end of their hooks, only of course he was always the one that got away, so there was never any evidence of such tales.

After supper, when his parents had gone to the pub, Tim had set up his rod and line on the side of the bank and settled himself down to wait. He had been watching a backswimmer as it paddled past him when a huge mouth came up from the depths and swallowed the insect whole. Tim, who had been lying back against the bank, sat up. He scanned the canal for another sighting of the fish that had swallowed the insect, but he saw nothing. In fact he had become so mesmerised by the patterns the dying light made on the water's surface that he had forgotten to watch his own line, and did not notice that it had gone suddenly taut until a young boy on the canalside shouted out, 'Oi, mister, you've caught summat!'

Looking to the line, Tim quickly grasped hold

of his rod before the great fish took it away with him.

'It's a big 'un,' the young boy said as he walked down to join him. 'Do you reckon it's a bream?'

Tim shook his head. 'I'm not goin' to jinx myself by sayin' what I think it is . . . ' he began, but fell silent as the battle to land his catch began.

The young boy bounced up and down excitedly, shouting out, 'Careful! You'll snap the line if you don't watch out!' or 'You'll end up wi' fish lips if you yank like that!'

All of which Tim found most unhelpful as he tried to concentrate on the task in hand. After what seemed like an age, he called out to the young boy to get him his net. The boy stood hopping from one foot to another until Tim handed him the rod so he could scoop the huge pike into the net. 'It's the Colonel!' Tim said, his heart fit to burst with the thrill of the chase. He carefully unhooked the pike from his line and had turned to thank the boy for his help when, quick as a flash, the boy had stuck his tongue out rudely and shouted 'Ta for the rod, mister!' before disappearing up the tow-path and across one of the fields.

Tim started to follow, but the fish was leaping about on the side of the bank as it made its way back towards the water, taking the landing net with it. Doubling back, Tim caught hold of the handle and managed to save his net from disappearing into the depths, but he was too late to stop the Colonel from making his escape.

Later, having heard Tim's story, Mr Bradley shook his head grimly. 'That lad sounds like one of the Gaspots. I'm afraid even if you see him again, it won't do to mention the rod. They're a nasty bunch and they'll turn on you if you try to get it back.'

Tim had felt terrible about losing the rod, which had been his father's before he had given it to Tim.

Now, Jimmy's voice interrupted his thoughts. 'Don't worry, a pal of mine's got a couple of rods we can borrow. Hardy's split cane . . . '

Tim raised his brows. 'Are you sure he won't mind us borrowin' them?'

Jimmy shook his head. 'Nah, they belong to his dad, not him. Carter doesn't fish himself, but his dad thought it'd be good for him to take up a hobby, so he tried a couple of times. He says it bored him rigid.'

Tim slapped his hands down on his thighs and stood up. 'Sounds good to me.' He turned to Patsy. 'Thanks again for the help, queen.'

★　★　★

As they left the cookhouse and headed back to their hut, Sheila had to trot to keep up with Patsy. 'I know you, Patsy Topham,' she said as she fell into step beside her friend. 'You want Tim Bradley for yourself. There's no way you'll give him the green light to go for this here . . . what was her name? Rosie O' . . . '

Patsy looked distastefully at her companion. 'Her name's Rosie O'Leary. And you're right. If

156

anyone thinks for one minute that I'd help dreary O'Leary get with *my* Tim . . . well, then they don't know me at all!'

Sheila clapped her hands together in delight. 'That's the Patsy I know and love. Tim's a handsome chap and decent to boot; he deserves a lot better than some dowdy canal girl.'

Patsy looked sharply at her friend, raising her brows, but before she could speak Sheila went on, 'Sorry. I wasn't including you in that statement. You know you're better than canal folk anyway; that's why you got out, weren't it?'

Reassured that Sheila was not making fun of her, Patsy nodded. 'Yeah, I s'pose you're right. And that's another thing me and Tim've got in common. We both left the canals to move on to bigger and better things.'

Sheila stifled a laugh. 'Workin' in the cook-house bigger 'n' better? Life aboard the canals must be much worse than I reckoned.'

Patsy stiffened. 'Don't you go makin' fun of me, Sheila Formstone! You were cleanin' pub lavvies before you joined up, so don't you start thinkin' you're better'n me, 'cos you aren't. Besides, who says I'm content wi' bein' in the cookhouse? It might be where you're happy to live out the rest of the war, but not me. I'm applyin' for a job drivin'.'

Sheila pouted. 'Okay, okay, keep your hair on! I were only sayin' — '

'Well don't!' Patsy snapped. She looked at her companion, who appeared to be downcast. 'I'm sorry if I were mean, but you know how much Tim means to me, and the very thought of — '

Sheila cut across her. 'Dreary O'Leary . . . '

Patsy grinned. 'Well, that's what she is. Tim deserves much better, and I'm going to make sure he gets it.'

Sheila opened the door to their hut. 'What you goin' to do?'

Patsy looked complacent. 'Not sure yet, but I'll think of something. And you're gonna help me.'

6

Over six months had passed since Rosie and Tim's meeting. Rosie had written to Tim twice but had yet to receive anything back, and had resigned herself to the fact that he would not be returning to the *Sally Anne* for Christmas. So far the winter was proving to be a mild one; it was typical, Rosie thought bitterly, that Tim would not be coming home for the one Christmas when any travel plans were unlikely to be hindered by bad weather.

With just a few days to go before the holiday, Harri announced her intention to decorate the main cabin and spent the entire morning making paper chains and lanterns, before stating that she was just nipping out to get their Christmas tree.

Maggie, who had overheard the last remark, leapt out of the main cabin, her voice shrill. 'A Christmas tree? On board a barge? Are you completely insane?'

Harri turned to face her. 'Quite possibly, but as I've never been professionally assessed it's impossible to say for sure.' She winked at Rosie, who hid a smirk behind her hand.

Maggie turned to her daughter. 'Surely to God you ain't goin' to allow her to bring a tree on board? There's little enough room with that bloomin' feathered fiend as it is.'

Rosie looked thoughtful. 'Well, it is only once

159

a year . . . ' she began, but found she was talking to empty air as Maggie, realising that her daughter was not going to refuse the other woman, shot back into the main cabin, muttering to herself as she went.

Rosie grinned quizzically at Harri. 'I take it you aren't really goin' to bring a Christmas tree on board?'

Harri gave an exaggerated wink and wagged a reproving finger. 'Wait and see. As you said, Christmas only comes once a year.' And with that she turned and began walking up the towpath, whistling 'Good King Wenceslas' as she went.

Rosie stood on the deck, a look of sheer disbelief on her face. Surely Harri wasn't really going to try to bring a Christmas tree on to the *Kingfisher?* . . . Hearing Pepè give a loud squawk, she shook her head. Harri had assumed that introducing a huge parrot complete with cage was completely acceptable, so why shouldn't she think the same about a Christmas tree? As Rosie turned to assess the main cabin a voice hailed her from behind.

'Coo-ee! Rosie — I'm back.' It was Babs. Rosie had completely forgotten that her other crewmate had gone off into the small village of Hadley to see if they were going to be showing a movie in the village hall that evening.

Rosie raised her brows. 'How'd you get on in the village? Are we to be entertained or is it another night of being crammed into the cabin?'

Babs was grinning from ear to ear. 'There's a dance on in the village hall.' She clapped her hands together excitedly. 'And while I was there, that feller what works on the cranes where we moor up seen me and asked if I'd like to go.' She danced a small jig of delight.

'Oh, Babs, that's wonderful . . . but which chap? There's more than one, you know!'

Babs giggled. 'Don't you go laughin' but it's the one what talks a bit funny. You know — Thimon, with the blond curly hair?'

Rosie shook her head doubtfully. 'I don't think I've ever heard of a Thimon . . . '

Pushing her fringe from her eyes, Babs sighed theatrically. 'You do know him. His name's Simon, but he says Thimon.'

Rosie scratched her head thoughtfully. She knew that Babs would not be making fun of her, but she could not grasp what the other girl was getting at. Holding her hands up in a gesture of mock surrender, she opened her mouth to speak, but Babs cut her off.

'The guy with the lisp. You know — he can't say his s's, so he says th instead. So Simon becomes Thimon, stool becomes thtool, and — '

Rosie interrupted, her voice unusually thoughtful. 'Stable becomes thtable . . . '

Babs frowned impatiently. 'Well, yes, I suppose so — ' she began, but Rosie was talking across her.

'How long has he worked in the yard, this Simon chap? And is he quite young, late teens, early twenties?'

Babs was looking curiously at her. 'Yeah. Well, I think so, anyway. Know him, do you?'

Rosie shook her head. 'No, I've never met him, but I think I may have heard him talking, a long time ago.' Her voice trailed off as she cast her mind back to the night that she had spent in Daisy's shelter. She remembered hearing the men talking outside, and how one of them, the one with the younger voice, had spoken in an unusual way. At the time she could not put her finger on what was wrong, but now, like an epiphany, it came to her as clear as day. He had had a lisp. It was only subtle, but when you're half asleep . . .

Babs was still speaking. 'Well, you'll get to meet him tonight, if you want to come along. He reckons a few of the fellers from the factories and the yards will be there, so you never know your luck, you might end up wi' a feller of yer own!'

'Hmmm? Oh yes, of course, that'd be nice . . .' Rosie spoke absent-mindedly, her thoughts still very much on the night in the shelter all that time ago. She searched her memory, desperately trying to remember what the young man's part in the conversation had been. But all she could recall was that he had been the one to discover the shelter, or so it seemed, and the man who appeared to be in charge had approved of his find. She tried to remember who had spoken of Daisy's using the field, and of Ken and Maggie and the *Wild Swan* . . . had it been the young man with the lisp, or one of the others? She shook her head impatiently. She would wait until tonight, go to the dance, and see if this Simon's voice matched her memory of the man outside the shelter. After all, though Rosie had never met anyone who lisped before, she supposed he could not be the only person in Liverpool with such an impediment.

★　★　★

'Can someone give me a hand?' Harri called from the towpath. Rosie and Babs were eating an early supper in the cabin before getting ready to go to the dance, while Maggie was preparing for 'a quiet evening in wi'out you lot breathin' down me neck'.

The older woman slapped a hand to her forehead. 'If that gel thinks she can bring a Christmas tree on to this barge . . . ' she began, but Rosie, who felt as concerned as her mother regarding a Christmas tree on board, did not wait to hear what she proposed to do about it but popped straight out into the crisp winter air.

She stifled a giggle. 'What a beauty. Mam, you really must come and see this . . . '

From within the depths of the cabin, they could hear Maggie making her way round the table, and as she pushed her head through the open doors Harri and Rosie both cried 'Ta-da!'

Maggie shot the girls a withering look. 'Oh ha ha, very funny!' she snapped, and returned to her supper.

Harri had been standing on the towpath, the sawn-off top of a small fir tree in her hands. Their Christmas tree stood at no more than a foot high. 'Come on, Maggie, where's your sense of humour?' Harri called after the older woman. 'I said I was gettin' a Christmas tree, I just didn't say how big.'

An impatient snort escaped Maggie's lips. 'You can ruddy well keep it in the engine room,' she called back, 'seein' as you're all so keen on operatin' the damned smelly thing!'

Babs, who had come out on deck to see what all the fuss was about, giggled aloud. 'I think it's cute, and it'll certainly brighten the place up a bit.' She shot a backward glance in the direction of the main cabin. 'Goodness knows, some of us could do wi' cheerin' up.'

Harri laughed and swung the tree up into her arms, addressing Rosie. 'Engine room it is, then?'

Rosie nodded. 'For now, but we'll see if we can fit it into the main cabin later, even if it's just for Christmas Eve and Christmas Day.'

Harri smiled happily. 'Are we goin' to do a sixpenny Christmas again this year? You know, each buy one present for no more than sixpence, and draw pieces of paper out of a hat to see who gives what to who?'

'I'm okay with that if everyone else is,' Rosie said, although she thought Maggie would probably not be as keen as she was herself. Last year one of the girls — Rosie thought it must have been Babs — had bought a small pot of pale blue eye shadow. Poor Maggie, who never wore make-up of any kind, had ended up with it, and had not hidden her disappointment. With this in mind Rosie had an idea. 'How about this year we all get summat practical, what any of us could use? You know, like a pair of socks, or some scented soap; that kind of thing? That way it doesn't matter who receives what gift, because they'll still be able to use it!'

Babs was disappointed, and Rosie suspected that the other girl had been planning to buy another item of make-up. If the truth be known, Babs was the only one on board who ever bothered with such matters, if you didn't count Harri's apparently endless supply of her trademark red lipstick.

Rosie placed the small Christmas tree in the engine room, secured the door behind her, and headed back to the main cabin, where Harri had already started on the plate of vegetable pie they had put aside for her, to be followed by a sugarless — but delicious — apple pie for pudding.

'These seamen's rations are great!' she enthused, holding a hand to her mouth so as not to spray the cabin with pastry crumbs. 'I'll be lucky if I'm able to put one foot in front of the other at this dance.' She turned to Rosie. 'If there's not many men, d'you fancy being my partner? I do a splendid quickstep and Daddy always says I take the lead in a foxtrot anyway, so probably better for me if I don't have a man to dance with!'

Rosie nodded. She had been secretly hoping that she would meet at least a few men at the dance, but she was not about to admit this to her crew as the three girls set off, each clad in her best dress, hair brushed until it gleamed and nails scrubbed until they shone.

The *Kingfisher* was moored at Tuppenny Corner, and Harri remarked that it was a good job they didn't have to go through the Panks' fields to get to the village, else they'd be looking like land girls by the time they arrived. She turned to Rosie. 'Have you had time to go and see Daisy and the foal again? I'm guessing he must have changed quite a bit by now.'

Rosie nodded, smiling. 'He's still as cute as ever, but he's getting cheeky now. You have to watch him when you go in the field, because he runs around like an idiot. But Daisy makes a wonderful mother, and doesn't get at all defensive when you stroke him.'

Babs hooked her arm into the crook of Rosie's elbow. 'Oh, I'd love to go and see them. D'you think we could go tomorrer mornin', before we set off?'

Rosie considered for a moment, then nodded. 'Don't see why not. I know the Panks won't mind. D'you wanna come too, Harri? It'll be early, though.'

Harri nodded eagerly. 'Do you know what they've called him?'

Rosie stopped in her tracks. 'Gosh! I forgot to ask. I know Mr Pank was struggling to find a name that wasn't too obvious, you know, like Blackie, or Jet — did I mention the foal's black?'

Harri nodded. 'He could call him Beauty, I suppose, after Black Beauty? That was one of my favourite books when I was growing up.'

Rosie wasn't sure. 'I think he was looking for something a bit unusual, so maybe not.'

Outside the village hall, an ARP warden was making sure that everyone entered and left the building without letting any light escape. He doffed his helmet as they walked towards him.

'Evenin', Rosie, Harri, Babs. All here for the dance, are we?'

Rosie smiled. It was old Reg Arkwright, one of the men who guarded the pillboxes along the canal. Every time the *Kingfisher* passed by his box he used to jump out, albeit rather slowly, and shout 'Who goes there', determined to pretend that he didn't know it was the *Kingfisher* and her crew. At first the joke had been amusing, but after a while it had got to be rather annoying, especially to Maggie, as Pepè would screech like a siren whenever the old feller jumped forth.

Realising no one had answered him, Rosie spoke up. 'Of course! Are there many in there, Reg?'

He pulled a face. 'Quite a few. They're ever so popular, these dances, although I'm afraid the women always outnumber the men, which is good for the likes of me, but I dare say a bit disappointing for you young gals.'

Rosie shrugged. 'Well, whatever happens I promise I'll save the last dance for you, Reg Arkwright — always assuming you've not had any other offers, that is.'

Reg chuckled and pulled off a mock salute. 'Right you are, Miss Rosie. Now get yourselves together, girls, I'd like to get you inside in one go. Can't risk any light escapin' . . . are we ready? Right then, in we go . . . ' As the girls huddled together he showed them through the door, making sure that it was shut tightly behind them before he lifted the blackout curtain up.

Once inside Rosie looked round. There was the familiar trestle table set up at the top of the hall, with two elderly ladies serving jugs of squash and what looked like sandwiches, should anyone wish to buy refreshments. One of the locals, a middle-aged man whom Rosie had often seen in the village shop, was operating a gramophone in the corner of the room, and the perimeter of the dance floor was lined with tables and chairs. As she continued to take in her surroundings a voice hailed her from across the way.

'Rosie? Rosie O'Leary, is that you? Come on, day-dreamer, it's me, Danny, from the train?' The voice that hailed her belonged to the man who had woken her from her nightmare when she had been on the train to go and see Tim. A slow smile formed on her lips. Danny Doyle was not as handsome as Tim, but then she was not as pretty as Patsy, so maybe that made things even.

Realising she had not responded, she gathered herself together and held an outstretched hand towards the young man as he approached. 'Golly, Danny! Fancy seein' you after all this time! How's the crane operating goin'?'

He pretended to polish his fingernails on the lapel of his jacket. 'Oh, I passed that easily; they're on about movin' me up to the offices next so's I can do the paperwork — you know, keep a record of what comes in and what goes out.'

Harri, who was standing close by, leaned forward. 'Do you think you might be able to fix it so we get the best jobs?'

Danny pretended to consider, but then shook his head, laughing. 'The fellers'd have my guts for garters if they thought there was any favouritism going on. Besides, I don't think that'll be part of my job. I'll just be checking stock, really.'

Babs appeared with three cups of lemonade and handed one each to Rosie and Harri. 'I've just seen Simon by the refreshments, and I promised him the first dance, so I'll have to be quick . . . '

Rosie caught hold of Babs's elbow and turned her to face Danny. 'Before you go I'd like you to meet someone. Babs, this is Danny. He's . . . he's . . . '

Danny spoke up. 'I'm a friend of Rosie's. Nice to meet you, Babs.'

Nodding, Babs took a quick swig of her lemonade before placing the cup on the table. 'Likewise, I'm sure. Now if you'll excuse me . . . ' She trotted off in the direction of a rather expectant-looking young man. Danny's gaze followed her until she and Simon merged into the crowd, and then he turned to Rosie.

'I say, I didn't know your Babs was a friend of Simon's?' he said.

Rosie shrugged. 'It's quite a recent thing, I think. Oh, of course, Simon works at the yard. I suppose you two must know one another?'

Danny pulled a face and shrugged. 'Not really, but I've seen him about quite a bit, especially down by the docks.'

As the music sprang into life, Harri gave Danny a nudge. 'Are you goin' to ask young Rosie here to dance, or can I have the pleasure of her company?'

Danny clapped a hand to his forehead. 'Blimey, I nearly forgot what I was here for.' He offered his arm to Rosie. 'May I?'

Blushing, Rosie placed her hand in the crook of his elbow, and as the two of them joined the others on the dance floor she could hear Harri — who was as tall as most of the fellers in the room — moaning that she wished she hadn't said anything because now she'd be left on the sidelines, again.

By the end of the evening, all three girls had danced the night away. Harri had got together with one of the farmhands from a nearby estate, much to the amusement of her friends, as Harri was a good foot taller than her partner, and they could hear his yelps as she kept trying to take the lead, which resulted in several squished toes — all of which belonged to the farmhand.

'That Danny seems like a decent enough chap,' Harri said, glancing sidelong at Rosie as they walked along the towpath back to the *Kingfisher*. 'Do you think you'll see him again?'

Rosie shrugged, then nodded. 'Bound to. He's training in the offices, so it's inevitable that we'll bump into each other sooner or later.'

Harri laughed. 'You know what I mean! Did he ask to see you again?'

Rosie gave a shy grin. 'You know as well as I do that finding the time for socialising isn't easy with the canals bein' so busy . . . '

'Aha! So he *did* ask to see you again. What did you say? Please tell me you said yes. He seemed ever so struck with you, and he's clearly a good sort, which is hard to come by on the canals — '

'Oi!' Babs cut in. 'What about my Simon? He's a good sort too, you know! And before you ask, he's takin' me to the cinema next time we're in Liverpool. I told him it should be okay to arrange for the day after Boxing Day.'

Harri held her hands up. 'Sorry, sorry, I wasn't implying that your Simon wasn't a good sort. He's always seemed fine whenever I've seen him loading up. But you're letting our Number One off the hook here. Come on, Rosie, spill the beans.'

Rosie gave them a wry look. 'I haven't agreed to anything, but if the occasion ever arises, and we're both free at the same time, I told him I'd be delighted to accompany him to another dance, or perhaps a meal out. Satisfied?'

Harri gave a contented smile and nodded happily. 'Good! It's about time you had a bit of fun. Now, if anyone's interested, Lord PeeWee asked me out too.'

Babs gave a shriek of laughter before hastily covering her mouth with her hand. 'Sorry. But, well, that's not his real name, is it?'

Harri gave a mischievous smile. 'No, I'm only pulling your leg. It's just that when he told me he was a farmhand on an estate, I assumed that's exactly what he was, you know, an employee, but it turns out his father *owns* the estate, so what with him being a little bit smaller than me I nicknamed him Lord PeeWee.'

Rosie's eyes widened. 'You didn't call him that to his face, did you?'

Harri laughed at Rosie's expression. 'His real name's Albert, Alby for short, and of course I called him that to his face. He's got a great sense of humour, and you can't hide the fact that I'm a good foot taller than he is. Besides, he should've been more forthright from the start and told me that his father owned the estate rather than making out that he was just a lowly farmhand, although he did admit that he's always been wary of gold diggers. Once we started talking he realised that I wasn't from round here, and when I told him that my family owns an extensive amount of land, that's when he decided to come clean.'

Babs snorted her discontent. 'Cheeky swine. Suggestin' that us Liverpool girls are only after a chap for his money. I'm from the city, but I wouldn't go for a man just because he's got money . . . has he got any brothers?'

This last remark caused all three girls to laugh so hard that Maggie, poking her head out of the cabin doors, accused them all of being drunk, which made them laugh even harder. Convinced she was right, Maggie shot back into the cabin, got her pillow and blankets and headed for the engine room. 'I'll sleep in here till you've all sobered up,' she snapped. The engine room doors slammed shut behind her, and a moment later the girls heard an anguished cry. 'What the hell?'

Harri, who was holding on to Babs for support, managed to gasp out, 'The Christmas tree!'

They all heard the splash, followed by the engine room doors slamming shut again. Giggling helplessly, Rosie and Harri leaned Babs over the side of the barge while they held on to the waistband of her dress. 'Get hold of the top, but try not to break it off, and we'll pull you back up,' Rosie instructed the other girl, who was snorting loudly as she tried to contain her laughter, making her sound like a pig with the giggles.

Once they managed to get the tree back on board, they took it up to the front of the barge, and Harri set it down on the empty cargo bed. 'Thinking back, we should have put it here in the first place, but I thought it might keep falling over. I hope its quick dip in the canal doesn't make it smelly! I don't think I'd much like having my Christmas lunch next to a pongy tree!'

Rosie giggled. 'We can sit Maggie next to it. She might think twice in future before chucking stuff into the canal!'

Babs yawned and stretched. 'Well, Maggie might not have a comfortable night's sleep tonight, but that won't stop me from gettin' a good night's kip. Come on, girls, let's get some shut-eye.'

When all three girls were tucked up in their cosy little beds, Rosie reflected on her evening with Danny. In some ways he very much reminded her of Tim. He had a good sense of humour and was very respectful of other people; he was sociable and got on well with both men and women. Unlike Tim, however, he had a quieter side to him, or perhaps a more secretive side. Maybe it was because they hadn't known each other long and he was being reserved, or perhaps it was the job he was training for — being in charge of the stock was a very important position — but there was a small part of Danny that came across as unusually serious. He had asked her lots of questions about her life on and off the canals, and had listened to her replies with interest. She, in turn, had asked him about his life, and here, Rosie thought, was where he seemed to be less talkative. He spoke about his job readily enough, and his social life, but as far as his upbringing and home life were concerned he gave mostly vague answers. She knew that he hadn't lived in Liverpool all his life, and that he was renting a one-bedroomed flat in the village. He had explained that he was an only child, like herself, and that his parents worked back in his home town, but when she asked what they did he said she would find the answer boring, and when she asked where his home town was he replied that it was near Manchester and she would never have heard of it. Not wanting to pry she had not dug any further, and his face had reflected nothing but openness and honesty, and yet . . .

Rosie turned over in her small bed. Thinking about it now, she thought perhaps his parents didn't work and he was too embarrassed to say so, and perhaps he was right and she would not have heard of his home town. She sat up and thumped her pillow into a better shape. Don't go looking for a mystery where there isn't one, Rosie O'Leary, and just be grateful that some feller, a *nice* feller, wanted to spend his time with you. And with this thought came another: she *would* meet Danny again. Why not? He was pleasant company and good fun to be with *and* he wasn't halfway across the country. With her decision made Rosie closed her eyes and let sleep take over.

★ ★ ★

There was much discussion over the next few days about where they were going to moor over the Christmas period. Maggie wanted to spend a traditional bargee Christmas at Tuppenny Corner, where they would sing carols on the towpath on Christmas Eve and on Christmas Day they would go to St Mary's for morning service along with every other bargee who had managed to find a mooring spot at the popular Christmas destination.

Harri and Babs, however, wanted to spend the holidays as close to the city as possible; Babs so that she might nip off and see her family, and Harri who also wanted to go home for a couple of days. Rosie understood her crew's desire to spend Christmas with their families; she just wished that Ken could have come home so that she would not have to spend Christmas alone with a miserable Maggie. However, to Maggie's credit, she did come up with a good idea. 'We can drop these two off the day before Christmas Eve and pick 'em up the day after Boxing Day. Does that sound fair?'

There was a murmur of agreement from the girls, Babs adding a rider that since that was the day she would be in Liverpool with Simon

175

the arrangement was ideal, but when Rosie asked her mother what Ken's plans for the holidays were Maggie shot her daughter the frostiest of looks then narrowed her lips into a snarl. 'Ken asked Hitler if he wouldn't mind leavin' Liverpool alone over the holiday period, and Hitler kindly agreed, so Ken says he'll come home.'

Rosie frowned. 'There's no need to get nasty. I were only askin'. It's been a while since we've seen him . . . I was just wonderin' if everythin' was all right?'

Maggie rounded on her daughter, her eyes positively spitting fire. 'What're you implyin'? You tryin' to say my hubby doesn't want to come home? 'Cos it ain't true! He's servin' his country, an' a damn fine job he's doin' an' all. Where's that Tim Bradley of yours? If we're talkin' about people avoidin' each other, what about him? Where's he at, eh?'

Rosie stood, perplexed. She had no idea why such an innocent question could have warranted such a combative response. She had not even remotely suggested that anything was wrong between her mother and Ken; she had just wondered what his intentions were for the holidays. She said as much to Maggie, who, despite the fact that she had calmed down by then and was looking slightly awkward, was not willing to listen, or apologise for her outburst. Instead, she marched off up the towpath and Harri, who had been at the front of the barge, gave a low whistle.

'Blimey, looks like you hit a raw nerve! Even

so, she shouldn't have gone off at you like that. Not right, and not fair. Must admit I'd quite forgotten that your mother was married. She never talks about her hubby, and as far as I know she doesn't get many letters either.'

Thinking about it now, Rosie realised that Harri was quite right. Her mother didn't talk about Ken, and Rosie could not remember the last time she had received any letters of any kind from anyone, let alone her husband. She looked at Harri, a puzzled frown etched on her face. 'Do you think there's trouble between 'em, then?'

Harri shrugged and raised her brows. 'No smoke without fire, and by God that was some fire you just lit under your mother. I reckon even if there isn't trouble in paradise, then it's something that's crossed your mother's mind . . . you know, made her wonder whether her husband's still wanting to be wed to her . . . '

Rosie clapped a hand to her forehead. 'Crikey! I wish to God I'd never said owt now, especially if we do end up spendin' Christmas alone together. Can you imagine?'

Harri smiled reassuringly. 'You can always come and spend Christmas with me. You'd be more than welcome, and goodness knows there's plenty of room at the manor.'

Rosie's eyes brightened at the thought of spending Christmas with Harri and her family, but how could she leave Maggie alone? She may not always get on with her, but the thought of leaving her on her own at Christmas was more than Rosie could bear. Shaking her head sadly, she declined Harri's kind offer.

'It's not like me mam's got parents or siblings of her own to visit. If she had I'd join you, but I can't leave her on her own — it just wouldn't be right. But thanks ever so for the offer.'

Harri nodded. 'I understand, but if you change your mind, let me know. I'll write down the address of the manor, and give it to you before I leave. Then, if the worst happens, you can come up and stay for a couple of days, okay?'

Rosie nodded and thanked her again, although she couldn't help noticing that the invitation only stretched to Rosie and not to her mother. She tried to imagine Maggie in a grand manor house: she would complain that the rooms were too big and the food too fancy, and then moan about posh folk in general. Rosie nodded her head thoughtfully. Harri had had the right idea.

★   ★   ★

It was the day before Christmas Eve and the women of the *Kingfisher* had exchanged their Christmas gifts. 'Can we open them now?' Babs asked excitedly. 'I want to see your face when you open mine, Maggie. I think you'll like it . . .'

Maggie looked at each woman in turn. Then, shrugging, she pulled the wrapper off the present that Babs had handed to her. Inside was a small bar of scented soap.

'It's Lily of the Valley. Rosie said it was your favourite.'

Maggie nodded. 'Thanks, Babs. Rosie's right, it is me favourite. Now you open yours.'

Babs carefully took the paper off a small bar of

chocolate. Her eyes shone as she flung her arms around an unsuspecting Maggie, and Rosie noticed that although her mother looked startled she did not pull away. 'Best ever!' Babs cried, then turned to Harri and Rosie and clapped her hands together. 'Come on, you two, get opening!'

When Rosie opened her present she started to laugh, and when Harri opened hers the reason for Rosie's mirth became apparent. 'Must be great minds thinking alike,' Rosie said, as both girls stood with exactly the same bag of assorted mints in their hands. 'Are you coming into the city to see the girls off, Mam?'

Maggie shook her head. 'You'll be faster wi'out me. Besides, I thought I'd take the time to do a few last minute chores.'

'I hope you have a nice Christmas, Maggie. We'll see you on the twenty-seventh,' Harri said as she turned to walk up the towpath to the canal basin.

Maggie didn't bother to reply, but she gave the other woman a half smile. How could they expect her to have a good Christmas when she knew full well none of the other women aboard the *Kingfisher* — Rosie included — wanted her around? None of them had ever said anything to her face, but she had noted the slight sighs and the exchanged glances, particularly when she had pointed out a mistake one of them had made. They never included her in their plans, and only ever asked her to join them after things had already been arranged. If they really wanted her to have a nice Christmas they'd bugger off

179

and not come back, she thought bitterly, though she knew there was no chance of that happening. The three of them got on like a house on fire, and in truth, Maggie knew that she was regarded as more of a hindrance than a help. Babs and Harri did not take well to criticism and seemed determined to worm their way in between herself and Rosie. If she were to speak her mind, she felt sure that it would only have one outcome, so rather than risk losing any relationship she had with Rosie she had come to a decision.

* * *

After waving goodbye to the two girls, Rosie walked into the city centre to do a bit of shopping before returning to the *Kingfisher*, where to her surprise she found her mother, clad in her Sunday best, coming out of the main cabin with a small holdall under one arm. 'Where're you goin'? I thought you wanted to moor up at Tuppenny Corner, so wherever you're off to you'd best be quick about it.' Rosie glanced down at her mother, but Maggie simply stared back without a word. Rosie frowned. 'Well? When do you think you'll be back? Or do you want to spend Christmas here now?'

Maggie looked round at the small table behind her. Rosie followed her mother's gaze, and saw an envelope lying on the otherwise bare surface. She looked back at her mother, then stepped on to the deck and made her way into the cabin. She picked up the envelope and turned round, only to see that Maggie had started off up the towpath, head down and walking quickly. Rosie hurried after her and grabbed her by the elbow, swinging the older woman around to face her. 'Just you stop there, Maggie Donahue,' she ordered. Flinching, she slit the envelope open, her lips moving silently as she read the letter in her hands.

Dear Roseanna, I expect you've already realised that life on the canals is not for me any more. I've always been bad at goodbyes, so I thought I'd leave you this letter instead. I applied to be a land girl some time back, and it appears me application must have gotten lost, because I've only just had a yes from the Ministry of Ag. Anyway, I'll write again when I know where I'm being placed. Hope all goes well for you. Merry Christmas! Love, Maggie.

Rosie glared at her mother, her hands trembling. 'How *could* you? To just up and leave without so much as a warning, and at Christmas time too. Have you no heart? I'd have been all by myself on Christmas day, and yet here you are, quite happy to just walk off without so much as a single goodbye.'

Maggie hung her head in shame. 'It weren't like that, I only made up me mind to go this mornin'. I would've said summat, only I thought I might change me mind last minute, and I didn't want to cause no upset.'

Rosie flourished the letter under Maggie's nose. 'Did you not think that leavin' me a letter tellin' me that my mother, my own flesh and blood, were goin' without even sayin' goodbye wouldn't upset me? Let alone leavin' us short one crew member . . . '

Maggie snorted. 'You don't need me. You made that obvious the moment them girls came aboard. The only reason I'm still here is 'cos I'm your ma; otherwise you'd have got shot of me long back, even a blind man could see that. I can't work the engine, which means I can't run the barge. You only need three people aboard the *Kingfisher*, and I'm just gettin' in the way. You'll all be a lot happier with me out of the picture, an' seein' as you ain't got the guts to get rid o' me yourselves I thought I'd do it for you. Bet you'll be off to that Harri and her stuck-up family the moment me back's turned. The only reason you're upset is because you could've been there already, livin' the high life and havin' fun . . . '

Rosie stood, her mouth gaping as she searched for words to contradict her mother, even though Maggie was right, life would be easier without her aboard the *Kingfisher*. She rarely came out of the main cabin and when she did it was to moan or whinge about something or other; she constantly sniped at the other girls, and there wasn't one morning when Rosie wasn't surprised to see that Pepè hadn't suffered an 'accident' during the night, but it didn't mean that Rosie wanted her to leave.

Maggie sniffed indignantly. 'You know it's true, that's why you aren't arguin'. In fact, you've not even tried to persuade me to stay. You

182

expect me to like Harri and Babs, but how could I when I know you prefer their company to mine? It were just a matter o' time before I left.'

Rosie finally found her tongue. 'But you're my mother . . . ' she began, but it was no use. Maggie had clearly made her mind up, so accepting defeat Rosie continued, 'You promise me you'll let me know where you end up?'

Maggie nodded. 'I'll be stayin' on a farm just outside Bootle for a couple of weeks and then they're sendin' me to somewhere in Norfolk for the duration of the war.'

Rosie hugged her, gingerly placing a kiss upon her cheek. 'I know things haven't been the same since Ken went off, but you're my mother and no matter what I will always love you. So you mind you keep yourself safe, and any time you change your mind and want to come back aboard the *Kingfisher*, you'll always be welcome.'

Maggie patted Rosie's shoulder and stood back, a small smile on her lips. 'I will, and mind you take care with those locks. You know what happened to your father.'

Rosie nodded, but a look of uncertainty crossed her face. 'Actually, I don't know exactly what happened to my father, just that it was a tragic accident . . . ' But even as she spoke Maggie had turned on her heel and was making her way up the towpath again, waving goodbye to Rosie over her shoulder as she went.

As Rosie watched her mother disappear from view, it occurred to her, not for the first time, that Maggie had no natural maternal instinct.

But then Maggie had never shown signs of affection for anyone, not even Ken, although Rosie supposed things must be different behind closed doors.

Stepping back on to the *Kingfisher*, Rosie was wondering whether to pack a couple of things into a small bag and take Harri up on her kind offer when a voice hailed her from behind. Turning round she gave an exclamation of surprise. 'Danny! What on earth are you doin' here? Shouldn't you be busy in the office?'

'I was, but then I overheard Pete sayin' as how your mam'd told him that she were leavin' the *Kingfisher*, and for him to keep an eye on you, so I thought I'd come down and see that you were okay.'

As Rosie wondered how to answer him, she realised, to her surprise, that she *was* okay. Maggie's leaving had upset her, but only because the older woman had chosen to inform her by letter rather than tell her face to face. She wondered what Danny would think when he realised that Rosie was not distressed by the fact that her mother had chosen to up and leave the day before Christmas Eve but was, if truth be known, relieved that Maggie had gone. The relationship between mother and daughter was a complicated one, which only Maggie understood and Rosie, while not understanding, accepted. Rather than go into detail she assured Danny that everything was all right, and that her mother had simply found life too cramped aboard a barge with three other women.

'Mam never liked the engine, and I think she'd

been looking for an excuse to leave ever since we got the *Kingfisher*. Once she knew I were okay for crew she seized her opportunity.' She searched Danny's face for his reaction.

Danny shrugged. 'Personally, I don't see how you canal folk manage to live in such small quarters at all. It must be hard, especially for married couples with children . . . ' He stopped abruptly as he realised the implication of his statement.

Rosie laughed. 'It's certainly no picnic, I'm sure. But it's something Maggie won't have to worry about now. Well, not until the war is over and she and Ken return to the canals — or I should say *if* they return to the canals. Ken may have a change of heart about life as a bargee now he's been in the army for so long.'

Danny peered over Rosie's shoulder into the main cabin. 'I've never been in one of the cabins. Would it be okay if I had a look?'

Rosie was both surprised and secretly delighted that Danny wanted to know more about the life of a bargee, so she took him down into the main cabin, carefully placing her mother's letter in her pocket as she did so.

She watched as Danny admired her cosy home. 'Gosh, it's actually bigger than I imagined, and so much more colourful. What's this?'

'Get stuffed!' Pepè squawked, causing Danny to hastily drop the blanket that covered the parrot's cage.

Rosie started to laugh, clutching her stomach with both arms as she tried to stop herself, but it

185

was no use. Danny's expression when the bird had screeched his warning was one of shock, horror and surprise, all rolled into one. Rosie's laugh was infectious, and within a moment both of them were laughing uncontrollably. As Rosie began to hiccup, she beckoned Danny to follow her back on to the deck.

'S-s-sorry about that,' she said, fighting to keep her voice even. 'We're just so used to Pepè that I forgot to tell you about him.'

Danny waved a hand. 'Don't worry, love, it's my own fault for bein' nosy. Is that all he says?'

Rosie rolled her eyes. 'I wish! But I'm afraid he's picked up a lot more than that in his time aboard the barge, and the crane drivers have taught him a few words we wish he'd forget!'

Danny chuckled. 'I'm afraid I can probably imagine the sort of thing they've said, especially when a load slips out.' He looked at Rosie thoughtfully. 'With your mam gone, what're you doin' for Christmas? Only from what I gathered you didn't expect her to be leavin' quite so sudden?' He blushed.

Rosie shrugged. 'I was goin' to go and stay wi' Harri and her family. She did invite me, but now I feel it's a bit of an imposition, because I told her I were stayin' on the *Kingfisher*.' She glanced around the barge. 'I thought it were just goin' to be me and me mam so I didn't go too mad wi' the food shoppin', but I s'pose I've got a fair bit for just one person.'

Danny rubbed his chin. 'I don't suppose you'd like to come over to mine for Christmas Day lunch? You'd be most welcome. My parents were meant to be comin' round but they've gone off to visit my Aunt Cissy and her family up north. I couldn't go with them because of work, so I've been left on my tod, and I don't fancy spendin' Christmas on my own. How about you?'

Rosie's heart leapt for joy. She liked Danny and the thought of spending Christmas Day on her own had not been appealing. 'I'd like that very much, but you know you'd be more than welcome to come here instead. I've not got a turkey, but I have got some lovely pork pies as well as a nice chunk of cheese, homemade pickles and a fresh loaf of farmhouse bread. Would that suit?'

'That'd suit just fine, but I insist you come to mine. You know what the bargees are like, and if they see you spending Christmas Day in the cabin of your barge with a man, you'd never hear the end of it, and neither would I.'

Rosie agreed. Goodness knows what sort of gossip they would spread if they heard that she was in her cabin alone with one of the canal office staff, but she guessed it would not be good, and they would persecute Danny too, accusing him in future of giving the best jobs to his lady friend. So they arranged that Rosie would go to Danny's at eleven o'clock on Christmas morning. No presents were to be exchanged, just food and company.

When Danny had taken his leave, Rosie went back into the main cabin and sat down on her bunk, marvelling at how much things had changed in just a few hours. This morning she had been dreading spending her Christmas Day alone with Maggie, but now she was looking forward to spending it with Danny. Feeling around under the bed, her fingers closed over the small pile of letters that she had received from Tim and pulled them out. She had felt sure that he would write to her around Christmas, and was disappointed that he had chosen not to; she had, after all, written to him. Maybe it was because he had fallen in love with Patsy. She knew the other girl had had her eye on him; she had made it plain that she intended to pursue him. Even so, it would have been nice to remain friends. But if that was Tim's decision, Rosie had no choice but to accept it. Adding her mother's farewell letter to the bundle, she carefully replaced the letters under the bed and came to a decision. Rather than hound Tim with letters and attention he did not wish to receive, she would leave him alone. If he ever chose to write to her in future she would indeed write back, but until that day came she would respect his wishes and leave him be.

7

As Tim walked over to the notice board to check for letters, he saw that Patsy was already there.

'Hello Tim. You look as if you've lost a pound and found a penny. What's up?' she asked, pushing an envelope in her pocket as she spoke.

Scouring the board for letters, Tim stuffed both hands in his pockets. He had felt sure that Rosie would write to him over Christmas, but there was not even a Christmas card. He could not think what had made his friend decide that she no longer wished to correspond with him, and as his eyes met Patsy's he voiced the thought that was uppermost in his mind.

'Are you writing to Rosie? Only I've not had a letter from her for a while, and I just wondered if she was okay.'

Patsy curled her hair with her finger and smiled sweetly at him. 'I must admit I haven't written yet; I suppose I've been a bit lazy. Besides, you know what it's like working the canals — you're always on the move and never near a post box. I'm sure Rosie means to write, it's just that she hasn't had time yet.'

Tim pulled a rueful face. 'I know, I know,' he said resignedly. 'I'm sure I'm worryin' over nothin'.' A thought struck him. 'You did remember to post those letters I gave you, didn't you? Only . . . '

Patsy pouted. 'Tim! I'm hurt. Of course I sent

those letters. I'm not a complete dope, you know.'

He laid a reassuring hand on her arm. 'Sorry, Patsy, I didn't mean anything by it.' Wanting to change the subject, he pointed to the envelope protruding from Patsy's pocket. 'At least one of us is getting mail. Who's that from? Your ma and. pa, or some lucky feller?'

Patsy giggled. 'It's not from any feller! You know you're the only man for me, Tim Bradley.' She pushed a blonde curl that had escaped its hairpin back behind her ear. 'Joking aside, if you ever need to talk I'm always here for you. And if it makes you feel any better, I promise I'll write to Rosie and let you know if she responds. At least that way it'll put your mind at rest, one way or another.'

Tim smiled and gave her shoulders a friendly squeeze. 'Thanks, queen, it means a lot. It's hard bein' so far away and not bein' able to talk to folk face to face. Have you been for lunch yet?'

Patsy shook her head. 'I was going to head down there once I checked the board.'

Tim offered Patsy his arm. 'I'm on my way there now. Fancy joinin' me? Only Jimmy's not goin' till later on, so if you turn me down I'll be eatin' me Christmas pud on my own.'

Patsy giggled, and was just about to link her arm through his when she appeared to remember something. 'I've just got to do somethin' first, and then I'll see you there, if that's okay?'

Tim smiled. 'Make sure you don't leave me standin' out in the cold all by myself.'

Hurrying away, Patsy called over her shoulder.

'Don't worry, I won't be more than a minute or so.'

Once inside her hut, Patsy drew the stiff envelope out of her pocket — it obviously contained a Christmas card — and walked over to the stove at the far end of the room. Opening the small door, she took one last look at the name of the sender before carefully pushing the card on to the smouldering embers. She watched while the envelope sprang to life as it started to curl in on itself, the flames licking the edges as it did so. When the sender's name had all but disappeared from view, Patsy closed the stove door and smiled to herself before heading for the cookhouse. As she approached, Tim gave her a wave. Grinning smugly, she waved back. You'll thank me for it one day, Tim Bradley, she thought to herself. When you come to your senses and realise that Dreary O'Leary is not the girl for you. I'm just helpin' you make the right choice, that's all.

Tim held the door open for her. 'Do you know,' he said casually, 'I was dreadin' Christmas away from my folks, but havin' you here seems to be making things more bearable somehow. Perhaps it's because we were friends before the war. Oh, look, a proper Christmas dinner — but then I guess you knew that already, what with working in the cookhouse an' all. And Christmas crackers too.'

Patsy collected a tray from the stack and headed for the counter. 'I'm just glad to be spendin' Christmas Day with one of me oldest pals. And as I work in the canteen, dependin' who's on shift I may be able to wangle us a bit extra.'

Tim raised his brows. 'Extra grub? Now that, Patsy Topham, is the way to a man's heart.'

* * *

Rosie stood outside the small terraced house on Abbot Street and looked at the address carefully written on the piece of paper in her hand. She'd found the right place all right. Knocking again politely, she had just decided that if there was still no answer she would chalk it up as a bad mistake and go back to the barge when, to her relief, she heard a muffled shout of 'Be right with you' coming from behind the door.

A moment or so later there was the sound of a key clicking in its lock, and when the door opened a rather flustered-looking Danny stood on the other side. 'Sorry, Rosie, only I rarely use the front door and I couldn't find the key, plus the sausages needed turnin' before they burnt to a cinder.'

Looking past Danny, Rosie could see a small haze of smoke coming from what she presumed to be his kitchen. She held out her offering of food, and Danny wiped a rather sweaty palm on his trousers before taking the pie and cheese from her outstretched hands. She slipped her coat off and for a moment they both stood awkwardly in the small entrance before Danny, remembering his manners, balanced both pie and cheese in one hand and took her coat with the other.

'Please, do come through. I hope you're not

too fussy when it comes to food, but looking on the bright side, at least you can be sure that it'll all be well and truly cooked, especially the . . . Argh!' Hastily placing Rosie's coat on one of the kitchen chairs, Danny rushed to the frying pan. He switched the stove off and carried the pan over to the sink where, holding it at arm's length, he gripped a fork and transferred the offending sausages on to a waiting plate. Rosie watched in some amusement as he turned the sink tap on and placed the pan under its flow; the resultant spitting hiss caused him to drop the pan into the sink before he turned to face Rosie with an apologetic grin. 'Sorry about that, love. I'm sure that once we've scraped off the burnt bits . . . '

Rosie looked at the black objects on the white plate. 'Once we've scraped off the burnt bits I shouldn't think there'll be anything left,' she teased. 'But not to worry. I've brought plenty of food, although I did leave Pepè in the *Kingfisher*, before you get your hopes up . . . '

Danny's eyes rounded in mock horror and he pretended to cough indignantly. 'Rosie O'Leary! The thought never entered my mind. Besides, I bet once we'd got past all those feathers there wouldn't be enough to fill even one of us.'

Rosie giggled. After the upset of her mother leaving, and the lack of any correspondence from Tim, this was just what she needed, she thought: someone who could be relied upon for friendship and company. She watched Danny pick up her coat and hang it carefully on the back of the kitchen door. She supposed that a lot of people would think it unseemly that a young woman was having Christmas lunch alone with a man she hardly knew, but there was something about Danny that made her feel safe. He had an air of honesty about him that seemed to run through to his bones. He began to slice the pork pie and cheese that Rosie had brought with her, and laid them carefully on the plates he had put out for their lunch. How nice it would be, she thought, to spend time with someone who wore their heart on their sleeve, no games, no hidden agenda, just plain, honest, friendship.

By the time they had eaten their dessert of bread and butter pudding — apparently it was the only thing that Danny had ever successfully cooked — Rosie felt that she would not need to eat for the rest of the day, even though Danny insisted she stay for supper.

'I'll never get through the rest of this lot by myself, and even if I did I wouldn't fit into my work clothes!' he said, a pleading look on his face. 'Please stay for supper. You'll be doin' me a favour, and then I can walk you back to the *Kingfisher*, and hopefully work off some of your delicious food as we go.'

Rosie had to admit she did not relish the idea of going back to an empty barge, with only Pepè and his spontaneous screeching to look forward to, so she accepted his offer, but insisted that he should come to the *Kingfisher* for Boxing Day. Reading his concern, she held up a hand. 'I won't take no for an answer, and if the bargees want to put about all sorts of rumours, let them. They can't prove anything because there's nothing to prove. You've been the perfect gentleman, and if I want to share my Boxing Day food with a friend, I shall.'

Holding his hands up in a gesture of mock surrender, he nodded reluctantly. 'Fair play, love. When you're right, you're right. Now, how about a quick tour of my quarters?'

Rosie nodded. She hoped she might learn something more about her host from his personal possessions, but he surprised her. As she started to stand up he waved his hand for her to remain seated and pointed a finger behind her. 'That there is my sofa, which converts into a bed; behind me is the kitchen — as you know — and over in the corner is my bathroom, such as it is. If you need the lavvy it's outside. Ta-da!'

Rosie giggled. 'It's not much bigger than the *Kingfisher*'s cabin. Still I don't s'pose you need much, bein' on your own an' all.'

'Precisely!' Danny said, looking satisfied. 'I've all I need right in this one room.'

After a cold supper of pie and mash — Rosie made the mash — Danny walked her back to the canal. 'I've really enjoyed myself today, and I may be wrong for sayin' so but I'm kind of glad that your mam left for the Land Army, 'cos if she hadn't I'd have had a right miserable Christmas Day on my own. I think we've gotten to know each other a lot better, too. Do you agree?'

Rosie nodded. 'Me mam's a strange one, allus has been, and I can't say I'm glad that she don't have a maternal bone in her body, 'cos I'd be lyin', but I am glad she's gone.' She looked hopefully into Danny's eyes. 'I hope that doesn't sound too harsh, only she's not been happy for a long time and I'm rather afraid she's been taking it out on everyone around her. When it comes to it I'd rather she was happy away from the canals than miserable on them.'

By this time they had reached the bow of the *Kingfisher*, and Danny helped Rosie on board before handing her the carefully wrapped leftover food that they would have for their lunch the following day. He stood back and placed his hands in his coat pockets. 'It doesn't seem selfish or harsh to me. It sounds like the behaviour of a child who loves her mother. You've got to be selfless to make sure that someone else's happiness comes before your own, and by lettin' your mam go wi'out a fuss you've done just that. You're very mature for your age, but I guess that's what comes with the responsibility of running your own barge.' He looked at the cover strapped over the empty cargo hold. 'Next lot for you's a load of cotton and grain, am I right?'

Rosie laughed. 'Never far from the office, are you? I've been meanin' to ask, only I don't want to appear rude, but do you regret not being able to join the services?'

Danny looked rather awkward, and Rosie was just beginning to open her mouth to take the question back when he interrupted her. 'It's okay, and a fair question. Of course I wish I could have done my bit for Britain, but with my asthma I'd have been a liability rather than an asset in any unit, so I'm much better off in the offices.' He looked shyly at her from under his brows. 'Some folk think that makes me less of a man because I can't go off and fight wi' the rest of them — '

'Not me,' Rosie cut in hastily. 'We can't help the way we're made, and it's not like you didn't want to go. Besides, someone has to make sure that vital supplies get carried across the country, and enough men have left the canals already. Take Simon, Babs's feller, for example. He's not joined up for medical reasons — I don't know what they are, just summat Babs said — but we need him to load the barges, so it's just as well he's here.'

Danny smiled at her. 'No need for explanations. I'm just glad you don't see me as unmanly. Talking of Simon, he seems a good chap. Does Babs know him well?'

Rosie shook her head. 'I dare say you know him better than Babs. She only met him from loading up cargo and the like, and they didn't get together until that dance. He does seem nice, though. It's a shame he has that lisp . . . '

Once more Rosie's mind returned to the conversation she had overhead outside Daisy's shelter. Before Babs had introduced her to Simon she had felt certain that he must be the young man with the lisp outside the shelter door, but after talking to him she was less certain. He didn't seem the sort to be involved with a group of men who she felt sure were up to no good. Rosie cast her eyes upwards. It had just been a dream, it must have been, and it was about time she put it to bed. She realised that Danny was talking.

'So I'll be here for eleven thirty? Give you a

hand with plating up?' He was looking at her, eyebrows raised.

Rosie shook her head and smiled. 'Sorry, I was miles away. It must be all that food. Yes, eleven thirty'll be grand.'

Danny grinned, then turned on his heel and walked slowly back up the towpath towards the basin.

A faint smile etched across her face, Rosie headed for bed. Checking on a sleeping Pepè, she had a quick wash before climbing sleepily between her sheets. I don't know what sort of day Tim has had, she thought drowsily, and I can't say I much care, because if I'm sure of one thing, it's that he's spent it with the dreadful Patsy who has, in all probability, got her man. Well, good luck to her, because I rather think I could grow quite fond of Mr Danny Doyle; at least he's not far from home . . . And with these thoughts, Rosie drifted off to sleep.

⋆　⋆　⋆

'Come on, Rosie, just try a little bit o' lippy. It's New Year's Eve, Danny's goin' to be at the party, and I should imagine he'll be expectin' a smooch around midnight.' Babs's tone was close to whining but Rosie was unyielding; she had never worn make-up and she was not about to start now.

'You can't make a silk purse out of a sow's ear, Babs Wilcox, so best you stop tryin', and even if Danny does expect a smooch at midnight, *a* there's no sayin' I'll be smoochin' wi' him, and *b* he won't want to end up covered in lipstick, so just you take your lippy elsewhere!' Rosie pushed her friend gently to one side as she dodged the tube of bright red lipstick that Babs was flourishing a couple of inches from her lips.

Babs sniffed haughtily, 'My Simon don't mind a bit o' lippy on him, not if it means he's had a smooch with me. I don't see why Danny should be any different.'

Rosie smiled apologetically. 'I'm not sayin' there's anythin' wrong with lippy, I'm just sayin' it's not for me. Me mam never wore it, nor do any of the other women on the canals — apart from you and Harri — so I s'pose it's summat I'm not used to or comfortable with. That doesn't mean to say there's anything wrong with wearin' it. Besides, it suits you two; I'd just end up lookin' like a clown.'

Babs relented. 'You're right, of course. None of the women on the canals wear make-up, but it's different in the city. When the war started me mam warned me about rationin' and the like, and how difficult it would be to get hold of some stuff. I must admit, I think for most of us girls the thought of goin' wi'out choccies was bad enough, but no make-up? It'd be like goin' out half dressed in the mornin', and you wouldn't want to do that!'

Rosie, feeling that Babs's attempt to get her to wear lipstick had ended for the time being, relaxed. Ever since Harri and Babs had returned from their holidays and found that Maggie had deserted her daughter, they had developed some kind of urge to 'fix' Rosie. The more Rosie told the other girls that she was fine, the more they were convinced that she needed their help. Harri had declared that Rosie should have come to the manor rather than spend her Christmas Day with a man she hardly knew, while Babs said that had she known, she would have left her family and returned to the *Kingfisher* to keep Rosie company.

'There really was no need,' Rosie had said as they stood on the towpath, watching the men from the factories load the *Kingfisher* with her cargo of cotton and grain. 'Danny is a lovely chap, a real gentleman, and we had a grand time. Besides, if I'd spent the holidays with one of you two, then poor old Danny would have been left on his own.'

Babs had wrung her hands fretfully. 'But you don't really know him, Rosie — or you didn't — so you were takin' a risk goin' to his house on your own. I blame your mother, of course; I mean, fancy leavin' a letter to let your kid know you were joinin' the Land Army. What kind of mother does that?'

Harri had shot Babs a warning look. 'The fact that Maggie left is no surprise to me, nor that she intended Rosie to find out by letter. She may not be the sort of mother that we can relate to, but then she's not had the same sort of life that our mums have had. It doesn't mean to say that she doesn't love her daughter, just that she finds it difficult to show that love.'

'Oh, but I — I didn't mean — ' Babs had stuttered, only to be saved by Rosie who placed a comforting arm around her friend's shoulders.

'Don't worry, queen, I know you didn't mean anythin' by it.' When Babs and Harri had first joined the *Kingfisher*, Rosie had noticed them exchanging glances whenever she referred to her mother as Maggie. When she had explained the reason they had nodded comprehension, but Rosie could tell that they still thought it odd. She knew that her mother was unusual, but if she accepted it, she thought that others should too.

But now, as they left the *Kingfisher* to go to the party in the village hall, Rosie felt that her life was in a far better place than it had been for a long time. With Maggie gone, peace and harmony reigned over the barge. Working conditions improved, as well as their cramped living conditions. She felt more relaxed about Pepè and no longer bothered to check his cage each morning to see if he had 'accidentally' escaped during the night. And while she wasn't exactly courting Danny, they had certainly formed a strong friendship; the kind that she and Tim had had before he left for the RAF, except that Rosie knew that Danny would welcome a romantic relationship. He hadn't said anything directly, but his eyes danced whenever she looked into them, and a special grin would make its way across his face.

As they made their way up the long path to the village Harri turned to Rosie.

'I haven't asked you for a while, but have you heard from that Tim feller recently?'

Rosie shook her head. 'Nope, and what's more I don't expect to either. I sent him a Christmas card, and I made sure it went two weeks before

Christmas Day, so there's no excuse for him not sendin' one back, even if just to be polite, but he didn't bother. I suppose he's no time for me now he's a high-flyin' mechanic, with that Patsy Topham on his arm.'

Harri looked over the top of Rosie's head and pulled a face at Babs. 'So does that mean you're going to give old Danny boy the green light if he asks you out on an official date? It's obvious to all that he's been dying to, but you're a bit like your mam when it comes to giving people the cold shoulder and you've made it pretty plain that while you're willing to be his friend, that's where it ends.'

Rosie frowned. 'I don't see what my friendship with Tim — or lack of it — has to do with me and Danny.'

Babs tutted impatiently. 'It's got everything to do with it, if it's Tim you're holding out for, and even though me and Harri have never clapped eyes on the lad, never mind seen you and him together, it's pretty obvious that you're keen on him, and not just as a friend. If Tim really has gone off with this Patsy you'd be free to look elsewhere, but you don't know for definite that he has, do you, and that's why you're holdin' back.'

Rosie felt a hot flush of embarrassment invade her cheeks. She hadn't realised that her feelings for Tim were so transparent. As far as she was aware she had never mentioned them, but of course she had spoken ill of Patsy, and for no reason other than that she thought the other girl was in love with Tim. Rosie cursed inwardly. She wondered who else knew how she felt about Tim, and gave a small groan of despair. What if Frog or Taddy had guessed? Would they tell Tim? Maybe that's why he was avoiding her, because they had told him and he did not feel the same way. Perhaps it had nothing to do with Patsy, and more to do with the fact that he simply didn't think of her in that way, and felt it best to break all ties rather than lead her on, or be accused of doing so. As the thoughts crowded in, Rosie began to make sense of them all. It wouldn't have mattered whether Patsy was on the same station as Tim or not; she could blame the other girl for taking Tim away from her until the cows came home, but in truth Patsy had nothing to do with it. Tim must have realised Rosie's true feelings for him the last time they met, and decided there and then that since he could not return them he would make a clean break so that they could both get on with their lives.

Feeling thoroughly deflated, she turned to Babs. 'It's true that I did have romantic feelings for Tim at one point, but that's not the case any more. And even though I know Danny has the same sort of feelings for me that I had for Tim, I want to be sure about my feelings for him before getting into a relationship that I'm not ready for.'

Rather to her surprise, Babs and Harri both appeared to accept this explanation without question. Harri removed her pipe from between her teeth. 'Very sensible, if you ask me. Too many people jumping into relationships these days without getting to know each other properly first, just because there's a war on.' She waved her pipe in Babs's direction. 'I hope you're taking your time with that Simon chap. There's no sense in getting married after five minutes just because you're worried you might get blown to smithereens!'

Babs looked horrified. 'Why on earth have you brought your pipe out with you? No decent feller in their right mind's goin' to go for a woman what smokes a pipe.'

Harri bowed her head and tapped her temple with the mouthpiece of the pipe. 'But I don't smoke it, you know that.'

Babs eyed Harri with frustration. 'You know darned well what I meant. What kind of chap is goin' to go for a woman who sucks a pipe, or holds one, or *has* one for goodness' sake?'

Harri shrugged. 'Can't say as I know, or care for that matter. I'm just goin' to bring the New Year in with my pals and have a bit of fun, and maybe a dance or two along the way. What's wrong with that?'

Babs appeared to consider. 'Well, nothing, I suppose, but what if Lord Pee Wee's there? Aren't you concerned that he may object to your pipe?'

Harri smiled smugly. 'I care not one jot! He either takes me as he finds me or he can go whistle. Besides, I'm pretty sure he's already seen it.'

Rosie looked at Harri with admiration. 'I wish I had half the confidence you have when it comes to men,' she said frankly. 'I think it's marvellous that you don't care how you're seen. I don't think I could be like that.'

Harri pulled a face. 'I suppose it's my upbringing. Mother always taught me that there are millions of people in the world so you mustn't compare yourself to any of them, because we're all individuals, with different views and different needs. You must just be yourself, and that way you'll stand out from the crowd and the right person will soon find his way to you.'

Rosie was impressed, as well as a little jealous. Why couldn't Maggie have given her advice like that? Far from being supportive, her mother had not given her any guidance at all when it came to the opposite sex, or life in general come to that. She had always been so concerned with the barge, their life on board and Rosie's ability to read and write that she had quite neglected the social aspects of her daughter's education. If I'd had a mam like Harri's, Rosie thought, I bet I'd have turned out totally different. And I reckon if I had the kind of confidence that Harri had Tim would want to be my boyfriend, because self-confidence is an attractive trait in itself.

When they entered the village hall it took them a moment or two to get used to the bright lights before they could take in their surroundings. Babs let out a squeal the moment her eyes fell on Simon, and she rushed over to speak to him.

Harri nodded thoughtfully. 'That's the way, play hard to get.'

Rosie let out a snort of laughter and hastily covered her mouth with the palm of her hand, nudging Harri in the side. 'Oh, Harri, you are awful. Poor Babs, she can't help wearing her heart on her sleeve, it's just the way she is.'

Harri smiled down at Rosie. 'I know, I was just playing. That girl has got a heart of gold and I'd hate to see her hurt by anyone, but Simon seems equally smitten with her. I just hope they don't rush into things because everyone else is doing it.' Spying Danny, who was getting himself something to drink, Harri continued, 'So you're not going to dump me and rush over to Danny then, I take it?'

Rosie shook her head. 'No, because you're quite right: just because there's a war on doesn't mean everything has to be done today.' She glanced around the room. 'Can't see Lord PeeWee anywhere. Can you?'

A throat cleared over her shoulder. 'Try looking behind you.'

Both girls turned and to Rosie's dismay 'Lord Pee-Wee' was standing right there. She stood for a moment or two, trying to find the right words, but Harri came to her rescue.

'Don't mind him, Rosie. He knows I have a pet name for him.'

'I may be small, but I would hope you don't see me as one of your pets,' Lord PeeWee said indignantly. 'Like that God-awful parrot of yours, what was his name again? Peter, Percy . . . '

Harri rolled her eyes. 'His name's Pepè, and he's not God-awful, he's as sweet as sugar and cuddly too.'

Lord PeeWee's eyebrows shot towards his hairline. 'Cuddly? Damned thing tried to take my finger off when I first met him! I don't call that cuddly. Vicious yes, but not cuddly.'

Rosie listened with amusement as the pair carried on the argument like an old married couple. Despite their differing opinions of the legendary bird, Rosie could quite clearly see the affectionate liking they had for each other. She glanced back to where Danny had been standing, and found that he had disappeared. Looking around the crowded hall, she spotted him talking to a couple of men in the far corner of the room. She had never seen either of the men in the canal offices, or at any of the lock houses, and as she stood wondering who they were and what they were doing with Danny, he caught her eye and waved. He spoke briefly to the two men, who turned to acknowledge her, and then, leaving the men behind, he made his way towards her.

'Wotcher! Everything okay? I wasn't sure whether you'd come tonight, but I'm glad you did. Can I bagsy a place next to you when we do 'Auld Lang Syne'?' Danny was speaking quickly, and Rosie thought he sounded nervous, although she could not think why; it was not as if this was the first time they had met.

She jerked her head in the direction of his companions. 'Who are they? I've never seen them around the canals before.'

Danny looked awkward. 'I'm not really sure who they are; I met them earlier today when they were looking for somewhere to stay and asked me if I could recommend anywhere. I told them to go to the Old Boot, 'cos I know they've always got a room spare there. They took my advice and the landlord told them that the village hall was having a bit of a shindig to celebrate the New Year, and that's why they're here now. They saw me, and came over to thank me for the advice.'

Rosie, looking into Danny's eyes, thought that she could see something hidden there, as if he was holding something back, but what could it be? His explanation was credible enough, and she could see no reason why he should lie to her. She chided herself. It was all this business with Tim that was causing her to try to read significance into everything that was said to her. She gave her friend a brief smile, then looked at the drink that he held in his hand.

'Oh, gosh, I'm so sorry,' Danny said quickly. 'Where are my manners? Would you like a drink, Rosie?'

The party was a huge success — they played blind man's buff, and musical chairs as well as musical statues — and by the time the evening was coming to an end and they had started the count-down towards midnight Rosie was quite worn out. She feared that Danny might try to kiss her, and never having kissed anyone before she was worried that she might do something wrong. But Danny, as ever, was the perfect gentleman, and as the clock struck midnight he lifted the hand he was holding and kissed the back of it. In some respects Rosie was quite disappointed, but at the same time she felt a sense of relief and assured herself that one day she would kiss him, just not today.

After a resounding rendition of 'Auld Lang

Syne' the New Year's Eve partygoers started to drift homeward in twos and threes. As Rosie bade Danny goodnight, he jerked his head towards Babs, Simon and Harri, who were making their way towards the door. 'Would you mind if I walked with you all for a while?'

Rosie pulled a puzzled face. 'Don't see why not. Any reason?'

Danny, who had been watching Simon and Babs walking arm in arm, shook his head. 'No, just fancied a bit of company for a while longer before I go back to the flat.'

As they headed towards the canal, Simon, who had been holding on to Babs the whole way, stopped and looked at his watch. 'Hope you don't mind, queen, but I've got to get back. Will you be all right to see the girls the rest of the way home, Danny?'

Danny was about to reply when Harri cut him off. 'Excuse me, but we're hardly shrinking violets, you know. We're more than capable of making our own way back.'

Simon chuckled. 'I don't doubt it; besides, that parrot of yours is enough to put any would-be criminal off. I don't s'pose there's a bargee between here and the Shropshire Union that hasn't heard all about Pepè by now.' Leaning towards Babs, he gave her a quick peck on the lips and started to walk up the path, bidding them all a Happy New Year as he went.

Danny turned to the girls. 'Well, it's been a grand evening, but I suppose I'd best be getting home too. I dare say you can all have a lie-in tomorrow, but I've got to be at the yard early, get the paperwork ready for the next load of deliveries.' He turned to Rosie. 'I really enjoyed myself tonight, Rosie. I'd like to do it again some time; how about a fish supper one evening? Maybe a dance in town?'

Rosie, knowing that Harri and Babs were listening with keen interest, nodded shyly. 'That'd be lovely, Danny. Pop in when you've got five minutes and we'll arrange something.'

Danny nodded, and before Rosie knew what was happening he had leaned forward, clasped her hands in his and kissed her on the lips. It was only a peck, but it was still on the lips, and before she could respond he had instructed the small party to have a Happy New Year and was off up the towpath, after Simon.

'Ooooo!' Babs squealed. 'Looks like someone's got a boyfriend! I *knew* he liked you, it's written all over his face. So, how was it? Did the earth move?'

Rosie giggled. 'Hardly. I mean, it wasn't exactly the kiss of the century, was it?'

Harri linked arms with the two girls. 'We all have to start somewhere, and I'm guessing that was your first kiss. Am I right?'

Rosie nodded shyly. 'You know it was.'

'Then you can only go up from here,' Harri said with a wink. 'C'mon, you two; we might not have to be up early tomorrow, but I'm whacked.'

As they approached the barge, Rosie suddenly held out a hand to prevent the girls from going any further. She put a finger to her lips, and beckoned them to follow her. When she was close enough, she held up a hand to her friends, sprang forward, and flung the cabin doors wide open. Pepè gave a loud shriek, followed closely by Babs. 'What the hell are you doin'?' Babs said, holding on to Harri for support with one hand and pressing the other to her chest in an effort to calm her beating heart.

Without answering, Rosie raced to the hold and ran her hand along the tarpaulin that covered the cargo. She shook her head, and went back to her friends, who were waiting for an explanation. She pulled an apologetic face. 'Sorry, but I thought there was someone on board.'

Harri looked curiously at Rosie. 'What on earth made you think that? I saw no lights, or even the slightest sign that we had visitors.'

Rosie shrugged. 'I don't know. It was just a feeling. Don't you think the barge looks different somehow?' As the words left her mouth, she remembered the time she and the girls had gone out for fish and chips and returned to find a bewildered-looking Maggie, who for some reason had also been convinced that they had had strangers on board the barge in their absence. A shiver ran down Rosie's spine. Her mother must have seen or heard something to make her think their privacy had been invaded, just as she did now, but what? There was nothing out of place, the doors had been shut just as they had left them, and the tarpaulin was tightly secured with no sign of missing cargo. Before the others could answer, she held up her hands. 'I give up. I don't know what I was thinking. I suppose it's been a long night, so the sooner I get to sleep the sooner I can stop imagining things.'

Harri, who had been inspecting the barge, agreed with her Number One. 'Staying up until the small hours certainly isn't going to make us any fresher. Best be off to bed; I'm sure all will seem normal in the morning.'

Later, in her dreams, Rosie was standing beside the *Kingfisher* watching a crane loading a cargo of coal on to the barge. 'Keep that bloody thing still, will you?' It was Eddie — one of the crane operators from the yard — and every time he tried to drop a load on to the barge the *Kingfisher* would drift sideways, like a feather on a pool of water. 'What this barge needs is more weight addin' to it. The damned thing's bobbin' round like a champagne cork.' As he released the load of coal on to the wooden deck, the *Kingfisher* dropped alarmingly into the depths of the canal.

'Take it off, take it off,' Rosie shrieked as she watched the water lapping at the top deck of the barge. 'One more piece and she'll go under!'

Pepè, who had been flying around their heads, swooped down and picked up a single piece of coal and the *Kingfisher* sprang back up and bobbed around on the surface of the canal once more.

Babs and Harri were standing close by. 'How on earth are we goin' to get the cargo to its destination? If any of us step aboard to start the engine, the whole thing'll go under,' Babs squeaked. 'Perhaps we could get your old mare to tow the barge?'

Rosie shook her head impatiently. 'Daisy's too far away, and besides she's not mine any more. I'll try gettin' on board real careful like, and see how we go from there.'

She gingerly stretched out one leg, and the next thing she knew she was standing on the deck of the *Kingfisher*, the two girls beside her, and they were making their way to their first drop-off point. As she turned to wave goodbye to the men who had helped load the barge, she realised that they were some way along the canal, probably not far from Pank's farm by the look of it. While they continued down the canal she arranged with her crew that they would moor at Tuppenny Corner and have their lunch before moving on. As the scene before her changed Rosie found herself tucking into a dinner of fish and chips and it was at this point that she realised she must be dreaming. There's no point in dreaming if you can't have a good time, so I'm going to dream a huge chocolate pudding, with chocolate sauce and chocolate sponge covered in whipped cream and cherries, she thought happily.

But before she could tuck into the treat the scene before her changed once again and now Harri was calling out to Babs to push them away from the bank so that they could continue their journey. Pepè was flying overhead, and suddenly a single tail feather left his body and floated down towards the barge. The three girls watched its descent as if mesmerised. The second the tail feather touched the tarpaulin, the *Kingfisher* sank to the bottom of the canal and Harri, Babs and Rosie found themselves floundering in the inky black water.

Rosie's cries for help had turned into gurgles as her mouth started to fill with the foul-tasting water. Looking to her side she saw Babs's head disappear under the surface and a ring of water appear where it had been, but before she could reach the spot a large barge pole was thrust into the canal and Babs emerged on the end of it, gasping for air like a landed fish. Rosie turned to see who their rescuer was and heard Eddie calling to her to grab hold of the pole. When all three of them were safe Rosie tried to tell him how relieved she was that he had been around, but Eddie had vanished. In his place stood the bearded man with piercing blue eyes who had been outside Daisy's shelter all that time ago, and as his gaze met Rosie's she saw a look of recognition cross his features. 'You!' he roared. 'It's all your fault.' He strode towards Rosie, the back of his hand poised to strike her, but before he reached her he disappeared and someone called 'Rosie, it's me, Tim. Don't worry, he's gone and I've called the scuffers.'

Tears coursing down her cheeks Rosie rushed to him, and as she embraced her old friend, she felt his lips kiss her cheek. 'Come on queen, you're safe now . . .'

Rosie turned her face to his and as their lips met he kissed her, tenderly at first and then passionately. Breaking away from him she whispered in his ear: 'Darling Tim. I knew you'd come for me, oh how I love you . . . ' She opened her eyes to look into his hazel eyes, but there was something wrong, they had changed; they were brown. Gasping, she realised that she had been kissing Danny. She gabbled an apology, but laughing, Danny shook his head.

'No need for apologies, love. I've been wanting a kiss from you for a long time.' His face was wreathed in smiles.

Rosie frowned at him. She had thought she was kissing another man; did Danny not care that she had been whispering Tim's name in his ear?

But before she could voice her thoughts the scene in front of her changed and instead of Tim or Danny, there was nothing but inky black. Rosie lay in the darkness, half awake, trying to make sense of it all; what did it mean? Was she still in love with Tim? She reprimanded herself. Dreams were just that; they meant nothing, and could give her no answers. Turning over in her narrow bunk, Rosie glanced at the small clock which hung above the cabin doors. It was nearly four o'clock; another few hours and she would be up and making the tea. Determined to sleep without dreams this time, she closed her eyes once more.

8

It had been several months since Maggie had left the *Kingfisher* and to Rosie's surprise she had received two letters from her mother, although the first was little more than a note giving Rosie her address and saying she was all right and hoped Rosie was, too. The second letter was more typically Maggie. The farm she had been sent to was in Dorset — not far from Ken, as it turned out — and the farmhouse itself sounded delightful. Maggie had described the buildings as belonging on a picture postcard, with stone walls, deep-set windows and a trellis of red and white roses taking over half of the house's façade. The farm itself was mainly arable but it did have a small amount of livestock, containing pigs, cows and some chickens.

I thought Pepè was bad with his screeching, but Plevin's cockerel takes some beating. He's up with the sun and don't he just let you know it! Damned thing needs to learn some manners, as not everybody needs to be up and at 'em so early. It wouldn't be so bad but he has a sort of domino effect on the rest of the animals. The cows start mooing, then the pigs begin to grunt, not to mention the hens who've been clucking since he woke them all up! Life's hard on the farm, but there's a lot more room than

216

on a canal boat. While Mrs Plevin's okay,
her hubby don't half like to be in charge and
bark his orders at you. It's always Maggie do
this and Maggie do that — he ought to be
told that people'll work happier if they're
asked to do summat rather than being ordered,
or even if he asked nicely, instead of acting
like a sergeant major. Some people are just
plain rude!

Rosie had grinned when she read that. Despite
Maggie's unawarenes of the fact, she and Mr
Plevin sounded remarkably similar; probably
why they don't get on, Rosie mused. I bet me
mam ain't backwards in coming forwards when
it comes to telling him to hold his tongue
neither. There's bound to have been some right
rows since she set foot on that farm. Rosie
imagined poor Mrs Plevin having to put up with
two strong, argumentative and bossy characters
under her roof. Lord only knows it was bad
enough having had one Maggie aboard the
Kingfisher, but the thought of two! The rest of
the letter ended much as it started, moaning
about how life was hard, unpleasant and unfair.
Finally, Rosie thought to herself, Maggie's
getting a taste of what it's like to work for
someone who treats you like a skivvy. I hope she
realises that that's how she used to treat me
before Ken came along.

Since that letter, though, Rosie had not heard
anything from her mother — she hoped that
Maggie and Mr Plevin had not come to blows
— and neither for that matter had she heard

anything from Tim.

Now, as they waited for Babs to come back from the post office, Harri spoke up. 'Ask the Bradleys next time we moor close to them,' she suggested. 'You can just drop it into the conversation, say you've written to him but not heard anything back and you're concerned for him.'

Rosie shook her head sharply. 'I'm not tellin' them that Tim's stopped speakin' to me. They'll want to know why, and if they write and ask him it would be embarrassin' all round. No, I'd rather leave things lie. I'm sure if there was anything wrong they'd let me know. Though I suppose I could always ask if he's okay and not mention the fact that I haven't heard from him for a while. That way they won't suspect anything's wrong.' She glanced at the clock over the cabin doors. 'How long is Babs goin' to take gettin' the mail? If she's fussin' that bloomin' pony . . .'

Harri rolled her eyes. Ever since Babs had seen the condition the pony who occupied Daisy's old field was in — they had nicknamed him Scruff — she had taken it upon herself to go and feed him apples and any other titbits she could get hold of, as well as giving him a groom with an old brush she had found in the field, every time they moored at Tuppenny Corner. Deep down Rosie appreciated Babs's care and concern, but she did worry as to what the owner might do if he thought someone was trespassing. He certainly hadn't seemed best pleased when one of Mr Pank's farmhands had interfered.

'That girl's gotta heart o' gold, but I don't think Scruff's owner would see it like that,' Rosie said. 'He must realise that *someone's* lookin' after his pony, though; he can't possibly believe that Scruff stays that clean all by himself.'

Harri was about to reply when Babs herself burst through the cabin doors, causing both women to jump. 'You've got mail!' she said, thrusting the familiar air force paper into Rosie's outstretched hand. She turned to Harri. 'Come on, queen, you can help me cast off. This calls for privacy.'

Rosie's heart gave a leap of joy. There was only one person she knew in the RAF and that was Tim, but glancing at the envelope she felt disappointment grow in the pit of her stomach. This was not Tim's handwriting. She took a knife and carefully slit the envelope open, but before she read the letter's contents she skipped to the signature at the end. Patsy! Why on earth would Patsy want to write to her? She'd never done so before, so why now? I hope it's not bad news, but there's only one way to find out, Rosie thought gloomily, and, smoothing the paper out, she began to read.

Dear Rosie,

I bet you are shocked that I am writing to you, and I must admit I always thought you were the last person I'd want to correspond with, but a guilty conscience has driven me to it. I know you've always had a soft spot for Tim Bradley, and I thought that if anyone was going to tell you the news it should be me. Tim told me that you know we're stationed together, but of course what you don't know is that we're now officially a couple. It happened one day when we were having our lunch together, but I won't bore you with the details. Tim is such a dear I know he wouldn't want to hurt anyone's feelings, but you can't help who you fall in love with.

I hope this news doesn't hit you too hard, dear Rosie, and I'm sure you'll find someone one day who will mean as much to you as Tim does to me. Please don't be angry with us because we've already agreed that when we get married — it'll be after the war — we will both want you to be at the wedding.

The letter went on at some length about the glamorous life that Patsy and Tim lived on the RAF station, but even though Rosie saw the words she could not take in their meaning as bitter tears trickled down her cheeks. So it's true, she thought miserably. Tim had finally gone and got together with the dreadful Patsy. No wonder he hadn't written for such a long time; he was probably too embarrassed to admit to Rosie that he had fallen in love, especially since Rosie herself had told him she was sure Patsy disliked her. He had dismissed it as being Rosie's imagination, but he must have realised that this was not the case.

Rosie read the first page again, then crumpled it up in her fingers. That dreadful girl had written to her not out of concern for her feelings but because she wanted to gloat that it was she, Patsy, who had won the heart of Tim Bradley, and not Rosie herself. She probably thinks that I'll end up a lonely old spinster while she goes off into the sunset with the love of my life. She doesn't care about Tim, Rosie thought bitterly; she just wants to see me unhappy. Well, I'm not going to let her think she's got the better of me —

Her thoughts were interrupted when Babs reappeared in the doorway. 'Me and Harri have been talkin' and Harri reckons — Oh, Rosie, what's happened?'

Rosie sat on the edge of her bunk, her shoulders shaking as she held the crumpled letter up for Babs to read. Babs did so, and when she had finished she sank to her knees and took Rosie in a comforting embrace. 'I know how this must look, but you have to remember, Rosie dear, war's a horrid time for everyone and it can make people act in a way they wouldn't otherwise. Tim may think he's in love with Patsy because she's close by and he knows her from before the war.' She smoothed her friend's hair back behind her ear. 'If I were you I'd wait until this whole dreadful war business is over and see what happens then.'

Rosie fished a handkerchief out of her sleeve and blew her nose noisily. 'Thanks, Babs. Perhaps you're right, but I'm not goin' to sit around waitin' for Tim to come to his senses. If Patsy really is the type of girl he goes for then he's not the feller I thought he was.' She glanced

221

towards the deck. 'Come on. There's no sense in me sittin' here feelin' sorry for myself, and besides, we've got work to do.' She gave Babs a watery smile. 'When we get to Barrowford Locks I'm goin' to see if Mrs Clutton's made any of them lovely scones; that'll cheer me up.'

* * *

Patsy came to the end of the letter she had just received, her eyes dancing. When she had written to Rosie, her plan, should Rosie ever write back, was to tell Tim that she had received nothing in return. But with the little gem she held in her hands she could do a lot better than that. She shuffled back on her chair and started again from the beginning.

My dearest Patsy,

Thank you so much for your kind letter informing me of all your news, and I must say, life in the WAAF seems to be suiting you very well. It is good to hear that you and Tim are both well and happy, and I'm afraid I must apologise for my long silence but I have been so busy with both work and life in general that I simply haven't had time to write. What with canal workers still in short supply we're on the go practically twenty-four hours a day, although I'll not deny that I have had some time for a bit of a social life, and that is how I came to meet Danny Doyle. He's very high up in the canal offices, and we actually met when I was on my way to meet Tim last, so if it hadn't been for that I might never have got to know Danny. Anyway, to cut a long story short, we met on the train, and things progressed from there. It's wonderful to have someone you can rely on so close to home, and it also means that I don't just have to dance with the girls at the village hops which we attend whenever we can. Can you tell Tim that I'm sorry I've not written for a while, but I promise I will when I have a moment or two to spare, though goodness only knows when that will be.

Patsy was beaming with delight. She had thought that Rosie would mention Patsy's engagement to Tim and of course, had she done so, Patsy would have been unable to tell Tim about the letter, but instead Rosie had gone on about her own relationship with this Danny bloke, whoever he might be.

Sheila, who was sitting on the bed opposite Patsy's, held her hand out. 'Give us a look, then. I helped you write the letter to that Rosie, so it's only right I should get to read her reply, although judgin' by the look on your face the poor beggar fell for it good and proper.'

Patsy handed the paper over and clicked her heels together with delight, but when Sheila handed the letter back to her the other girl was not as congratulatory as she expected. 'Talk about fallin' into a trap and servin' yerself up for lunch — that poor mare's stitched herself up good and proper.' She eyed Patsy shrewdly. 'I don't know Rosie, I only know what you've told me, but this doesn't sound like a devious schemer to me. I hope you're telling me the truth, Patsy Topham, 'cos I wouldn't like to think I'd had anything to do with hurting someone who's done nothing wrong.'

Patsy glared over the top of the letter at her friend. 'You can shut your trap if you're calling me a liar, 'cos I don't tell lies,' she snapped, surreptitiously crossing her fingers behind her back. 'Rosie O'Leary has tried every trick in the book to steal Tim out from under my nose, pretending that her mother was like some sort of wicked witch and she really needed a friend, and the poor sap — Tim, I mean — is too nice to see the truth.' She flicked the paper with her fingers. 'Well, he's gonna see the true Dreary O'Leary now, and in her own hand too.' She eyed Sheila contemptuously. 'It's a bit late to be developing a conscience now, and if you're thinking of telling Tim what I did I'll say it was all your idea.'

Sheila held up her hands and shook her head. 'Steady on, I was just saying, that's all. I won't be telling anyone anything 'cos I'm keeping out of it, and if you ask me that's what I should have done in the beginning.'

Patsy sniffed scornfully and wagged a finger at the other girl. 'I didn't need you to help me write that letter. I'd have done just as well on my own, Sheila Formstone — you were the one who wanted to have some input. In fact, you insisted on it.'

Sheila heaved a sigh. 'All right, all right, you've

made your point. So what's your next move?' She eyed her friend incredulously. 'You're not going to show him that, are you?'

Patsy scoffed. 'Of course not. You read it — she mentions summat about me and Tim bein' happy together. That would be hard to explain, so I'll just give him the general gist of it.' She glanced at the clock on the wall of their hut. 'Crikey, we'd best get a move on else Cook'll have our guts for garters.' She carefully folded the letter and put it into her apron pocket. 'When you think about it, I've done nowt wrong. I didn't force Dreary to have a relationship with another man, and in a way, it's a good job I wrote that letter, 'cos now I can be there to support Tim when I tell him. Besides, he's the one who asked me to write to her in the first place.'

Sheila shook her head disbelievingly as they left the hut. 'But the only reason he asked you to write was because he thought she'd stopped writing to him, and he only thought that because you've been destroying her letters to him. I don't s'pose he'd be best pleased if he knew you'd never posted his letters to her, either. Beats me why he ever asked you to mail them for him anyway.'

Patsy raised her brows. 'Because I offered, silly. I'm fed up with this conversation. What's done is done, and by the sound of it Rosie and this Danny are more than happy together, so maybe I've done everyone a favour.'

Sheila sighed resignedly. 'I s'pose Rosie's quite lucky, really. At least she knows her feller's relatively safe and she can see him at the end of his working day.' She looked at her friend. 'Working in a canteen is a bit like working in a pub, don't you think? You get to meet most folk on the station and have a chat with them, even if it's only for a moment or two.'

Patsy looked at her friend grimly. 'You're right. You get to know everyone, and even if it's just a little bit it makes it all the harder when they fail to return from a mission.' She glanced at her feet as they walked towards the cookhouse. 'I do love Tim, you know, and I'm glad he never made it as air crew, because the thought of him going up and never coming back would be more than I could bear. And I know I've been a bit sly about the whole Rosie thing, but I've been in love with Tim for longer than I can remember, and if he went off with Rosie, well, it would be as bad as him becoming air crew as far as I'm concerned.'

Sheila, who was a rather squat, frumpy individual, eyed the leggy blonde who appeared to have it all and shook her head sadly. When they first met she would have given anything to look like Patsy. But now, seeing how hard her friend was trying to woo her man, it occurred to Sheila that it didn't matter how beautiful you were, sometimes beauty was not necessarily what a man was after.

Summer 1943

Tim was elbow deep in the engine of a Halifax when a familiar voice called down to him. 'You comin' for lunch? Only we've a whole heap of work to do on that bomber, and it won't all get done today whether you miss your lunch or not.'

Tim sighed and pushed himself out from underneath the plane. 'Tell me about it. Everyone keeps saying we're winning the war, but it seems like we're still having the same amount of repair work to do . . . '

Jimmy raised his brows. 'I'd rather be doing repairs than missing a plane altogether. Look on the bright side. At least this lucky lot returned home safe, even if there is more work than we can manage.'

Tim fished an oily rag out of his pocket and proceeded to smear oil from his fingers on to the rag, whilst at the same time no doubt transferring some of the oil from the rag back on to his hands. 'That's true, and I'm not complaining, not really, it's just been such a long time since I had any leave . . . '

Jimmy frowned at his companion. 'You mean, since you took any leave. You know as well as I do that you've been issued with leave on more than one occasion, it's just that you don't want to go back . . . '

Tim waved the rag at Jimmy. 'If you're talking about Rosie, then you're wrong. She's not the reason why I've not gone back. It's the thought of being cramped up in a tiny barge with my folks again. It's funny really, because it never bothered me when I was working on the canals, but then I suppose I never knew any different. Now I've been in the RAF for a few years I've got used to having lots of space and room, not to mention privacy.' Tim chuckled at the look of surprise on his friend's face. 'Believe me, Jimmy, there's plenty of privacy here in comparison to a barge. It's something I've been thinking about a lot lately. Everyone reckons the war can't go on too much longer, and it does look like we're winning, but what'll I do when we get demobbed? I can't picture myself back on the canals, but apart from being in the services I don't know any other kind of life. I don't fancy stayin' in the RAF, and I don't think I could stand to go back on the canals, and I'm no pen pusher . . . '

Jimmy raised his brows, a quizzical look etching his features. 'Are you pulling my leg? The best mechanic this station has ever seen, and you reckon you haven't got what it takes to make it on your own in the big wide world? Any garage in its right mind will snap you up — that's if you don't decide to open one of your own, of course. You could rent somewhere . . . '

Tim stopped walking, a thoughtful frown creasing his brow. 'Golly, I'd never thought of that. Do you think I could make a go of it — on my own, I mean?'

Jimmy appeared to consider. 'You wouldn't necessarily have to do it alone. I'd like to think I'm not too shoddy when it comes to all things mechanised, and I wouldn't mind goin' into partnership with you.'

Tim's face lit up, his eyes shining as he clapped his friend on the shoulder. 'Jimmy, are you serious? Only I'm game if you are . . . me mam and dad would be okay with it, I'm sure, 'cos I bet they've got used to havin' a bit of extra space without me on board.'

Jimmy held out a hand. 'Hold on, hold on. We'll have to look into things, see what's what, price things up . . . but providin' it makes good business sense, and we can afford it, then yeah, count me in.'

Taking Jimmy's hand in his own, Tim shook it firmly. 'Deal. All I've got to do now is break the news to my parents, although I'm sure they'll be glad to know I'll not be a burden to them when the war's over. I'll take a forty-eight as soon as Sarge can spare me. Tell you what, I'll go and see him straight after lunch, strike while the iron's hot, as they say.'

Jimmy grinned at his friend. 'Might give you a chance to see what's what with Rosie as well. You never know your luck — her and that Danny bloke might be a thing of the past. But if they aren't, I suppose there's always Patsy. She seems real keen.'

Tim waved a dismissive hand. 'Patsy's like the little sister I never had. Besides, I'm sure she doesn't see me in any other way than an older brother.'

Jimmy let out a low whistle. 'They say there's none so blind as those who will not see, and if you can't see how keen Patsy is on you . . . She's a real stunner, and there's not one bloke on this station who wouldn't swap places with you when it comes to Patsy Topham. Perhaps you should let her know you're not interested and give the rest of us a chance.'

Tim was about to correct his friend, tell him he was wrong, but when he pictured Patsy's pretty little face looking up at him he began to think that maybe there was something in what Jimmy said. As far as Tim knew, Patsy had at least half a dozen men all vying for her attention at any one time, yet she chose not to link up with any of them. Rosie had mentioned something about Patsy's liking him, too, at one point. He scratched his chin thoughtfully. Was he really that ignorant of his old friend's feelings? He'd just assumed that she was being fussy; having the pick of the crop she was waiting for someone really special to turn up. But now, as he walked towards the cookhouse with Jimmy, he conjured up an image of her face as he stood in line waiting to be served. Tim's brow furrowed as he pictured those wide, blue, adoring eyes as she looked hopefully at him; he had always assumed he got extra grub because they had known each other before the war, but now . . .

'Penny dropped, has it?' Jimmy chuckled. 'Blimey, I'd give me right arm to have Patsy look at me the way she looks at you, yet you seem to have it bad for Rosie. I can't wait to see what she looks like, although I can't imagine a woman more beautiful than Patsy . . . '

Tim shook his head. 'Rosie may not be what you'd call a stunner, but to me she's the most beautiful girl in the world, and I just don't see Patsy that way.' He waved a reproving hand as Jimmy began to protest. 'Oh, I know she's what you might call a pin-up, but she doesn't do anything for me. Rosie's got depth. She's funny, quick-witted and kind, and her eyes . . . ' He looked up at the sky as his mind formed a

230

picture of Rosie. 'They say the eyes are the window to your soul, and in Rosie's case it's true; her soul holds more beauty than any other woman I've ever met.'

Jimmy was staring at Tim. 'Crikey, boy, you've got it worse than I realised. Does Rosie know how you feel?'

Tim pulled a face. 'I thought she did, but I suppose I never actually said how I felt. Us chaps don't, do we? But with hindsight, mebbe I should have. I did try the last time I saw her at Buxton, but like I told you, she was either in a rush to get off or she shunned me.'

'Faint heart never won fair lady, that's all I'm gonna say,' Jimmy began, but seeing the look on Tim's face he said no more.

'No point in crying over spilt milk, either. All I can say is, if I ever get the chance again to tell Rosie how I feel, then I won't hesitate, or let her walk away.' Tim glanced at his wristwatch. 'Anyway, no point in goin' on about it. Best stop daydreaming and get a move on. I think I'll skip pudding today; that way I can go and see Sarge without losing any time on the job.'

★   ★   ★

'Keep it coming, down a bit, down a bit . . . stop!' Rosie unhooked the sack of rice off the crane, and as she waited for Eddie to collect the next one she watched the men loading up the other end of the *Kingfisher* with grain. Babs and Harri had gone off to the office to show Pete their union cards — some of the bargees had been threatening a strike, claiming that the *Kingfisher's* crew were not all in the union — and Rosie had said she would keep the work going while they were gone. It never ceased to amaze her how the men of the canals still resented an all-female crew. She had never caused any of them to lose wages — there was after all plenty of work to go round — and the *Kingfisher* had never caused any damage to the locks or any of their barges. She had turned a blind eye to their many unlawful antics, and bitten her tongue on more than one occasion when a farmer had asked her outright if she knew who had been stealing from him, yet they still wanted her off the canals. She had voiced her thoughts to Danny, but he had shrugged, stating simply, 'You know what the fellers are like. Probably having a bit of fun with you, that's all.'

His response had angered Rosie. She didn't call it 'having a bit of fun' when some fool of a man cast them off in the middle of the night, so that they ended up bumping into another barge, causing a furious row between the crews of the *Kingfisher* and the *Marlow*, all of whom had been asleep in their bunks at the time of the collision. Or the occasion when they went to fuel up and instead of letting the girls fill the tanks themselves the feller had insisted on doing it for them. Fortunately Babs had been keeping a careful eye on him, and when Rosie took out her purse to pay she had said, 'Hang on a minute, Rosie — I think you'll find there was a problem with the line. Take the nozzle out, there's a good chap, so we can see if she's full or not.'

The man had positively glowered at Babs. 'You callin' me a cheat? I was just about to check if you was full before you butted in.'

Babs smiled sweetly at him. 'Oh, I *am* sorry. My mistake. Only when you said 'there you go', I thought you meant you'd finished. Rosie dear, you heard the man, we're not full yet. Best wait before you pay . . . '

While he did eventually fill the barge with diesel, it had made for a very awkward moment, and even though he never tried that trick again Rosie was sure that he was giving them dirty fuel, because they were continually having to clean the fuel line. She had got tired of complaining to Pete, who, while he sympathised, told her that there was very little he could do. 'At the end of the day there's more of them than you, queen, and if they decide to go on strike then I've had it. I'm sorry, and I wish I could help you, but . . . '

Rosie knew he was right. 'You're just trying to keep the peace best you can. I understand that, Pete, same as I have to remember that Babs and Harri are only here for the duration of the war; after that they'll be gone and I don't know what I'll do then, running a barge on your own just can't be done, and I've no idea if Maggie will come back. Even if she did, I can't see the two of us running a barge together again.'

Now, with the *Kingfisher* nearly loaded up, Babs and Harri returned from the office. 'Yoohoo, we're back!' Babs called out as she stepped aboard the barge. 'Stupid men. I don't know why they bother any more, you'd think they had nothing better to do with their time than try to create trouble for us.' She glanced at the cargo. 'Looks like we're about ready to cover up.'

Harri nodded and began to walk over to the far end of the barge, but Simon waved a hand at her. 'It's okay, queen, we'll start this end if you gals do that 'un, only we've got a fair few to load up today and we want to get a move on — no offence.'

'If it means we get under way quicker that's fine by me,' Babs muttered. 'Sooner we get going, sooner we're away from that lot of backstabbing . . . '

Rosie placed her hands on her hips. 'Don't go gettin' worked up. They're not worth it, and besides, that's what they want, to get you all on edge so you'll end up leaving, and you're not going to give them what they want, now are you? So let's get the cover strapped down. Harri, you can start the engine, and then let that bird of yours out of his cage for a bit. I like to watch him when he flies alongside us.'

Harri nodded. 'Pepè likes to spread his wings, and it gives me a good opportunity to give his cage a thorough clean.'

Simon, who had finished strapping the cargo down, wandered over to the main tiller of the *Kingfisher*. 'You thtill on for the danth tonight, queen? And you good ladieth too, of courth,' he added, indicating Harri and Rosie.

Babs pulled a face. 'Don't know as I can be bothered, to tell the truth, Simon. I wouldn't

234

be surprised if we came back to find some of the waterway whingers had chucked half our cargo in the drink.'

Rosie giggled. Waterway whingers was the name Babs had come up with for the bargees who complained about the girls on a regular basis. But one look at Simon's face told Rosie how disappointed he was. 'Of course we'll come to the dance, Simon. Babs is just havin' a bad day, that's all.'

But Babs continued to pout. 'I'll see how I feel. I may see you there, but then again I may not.'

Simon frowned. 'Come on, queen, you can't let me down, and your palth want to go. You can't thtay on the barge by yourthelf — it wouldn't be thafe.'

Babs looked sharply at him. 'Why? What will happen to me if I stay on my own?'

Simon's Adam's apple bobbed nervously in his throat. 'Well, nothing, I ecthpect, but you never know . . . '

Rosie, feeling sorry for Simon and the hole that he appeared to be digging for himself, cut in. 'I think Simon's trying to say that you'll feel better for getting away from the canal for a bit. Goodness knows, we'll all feel better for it.' She looked at Simon and could see the relief in his face. 'That's right isn't it?'

Nodding, Simon cleared his throat. 'I won't be able to join you thtraight away, but I'll be there ath thoon ath I can. Only I'll have to have a wash after work — we've got coal on today.'

Babs looked sullenly at him. 'I suppose I could

235

make it, although I can't promise I'll be in a dancing mood.'

Simon's face became wreathed in smiles. 'That'th more like it,' he said, picking up a pole from the canal bank and giving the *Kingfisher* a hefty shove, as the two men from the front of the barge jumped back on to the path. 'Thee you later, ladieth!'

As they slowly set off along the canal Rosie leaned over to Babs. 'He's ever so keen on you, and he's such a nice feller; try not to be too hard on him. He's not one of the waterway whingers, you know.'

Despite her bad mood Babs let a giggle escape her lips. 'I know he's not, it's just men in general I have something against at the moment. I like working the canals; you get to meet so many interesting people, and the countryside's beautiful — even with the pillboxes and barbed wire defences — so why do the men have to try and spoil things for us?'

Rosie shook her head. 'Beats me, but if you don't go out there and enjoy yourself you're letting them win. They want the canals to themselves, and if we let them push us out, even a little bit, then they've succeeded.'

Babs watched Pepè as he glided over their heads, just below the trees. 'I wish I could fly.'

Rosie, who was also watching the graceful parrot, nodded. 'To be as free as a bird, you mean?'

Babs looked sideways at her friend. 'No, so I could go and poop on their boats during the middle of the night without them knowing.'

236

Rosie let out a hoot of laughter. 'Babs! You can't say things like that . . . '

As the two friends guided the barge up the canal, they burst into giggles whenever Pepè flew over the top of them.

By the time they got to Tuppenny Corner the general mood on the barge had improved greatly, and all three girls were looking forward to an evening out. 'Can we go for fish and chips before the dance? I fancy a bit of a treat, and then on the way back perhaps we can call in on Scruff. It's light enough to see our way across the fields without fear of rabbit holes,' Babs said, as she tied the *Kingfisher* up for the night.

Rosie raised her brows at Harri. 'Fine by me. You?'

Harri nodded. 'Never been known to turn down a fish supper yet, and never will be either. Although we'd best take some treats for Scruff, otherwise he gets too overbearing, and I don't fancy being nudged all the way across the field.'

Later that evening it was a jovial little group that set off towards the village. Rosie was wearing a beautiful blue frock that she had picked up from Paddy's Market the last time they had been in the city. None of her old clothes fitted any more. She had arranged her hair into a neat bun at the nape of her neck, and despite her objections Babs had managed to place a small dab of rouge on her cheeks.

'Now that wasn't hard, was it?' Babs had said, a huge smile on her face. 'One of these days I'm going to get that lippy on you if it kills me.' A thought occurred to her. 'Is Danny going to the dance? I've not heard you mention it.'

Rosie shook her head. 'He said he had summat on tonight. Not sure what, but I think it was something to do with stocktaking.'

Harri pulled a face. 'He's always working, that one. Doesn't he know that all work and no play makes Danny a very dull boy?'

Rosie chuckled. 'Some folk are born to work, and I suppose Danny's one of them. Besides, if stock goes missing — and we all know what some of the bargees are like — then he's got to do something about it. And you can't check stock while cargo's being shifted in and out of the sheds during the day, so he has to work in the evenings.'

Babs wrinkled her nose. 'But who on earth would want to nick sacks of grain? I could understand if it were gold bullion we were transporting, but grain?'

Rosie stopped walking. 'Blimey, I hope we aren't goin' to be talkin' shop all night.'

'Oh, God, I hope not,' Harri said, her tone clearly heartfelt. 'I only agreed to come to this dance so that I could get away from work for a bit.'

Babs giggled. 'Sorry. I were only askin', but you're right, talkin' about work's no fun, so let's go and get our supper. I can just taste those golden brown crisp chips, and the crunchy batter . . . '

Rosie's mouth had started to water. She looked at her friends, a smile spreading across her cheeks. 'Last one there . . . ' The rest of her words were lost as she raced along the streets, her fellow crew members pounding along behind her. As she stopped to open the door she was barrelled into by Harri and Babs, who had been racing for second place, and the three of them almost fell inside, much to the annoyance of the shop owner, whose grumpy features showed his displeasure at their ungainly arrival.

'Watch out — you'll be through the glass if you're not careful. I'll have no horseplay in here,' the man said as he adjusted his overall, which had once been white but was now stained with the lard they used to cook the chips in.

Rosie apologised and tried to placate him by saying that they had only been in such a hurry because they could not wait to taste his delicious fish and chips, but from the arms folded across his chest and the defiant look on his face it was obvious that the man could not easily be buttered up.

After what proved to be a pleasant evening of food and dancing the girls headed back to the *Kingfisher*. Rosie linked arms with Babs and gave the other girl a friendly squeeze. 'Simon was so pleased to see you, Babs. Everyone could see how relieved he was that you'd turned up. It wouldn't surprise me if he popped the question one of these days.'

Babs looked horrified. 'God, I hope not! I mean, he's a nice bloke an' all, but I'm not ready to get tied down for a long time yet.'

Reaching the fence that bordered Scruff's field, they climbed carefully over. 'Good job none of us are wearing stilettos,' Harri grumbled as she examined her shoes. 'Next time I'm only coming to see Scruff if I've got my wellies on. It's getting dark, and what's the betting I stand in one of his piles of — '

'Shh!' Rosie hissed.

'I wasn't going to swear,' Harri said, looking hurt. 'I was only going to say — '

Rosie pulled her back to the fence, where Babs was already crouching, looking worried. 'There's someone in the stable. I can see a light on, and it kind of blinked on and off, you know, as if someone walked across the beam.'

Harri followed her friend's line of sight, and as comprehension dawned she sank down next to Babs. 'You think it's the feller that owns Scruff, the one who said he didn't want people in his field?'

Squatting down herself, Rosie nodded, then let out a small groan. Scruff, who must have been grazing in the far corner of the field, had recognised them, and was heading in their direction. 'Did either of you bring any treats? If so, throw them towards him so that he stops to eat them. Otherwise he's going to give us away.' Harri gave Rosie the thumbs up, and she and Babs pulled such a large quantity of titbits out of their pockets that Rosie had to suppress a giggle. 'Good God, no wonder he's so happy to see you!'

Babs placed a hand in front of Rosie's mouth and pointed towards the stable. Four men were now making their way out of the door. Their jackets were slung over their shoulders and their shirtsleeves were rolled up above the elbows, giving the impression that they had been hard at work. The man leading the group was carrying the lamp. Scruff raised his head. Quickly, Harri threw an apple, and it landed with a soft thud in the grass. 'There you go, greedy guts. That should keep you happy for a bit,' she said in a whisper so quiet that Rosie barely heard her. Unfortunately, no one had told Scruff about being quiet, and as he walked towards the apple he let out a nicker as if to thank Harri for her offering.

The man with the lamp paused and looked over to where the pony stood munching happily. 'Bloody stupid animal: near on give me a heart attack,' he said, much to the amusement of his fellows. 'Soon as we've finished our business in these parts, I'll send him for glue!'

One of his companions appeared to take exception to the threat.

'You leave him be. Don't forget he does his share of the work, as well as keepin' them with long noses out of — '

The first man snorted. 'He's doin' a better job than that lad of yours, I know that much! You can tell him from me, if he don't manage to keep that gaggle under control it'll be me he has to answer to.'

The man who had stuck up for Scruff raised his hands in a bid for calm. 'He's doin' his best. We ain't 'ad no problems, have we? Besides, if it weren't for him you wouldn't be 'ere now, so truly speakin' you should be grateful.'

The leader stepped towards him, but was stopped by a third man, who steered him in the direction of the lane. 'Bertie, leave it be. You're

241

just tense, that's all. Everyone is. But Andy's right, nowt's gone wrong so far, and I'm sure his lad won't let us down. Besides, we need him at the other end . . . '

The men walked on, and their voices became too distant to hear. Rosie, whose heart had been in her mouth the whole time, let out a shuddering breath. She had recognised the man in front. It was the man she had seen when she spent the night in Daisy's shelter. Probably, she thought, with the same lamp too. So it had not been a dream after all. She had to tell Tim. He may have been keeping his distance, but surely he would want to hear about this? And it would be an excellent excuse to ring him. But when would be a suitable time? She didn't even know if he was at the same station any more.

'I wonder what they were doing in Scruff's stable?' Babs's voice brought Rosie back to the present. 'Shall we go and have a look? I'm pretty sure the last feller put the padlock back on, but you never know . . . '

Harri grimaced. 'It's none of our business what they were doing in there, and besides, according to Mr Pank, the feller that owns Scruff doesn't want people in his field. Can you imagine what he'd say if he caught us snooping around his stable? Besides, I can't imagine anything they keep in there being of any interest to us. You know what fellers are like — it's probably fishing gear or summat equally boring.'

Rosie, however, very much wanted to see if they could get into the stable and find out what was going on in there, if anything. If she could

242

ring Tim with some kind of evidence that the men were up to no good, he'd have to believe her.

Leaving Babs and Harri to argue over the necessity to poke their noses into other people's business, she strode towards the stable. When they caught up, Babs looked at her excitedly. 'You think there's summat worth seein' in there, don't you, Rosie?' She turned to Harri. 'See, even our Rosie thinks there's summat shady going on.'

As they neared the stable door, Harri let out a sigh of relief. 'Padlocked. Let's go home.'

'Oh, come on, we're only havin' a bit of fun. Where's the harm in that?'

'Where's the harm? *Where's the harm?*' Harri shook her head in disbelief. 'Trespassing, breaking and entering, and being general nosy parkers, and that's just for starters.'

Babs rolled her eyes. 'It's a bloomin' stable, not the Bank of England!'

'Every man has a right to his privacy. Just because you want to have a good look round is no excuse for what you're doing.'

Babs grinned. 'I think you'll find it is. But if it makes you feel any better, when they haul us before the judge I'll swear we forced you to come at knife point, eh, Rosie?'

But Rosie was not listening. Instead she was sliding her hands across the rough timber of the shelter walls, searching for a hole. When she found one she placed her eye against it, only to draw back, tutting to herself. With the light fading outside, it was far too dark within to see anything. Remembering how she had first taken refuge from Scruff, she walked round the stable until she could squeeze between it and the bordering fence, noting as she did so that she must have grown somewhat, as it was a good deal tighter than it was the last time she had been here. She sidled towards the far corner, scouring the planks for any way in, and noticed a repair that someone had done a long time ago to the bottom of the wall. The space was too tight to bend down and poke around, so she climbed over the fence and, kneeling down, put her hands back through, gripped the broken plank and pulled gently. The wood gave way, and a smile spread across her face. Harri and Babs were watching her from the corner, and as Rosie slithered through the fence and squeezed into the gap Babs gave a squeal of delight. 'She's in, she's in! Can you see anything, or is it too dark? Hang on a mo . . . Harri, have you got that torch of yours, the one you keep on your head?'

Harri sighed dramatically as she unwillingly pulled a small torch from the knot in her headscarf and handed it to Babs, who, following Rosie's example, climbed into the adjacent field and pushed it through the fence into the hole, saying as she did so: 'There you go, queen, take a gander with that.'

'Ta.' Rosie flicked the torch on and paced around the interior of the stable, flashing the beam into every nook and cranny, searching for anything that would indicate that the men were indeed up to no good. There was a small cart in one corner, and a few empty crates were stacked

244

up against the walls. More crates had been pushed together to form a kind of table, and as she looked more closely she could see that it held a couple of empty whisky bottles plus four small glasses, and a pack of playing cards. Gambling. I bet that's what they're up to, drinking and gambling.

She gave a disappointed sigh. It was hardly the crime of the century; in fact she wasn't sure if it was a crime at all to play cards and drink whisky. She knew that liquor was hard to get hold of, but these bottles could have been from before the war. She continued with her search, but apart from a couple of forks and a quantity of old hay which looked suspiciously similar to the pile she had snuggled up in all those years ago there was little else in there, so after one last look round she slid out the way she had come in and carefully placed the wood back over the hole.

Babs raised her brows and rubbed her hands together eagerly. 'Well? Where's the gold?'

Rosie shrugged. 'Sorry, queen, but there's nothing exciting to be found in there, unless you like empty whisky bottles and a game of cards. Here's your torch, Harri — thanks for the loan.'

Babs was pouting. 'What, not even a locked chest?'

Seeing her friend's disappointed face, Rosie gave her an apologetic smile. 'I'm afraid not even that, just a few empty crates, some old hay and a couple of gardening tools, probably to clear out the muck . . . oh, and a small pony cart.'

Harri, who had been on tenterhooks the whole time Rosie had been inside the stable, clapped her hands together. 'Satisfied? Then for goodness' sake let's get out of here before someone catches us. Honestly, you two don't half like to court danger! And for what? Nothing, that's what; it's not against the law for a man to have a drink and a game of cards, you know.' Shaking her head, she made for the gate that led to the towpath.

Trotting to catch up, Babs defended her curiosity. 'They could still be spies, though . . . '

Rosie trailed behind, listening to Harri telling Babs to 'leave well alone' as Babs tried to argue a case for being suspicious, Rosie was unwilling to join in what was rapidly becoming a pretty heated discussion. In truth, she was dismayed. She could tell Tim that the men were real enough, and that she had broken into the stable and found proof that they spent some time there, but the burning question still remained. Why lock a stable that contained nothing? She assumed the cart held some value, but would it be worth locking up? She supposed she could ask Danny's opinion, but thought better of it. No matter whom she spoke to, it was still going to sound like a game that only children would play. She caught up with the other two and took hold of Babs's elbow.

'You aren't goin' to tell anyone about this, are you? Only they may think that we're interfering with matters that don't concern us . . . '

'And they'd jolly well be right, wouldn't they?' Harri said defiantly. 'I said that we shouldn't go in there, but did anyone listen to me? Oh no, it was just boring old Harri — '

'I didn't say that, and neither did Rosie,' Babs said irritably. 'And of course I won't go sayin' anything. They'd think I were soft in the 'ead.'

Harri raised her brows but said nothing. Rosie smiled at the other girl. 'I don't think anyone would think that, but I know what you mean, so best we forget all about it, eh?'

'Hallelujah!' Harri said, holding her hands up in exasperation. 'Now let's get back to the barge. All this sneaking about has fair worn me out!'

9

Maggie had grimaced as she entered the pigpen. Out of all the jobs on Plevin's farm, she hated this one the most. When she had first arrived she had thought pigs to be nervous creatures, like the ones in the fairy tale, but the truth was the exact opposite. The boars had tusks that could penetrate your wellingtons like a knife going through butter and they were not shy retiring creatures at all, but bolshie and stubborn. The big bad wolf would have his work cut out if he met Wilbur, the Plevin's prize boar, she thought bitterly as the obstinate creature refused to do as he was told, forcing Maggie to jump over the pen wall, landing her in a heap of pig manure as she fell. Now she knew where the term pig-headed came from, she realised as she bashed her knees on the pig board, which was used to steer the pigs from one pen to another.

Maggie had been at the farm for almost a year now and was starting to get into the swing of things. As long as you knew that no animals were like those depicted in fairy tales but were in fact dirty, smelly and constantly hungry with no reservations when it came to standing on your feet or barging through you as if you didn't exist then you got along just fine.

'Make sure you always keep your eye on 'em, never turn your back and don't try to stand in their way if they start runnin',' Mr Plevin had warned her when they were taking the cows down the lane to graze in one of the summer pastures. 'If summat spooks 'em, the whole herd'll bolt and won't take no notice of you swingin' your bit o' pipe at 'em. You wouldn't be the first farmhand to get killed by a stampede and you wouldn't be the last either. Your job is to guide them, so don't go standin' in their way should things go wrong else you'll go down like a skittle, albeit a very flat one!'

Now, as Maggie herded the last of the piglets into the neighbouring pen, she reflected on the difference between life on the canals and life on the farm. All in all, she preferred the farm; she just wished she was the one giving the orders rather than having to take them. Ken, she knew, had worked his way up through the ranks and was now in charge of his own ack-ack battery, but there was no way of working your way up the farming ladder. You either owned a farm, or rented one, or worked for someone who did.

On reflection, she knew that life on the canals had never really been for her, but after she met Jack O'Leary it had seemed to be all she wanted. She and her parents had been staying with her aunt and uncle in their little cottage in Ellesmere Port, and Maggie and her cousin Lily had wandered down to the towpath to watch the brightly painted barges as they travelled back and forth along the canal. At the time, opening and closing the locks for the travellers had been novel enough to be fun, and it was at one of those locks that Maggie met Jack. She smiled wistfully at the memory. She had been impressed by the way he had managed to single-handedly navigate his barge so close to the gates without touching them. All the other bargees they had seen that morning had help aboard, but Jack was on his own. He smiled and waved at Maggie as she called out to him to pass her his lock key so that they might open the gates for him.

'Very thoughtful of you I must say,' he had said as he leaned towards her, holding the key out as far as he could so that she might grab it safely. 'You make sure you're careful round these locks, though; they can be dangerous if you get caught in them, and it wouldn't do to see a pretty little thing like you getting hurt.'

Even now Maggie's tummy turned a somer-sault at the recollection. His face was bronzed from the reflection of the sun off the water, and his teeth gleamed white against his skin. The top buttons on his striped shirt were undone, and he had rolled the sleeves up over his elbows, allowing Maggie to see his strong forearms as he held out the key. As she took the metal object from him, Maggie looked directly into his upturned face. The strong jaw, straight nose, and clean-shaven features appealed to her immedi-ately. Her eyes had travelled down to his open-necked shirt and a glimpse of broad chest, and she thought she had never seen a man so utterly handsome in all her life.

'Come on! What's the hold-up?' Lily had called.

Maggie could have stayed and admired Jack all day, but it was not becoming to stare, so she ran back to join her cousin, clasping the key in her hand as she went. Once they had seen Jack safely through the gates, Maggie grinned at Lily. 'See that man, the one on the boat we just let through?'

Lily cast a lazy glance in the direction of the barge. 'Yes?' she said, her tone disinterested.

'He's the man I'm going to marry!' Maggie had giggled, though in her heart she knew that she was serious.

Lily spluttered as she laughed. 'Hah! Your mam'd have a fit! There's no way on earth she'd let you marry a bargee!'

Maggie's eyes had narrowed. 'She can't stop me; I'm sixteen and I'll do as I damn well please.'

Now, as she wielded the fork around the straw in the pigpen, a tear trickled down her cheek. She had never been so in love as she was with Jack; not even Ken could take his place. Part of her wished she had never gone to visit her cousin in Ellesmere Port, or at least that they had not gone down to the canal that day, for while meeting Jack O'Leary had been the best thing that ever happened to her, losing him had been the worst. She had turned her back on her parents and her home, just to be with the love of her life, and where had it got her? Widowed at a young age, a single mother, working on a barge, which she had never really enjoyed. Without Jack, the memories evoked by every mile of the Shropshire Union Canal were too painful to bear, so she had returned to her home town and started on the Leeds and Liverpool Canal, and ten years later Ken had come into her life. Ken was a good man, but he was no Jack, and no matter how much she tried Maggie could not get away from the fact that she was still deeply in love with her first husband.

She rested her chin on the end of the fork handle. She supposed Ken must know that while she loved him, and enjoyed his company, he hadn't completely won her heart. But how could he, when it still belonged to Jack? She shook her head miserably. What an awful mess. She knew that she could make Ken a good wife, but not on the canals. Too many memories of Jack were heaped in every lock she traversed.

Her thoughts wandered back to the day of his death. The bright blue sky, the butterflies fluttering from one flower to the next, and the bees joining the butterflies in search of their amber nectar. Rosie was coming up for her fourth birthday, and Jack had insisted she was old enough to help with various chores around the boat. The two of them would wind the big mooring ropes together, and push the barge off the banks using the long pole. Rosie had loved turning the big lock key best; seeing her little hands next to her father's as she 'helped' him wind it was one of her favourite things, despite Maggie's misgivings.

'Locks is dangerous, Jack O'Leary,' she had warned him on numerous occasions. 'Our Rosie shouldn't be anywhere near them. I know you like to include her in the running of the barge, but some things are best left alone.'

'She's the daughter of a bargee,' he would reply, feeling that she was being overbearing, 'and she needs to know what to do. Besides, look at her little face. She loves it!'

But on this particular morning someone had got to the lock before them and had already begun to open the gate. Rosie had been full of disappointment — this was her and her daddy's job. She was running, looking directly at the man, calling out to him to stop, but the rush of water was too loud for him to hear her, so he kept turning. Watching Rosie's line of direction, Maggie realised the horror which awaited their daughter and screamed a warning. Jack, who had been making his way up to the lock gates, turned . . .

Now, with the tears streaming down her cheeks, Maggie had lifted her chin from the fork handle in order to wipe them away when a hand descended on her shoulder and made her jump. The farmer's wife had heard the sobs coming from inside the pigpen and come in to investigate.

'Oh, my poor dear,' she soothed, brushing Maggie's hair back from her face. 'Whatever's got you so upset?' Her eyes narrowed and her tone became sharp. 'It's not summat Mr Plevin's said, is it? That man . . . '

Laughing shakily, Maggie shook her head. 'No, it's nothing Mr Plevin's said, not this time.'

Mrs Plevin pulled a face. 'Glad to hear it. He can be so insensitive, but if it's not him, then what? Or am I stepping out of line?'

Sniffing, Maggie searched her pockets for a handkerchief, before remembering that she had pushed one up the sleeve of her shirt earlier that morning. Taking it out, she blew her nose and smiled apologetically at Mrs Plevin. 'Just memories of my first husband, that's all . . . thinking of when we met, and our last day together . . . '

Mrs Plevin smiled sympathetically. 'Mebbe you should go back to the canals; I dare say you're feelin' homesick. You told us you lost your first hubby to a lock accident, and now your second man's gone off to join the army, God bless him.' She placed a comforting arm round Maggie's shoulders. 'It's a lot to lose in one lifetime, and you're not even halfway through yours, God willing. Why don't you go back, even if it's just for a weekend?'

Maggie held up a hand. 'Thanks, Mrs Plevin, but I couldn't. Besides, I don't think it would help. If anything, it might make things worse. My days on the canals are over, and while I don't know what I shall do when this dreadful war ends I do know that I shan't be goin' back on any barge.'

Mrs Plevin looked taken aback. 'But what about your gal? Rosie, isn't it? Surely you'll want to see her again? She is your daughter, after all.'

Maggie smiled feebly at her host. 'It's a long story, and one I shan't bore you with today . . . ' she prodded the pig manure with the end of her fork, 'and as your husband is so fond of sayin', 'these animals won't muck themselves out', so if you'll excuse me I'd best get on wi' the job in hand, so these creatures can get back into a nice warm clean bed.'

★　★　★

It was the morning after their unexpected evening adventure, and Rosie was pumping up the primus, ready for the morning tea. When she had lit the small stove, she placed the kettle on its ring and sat back on her haunches while she waited for the water to boil. When they had returned to the *Kingfisher* the previous evening she had once more got the feeling that there was something different about the barge. She had searched it from top to bottom and checked the cargo, and even after she had found nothing wrong she had checked it again, lifting the tarpaulin and tying it down again before settling back in the main cabin, where she had tossed and turned throughout the night, much to the annoyance of Harri.

'It's all that snooping and sneaking you and Babs got up to earlier. It's given you all sorts of ideas,' Harri had warned, waving a reproving finger at Rosie. 'You were convinced those men were up to no good, but you were wrong, so now you've turned your attention to the barge, and you're wrong about that too. Why can't you just leave things be?'

'It's like an itch,' Rosie had explained apologetically. 'You've got to scratch it even though you know it's the wrong thing to do, and the more you scratch the more you itch.'

Harri had shaken her head and pulled the covers up around her ears. 'Well, if you ask me you're better off leaving that particular itch alone. Don't forget my father's a landowner, and even though I may not always agree with his stuffy ways, I do agree with his stance on trespassers. Whether you own the land or rent it, if you're the

255

one paying for it others shouldn't feel free to walk through it without your permission. Those fellers, no matter who they were, have the right to be there 'cos they pay their way; we're the intruders, not them. We were the ones prying into their business, ergo, we're the ones in the wrong. Like it or lump it, Rosie O'Leary, you know I'm right.'

Rosie had frowned. 'Not if they're up to no good, though,' she had said, her tone resolute.

Harri leaned up on one elbow. 'But they weren't though, were they? There was nothing suspicious in the stable, or outside it for that matter. Perhaps they just need a quiet place where they can get a bit of peace from work and family life. Perhaps a quiet game of cards . . .'

'Gambling, you mean?'

Harri lifted her elbow and thudded back on to her mattress. 'Rosie O'Leary, you're a lost cause. I . . . give . . . up!'

Rosie had bitten her lip as she fought back a giggle. Of course she knew she was in the wrong and Harri was right, but she also knew that when those men had visited the stable years ago they had talked of war being a profitable thing and the stable being handily placed for their purpose. She would find out what they were up to if it was the last thing she did, and when she knew what it was she would tell Tim. He would be interested even if Harri was not.

Now, as steam started spouting out of the kettle, Rosie warmed the pot, spooned in the tea, poured in the boiling water and gave it a good stir. She had always kept a diary, ever since she was little — Maggie had encouraged her, as it was good writing practice — so she would fetch it when she got a minute and look over what she had written since the night in the shelter with Daisy, to see if there was any kind of pattern or clue to what it might be being used for now. When she had something firm to go on, she would give Tim a ring, and if he wasn't at the station any more she would talk to the Bradleys, find out his whereabouts from them. He had been her confidante from the start, so it was only natural that she should turn to him now.

Having refilled the kettle, Rosie called to her crew. 'Tea's up!' she said, knocking briefly on the roof of the main cabin. 'I made some porridge while you two were still snoring the morning away, so get yourselves dressed and we'll have us some brekker before headin' off.'

Later that morning, secure in the knowledge that Harri and Babs were more than capable of running the *Kingfisher* on their own, Rosie sat in front of the main cabin, her legs dangling over the water as she thumbed through the pages of her diary. So far as she could make out the overheard conversation had been an isolated incident with nothing untoward happening directly before or after it. She had also gone back to the night when Maggie had thought someone had interfered with the *Kingfisher*. It had been on a Wednesday, when all four women had been off for the evening. The first time she herself had thought she detected something different about the barge was on a Tuesday, and as last night was a Thursday she ruled out any significance regarding the day of the week. The only thing that the incidents did have in common was that they had all occurred when they had been moored at Tuppenny Corner.

Rosie drummed her heels rhythmically against the hull of the boat. She had also noted that there had been lots of other times when they had gone into town while being moored at Tuppenny Corner and noticed nothing untoward on their return.

She snapped her diary shut and stared into the murky water. She would just have to keep her wits about her every time they moored at Tuppenny Corner, and see if anything else happened. If it did, she would make a careful note in her diary and take it from there.

★   ★   ★

Tim had returned from his trip home to see his parents. He had hoped to see Rosie too, but much to his disappointment the *Kingfisher* was nowhere near the *Sally Anne* at the time. He had asked his mother, as nonchalantly as he could, whether she knew anything about a Danny who worked in the offices, but though she had said she did know of him she could give very little detail, except that he seemed a nice enough chap and was good at his job.

'From what Patsy Topham said, this Danny and Rosie O'Leary are quite fond of each other,' Tim had ventured as the Bradleys were walking along the tow-path on their way into the city for lunch.

258

'Can't say as I've heard that, but it wouldn't surprise me,' his mother had told him. 'Rosie O'Leary's turning into a real nice young woman, and it has to be said that since her mother left the barge she's really come into her own. Although I must say, Tim, I don't want to spend what little time I have with you talking about Rosie O'Leary and some chap from the canal offices. I know you and Rosie are good friends, but I thought that's as far as it goes, or am I wrong?'

Tim had shaken his head hastily. 'I'm just concerned for her welfare, I suppose. As you say, she's a good girl, and I wouldn't like to see her taken advantage of by some fancy high flyer.'

Tim's father had covered his laugh with a cough, then cleared his throat. 'Of course you're not interested in her, Tim, anyone can see that.' He had winked at his son, but stopped grinning when his wife jabbed him sharply in the ribs with her elbow.

'Stop your teasing, Will Bradley. If our Tim says he's only concerned for Rosie's welfare then I believe him. But I said it before and I'll say it again: I have precious little time with my son as it is and I will not spend it talking about other people's concerns, however nice they are. Understood?'

Both Bradley men had nodded their understanding, and the rest of Tim's limited stay had been spent talking of the new venture he and Jimmy planned to undertake as soon as they were demobbed. Will's face had shone with pride as he listened. 'I think it's a grand idea, our Tim!

Do you think you'd be able to set up near to the canal so's you could take in passing barge trade as well as motor vehicles and the like? Only if you could, I reckon you'd be set for life. Everyone on the Leeds and Liverpool knows you're a whiz with engines, and that were before you was RAF trained. Now you've got that under your belt an' all, well, the sky's the limit, if you'll pardon the pun.'

Tim had listened as his father continued to talk, but inside his head all he could think about was Rosie and her alleged relationship with Danny, and how he could find out the truth behind it. His mother had not seemed suspicious when he enquired about Rosie, so if the Number One of the *Kingfisher* had a problem with Tim she had certainly not aired her thoughts abroad, for had she done so the bargee grapevine would have been in full swing and everyone would have been talking about it.

When his forty-eight was over Tim had asked his mother if she would pass on his best wishes to Rosie and tell her how sorry he was that he had been unable to see her on this trip. 'Hopefully the next time I have leave it will be for a bit longer, so I'm sure I'll manage to catch up with her then.'

His mother had promised that she would pass on the message, and had stood on tiptoe to give her son a kiss goodbye. 'I know your father were teasin' about you and Rosie, but I'm guessin' there were some truth in what he said. Don't go frettin' over some young gal who's hundreds of miles away from you, son. War's a funny old business and it causes folk to act peculiar. Just you make sure you take care of yourself on that airfield of yours, and don't go daydreamin' about things you have no control over.'

Now, sitting on his neatly made bed, Tim sucked the end of his pen thoughtfully as he attempted to write a letter to Rosie. Trying to keep the contents casual while hoping to find out if there was a problem between the two of them was not proving an easy task.

Dear Rosie, I was so sorry that I never managed to catch up with you on my recent bit of leave, as I would very much have liked to have seen you. I am still stationed in the same place and the number is the same, so if you have a moment or two free it would be nice to catch up.

Tim scanned the page before him before crumpling it up into a ball and throwing it into the growing pile that was slowly taking over the wastepaper bin. Why had she stopped writing to him? Even if she was with Danny that was no reason for her to give him the cold shoulder. He had said as much to Patsy, thinking that another woman might be able to explain it, but instead of coming up with an answer she had appeared annoyed that he still persisted in trying to retain a friendship with the other girl.

'Beats me why you give two hoots about her. She hasn't replied to your letters in ever such a long time, and you know from what she wrote to me that she has another feller . . . ' She had pouted, clearly hurt by his persistence. '*I'd* never treat you like that, Tim Bradley. That girl don't know how lucky she is to have a feller like you as a friend. If you take my advice you'll stop pursuing someone who can't even be bothered to write to you, and start looking for a girl who'll treat you right.'

Tim had felt sure that Patsy was referring to herself, and he could not help feeling flattered. Most of the men on the station — including the officers — had noticed Patsy's beauty, and any one of them would have given a good deal to have her look at them the way she looked at Tim. What was more, the two of them had been friends ever since Tim could remember and even though he knew Rosie had reservations about her, he had always found her to be good fun and a good pal too.

He pulled another piece of paper towards him. Patsy was right about one thing. Why *did* he persist in trying to pursue a friendship with Rosie? It didn't make sense that he was chasing after someone who had shown no interest when he had one of the most beautiful girls on the station begging for his attention.

He glanced at the clock on the wall of his hut, pushed back his chair and placed his pen in his pocket. Picking up his irons, he set off for the cookhouse. He wondered if Patsy was still annoyed at him for taking the forty-eight. When he had told her of his plans she had slapped a lump of mashed potato into the middle of his stew so hard the gravy had splattered his overalls, and even though she had uttered the word 'sorry' the cold icy glare she gave him had said otherwise. A smile began to curl on his lips. Patsy had always been feisty. Growing up on a working barge was hard enough for a boy, and he supposed that girls had to be really tough in order to cope, especially around the likes of Frog and Taddy who were relentless in their teasing.

Since he had joined the RAF Tim had kept in contact with Frog and most of his pals from the barges, many of whom had either joined the forces or left to work in one of the munitions factories. It seemed that all of them had sought a different life and the war had been a good excuse to get off the canals once and for all. Frog had said in his last letter that when the war was over he wanted to stay in the army and see a bit of the world. Tim knew that Patsy did not wish to return to the canals after the war either.

'I'll stay on if the WAAF will have me,' she had said one crisp autumn morning as she served him breakfast. 'I couldn't go back to being cooped up on a barge with Mam and Dad. To be honest, since they've both joined the services too, I don't think they'll be wanting to go back either.'

Tim paused, his hand resting on the cookhouse door. He thought about how their lives might have turned out if Britain had not gone to war with Germany. Would they all have carried on working the canals? He pulled a rueful face. It was quite likely that they would, not knowing any other life. It was strange to think that even when the war was over things would never go back to the way they were. He knew from Rosie that finding people to run the barges was nigh on impossible. Surely no landlubber wanted to swap their house for a cramped-up barge, where the work was hard and pay was poor.

Looking at it logically, if there were fewer people supplying transport along the canals, then producers and manufacturers would turn their attention to the road network or the railways, and then what would become of his parents? They had been on the canals all their lives, and knew nothing else. Perhaps they would take early retirement, or maybe his father could work for Tim and Jimmy in the garage. Come to think of it, what would happen to Rosie? She was far too young to retire, yet she had shown no sign of wanting to change her way of life. He supposed this was what made her stand out from all the other youngsters on the canal, most of whom had been desperate to leave by the time they reached their teens. Rosie had remained loyal to the canals, and the need to keep the country's supplies on the move.

As ever, Tim's thoughts came back to Rosie's apparent lack of interest. He knew that he was popular amongst the women on the canals, and his pals at the station often teased him about the number of WAAFs who were keen to be seen on his arm, so why not Rosie? He had always been kind to her, never teased her about her life with Maggie, as Taddy had done. In the run-up to his leaving they had spent as much time as they could together; and years before that, he had been the one who had taught her how to swim in the Scaldy when they were just kids, and the art of catching brown trout in the pools when they were older. Looking back, it occurred to Tim that unlike other girls Rosie had never tried to impress him, or pretend to be someone she wasn't; she had always remained the same dear Rosie.

He pushed open the door to the cookhouse and walked over to the counter, keeping an eye out for Patsy as he did so. He would have valued a woman's opinion on what to put in his letter, but he knew that asking Patsy would probably result in half his dinner's ending up on his overalls again.

'Stew and tatties is all I've got left, although there's some jam roly too if you want pud.' It was Sheila, Patsy's friend.

Tim nodded and held his tray out. 'Patsy not on lunch duty?'

Sheila shook her head. 'She's gone home for a few days, although where home is I'm not exactly sure. She said she was goin' to stay with some feller called Taddy and his mam.'

Tim nodded. 'The Madisons. They run a working barge — Patsy helped them get it up and running when their old one got destroyed in a bombing raid.'

Sheila shrugged. 'All I know is she's not going to be back for a week, so I'm covering for her as well as doin' me own work.' She put the plate of stew on Tim's tray, then held a ladle of custard above a bowl of jam roly-poly and raised her brows.

'Yes please,' Tim said. 'I've just come back from a quick trip home myself. It was good to see my mam and dad, but it's not much fun being crammed into those tiny bunks.'

'You see that Rosie?' Sheila said, regretting the question as soon as the words had left her lips.

Tim shook his head. 'How do you know about Rosie? Has Patsy said something?'

Sheila shrugged. 'I'm too busy to stand here chattin' to you all day.' She turned to the next person in the line: 'Stew and bread do you? Only he's just had the last of the tatties . . .'

Tim took his tray and sat down at one of the melamine-topped tables. He watched Sheila as she scooped stew on to plate after plate and exchanged a few words with every recipient. If the girls in the WAAF were anything like canal folk, he expected that they all probably knew about Rosie and how she was ignoring him.

He wondered whether Patsy might bump into Rosie on the canals. He was surprised that Patsy — who claimed to hate barges now — had chosen to spend her leave with the Madisons, but then what was the alternative?

He supposed that most canal folk went back when they had a bit of leave, just as he and Patsy had done. In a few months' time it would be Christmas, and although he did not relish the idea of being cooped up on an iced-in canal barge he would ask his sergeant if he might spend a few days with his parents. He knew it was unlikely that Rosie would be working over the Christmas period, and if she stuck with tradition she would moor at Tuppenny Corner along with the Bradleys, the Madisons and as many others as could fit, so that they might enjoy the holiday together, singing carols, swapping stories and going to the pub to see in the New Year.

Tim put his empty plates on one of the trolleys and headed for the exit, where he dutifully dipped his irons into the tank of steaming water. Checks were regularly made to ensure that everyone kept their cutlery clean and Tim was not going to risk getting in trouble for dirty irons, not when he intended to ask for leave at Christmas. After giving them a good swill around in the water, he left the cookhouse and made for his hut. He would ask his sergeant about his leave straight after drill in the morning. Get the request in early, he thought, and maybe I'll stand a good chance of going home.

If his request was approved then Tim would write to his parents and make sure they knew of his plans in time to bag their place at Tuppenny Corner, though he would also ask them to keep his return quiet so that he might surprise his pals. He pictured them all holding candles in their mittened hands and singing 'Good King Wenceslas' at the tops of their voices, and how surprised they would be when he strolled up behind them and joined in the merriment. Feeling confident and optimistic, Tim entered the hut and eyed the half-full wastepaper bin. Letters were impersonal, a waste of time. Face to face was the only way to solve any problems that he and Rosie had, and if he got his way this Christmas was going to be one to remember.

After changing into his issue pyjamas Tim slid between the itchy blankets and visions of the holiday formed in his mind once again. Taddy would squeal with delight at the sight of his friend, and Rosie would rush forward to envelop him in a tight embrace, delighted to be with her beloved Tim. A smile formed on his lips as he closed his eyes and settled down for the night. Yes, this Christmas would be one to remember, just him and Rosie and no sign of Danny. With this image foremost in his thoughts, Tim dozed off into a dream world of roast turkey, Christmas crackers, and hot Christmas pudding, all served to him by the wonderful Rosie O'Leary.

★　★　★

Danny scratched his head. Whenever he did a stock-take he expected, if anything, to find that something had gone missing, so to discover that he had five extra sacks of cotton was something he had not anticipated. He was sure that all the barges had gone out fully laden. He had the paperwork on his office desk to confirm it, yet stacked in front of him were five sacks of cotton. He had even nicked the sewing on the top of one of the sacks and placed a finger and thumb inside, pulling at its contents to confirm that it was indeed cotton. He scratched his head. How on earth was he meant to explain this to his bosses? It would be harder than saying that stock had gone missing, because unfortunately some of the bargees were known to be light-fingered, as were some of the dock workers, as well as the factory folk. Taking stuff was more or less expected, but *adding* it? Danny stuck his pencil behind his ear, left the shed and set off for his office. He was determined to get to the bottom of this, preferably without having to inform anyone else of his mistake. Because it must be his mistake, even though he could not fathom how it had occurred. It was true that they had been extremely busy, with barges loading and unloading all day, as well as shipments being brought in from the docks for storage, but surely, he thought as he opened his office door, he had not lost track of any of the cargoes?

He groaned as he imagined the fuss someone was going to kick up when they discovered that their order was short. First they would blame the unsuspecting bargee, then they would look to the canal offices, and eventually, of course, they would come to Danny. Sighing, he sat down at his desk, pulled the piles of paperwork towards him, and began to wrestle with the numbers on the sheets as he tried to make sense of it all. Could he have given someone five sacks of coal instead of cotton? But that was impossible, as he would have to be five sacks of coal down in the yard, and he wasn't. Everything was accounted for and in its place. Maybe someone had brought the cotton in towards the end of the day when he had been busy elsewhere and just dumped the sacks down before shooting off home? He grimaced. It was the only possible explanation, as nothing else made sense. He tapped the papers into a neat pile and placed them in one of the many filing trays on his desk. One thing for sure: he'd be having a few words with the culprit when he found them. *If* he found them.

Glancing at his wristwatch, he unhooked his coat from the back of the door, then locked his office for the night and made his way back to the shed. As he approached the open doorway he frowned in perplexity. That's funny — I could have sworn I closed the door when I left, he thought. He peered round the doorway and called, 'Anyone here?' There was no reply, and he was just about to lock up for the night when to his amazement he saw that the extra sacks of cotton were gone. He stepped inside the shed and walked over to where the sacks had been some ten minutes previously.

Danny was flummoxed. Where could they be? He had definitely seen them, he was sure of it. But it had been a long day, and he was very tired. He couldn't have imagined it, could he? He shook his head. Having more stock than he should have was wrong, and now things were right again. Should he mention it to his superiors? But he was the only one who knew that anything had gone awry, and seeing that it all seemed to be back in order he felt it wise to let sleeping dogs lie. Stepping out of the shed, he carefully locked the door behind him before going back to his office and double-checking that he had locked that door properly too. If I'm making mistakes because I'm tired I mustn't take any chances, he thought as he gave the handle an experimental turn. Satisfied that all was secure for the night, he left the yard and headed home to an unappetising tea of cold Woolton pie and some bubble and squeak which he would hot up in the frying pan before turning in for a good night's sleep, something that he obviously needed.

Patsy stood in the canal basin watching the barges being loaded ready for their next deliveries. Things had changed a lot since she had left the canals, and not for the better in her opinion. Before the war, even though life had been hard, the bargees had made time to socialise and have a good time in the pub at the end of the working day. The children would play games of hide and seek or duck duck goose while stealing sneaky sips of their parents' beer. But now, with the workload trebled, a lot of the barges ran well into the night just to keep up with the demand. Mrs Madison and Taddy were doing a grand job aboard the *May Bell*, but while Patsy had once longed for Taddy to become more mature and less like an annoying wasp, looking at him now she knew that she had preferred the happy-go-lucky, cheeky little boy he used to be. He had grown up a lot, and had no time any longer for play or tomfoolery. His childish ways had all gone; along, it seemed, with his childhood.

She watched as the *Kingfisher* came slowly along the canal, eventually joining the queue of barges waiting to be loaded up. She saw one of the new girls, the short blonde one, jump from the barge to the towpath. Rosie threw a mooring rope to the girl, who caught it first time and quickly tied the barge up to one of the posts. One of the men operating the cranes left his position and came to greet the women. He placed an arm round the young blonde and kissed her on the cheek. Patsy recognised him: it was Simon, who had come to work in the yard not long before she had left. As she stood watching, Mrs Madison called to her from street level.

'Come on, Patsy, I've finished in the offices. We can go into the city now, if you're ready?'

Turning, Patsy climbed out of the basin to join her hosts. 'I see one of the *Kingfisher* crew has made a new friend,' she said, jerking her head in the direction of Simon and Babs.

Mrs Madison pulled a rueful face. 'Don't ask me, I'm not one to judge, and besides, he seems like a grand chap, not like the rest of 'em.'

Patsy raised a quizzical brow. 'What do you mean? The rest of who?'

Mrs Madison considered. 'The Gaspots.' She held up a hand as she saw Patsy's look of surprise. 'He's the only one here, and he's been warned that no one don't want no trouble. Like I say, he seems okay, and the others ain't come sniffin' round, but you have to be careful. They brought a lot of grief when they was on the Leeds and Liverpool. Allus gettin' into fights, or drinkin' too much.' She nodded in the direction of Simon. 'From what I hear he's not put a foot wrong, and just 'cos one dog's got fleas you don't shoot the pack.'

Patsy's brow furrowed. 'I'd forgotten all about the Gaspots; it's been a while since I've heard their name mentioned. Didn't they move on to the Shropshire Union, reckoned it was better money or summat?'

Mrs Madison looked awkward. 'That may be

what they tell folk, but in truth they got chucked off this stretch.'

'So do Simon's parents work the Shropshire Union too, then?'

Mrs Madison shook her head. 'No, his dad's a docker, and a right rough 'un too, and I don't know owt about his mam.' She pulled a face. 'I must say, I'm quite surprised that Rosie's allowin' one of her crew to date Simon but then again I s'pose you can't blame him for his kin. On the other hand, they do say the apple don't fall far from the tree, so by all accounts Rosie'd best hope they're wrong.'

Patsy nodded her head wryly. 'Well, you say he's not put a foot wrong yet.'

Mrs Madison pulled a face. 'I suppose I should say summat to Rosie, but then it's none of my business. Besides, I've enough problems of me own without gettin' involved in other folk's lives.'

Patsy dropped her gaze to the path in front of her in an effort to hide her amusement at this last statement. Mrs Madison was often considered to be one of the worst offenders when it came to gossip on the canals. Getting involved in other bargees' lives was something of a hobby to her.

Patsy caught Taddy's grin out of the corner of her eye. 'That's right, Ma, we all know as how you mind your own business, and don't go pokin' round in other people's affairs.' He winked at Patsy. 'Have you told Patsy about how Maggie has left the *Kingfisher* and her and Ken's marriage is on the rocks?'

Mrs Madison's eyes widened and she placed a hand on Patsy's arm. 'Now, Patsy, you mustn't tell anyone, 'cos I don't know if it's entirely true, but . . . '

Patsy suppressed a giggle as she half listened to Mrs Madison gossiping about the Donahues, and gave Taddy a wry smile. She was glad to see that her young friend had not lost all his cheeky ways.

By the time Mrs Madison had finished imparting her unconfirmed news, she had a satisfied smile on her face. 'Remember, don't you go sayin' nothin' to no one. Now how's about a bit of brekker before we see you off on your way back to your station?'

Patsy nodded. 'We'll go to that little café on Lime Street, but it's my treat.' She waved a hand as Mrs Madison started to protest. 'No, I insist. You've put me up all week and made me feel right at home, so this is my way of saying thank you.'

Taddy's face split into a wide grin. 'Can I have a scone? I love the ones they do there. They're huge, and the jam's all thick and sugary.'

Patsy ruffled the mass of curly hair that topped Taddy's head. 'You can have whatever you like, chuck, especially as I, for one, will be havin' some of that delicious hot chocolate they serves up.'

Taddy's eyes shone with delight and just for a moment Patsy caught a glimpse of the cheeky, carefree little boy she had left behind.

★　★　★

Rosie stood outside the offices waiting for Danny to lock up. He had promised her an evening of cinema, food and, if time allowed, dancing. Harri and Babs had gone through their usual routine of trying to get Rosie to wear just a little bit of make-up, but she had stuck to her guns and refused.

'Danny and I aren't a couple, and even if we were, no amount of paint or powder would make this look any better,' she had said, pointing a finger underneath her chin.

Babs had rolled her eyes theatrically. 'You'd be so pretty, Rosie O'Leary, if only you'd try, and I bet you'd have more than one boy rarin' to take you out.'

Rosie looked aghast. 'I don't want *any* boys rarin' to take me out; I've told you a thousand times, Barbara Wilcox, I haven't the time for a relationship and quite honestly, I don't know how you manage to juggle Simon with everything else in your life.'

Harri had raised a quizzical brow. 'So is that really any boy, or would you make an exception for, oh, I don't know, someone like Tim?' The tall woman had jerked out of the way as Rosie pretended to take a swipe at her.

'Even Tim,' Rosie had chuckled. 'Now leave me be or I shan't be goin' anywhere with anyone.'

Babs had heaved a sigh and held her hands up in submission. 'Fair enough. We were only tryin' to help.'

Now, standing outside the canal offices, Rosie began to feel that her friends might be right. She knew that she wasn't particularly attractive, and maybe a little bit of make-up would make her look half decent ... but it was too late now. Danny had appeared at the door of his office and was locking it behind him.

He turned to greet her. 'Sorry I'm late, but with more and more shipments coming in we're run off our feet, although I don't need to tell you that. I bet you hardly have time to think with all the extra work that's come your way.'

Rosie nodded. 'We've been taking it in shifts, the girls and me, to run the boat into the small hours of the morning just to get the deliveries out. The intention was for Harri and Babs to run their own barge when they first came on to the canals, but to be honest I don't think I could have coped without at least one of them by my side, and of course we make a great team. Arnie — the one at Bank Newton locks — reckons we're like a well-oiled machine.'

Danny tilted his head to one side. 'I must say, there's not many that run their barges as efficiently as the crew of the *Kingfisher*,' he said as he led her up out of the canal basin, and just for a moment Rosie had a sense of déjà vu. The last time she had trodden this path with a feller had been when Tim had first escorted her out on to the streets of Liverpool. She remembered buying a dress at Paddy's Market before they went to one of the cinemas and watched *Robin Hood*.

She glanced at Danny as she reflected how much her life had changed since those bygone days. It was no more than five years ago that she first set foot in the big city without Maggie by her side, and yet here she was, Number One of a barge, with two crew members serving under her, her mother a land girl in the south of England, Tim in the RAF, and more friends than she had ever had in her life.

Danny spoke about his work as they walked, but Rosie found her mind wandering to other things. The girls were sure that Danny wanted more than friendship with Rosie and at one time she had thought they were right, but with their work commitments it meant that they hardly ever got a chance to meet. Danny often worked late into the evenings — as did Rosie — but even so she felt that if he had really wanted more than friendship he would have tried his hardest to make it happen, whereas instead he appeared indifferent. She supposed that his feelings had changed, or he might of course have found someone else. Once again her thoughts turned to Tim. Perhaps that was the way he felt too. She had, after all, known Tim much longer than she had known Danny. So what would she do if Tim turned up on her doorstep and announced that he wanted to go out with her? Rosie chided herself inwardly; that was never going to happen, so what was the point in even thinking about it? Besides, after all this time of no communication she would have a few questions to ask him if he did suddenly turn up on her doorstep.

'Here we are. I thought we could see *Casablanca*, or have you already seen it? Only it's got a bit of everything . . . Rosie?'

Rosie smiled apologetically at Danny. 'Gosh,

277

I'm sorry, I'm afraid I was miles away. *Casablanca?* No, I've not seen it yet, but I've heard it's terrific.'

Danny looked curiously at her. 'You sure you want to go out this evening? You sound awfully tired, and I know you haven't long got back from your last delivery. We could always make it another time.'

Rosie linked her arm into his. 'Don't you worry about me. I was just daydreaming, that's all, and I can't think of anywhere else I'd rather be than here, so we'd best get in this queue before it grows any longer.'

Seemingly reassured, Danny led her to the end of the queue. 'It's not too bad at the minute, so with luck we'll get good seats.' He tilted his head. 'You daydreaming about anything special, then?'

Rosie chuckled. 'No, just work.' She hoped he would not see the blush that was starting to invade her neckline. Why had she lied? She and Danny were not a couple, so why had she not told him the truth? Surely if she really believed that Danny only wanted to be friends it wouldn't matter if she talked about Tim? Much to her relief, the queue in front of them started to move forward, and the subject was dropped.

By the time they emerged from the depths of the cinema, nearly two hours had passed and Rosie was famished. 'Can we go for fish and chips in the cinema café?' she asked Danny, crossing her fingers behind her back, hoping that he would say yes. 'You're right — I am rather tired, and I don't think I'm capable of dancing.'

Danny placed a friendly arm round her shoulders. 'Fine by me, queen. An early evening would suit me too. Besides, I'm having a grand time as it is.'

As they took their seats at a small window table, Danny hailed a waitress before turning to Rosie. 'From what you said outside I take it we'll be having the house special? Fish and chips?'

Rosie giggled. The cinema café had a very limited menu, but she had been assured by Danny that the food was good in both quality and quantity. 'Yes, that's fine by me. And I'd love a cup of tea.'

Danny nodded as the woman arrived at their table. She was in her late sixties and wore a surly expression. She frowned at the pair as she stood with her pen poised over her pad. 'Yes?' she said, her tone disinterested, her eyes fixed on the large round clock which hung on the wall behind the counter.

'Fish and chips twice and a pot of tea for two, please,' Danny said promptly.

Rosie was looking carefully at the waitress who was serving them. She reminded her of someone, but she could not think who it was. The expression was surly enough to be Maggie's, but that's where the similarity ended. Rosie tried to make a connection between the face and her memories but failed to come up with an answer, and as the woman left to get their order she leaned across the table to address Danny. 'I'm sure I know her from somewhere. She reminds me a bit of me mam, you know, bein' bad-tempered an' that, but that's not it. I'm sure

I know her from somewhere else . . . '

She stopped short as the woman returned and proceeded to set cups, teapot and a small milk jug down on the table in front of Rosie. As she turned to leave, Danny held out a hand. 'Any chance of a pot of extra water? I don't believe they've started rationing that yet,' he said with a smile.

The waitress did not appear to think that was funny, and rather than answer she simply scowled and walked away, to return a few seconds later with a small metal jug which she grudgingly banged down next to the teapot. She looked from Danny to Rosie as if daring them to ask for something else before turning on her heel and leaving. Danny raised his brows. 'I wouldn't like to meet her down a dark alley.'

Rosie smothered a giggle. 'That face of hers would turn milk sour! I know the war is no fun for anyone, but she might at least try to crack a smile.' The woman returned and plonked their plates of fish and chips in front of them, and as she did so, Rosie gave a little cry, causing the woman to jump. 'Oh, sorry,' Rosie muttered. 'I've just remembered something.' The waitress shot her a glare that would have silenced an army before walking stiffly from the table. Rosie tapped Danny's plate with her knife. 'It was the smell. I know exactly where I've seen that woman before. Tim and I had gone exploring in Liverpool and on our way home we stopped for fish and chips. She was in the queue with us, and she was awful. She hates bargees, and the way she spoke about us was terrible. She really upset me at the time.'

She looked disdainfully at the woman, who was standing behind the counter. 'Well, it seems that it's people in general she don't like, so don't you dare give her a tip, Danny Doyle.'

Danny smiled. 'Don't you worry, I won't.' He jerked his head in the waitress's direction. 'So what's she got against bargees?'

Rosie shrugged. 'No idea, but she said we were no better than gypsies. Tim put her in her place, though.'

To her surprise, the repetition of Tim's name appeared to unsettle Danny. 'The one in the RAF? Do you still speak to him then?' he said.

Rosie put down her knife and fork. There was nothing wrong with Danny's innocent enquiry, but it made her feel awkward. 'I haven't heard from him for a while. Why?'

Danny shrugged. 'Just wondered. I don't fancy some feller turning up halfway through my supper and asking me what I'm doing with his girl.'

Rosie stiffened. 'Well, there's no fear of that, as I'm not anybody's girl, nor do I have any desire to be.' What had started off as a pleasant evening with a good friend seemed to be going awry, and silly as it seemed she wished that she had never mentioned Tim, or come to this café and seen that awful woman again. She glanced at Danny, who seemed to be busying himself with his supper. She had not meant to be so short with him, but she still found talking about Tim painful. She leaned forward and placed a hand on his. 'Don't let's fight. I've had a wonderful time.'

281

Danny glanced up briefly before looking back down at his plate. 'Who's fighting? I just asked a simple question. I'm sorry if I offended you.'

Rosie sighed. 'You didn't offend me. As I said, I'm tired. Perhaps you were right when you suggested we come out on a different day.'

Danny put his knife and fork down on his plate and pushed his seat back. 'No, it's my fault. I shouldn't have asked personal questions. It's none of my business whether you speak to Tim or not. It's been a grand evening, and I'd like to do it again some time. So can we start afresh?'

Rosie nodded, a smile returning to her lips. 'Sounds like a good idea to me. These fish and chips look scrummy, and you were right about the portions too. I shan't be wanting a pudding, that's for sure.'

Danny smiled, the relief clear to see on his face. 'Next time we'll go somewhere different for our tea, agreed?'

'Definitely,' Rosie said, thankful that their evening was back on track. Picking up her knife and fork again, she tucked into the plate of food in front of her.

By the time they were ready to leave the surly waitress had gone into the back somewhere and a far more cheery woman stood at the till waiting to take their payment. She totted up the amount on the chit in front of her and spoke directly to Danny. 'That'll be two bob, please, luv,' she said, a friendly smile splitting her rosy cheeks.

Danny handed over the money, plus a bit extra. 'Here. I normally tip the waitresses, but that one can forget it.' He nodded his head in the direction of the door through which the other waitress had disappeared. 'I don't mind you getting it, though. At least you look pleased to see us.' He placed the coins in the large woman's outstretched hand.

'You mustn't mind Ronnie. She's the same with everyone, so don't go thinkin' it's owt personal,' the woman said.

'We already know,' Rosie told her. 'I bumped into her years ago, and she got right nasty 'cos she knew me and my pal were off the canals. We were only kids so she didn't mind her tongue, and she let us know what she thought of canal folk all right. Said we were no better'n gypsies, although what she's got against them either . . . '

The woman behind the counter glanced over her shoulder and leaned forward, placing a chubby hand on the till to keep her balance while she spoke. ''Er daughter run off with a bargee years back, got married, the whole lot. Ronnie told her if she went she'd never be welcome back. I suppose she thought her gal wouldn't leave, but she did, and ever since then Ronnie reckons that all canal folk are thieves what kidnap people's kids — '

''S'no more than the truth!' a sharp voice snapped at the back of the waitress, causing all three to jump. 'Runned off with the feller and his brat of a kid when she were no more than a child herself . . . and where's it got her? On her own, looking after someone else's kid, that's where.'

'On her own?' Rosie asked, despite herself. 'What happened to her husband?'

The woman sniffed disapprovingly. 'Died, not

283

long after they'd got wed either, from what I 'eard.'

'How awful,' Danny said, his brow furrowed. 'What happened?'

The woman shrugged. 'Summat to do wi' savin' his brat from the locks, I were told; he got crushed by the gates. Makes no odds 'ow it happened, point is 'e left my gal lookin' after his kid, with no future to speak of. She give up everythin' — a nice home, her family, the lot — to be wi' him.' She placed her hands on her hips. 'If I'd had my way, she'd have chucked the kid in the workhouse.'

Rosie looked horrified. 'What a dreadful thing to say about your daughter. I don't blame her for not wanting to come back. How could you suggest she give up her child — *your* grandchild — to the workhouse?'

The thin woman leaned forward beside her workmate. 'Don't you listen properly, cloth ears? It weren't her kid, it were 'is, so not my grandchild, nor her problem.'

Rosie shook her head disbelievingly. 'I think your daughter sounds lovely, bringing up a child that's not hers. That's what you call real love, that is, although I'd very much doubt you'd know.'

The older woman rallied. 'I don't have to stand 'ere and listen to you judgin' me.' She turned to her work companion. 'And I'll thank you not to go gossipin' about my personal life, thank you very much.' She stalked off into the back room and had almost disappeared from sight when she called over her shoulder, 'I never minded bargees or canal folk until my daughter got took from me. You've Jack O'Leary to thank for that!'

★   ★   ★

'Rosie . . . can you hear me? Oh, look, I can see her eyes moving. I think she's coming round.'

When Rosie opened her eyes she could see Danny and an unfamiliar woman hovering over her. She sat up sharply, only to feel her head swimming with the effort.

'Steady on, queen, you've had a bit of a shock . . . ' the fat lady said, her round friendly face oozing sympathy and concern.

Rosie blinked as she tried to make sense of her surroundings. 'What happened? Where is this?'

Danny looked briefly at the lady next to him, then shook his head. 'We're in the cinema chippy. Perhaps it'd be best if we got you back to the *Kingfisher*. We can talk there.'

Rosie nodded, then grimaced. 'Did I hit my head on something? It feels quite painful.'

Danny looked guilty. 'I'm afraid I wasn't fast enough to catch you, and you hit your head on the table.' He indicated one of the square tables that filled the café. 'Try not to talk. I'll get a taxi to take us back to the canal.'

Rosie started to nod, then hastily gave him the thumbs up instead. She looked into the other woman's face as Danny left to hail a taxi. 'How embarrassing. I've never fainted before. Did I damage anything?'

The woman, who was looking rather awkward,

shook her head. 'Blimey, queen, you've nowt to apologise for.' She glanced behind her. 'She's the one that should be apologisin', not you.'

Rosie tried to turn her head but could see no one. 'Who? And why should they apologise?'

Danny loomed into view. 'C'mon, queen, not here. I'll explain everything later.'

Rosie allowed Danny to help her to her feet, and as they passed the table where they had been seated she gave a small chuckle. 'I didn't faint because you tipped that mean old woman, did I? Oh, oh, oh!' She clutched the back of her head.

Danny looked worried. 'Is it your head? Does it hurt? Do you want to sit down?'

Rosie held up a hand. 'I've just remembered why I passed out,' she said, her voice hoarse. She looked at Danny, tears brimming in her eyes. 'Oh, God, Danny, please tell me I've had a bad dream . . . please tell me it's not true.'

Danny hung his head and took a deep breath. 'I wish I could, Rosie, I really do.' He glanced in the direction of the counter. 'She's gone; as soon as I told her who you were she took off like a jackrabbit. I'm so sorry, Rosie, truly I am.'

Rosie sank into one of the chairs at their table. 'Why? Who would say such horrible untrue things about my mother?' Rosie's eyes rounded with horror as she remembered more pieces of the conversation. 'Danny! My dad — Jack — she said that he died saving me . . . Danny, am I really the reason why my father's dead?'

Danny looked nervous. 'I'm afraid I don't know the answer to that, queen. But I wouldn't listen to everything she says; by all accounts she hasn't seen your mother — Maggie — for a long time, and as far as your father and the rest of her poison is concerned you're better off speaking to the only person who can give you the answers.'

Rosie looked into Danny's eyes. Tears trickling slowly down her cheeks, she gave a small nod, then winced. 'Maggie.'

10

Patsy was an extremely good dancer. She was always in great demand at the NAAFI dances, and tonight would be no exception. She and Sheila had spent the greater part of an hour primping and preening in front of the small hand-held mirror that Sheila's mother had given her as a birthday present, making sure that the sparsely dabbed rouge had been correctly placed and the dashes of mascara were being put to best effect, although Sheila still said that the mascara made her eyelashes feel too lumpy.

'What do you expect?' Patsy had snapped irritably. 'I've had this since before the war. It's a wonder there's any left in it at all.'

Sheila's contribution to the make-up had been one of her grandmother's old lipsticks, which even she admitted felt greasy and had a musty scent.

After checking their reflections for the last time, the two girls had headed for the NAAFI, where Patsy soon found herself whirling around the dance floor while Sheila, who was not keen on the faster dances, went and got the refreshments, which tonight would be two glasses of ginger ale and a couple of custard creams.

As she stood in the queue, she felt a tap on her shoulder and to her surprise found that she was looking into Tim's cheery countenance. 'Fancy a turn on the floor?' he asked, as they shuffled forward.

Sheila pulled a face. 'Not yet, and if you want to dance with Patsy you'll have to be pretty quick. She's like Ginger Rogers that one, what with all the fellers linin' up to take their turn. You'll be lucky if you get a look in.' She looked Tim up and down.

He chuckled. 'I get the impression that you're not too keen on me,' he said, tilting his head to one side.

Sheila shrugged. 'I don't mind you either way, but I'm not keen on the way you treat our Patsy, although why she still holds out for you I do not know. Look at her now.'

As the music stopped Tim turned his attention to the dance floor, where he saw the airman who had been dancing with Patsy being quickly replaced by another. The music started up again and the couple whirled away around the dance floor.

'So, are you comin' to sit wi' us or are you wi' your pals?' Sheila enquired as she held the two glasses of ginger ale precariously in one hand while balancing the plated biscuits in the other.

Tim got himself a drink and nodded to Sheila. 'I wouldn't mind catchin' up with Patsy, you know, after her trip home. See if she's got any news for me,' he said, his voice muffled by the biscuit out of which he had just taken a large bite.

Sheila shrugged. 'She didn't say much to me.' She looked up at Tim from under a thick fringe of lashes. 'If you're after news of that Rosie then

I know she didn't speak to her directly, although she did say something about the crew of the *Kingfisher* hanging out with ne'er-do-wells.'

Tim frowned at Sheila. That didn't sound like his Rosie. She had always been very particular about the company she kept, and he couldn't see her socialising with the wrong sort. He placed his glass of ginger ale down on the table and stood up. 'I reckon I will have that dance with Patsy. I shan't be a mo.'

As he crossed the dance floor he heard Sheila protesting behind him. 'Hang on, she's with someone . . . ' But the music stopped, and before anyone else had the chance Tim scooped Patsy into his arms and his old friend found herself looking into the handsome face that she knew so well.

'Tim, I — I didn't know you were here,' she said, the surprise in her tone evident.

Tim shrugged. 'I'm not the best at social events, I know that, but I've not seen you since you got back, so knowing how much you love to dance I figured I'd find you here.'

The music started, and much to Patsy's joy it was a slow number. Tim pulled her close and the pair made their way around the floor at a leisurely pace. Patsy snuggled into his arms and laid her chin on his shoulder. 'There's not much to tell you. The only people I saw on the canals were Mrs Madison and Taddy, though I can tell you that Taddy's grown up an awful lot, much more than I thought he would in such a short time. I suppose that's what war does to people.'

As Tim nodded his agreement Patsy felt his

cheek brush past her ear, sending a shiver running down her spine. 'Didn't you see anyone else? Only I've just spoken to Sheila and she said something about the crew of the *Kingfisher* hanging around with a bad lot?'

Normally Patsy would have been annoyed that someone had passed on something she had told them, but for once, she thought, this might not be a bad thing. It would not look as though she herself were out to stir trouble by tittle-tattling to Tim directly. She chose her words carefully. 'That's what Taddy's mother thinks; but I can't really say because I don't know the chap concerned.'

Tim pulled himself back so that he could look directly into her eyes. 'A feller? Is it that Danny bloke?'

She shook her head. 'No, not him. I didn't see him at all. She meant one of the men who operates the cranes; I think she said his name was Simon. He's one of the Gaspots.'

'A Gaspot? What on earth are they doin' hangin' around with the Gaspots? Everyone on the canals knows they're a bunch of no good, thieving — '

Patsy feigned surprise. 'Oh, so you've heard of them too? I must admit I don't know any of them personally — Mam allus told me to steer clear of folk like them — but it seems Rosie and her lot are always goin' to dances with them, or out for meals . . . from what Mrs Madison said, they're well in together.'

Tim stared into Patsy's upturned face, searching her wide blue eyes for signs of deceit,

291

but found none. So it was true. Rosie really had taken to going about with the wrong sort.

He wondered what on earth had happened to Rosie to make her hang about with the likes of the Gaspots. His parents had not mentioned it, but he knew they had no time for getting involved in other people's business. Hadn't his mother actually said she didn't want to talk about Rosie? He shook his head. All this time he had been wondering why Rosie O'Leary had snubbed him, while she, Rosie, was off with the likes of the Gaspots.

He held Patsy close to him once more. Here was Patsy, a little feisty, rough round the edges too, and definitely a handful, but she would never ignore him to hang around with the likes of them. He felt the anger begin to rise in him. What a fool he had been, believing Rosie to be innocent, honest and vulnerable! But no — he couldn't envisage someone like Rosie with a bunch of criminals. Doubt reared its head. Perhaps it had been a one-off, before Rosie found out who they were? But then again, she had distanced herself from Tim. Shrugging, he came to a decision. Gaspots or not, he would not waste any more time mooning over someone who couldn't give two figs about him. As the music faded he bent forward and kissed Patsy gingerly on the mouth. For a moment he wondered if he was doing the right thing, and he was about to pull away and apologise when Patsy's hand slid up the back of his neck and she kissed him back. As the music stopped, Tim pulled back and smiled into her upturned face. 'I hope I haven't overstepped the mark . . . ' he began, but she placed a finger on his lips.

'I have been waiting for you to do that for ever such a long time, Tim Bradley, and I must say it was well worth the wait.'

Tim grinned, and when an airman approached Patsy to ask for the next dance he was delighted when she said she was going to sit this one out. Slipping his hand into hers he led her to the table where Sheila was waiting with their refreshments and pulled out a chair for her before excusing himself and heading for the lavatories.

'My, my, my! Someone looks like the cat that got the cream,' Sheila said, her face full of curiosity. 'What did you say to get that smooch?'

Patsy leaned forward and took one of the glasses. 'It's all thanks to you telling him about the crew of the *Kingfisher*. Once he realised that Rosie was knocking around with the likes of the Gaspots he made up his mind that I was the girl for him.'

Sheila frowned. 'But I thought you said that it was her mate Barbara that was with that Gaspot feller, and that he seemed to be okay. It was his father who was a wrong 'un — ' she began, only to be cut short.

'I didn't go into explanations. It's not my fault if Tim got the wrong end of the stick, is it?' Patsy said, giving her friend a warning look. 'Don't you go beggaring this up for me, Sheila Formstone. You've done your bit, and I'm grateful, but now let's leave sleepin' dogs lie, and if the time ever comes when Tim finds out his mistake, let's just hope that it'll be too late, 'cos I'll have his ring on my finger.' And with a grin so wide she made the Cheshire cat look like the Mona Lisa, she took a bite out of her biscuit.

★ ★ ★

With barely a month left before Christmas, Rosie decided that she would leave the confrontation with her mother until the New Year. She had, of course, told her crew all about the evening with the awful woman at the cinema café, and when all three girls had gone back to confront her a few days later they were told that Maggie's mother had left that evening and never returned.

'Blimey, it caused a real stir. The manager went bonkers. Left us short-handed just before the Christmas rush, she has.' The waitress had looked pleadingly at the three girls. 'I don't suppose none of you is after extra work?'

They had all shaken their heads. 'Where does she live?' Babs had asked the other woman politely. 'Only Rosie needs some kind of explanation . . .'

The large woman had shaken her head sadly. 'She's gone, queen; not just from 'ere, but from her 'ome an' all. Seems she's runnin' away from the carnage.'

Rosie had nodded. 'Can't say as I blame her. If I'd talked a load of rubbish like her, I think I'd be off an' all.'

Harri and Babs had exchanged glances. 'Come on, Rosie. There's nothing here for us, so we may as well be getting back,' Harri had said, giving the waitress a sympathetic smile as they trooped out of the café.

Now, Rosie took the ticket from the canal office and headed back to the *Kingfisher*. As she climbed on board she held the ticket up, calling to Harri as she did so, 'Cotton, and when we get there we're to pick up another cargo of coal and take it up to Leeds.'

Harri gave Rosie the thumbs up and turned to Simon and Babs. 'Way you go!' Babs stepped from the loading area to the deck of the *Kingfisher* to guide the first stack of cotton sacks on board. When she had steadied the stack over the spot she wanted, she waved at Simon and he gently lowered the sacks until she signalled him to stop by raising her hand. Quickly, she slipped the rope from the stack and gave him the thumbs up. When there were only a few sacks left to load, Simon called out to one of his mates to help with this last lot while the girls started tying down. Rosie knew that they only received this privilege because Simon and Babs were a couple, but she was grateful none the less, even though the other bargees had shown their disapproval with snide comments and remarks. It meant that they got away just that little bit sooner, as once Simon and his mate had put on the last few sacks they would start tying down at their end and work their way round to meet the girls.

When they had finished, Simon jumped down from the crane and untied the *Kingfisher* from its moorings. 'Thee you girlth tonight at the danthe,' he said as he threw the rope to Babs, who waved and nodded.

As they headed down the canal Harri approached her Number One. 'Is Danny going to make it to the dance, do you think?'

Rosie shrugged her shoulders. After the incident in the café she and Danny had hardly seen each other. She knew that it was mostly down to their work schedules, but she also knew that it was partly because she did not wish to discuss the events of that evening with him. 'I didn't get the chance to ask him. Besides, he'll probably be doing a stock-take.'

'He must be the hardest workin' feller in the yard. I hope they pay him properly,' Harri said. 'You'll have to make sure you ask him next time, otherwise he might think you're avoiding him.'

Babs carefully sidled down the barge towards Rosie. 'Want me to have a go at the tiller? That way, if Harri cleans Pepè out he can have a bit of freedom, and you can make us teas and put your feet up before we moor for the evening.'

Rosie nodded, glad to get away from the questioning. She waited until Babs's hand was firmly on the tiller, and then ducked down into the cabin, only to be brought up short by the sight of Harri's large bottom looming at her from the depths of her bunk and the sound of a muffled voice cooing, 'Come on, sweetie, Mummy's got some nice sunflower seeds for good boys who do as they're told. You come here and you can have them.'

'Get stuffed and pass me the whisky,' came the response from Pepè, causing Rosie to hoot with laughter and Harri to shriek with pain as Pepè lunged at her, trying to peck her out of the way.

Manoeuvring in such a small space was not easy for someone as big as Harri, who was shuffling backwards as fast as she could. As she slid to the floor, Pepè shot past them both, and Rosie heard him land on the roof of the cabin. Holding her sides, she apologised for her mirth as Harri rubbed the top of her head.

'Bloomin' bird. Why'd he have to do that? And what on earth was that he said?' she said, as she checked for signs of blood on her fingertips.

Rosie, who had by now managed to control her laughter, shrugged. 'As far as I could make out he told you to get stuffed and pass him the whisky.' She pursed her lips in an effort to control her amusement.

'Have the bargees been teachin' him rude words again?' Harri said, and judging by the scowl on her face she, unlike Rosie, could not see the humour in the situation.

Rosie shrugged. 'I don't think anyone's deliberately taught him rude words, but I will agree that the men seem to enjoy hearing him saying certain things . . .'

Standing up, Harri smoothed her hair down then picked up the brass cage and headed for the cabin doors. 'I just know my father's going to be in his element with his 'I told you so's when he hears Pepè talking gutter language, especially if he does it during one of their soirees.' A chuckle escaped her lips as she envisaged the shocked faces of high society. 'Mummy does love her little Pepè.'

Rosie shook her head in amusement. It was quite clear that if Pepè told the Swires' guests to 'get stuffed' it would make Harri's evening. However, it was time to turn to the task in hand: meat and potato pie with some of last night's mash, and blackberry crumble with custard for pudding. She lit the small stove and set about the arduous task of cooking a meal for three in such a confined space.

By the time Harri had caught Pepè and put him back in his clean cage, the girls' tea was plated up. As they ate, they discussed their plans for the evening.

'If that Simon reckons he's goin' to bobby off again for half an hour halfway through the night he's got another think comin',' Babs said, her face set in a determined expression. 'I know he's only steppin' out for a fag, but I don't smoke and I feel like a right lemon standin' there waitin' for him to come back.'

'Half an hour?' Harri said, her eyes wide with astonishment. 'How big's this cigarette he's smoking? It doesn't take half an hour to have a smoke. What's he up to?'

Babs rolled her eyes. 'He's talkin' to the other fellers, reckons he's doin' a bit of business . . . I know a lot of folk do a bit of work on the side, but I don't like to get involved, so I don't ask any questions. As far as I'm concerned Simon's my wartime fling, but when the war's over and things go back to normal I'll likely as not be back in the city, so no point in tryin' to interfere or change the feller. It just gets on my nerves, that's all.'

A thought struck Harri. 'That reminds me: Pepè started swearing earlier. You don't reckon

Simon and his pals have been teaching Pepè rude words for a laugh, do you?'

Babs chuckled. 'I wouldn't put it past him. Boys will be boys after all, and I know they all find it highly amusing when Pepè gives tongue while we're loading up.'

An annoyed frown etched Harri's brow. 'Well you can jolly well tell him to stop it. When the war's over I'm going to have to put this bird in solitary confinement until he's unlearned everything he's heard over the past few years.'

After they had finished their pudding, the girls got ready for their evening of dancing. Waiting on the towpath while her friends put the finishing touches to their make-up, Rosie surveyed the *Kingfisher*. Considering the number of times that Harri had driven the boat into the canal bank, or worse still someone else's barge, whilst she was learning to navigate, the boat was in tiptop condition. There was one slight mark where she had rammed into one of the five locks on the Bingley Rise, but Rosie had kept her eye on it and so far the damage did not seem to be getting any worse. She was pretty sure that Maggie had suspected that Harri would sink the barge within the first few months, but Harri had proved them all wrong, and now she probably turned the barge round better than any of them, without touching a single reed.

'Right-ho, let's be off,' Babs said, stepping on to the bank. 'Simon said they've got a new band playing tonight. He reckons they're really good, so it looks like we're in for a treat.'

As they headed towards the village, Rosie

decided that the next time the *Kingfisher* unloaded she would apply some waterproofing paint to the area where Harri had hit the lock. The gash was high enough to attend to without having to go into dry dock, yet low enough when the barge was fully loaded, as it was now, to sink below the waterline, meaning that corrosion would eventually set in.

The dance itself was much like all the others she had attended, only of course Danny was not there. She watched Simon and Babs as the pair dipped and swayed their way around the fishbone floor, Babs giggling every time Simon spun her around. Remembering how Babs had said she didn't think she would carry on seeing Simon after the war, Rosie wondered how Simon would take the news. She knew he had come to the shipyard not long before war had been declared, so she supposed he must be local to the area. As Rosie watched them, she could not help but notice that Simon seemed to be keeping his eye on the clock, which was set above the entrance to the hall. Probably going to meet his pals, Rosie thought; Babs would not be best pleased.

She glanced around the room and eventually spied Harri spinning her partner around as if he were caught in a whirlwind. Rosie smiled to herself. When it came to Harri and Lord PeeWee, she would have put money on their having nothing to do with each other once the war was over, but after discussing the matter with her friend she was surprised to find that Harri and Lord PeeWee were, on paper, perfect for one another.

'Plus we get on like a house on fire,' Harri had

explained to Rosie as they had made their way to the dance earlier in the evening. 'Both our fathers rear rare breeds, and they'll get some champion stock if the right deal is negotiated.'

Rosie had looked horrified. 'Like an arranged marriage? Surely you won't have to marry him if you don't want to?'

Harri had laughed at the look of disapproval on Rosie's face. 'Of course not, you goose! But I do like him. He's got a good heart, and he sticks two fingers up to the hierarchy, a bit like myself.' She appeared to consider before continuing. 'He reminds me a bit of Pepè in some respects — '

She had got no further, as the roars of laughter from Babs and Rosie drowned her out. 'You mean short and feisty with a colourful vocabulary?' Babs said in between giggles.

Harri had nodded. 'But not the colourful vocabulary bit. At least, he's never sworn in front of me.'

'Which is more than we can say for Pepè,' Rosie had added, holding on to her sides as she did so. 'Ooohh, ow, I've got a stitch.'

Harri had raised a cynical brow. 'He's just a dumb animal. You can't blame him for his bad language.'

'Are we still talking about Lord PeeWee?' Almost helpless with laughter, Babs dodged a playful swipe from her friend.

'That'll do, you two. I refuse to talk about my love life if you're goin' to take the mickey,' Harri said, folding her arms in defiance.

Babs leaned on Rosie for support as the two girls tried to quell their giggles. 'Sorry, Harri. We were just playing. Lord PeeWee's a real catch, and I'm glad you aren't being forced into marrying someone you don't want to.'

Now, as Rosie watched the pair gliding their way across the dance floor, she found herself picturing Harri and Pepè doing the same dance. Good old Harri, she thought. She can take a joke as much as the next woman, if not better. I do hope she and . . . Rosie racked her brains as she fought to remember Lord PeeWee's real name. Ah, that was it. Alby. I do hope that Harri and Alby will be happy together.

'Evenin', Miss Rosie. Hows about takin' an old feller for a turn on the floor?'

Rosie turned and saw Reg Arkwright giving her a wide toothy grin as he held out a hand. 'C'mon, queen; can't see you stood on your own all night!'

Rosie took his hand and smiled at her peculiar-looking suitor. 'Thanks, Reg. I hope Mrs Arkwright won't mind.'

Reg chuckled. 'When you're married to a chap as handsome as me you have to realise that there's allus gonna be plenty of women after your hubby, but the missus knows I'd never do her wrong.'

Rosie liked Reg. He was always cheerful, and she thought now that she had never seen him looking down or glum. 'You're quite the Fred Astaire — I had no idea you were such a good dancer,' Rosie said honestly, as Reg guided her expertly to the tune that the band had struck up.

Reg nodded modestly. 'Me and the missus used to do a lot of dancing before the war, only now she does the fire watchin' in the city, as do I if I'm not keepin' an eye on the doors here, of course.' He tilted his head. 'How's your mam gettin' on? Last I heard she were enjoyin' life on the farm.'

Rosie felt herself stiffen. Reg's question regarding her mother had been unexpected. She searched his withered face for clues. Did he know? Was that why he'd asked the question? As she looked into his eyes she saw nothing but innocence. She chided herself inwardly for doubting this friendly old man. Remembering that he had asked a question, she decided to keep her answers brief. 'Yes, I believe so.'

Reg gave a satisfied nod. 'Good-oh. Are you goin' to see her at the farm? Far as I know you've not 'ad a break from that barge in ever such a long time. It'd do you good to get away.'

Rosie longed to tell Reg the truth, to ask him what he thought, but she knew that he would not be able to give her any answers. She had been pushing what she'd heard to the back of her mind, hoping that if she ignored it, let things be, she would never have to know the whole truth and could carry on as things were. But in her heart she knew this was impossible. She had to see Maggie, to confront her with the dreadful woman's accusations, if nothing else to find out what had happened to her real mother . . . Rosie made up her mind. 'I'm going to write to her and arrange to see her for a few days as soon as she's free,' Rosie said, her heart racing as the words left her lips. 'Thanks, Reg.'

Reg looked puzzled. 'What for?'

Rosie smiled. 'For dancing with me, and helping me come to a decision.'

Reg shook his head. 'Beats me if I know what you're on about, queen, but if I've helped you in some way then I'm glad.'

Later that evening, as the three women made their way back to the canal, Babs showed them a present Simon had brought her.

'Whisky! Blimey, where'd he get it from?' Rosie said, as she examined the bottle that Babs had handed her.

Babs shrugged. 'Told you, I don't ask questions, although I must say I'd have preferred some make-up, but he said whisky was all he could get.'

Rosie passed the bottle to Harri, who examined it closely. 'Looks the real deal to me. If you don't want it . . . '

Babs gave her friend a wry look. 'I didn't say that, did I? Just that I'd have preferred summat else. Besides . . . ' she took the bottle from Harri and held it up for inspection, 'I may be able to swap it.'

Aboard the barge, Babs tucked the bottle into one of the cubbyholes. 'I reckon he only give it me 'cos I told him off for leavin' me again. Mind you, I wasn't on me own for long. That Charlie from the yard filled in for him. He's a pretty good dancer, and . . . ' she turned her back on the others as she stepped into her pyjamas, 'he's asked me to go to the cinema with him.'

Rosie feigned shock. 'Barbara Wilcox! You naughty girl. I thought you were spoken for.'

As Babs slipped between the sheets she gave

Rosie a very prim look. 'Not me, queen. All me and Simon have done is a cuddle and a smooch, and apart from the dancin' he's never asked me nowhcre else. If he wants my affections he'll have to try a lot harder.' She giggled. 'And he can keep his bloomin' whisky. Next time, it's make-up or nowt!'

Rosie laughed and took out her diary, as she did every night. It had been a while since anything unusual had happened, and she had begun to think she was wasting her time. Idly, she looked round the cabin. They no longer checked on Pepè when they had been out for the evening, as his angry shrieks on being disturbed had woken several bargees on occasion, resulting in heated words the next day. Now, sitting up, Rosie stared hard at his cage. Its night-time blanky was pulled over the top of it, as it should be, but something was amiss. She slid out of bed and trod carefully across the floor of the cabin. The blanket looked almost black, which was wrong because it was a light grey. Gingerly, she put thumb and forefinger on the corner of the blanket and lifted it. Much to her relief, but to the others' annoyance, Pepè swore.

'What on earth are you doing?' Harri said sleepily. 'I was just nodding off.'

When Rosie spoke her voice was worried and confused. 'Pepè's wet . . . and so is his blanket. Harri, look at him. Someone's been in the cabin.'

* * *

Harri crossed the small cabin and removed Pepè's blanket, noticing the drips of water on the floor of the cage. She opened the door and carefully placed a hand inside. 'Shush, little fellow, Mummy's not going to harm you,' she cooed softly as she stroked his feathers. She removed her hand, closed the door and replaced the blanket. 'He's definitely been in some water and so has his blanket, but his cage is dry. The drips on the floor-paper must have run off him. So whoever came in managed to get Pepè and his blanket wet, but not his cage.'

Babs was leaning up on one elbow. 'Mebbe he was making a riot and someone squirted him with water to try and shut him up.'

Harri shook her head. 'If they'd thrown water over him, the paper would have got it too, and if they'd just thrown it on the blanket he would have stayed dry.'

Rosie looked keenly around the small cabin. Reaching up to the cubbyhole, she checked their documents. Everything was in its place. 'Do either of you have any money hidden away, 'cos if so, you'd best check it's still there. Nobody breaks into a barge for the fun of it, and if they'd been after Pepè they would have taken him, not just given him a bath.'

Babs fiddled about under her mattress and withdrew a small wallet. She peered inside and poked around with her forefinger. 'Still here, not that there was much to take. How about you, Harri?'

Harri shook her head. 'Any spare cash I have usually gets spent on treats for Pepè. Either that

306

or I put it straight into my savings account down at the post office.'

Both girls looked expectantly at Rosie, who shrugged. 'I'm the same as Harri. Any spare cash I have goes straight into my savings account.'

For a moment they all sat silent as they contemplated their uninvited visitor. Eventually Rosie spoke up. 'I'll check the cargo in the morning. I'm not poking around in there tonight, but I doubt any of it's been nicked. Who'd want a load of cotton? Besides, they wouldn't come into the cabin if they only wanted to steal the cargo.'

Harri raised an enquiring brow. 'Are you going to report it?'

Rosie pulled a face. 'Who to? And what would I say? Someone gave Pepè a bath? Nothing's actually missing, and there's no damage done. It might be one of the bargees playing a prank. Pepè's ruffled a few feathers in his time with his squawking, so I suppose it could be that.' She thought for a moment. Maybe he had gone off like a siren and someone had decided to set him free in the hope that he would get lost and never come back. But then how had he got back in his cage, and replaced his blanket? No, that did not make any sense at all. 'Let's leave it till the morning. Maybe we'll see things more clearly after a good night's sleep.'

With nothing more to say on the matter, the crew of the *Kingfisher* settled down for the night, each girl trying to work out the mystery as she drifted off to sleep.

★ ★ ★

Rosie sat on the towpath gazing into the canal, her inspection of the *Kingfisher's* cargo complete. The cotton sacks were all accounted for, each one as full as it had been when loaded into the hold in Liverpool. She chewed her lip thoughtfully. All three women had spent the whole of breakfast discussing the previous evening's events. None of them had come up with any feasible ideas as to how Pepè and his blanket had got so wet, or why. As she stared into the water she had almost slipped into a trance when Harri appeared by her side holding a mug of tea. 'Come on, Rosie, we'll just have to lock the cabin doors in future. There's no sense in wasting time going over old ground.'

Rosie glanced up at Harri and took the mug of tea. 'It's not the first time we've had suspicions about people being on board the barge though, is it, Harri? What if they come back while we're asleep?'

Harri averted her eyes. 'Do you want me to get rid of Pepè, is that what you're saying?'

Rosie looked astonished. 'No, no, that's not what I'm saying at all. If anything I feel safer with Pepè on board. I've thought about whether someone intended to get rid of him — you know, let him out on purpose — but that can't be the case, because if it were he'd be gone. I don't know how he got wet or why, but whoever broke in was not after Pepè.'

Harri settled down on the bank next to Rosie. 'So if not Pepè, then what?' she asked, her tone puzzled.

Rosie shrugged. Her eyes fell on the hull of the

barge as she took a large swig of her tea. The gash that Harri had made did not seem to be getting any worse. Rosie hated the idea of asking any of the men for help, especially if she had to tell them how the accident had happened, although she was pretty sure they had all known about it. The lock keeper had not been happy when Harri had pushed the boat — at full speed — forwards instead of backwards, and he was bound to have gossiped to the other bargees about it. She was just wondering how much they would charge to fill in and overpaint the gash when a thought struck her. 'Harri, d'you see where you hit the barge?'

Harri rolled her eyes. 'Not that old chestnut again! How many more times do I have to say I'm sorry — '

Rosie cut across her. 'I'm not complaining about it, I'm just asking can you see it?'

Harri frowned. 'Of course I can see it. I'm not blind.'

Rosie folded her arms and raised her brows at Harri. 'Well, I couldn't see it yesterday when I was waitin' out here for you and Babs.'

Harri looked confused. 'I don't understand what you're trying to say . . . can you see it now?'

Rosie sighed dramatically. 'Course I can see it now, but I couldn't yesterday, and do you know why?'

Harri opened her mouth to reply, but before she could speak Rosie continued, 'Because yesterday that gash was below the waterline.'

Harri pulled a face. 'So the water level's

dropped in the canal? You think there's been another breach?'

Rosie shook her head impatiently. 'No, what I'm saying is that the weight on board the barge has changed. It's lighter today than it was yesterday.'

Harri looked down at her ample frame. 'Are you saying that I'm too fat?'

Rosie giggled. 'Don't be silly. But there's certainly something odd about the *Kingfisher*, and I'd bet a pound to a penny it has something to do with Pepè's skinny-dipping last night.'

Harri frowned. 'Are you sure there isn't a tide on the canal? You know, like the seaside? I bet there is. It is water, after all.'

Rosie pulled a face. 'Not that I've ever heard folk speak about, but I bet my old mate Tim would know.'

Harri looked curiously at Rosie. 'I don't suppose you intend to ask him, do you?'

Rosie gave a snort of contempt. 'Not on your life! I've managed all this time without the help of a feller and I'm not going to start asking for advice now. And don't you go saying owt either. The last thing I want is the canal folk thinking we're ignorant; they already think we're useless as it is.'

Harri shrugged. 'Well, it makes no odds to me as far as I can see — unless we were sinking, of course — so I say let it be, and let's get on.'

The girls cast off, but deep down in her heart Rosie could not help but think that Harri was right and that this would be a good excuse to ring Tim. And I will one day, she mused, just not

310

today, because I have to see Maggie first and find out the truth from her. She called to Harri and Babs to take control of the barge while she disappeared below deck and fished out her notepad and pen. Strike while the iron is hot, she thought to herself.

Dear Maggie . . .

★ ★ ★

Patsy tidied her bed things into three neat biscuits. Being a bargee meant that you had to be very neat and organised, so joining the WAAF had suited Patsy well. Her drill sergeant often advised her fellow WAAFs to follow her example, which did not win her many friends among the other girls, but as far as she was concerned life could not have been any better. A few weeks had passed since Tim had kissed her, and the pair had spent most of their free time since then together, either going to the local dances or having a meal out in the city. Tim was the perfect boyfriend, he was attentive, caring and fun to be with, and Patsy was the envy of many of her fellow WAAFs, who all commented on what a handsome couple they made.

And yet something troubled her. She looked down at her perfect biscuits, then checked her reflection in Sheila's hand mirror. As usual her blonde curls were pinned neatly in place and her lightly tanned skin was flawless. Yet as she glanced at the image in front of her her eyes met and she hastily replaced the mirror. She liked Tim, she liked him a lot, but even though everything should have been perfect, it wasn't. Glancing at the clock on the wall of the Nissen hut, she saw that she still had ten minutes before she needed to report for duty.

Sitting down on the edge of her bed, she reviewed her relationship with Tim. She had been the cat who had got the cream and triumphed over her rival Rosie O'Leary. She frowned as a picture of Rosie formed in her mind. If it weren't for that dratted girl everything really would be perfect. But why should Rosie O'Leary have any influence over Patsy and Tim? Neither of them had heard from Dreary O'Leary for a long time, yet she was still an element in their lives.

I won Tim fair and square, she thought, even as a pang of guilt-ridden doubt rose in the pit of her stomach. Patsy folded her arms defiantly. While she may have played a small part in the disappearance of Tim and Rosie's correspondence, it had been Rosie's association with Simon Gaspot that had been the main reason for Tim's choosing Patsy. Sheila had been the bearer of bad news on that occasion, and while Patsy could not be held responsible for Tim's misinterpretation, she knew that his relationship with her had been a direct result of his and Sheila's conversation. Patsy tried to tell herself that even if Tim knew that Rosie was not directly involved with Simon, or that Simon himself did not have the same reputation as his father, he would not change his mind. Would he?

Patsy placed the heels of her hands under her chin. For a long time she had wondered what the problem between them had been, and now, thanks to her pal Sheila, she had her answer. She could not claim Tim for her own while he did not know the whole truth, something which her friend Sheila had gleefully pointed out to her earlier that morning. 'All that sneaking around and conniving may've got you what you wanted, but you're going to spend the rest of your life scared that he'll find out the truth, and what he'll do when he does is anybody's guess.'

'He'll see it from my point of view. He'll know I was only looking out for him, and anyway it'll be too late. He'll be head over heels in love with me by then.' She pouted defiantly.

Sheila's brows shot towards her hairline. 'Do you really believe that? How can he be in love with you when he doesn't even know you?'

Patsy had scowled. 'Of course he knows me. What are you talking about?'

Laughing, Sheila shook her head. 'No he doesn't. Tim thinks he's in love with an honest, caring woman who would always tell the truth. He doesn't know his whole relationship is based on a huge lie.'

'Shut up!' Patsy had shouted as she stormed off, slamming the door behind her as she went. As she strode angrily across the yard she tried to dismiss Sheila's accusations. How dare she? Patsy was not a liar; she had only told Tim a small fib, which was certainly based on the truth. At most you could say she had been slightly deceitful, but surely he couldn't hold that against her? But as the morning wore on, Patsy had come to a painful decision. She was lying to Tim, and that was why she had to speak to him.

Now, taking a deep breath, Patsy stood up. If she really wanted Tim for her own she would have to be honest with him. But how would he feel if he knew that she had interfered in his friendship with Rosie? Surely he would understand that Patsy had only acted out of her love for him; perhaps he would not mind that she had meddled with his personal affairs . . . Smoothing down her starched white apron, she headed for the door of the hut. There was only one way to find out how Tim would react and that was to confront him, spill the beans and see what came of it.

As she opened the cookhouse door she saw Tim walking towards the parade ground. She was about to call out to Sheila that she would be a few minutes late, but then she changed her mind. Maybe, if she just gave their relationship a little longer, she could learn to live with her deception. Besides, what good would telling him do anyway? Not only could she lose Tim but he might even end up turning to Rosie for comfort . . .

Sheila was scowling at her. 'Are you comin' in or not? There's spuds what need peelin' and I ain't doin' them on me own. When this war's over I swear I'll never peel another spud again as long as I live.'

Her mind made up, Patsy let Tim continue on his way. 'Pass me a knife,' she said, and settled next to her friend.

11

Spring 1944

Maggie was sitting at the big kitchen table eating a bowl of porridge laced with honey. It was her turn on early milking — something she quite enjoyed — and so far only herself and the other land girl, Penny Roberts, were awake on Plevin's farm.

'I'll stick us a couple of slices of toast on. It's right sharp out there this mornin' and I want a full belly before I venture into the milking shed,' Penny said as she scraped the last bit of porridge from her bowl. 'I'm goin' to have some damson jam on mine; d'you want the same?'

Maggie shrugged. 'I'm easy. I'll have whatever we've got the most of.' She took a large gulp of her tea and turned her attention back to the letter she had received from Ken the day before.

My darling Maggie, I was so glad to get your last letter. It sounds as if farming life is really suiting you. I was worried for quite a while that my suggestion that you get away from the canals had been a mistake, but it seems that you've taken to it like a duck to water.

Maggie smiled. When she had first joined the Land Army, farming had seemed like a hard, dirty, smelly job, but after a while she had found that she rather liked the odour of the animals, and the hard labour had done wonders for her figure. There was always something different to

315

do, whether it was milking cows, herding pigs, feeding the chickens or mucking out; you weren't always doing the same thing as you were on a barge. The freedom had done her the world of good, too. She had had time to think, to be away from the constant reminder of Jack O'Leary and the life that should have been. On the farm, no one cared about your past or where you had come from. All they were interested in was the welfare of the animals and getting the chores done. She continued to read.

You mentioned that you might try to get a smallholding after the war and I think it's a wonderful idea. When I was a small lad I always dreamed of renting one of the farms that you see along the canal. It's always seemed an idyllic life, but I've no knowledge of what to do or how to do it. On the other hand, now you've been farming for a while you know exactly what is required to run a smallholding and how to do things properly. I do believe that we could make a really good go of things together.

When Maggie had suggested a smallholding, she had worried that he would reject the idea without thought and was delighted to find that he was just as excited over the prospect of running their own farm as she was.

I'm so glad that you've finally found your calling. With luck, it will put a lot of ghosts to rest and allow you to move forward with your life. I don't suppose you've seen Rosie? I really think you should, because it would help you to draw a line under the old one. Rosie's ever such a good kid, and I'm sure she'll understand.

Maggie raised her brows. Ken always made everything sound so simple. She wished she felt the same, but she didn't. Since Jack's death, she had found sharing her feelings almost impossible, and tended to sweep matters under the rug rather than face them head on. She knew now that was why she had thrown herself into running the *Wild Swan*. But though the feelings might have been buried they were still there, just waiting for you to stand still long enough for them to make their way back to the surface. Being away from the canals had freed Maggie to address her past and the emotions that went with it. On reflection, she now regretted that she had either hushed Rosie up or changed the topic whenever the child had brought up the subject of her father. It had been unfair, but at the time it was the only way that she had been able to cope. Rosie needed to hear about her father, to learn about their life together, and the only person who could explain things to her was Maggie. It would not be easy, and a lot of painful memories would be raised, but she knew that she must do so, for Rosie's sake as well as her own.

Now that winter is more or less over it would be an ideal time for you to pay the girl a visit, if they can spare you down at the farm, that is. I would offer to come with you when you go to see her, as a bit of moral support, but I really think this is something that you and Rosie should address alone.

Maggie put the letter down and thanked Penny for the toast which the other girl had put in front of her. 'You're ever so lucky, you know,

317

bein' able to write to your feller,' Penny said as she sat down opposite Maggie. 'I don't even know where my Eddie is. Just some stupid telegram saying that he was missing in action. It doesn't tell you much, does it? For all I know he could be hiding somewhere until he can get back to his unit, or he could have been taken prisoner.' Penny was silent for a moment, then went on, 'I daren't think of the alternative, because I can't, you see. I have to believe . . . '

Maggie hastily placed Ken's letter in her overall pocket before leaning across the table and clasping the other woman's hands in her own. 'You've told me a lot about your Eddie, and he sounds like a bright feller who knows how to look after himself. Plenty of men outwit the Nazis, and I bet your Eddie is one of them. The war can't go on much longer, you watch, and when everything settles your Eddie'll come out of the mist like one of them soldiers in the movies.'

Penny sniffed and gave Maggie a watery smile. 'He will, won't he? I bet they'll even make a movie about him and his escape one day.'

Maggie patted Penny's hands and leaned back in her seat. They had all been in the kitchen the day the telegram had arrived. Mrs Plevin had been expecting word from one of her cousins regarding some stock that they were having problems with, so when Mortimer had arrived on his bike they all thought the message was for her. When he asked for Penny Roberts you could have heard a pin drop. Mrs Plevin had asked Penny if she would like to read the message in private but Penny had shaken her head. The whole kitchen seemed frozen as Penny's lips moved soundlessly while she read. When she had finished, she folded the telegram neatly and addressed the assembled workers.

'My Eddie is missing in action, but he's not dead,' she had said quietly.

'How do they know he's not — ' Mr Plevin had started before his wife had landed him a sharp kick in the shin.

Penny had fixed him with a resolute glare. 'Because he's not. And now, if you'll excuse me, I need to go and feed the chickens.' She stood up and went to the kitchen door, and as she slid her feet into her wellies she spoke with her back to the other three. 'If I hear any more I shall be sure to let you know, but until then I don't want to talk about it; I hope you understand.'

There was a general murmur of agreement and Penny had closed the kitchen door softly behind her as she went out.

That was months back, and so far no further news had come through. Maggie understood the other woman's need to hide her emotions — she had done the same after Jack died — but she also knew that eventually everything would catch up with Penny, and she was determined to be there for her when it did. She had said as much to Ken in one of her letters.

If Eddie's been killed that poor woman's going to need help to recover, and she's like me, no family to help her through it. I know how hard it is to cope on your own, and all those feelings she's bottled up are going to explode like a

319

*champagne cork what's been shaken up. I won't
let her do it alone. I couldn't bear to see
someone else go through the pain that I did.*

Penny's voice brought Maggie back to the
present. 'Come on, best get started. I'll eat this
en route.'

Maggie scraped back her chair and passed
Penny her wellies. Unbeknownst to Ken, Maggie
had also received a letter from Rosie, asking if
she might visit her mother on the farm. After
speaking to the Plevins Maggie had responded
saying that any time would be fine; she did not
add that as far as the farmer was concerned
Rosie would be more than welcome as a free pair
of extra hands.

As the two women crossed the farmyard Maggie
breathed in the chilly morning air. She loved
mornings like this. It was so peaceful: no birdsong,
no tractor chugging its way across the fields; even
the chickens were still asleep in the henhouse. As
she entered the cowshed one of the cows mooed
a welcome, a sign, Maggie thought, that the
farming day was about to begin.

★   ★   ★

The crew of the *Kingfisher* were working harder
than ever to catch up with their deliveries. They
had just dropped off a load of coal to a
merchant, and, looking at her watch, Rosie said,
'We've just got time to nip to the post office to
see if there's any mail. Anyone else want to
come?'

Babs said she would, but Harri wanted to stay

320

with Pepè. 'He's not been getting out much over the winter, so I think I'll let him stretch his wings a bit while you're gone. But if you see anything you think I'd like and that isn't on ration, get it for me and I'll give you the money, later, if that's okay?'

Rosie gave her the thumbs up and she and Babs set off. The walk was a pleasant one through some beautiful countryside, and the quickest way was across the fields, but there had been quite a lot of rain lately and instead the girls walked along the lane, with its high hedgerows and grassy track down the centre of the tarmac. When they finally reached the post office Rosie asked whether the *Kingfisher* had any mail, and was surprised when the postmistress handed her a good few envelopes.

'Makes you wonder how many of these have been caught up in transit when you get a few together like this, don't it?' she said as Rosie hastily sorted through the pile.

'It certainly does. Here you go,' she said, handing Babs three envelopes. 'And there's four for Harri.'

'None for you?' Babs said, raising her brows in surprise.

Rosie nodded. 'Just a couple.' She looked at the writing on the envelopes. 'Gosh — this one's from Maggie, but *this* one,' she paused, a mixture of concern and joy on her face, 'this one's from Tim.'

Babs's eyes widened. 'Crikey, there's a turn-up for the books. Are you goin' to read them now?'

Rosie shook her head as she carefully placed

321

her and Harri's envelopes in her dungarees pocket. 'I'll wait till we're back at the barge. Come on, let's get going.' But before she could go any further Babs held up a hand.

'Slow down there. I know you're the Number One, but we said we'd get summat suitable for Harri if we saw owt and I reckon she'd love a bit o' liquorice.'

Rosie looked at the jar Babs was pointing to. 'Come to that, I'd like a stick or two myself. Hang about, I've got a few pennies here somewhere . . . ' She fished around in her pocket and pulled out a few sticky coins, which she handed over to the postmistress with an apologetic smile. 'Sorry about the fluff. I s'pose the sticky stuff's treacle from the butty I made for Daisy and her foal yesterday.'

The postmistress shrugged complacently. 'Money's money, queen, fluff or not.'

Back on the barge, Rosie handed each of the girls a stick of the liquorice before heading off to her favourite spot on the hull, where she intended to sit and allow her legs to dangle freely over the front as she read her post. 'You two okay to cast off while I have a read?'

Harri nodded. 'Aye aye, cap'n,' she called back, before sinking her teeth into her liquorice stick and pulling at it until a piece broke off.

Rosie carefully slit open the envelope from Maggie, her heart pounding as she read the short note in front of her. Maggie said that it was good that Rosie was able to come to the farm as they had not seen each other for such a long time and she thought that Rosie would enjoy a change of scenery. Rosie raised her brows. She doubted whether her mother — or should she always think of her as Maggie now? — would be pleased to see her when she voiced the thoughts that were uppermost in her mind.

Carefully placing the letter under her leg to keep it from blowing away, Rosie turned to Tim's envelope. She looked hard at the writing on the front, as if she hoped she could read the contents without actually having to open it. What if it said that he never wished to see her again? What if he planned to stay in the RAF and this was his farewell letter? Rosie continued to stare at the unopened envelope. She felt she could not bear it if she knew for certain that he was cutting all ties with her, and if she didn't open the letter she would never know for sure, so could carry on as if all was well. But in her heart she knew that the letter would always call to her, telling her to read it, and sooner or later she would do its bidding. So, taking a deep breath, she slit the envelope open and began to read.

My dearest Rosie, I am so sorry if it appears that I have forgotten you, as nothing could be further from the truth. I have a lot to explain and it cannot be done in a letter. I hope that you are not too angry with me for my apparent lack of interest, and if you will ring me I will tell you what's been going on. I had planned to come home over Christmas, but my sergeant said no go, so I couldn't. But as soon as I do have some leave I would very much like to come and see you — if you're willing to see me, that is? I have changed stations, for a reason I will tell you when we meet. Please, queen, just give me a chance to explain.

The rest of the letter contained very little information other than chit-chat about the weather and his general welfare, and a telephone number. Rosie turned the page over, expecting to see a PS regarding Patsy, but there was none. She thought this was odd, unless, of course, the reason why he wished to speak to Rosie was so that he could tell her in person he was with Patsy. If that was the case, Rosie thought bitterly, he could keep his news to himself. She got to her feet and made for the cabin to bundle the letters with all the rest.

Harri and Babs, who had been giving their friend some space, exchanged glances. 'All good, I hope?' Harri ventured as Rosie approached.

'Mam's agreed I can go to the farm, and Tim wants to talk. Other than that, there's not much to tell.'

Babs brightened. 'It's going to be good for you and your mam — er, Maggie — to talk. We could come with you if you like? I'm sure the canals could cope without us for a couple of days.'

Rosie smiled at her friend's suggestion but shook her head. 'Thanks, but this is something I've got to do on my own. Besides, I need Maggie to talk freely, not clam up 'cos she's worried about what other folk will think.'

Babs nodded agreeably. 'And what about Tim? If he wants to talk that's a good thing, isn't it?

You've not spoken in an age, so it'll give you a chance to clear the air.'

Rosie shrugged. 'Depends on what he has to say, I s'pose. What did you two get in the mail? Anything good?'

Harri rolled her eyes. 'Can you believe that my parents told the rellies to give them their letters so that they could pass them on to me, rather than explain that I'm working on a barge?' She shook her head in disbelief. 'They don't understand that what we're doing here is essential to the war, they only have to hear the word 'barge' and it conjures up poverty.' As she felt Babs's elbow nudge her in the ribs Harri remembered her company and glanced at Rosie, quickly adding, 'Not that I think that at all, Rosie, it's just that they're frightful snobs . . . '

Rosie held up a hand. 'Don't worry — there're plenty of folk who look down on bargees. I used to take it personally, but it's like water off a duck's back now.'

Babs gave a heartfelt chuckle. 'I grew up on the Scottie and still live there — when I'm not on the barge, that is — and when I tell people you can see the look of disapproval on their faces. But like you, Rosie, I don't let it bother me. I'm honest, hard-working and trustworthy, which is more than can be said for them that judge me.'

For the first time, Rosie looked at her friends in a different light. They were kindred spirits. Babs and Harri might both be from the land, but they had all been judged by where and how they lived, and through no fault of their own had been treated unjustly. She turned her gaze to Harri, who came from the other side of the tracks, as it were, yet had only ever treated her and Babs with respect. She turned back to the little blonde. 'You're right — it's not where you're from, it's who you are. Take the three of us, for example. I bet there's folk on the Scottie that look down on the bargees, and probably vice versa, same as those who have money will look down on both bargees and the folk from the Scottie with equal disgust.'

'And there're those from the Scottie and the canals who dislike the gentry. It's a funny old world,' Harri mused. She turned to Rosie. 'So, are you going to give Tim a call? Find out what's what?'

Rosie nodded. 'Not yet, though — I want to have a think about what I'm going to say to him first. Up until now I thought that if I ever spoke to Tim again it would be to give him a piece of my mind, but now I'm not so sure.' She tilted her head to one side and looked thoughtfully at the other girls. 'I told Tim a long time ago about some men I'd heard talking outside Daisy's old shelter — Scruff's stable — but at the time we thought it must have been a dream. I was thinking I might ring him and tell him about the men we saw there, and while I was at it I thought I'd tell him about Pepè and his late night dip. What d'you think?'

Harri shrugged. 'Can't see as it'd do any harm. We could use an outsider's opinion. You never know, he may have heard something useful himself. Maybe that's why he wants to speak to you.'

Rosie considered. 'I hadn't thought of that, but in any case it would make speaking to him a bit easier if I had something to talk about which didn't concern him and Patsy.' Taking a deep breath, she continued, 'So I'm goin' to see me mam first. That way I'll have plenty to talk about.'

★ ★ ★

When Rosie arrived at the small village of Willoughby she marvelled at its charm. All the cottages were whitewashed and had deeply thatched roofs. The gardens were well kept — most of them seemed to be vegetable plots, although Rosie felt sure that before the war they would have been given over to roses, geraniums, hyacinths and a whole variety of other plants. Stepping off the bus, she turned to the driver. 'I don't suppose you could tell me where Home Farm is?'

Leaning forward in his seat, the driver pointed down the lane. 'You keep goin' down that lane and don't stop till you reach the Whistlestop pub. Call in there and Mrs Reading will give you directions as well as a nice drink of lemonade if you're lucky.'

Rosie thanked the man and headed off down the lane he had pointed out to her. Looking at the hedgerows towering over her head, she mused that she could have been making her way to Pank's farm to see Daisy and Merlin — a name Mr Pank had chosen because he said that the foal was like a magician when it came to getting out of fields — up Tuppenny Lane. It was too early in the year for any fruits to be growing in the hedges but Rosie guessed that they would be heavily laden come the autumn.

As she walked, she wondered how she would broach the subject of the terrible woman in the cinema café and her accusations. Each time she envisaged Maggie standing before her, she found that even in her dreams words failed to come forth. How did you ask your mother if she *was* your mother? Now, too late, she regretted not involving Tim with her problems. He always knew what to say; if he'd been with her in the cinema café that day, Rosie felt certain that the whole matter would have been laid to rest by now because, unlike Danny, Tim would have insisted on getting at the truth then and there. She felt a twinge of guilt for thinking that Danny could have done more, but she could not help it.

After what seemed like a good half hour Rosie saw a large whitewashed house looming ahead of her. Above the entrance was a sign which depicted a train with the word *Whistlestop* written above it.

She pushed on the studded oak door, expecting it to be heavy, and was surprised when it opened easily under her touch. Stepping inside, she could not have been more pleased. The ceiling was only a couple of feet above her head and all sorts of brass ornaments hung from the beams. On the far wall a fire hissed and crackled in its iron grate, while the long wooden bar in front of her had been polished until it shone.

As she approached the bar, a young woman emerged from a small door which led into another room. 'Hello dear. What can I get for you?' she said, a warm and friendly smile lighting up her features.

'I've just got off the bus and the driver told me to come and ask Mrs Reading for directions to Home Farm,' Rosie said, hastily adding, so as not to appear rude, 'though I would also very much like a glass of lemonade if there's one going?'

Wiping her floury hands on her apron, the woman nodded and stepped behind the bar. Reaching below the counter, she pulled out a bottle of White's lemonade. 'This do you? We do home-made in the summer, for the tourists, but it's not worth the trouble out of holiday season.'

Rosie nodded. 'That'll do nicely. Thank you. It's a lovely place you've got here. I take it you're Mrs Reading?'

'Aye, that I am, so what brings you to this neck of the woods? By the sound of your accent I'd say you were from up north? Hint of Liverpool as well as Yorkshire in there if I'm any judge; probably means you travel around a bit?'

'I'm a bargee on the Leeds and Liverpool Canal, so I suppose my accent is a bit mixed up.'

The woman nodded knowingly. 'That'd be it. Must be lovely travelling the canals. Hard work, I expect, but still beautiful scenery to be working in.'

Rosie nodded gratefully. She had half feared an accusation of her being a gypsy, and wanted to set the record straight before a misunderstanding occurred. 'You've not got it so bad here either. The village the bus stopped in was like summat out of a postcard.'

Mrs Reading chuckled. 'Aye, it's not as bad a place to live as some have got, I don't suppose.' She handed Rosie the glass of lemonade and waved a hand as Rosie dug around in her pocket for the money. 'Don't you fret about payin'. It's a pleasure to have a nice bit o' company what's female. Out of season it's mainly workin' men that get comin' in.' She tilted her head to one side. 'Sorry, what did you say you were wantin' at Home Farm?'

Rosie shook her head. 'It's my — my Maggie. She's in the Land Army and I've not seen her for a long time, so I said I'd pop by.'

The woman looked at Rosie shrewdly. 'You're too young to be anyone's mum, so who's 'my Maggie' when she's at home?'

Rosie's mind worked quickly as she sought for a response. 'She's my aunt.' As soon as the words left her lips she regretted them, but how could she explain to a total stranger that she called her mother — if she was indeed her mother — Maggie? It was easy with canal folk: they knew the status of a Number One.

Looking at Mrs Reading, Rosie saw the other woman nod diplomatically. 'Hope you don't think I'm pryin' . . . '

Rosie shook her head hastily. 'Not at all. I suppose I'm not altogether with it — the journey was a long one, with plenty of changes and delays . . . but the lemonade's lovely.'

Smiling, Mrs Reading wiped the bar top. 'Getting to the farm's pretty easy from here . . . '

The landlady's directions were easy enough to follow: second left and third right, then keep going and you'll see the farm in front of you. However, the lanes were long, and by the time Rosie reached Home Farm she realised that dusk was starting to fall. 'I should be in time for tea' was the first thought that entered her head, but her heart was beginning to pound. I'm going to have to pretend there's nothing wrong for the entire evening. I dare say the Plevins will want to meet me, and I'll be introduced as Maggie's daughter ... I should have stayed at the Whistlestop overnight and come first thing in the morning. That way I'd have had the whole day to talk to Maggie privately. She paused by the big five bar gate which shut the farm off from the lane. Perhaps I should go back to the pub.

'Wotcher!' a voice coming from behind caused her to jump. 'I didn't think you'd get here this evening.'

Rosie turned, and to her surprise found that the cheerful tone belonged to Maggie. A mixture of emotions held her speechless for a moment, and before she could recover another voice called, 'Come on, Maggie, let's get these cows sorted before — Oh, hello. You must be Rosie.' The speaker was a plump, friendly-looking woman with greying hair pulled back into a bun, although most of it had successfully escaped during the course of the day. 'I'm Mrs Plevin.' She smiled broadly at Rosie.

Remembering her manners, Rosie shook the older woman's hand politely. 'That's right, I'm Rosie. It's nice to meet you, Mrs Plevin.'

Maggie laid an uncharacteristically gentle hand on Rosie's shoulder and guided her towards the house. Despite the awkwardness of her situation, when they reached it Rosie stopped and stared in awe. Up one wall grew a creeper, which had already started to bud, while the cobbled stable yard reminded her of the Panks', although the stables themselves were a lot larger and considerably better maintained.

Maggie brought Rosie back to the present by rubbing her shoulder. 'Lovely isn't it? I can't wait for you to meet all the animals, but best leave it until the mornin' for that. Don't want you gettin' trodden on or kicked on your first day, do we?'

Rosie shook her head. 'Definitely not, nor on my second day either.'

Maggie laughed, but instead of the sharp or snide laughter that had characterised her in the past, this was a soft chuckle of genuine amusement. Rosie followed her into the farmhouse kitchen. Much to her surprise and relief, the room was heaving with people. Mr Plevin was sitting next to a huge open fireplace, which had an Aga fitted into it. Penny was standing beside it enthusiastically plating up some delicious-smelling food, while two older men who Rosie assumed were farmhands were sitting at the table, one reading a newspaper, the other twiddling a penny piece between his fingers. The inhabitants of the kitchen were all friendly, eager to make her acquaintance and speaking highly of her mother and her work on the farm.

'She's a grand lass, your mum,' Mr Plevin assured Rosie, who could not help noticing that Maggie raised her brows in surprise under his praise. 'Bit slow at first . . . '

'Leonard! Can't give a straight compliment, can you?' Mrs Plevin tutted at her husband, then turned to Rosie. 'Your mum's been a marvel. She's a natural with the beasts and doesn't mind a bit o' hard graft.' She looked into Rosie's face and placed a hand on the younger woman's shoulder. 'Dearie me, petal, you look worn out. Penny, give this gal the first slice o' that fish pie and she can get it down her before she goes for some rest. All these people is too much for a young 'un after a long journey like what she's had.'

Penny obediently set one of the plates in front of Rosie and handed her a fork. 'Once you've had some of Mrs Plevin's fish pie you'll feel right as rain. It always sets me up a treat.'

Rosie thanked her and tucked in. One by one the other diners began their evening meal, and Rosie listened to the general chat about their day's work. Everyone had a different tale to tell about the welfare of the animals, or how the crops seemed to be getting along. It seemed strange to Rosie to hear Maggie talking about matters that did not concern the canals. She chatted happily about the cows, referring to them by name and reporting how much milk they had produced compared to the previous day. Listening to her, Rosie thought, you would never have believed that she had not been born on a farm, she seemed so at home here.

After the meal was finished, Rosie said goodnight and followed Maggie to the room in which she was to stay for the next couple of days. 'It's just up here,' Maggie called over her shoulder as Rosie followed her up the steep and narrow staircase. 'There's a gazunder where you'd expect to find it . . . ' She opened a small wooden door and indicated that Rosie should go in first. Inside there was only enough room for a bed and a chest of drawers, on top of which there was a large ewer and basin. 'My room's across the hall from yours,' Maggie went on. 'Give me a shout in the mornin' — no, better still, I'll wake you up in the mornin' and bring you some fresh water. That okay?'

Rosie nodded wearily, and putting a hand out to stop Maggie from leaving she added, 'Sorry I'm not being very sociable. It's just that I'm so tired . . . '

Maggie placed a hand under Rosie's chin and lifted it until their eyes met. 'You really do look done in. But the food's done you some good, and when you've had some brekker in the mornin' . . . I know you like your porridge so there'll be plenty of that, and some toast too.' She gave her tummy a playful pat. 'We eat well here; probably not as good as a seaman's ration, but well enough.' She leaned forward and kissed Rosie's forehead. 'Goodnight, petal. See you in the mornin'.'

As Maggie clicked the door shut, Rosie dropped her rucksack on to the bed and sank down beside it. What a day it had been, up at the crack of dawn, then the long journey with multiple stops, squeezed into a carriage with screaming children and snoring veterans. And then there had been the peaceful bus journey, the vehicle winding its way through the narrow country lanes until it reached the village where Rosie had alighted.

She looked at the small, discoloured face of her wristwatch. It was nowhere near time for bed, but what with the arduous journey as well as the prospect of her forthcoming conversation with Maggie and its uncertain outcome she felt completely washed out. Slowly, she changed into her night things and padded over to the ewer, which to her surprise contained fresh warm water. She poured some into the basin and dipped her face flannel into it, then pulled the flannel across the back of her neck and over her face, savouring the feeling as the warm water cleaned the day's sweat and muck away. Without bothering to dry, she slipped between the crisp linen sheets and pulled them up around her ears. She closed her eyes. I must not think about Maggie and our talk tomorrow, she thought wearily. I must not . . . I must not . . .

★   ★   ★

Harri rolled her eyes in disbelief. 'Nothing has changed in the last five minutes. Now for goodness' sake will you come back in so's we can get to bed?'

Babs pouted. 'Rosie's never left the barge overnight before. She's trusting us to look after it whilst she's gone, and I for one am goin' to make

335

sure that everything's shipshape when she comes home.'

'You've checked the tarpaulin three times that I know of, the engine room umpteen times . . . what exactly are you expecting to go wrong? We're carrying cotton, not coal, so it's not likely any of the villagers will come down during the night to snatch a bucketful, now is it?'

Babs shook her head. 'I suppose I'm just anxious about Rosie visitin' her mam. I mean, how do you tell your mam that you know she ain't really your mam?'

Harri grimaced. 'I must admit, it's not something I'd want to do. Especially with someone like Maggie! I realise now that the reason she's not a natural mother is because she's not a mother at all, but it goes further than that: she's pretty horrid all round. I can't imagine there'll be tears of shame and sorrow when Rosie tells her she knows; more like tears of anger or resentment with that one.'

Babs wrung her hands. 'I *wish* she'd let us go with her, just for moral support. Even if we stayed in a nearby pub or summat, at least we'd be on hand for her.'

'I know, but you have to let Rosie do things her way.' Harri smiled wistfully. 'When we first joined the *Kingfisher*, I never saw myself with a boss like Rosie. Someone I'd end up caring about, I mean.'

'I know what you mean. I thought I was goin' to end up on a barge with someone like Captain Thorne of the *Sea Hawk* . . . ' Babs said dreamily.

Harri raised her brows. 'You thought that someone like Errol Flynn was going to be your Number One?'

Babs chuckled. 'Not really, but I did *hope* I might end up with someone like him.'

The girls had been changing into their night things whilst this conversation took place, and just as she was about to climb into her bunk Harri found herself having to put out a restraining arm to stop Babs from doing one more inspection of the barge in her nightie. 'Bed, Babs Wilcox, or I'll take Pepè's blanky off!'

Babs held up her hands in mock surrender and climbed into the small bunk. 'All right, all right, no need for threats. I'll go to sleep like a good girl.'

Harri grinned. 'And dream of Errol Flynn, no doubt!'

Settling down to sleep, Babs listened to the creaking of the hull as it cooled, whilst the water lapped gently against the wood. She smiled to herself. Both were good ingredients for a lullaby. Snuggling down, she soon drifted off to sleep.

It seemed as though she had hardly closed her eyes for more than a few minutes before she was rudely awakened. As she peered into the gloom, wondering what had disturbed her, her eyes fell on the clock; it was midnight, which meant that she had been asleep for quite some time. Sitting up in her small bunk, she rubbed her eyes, and looked over at Harri, to see if she was lying on her back snoring. She wasn't, which meant that something else was responsible for disturbing Babs's sleep. Casting her eyes around the room she could see nothing amiss, and she was about to lie back down when she heard the rattle of chains. This time she leaned over the small gap between the bunks and gently shook Harri's shoulder.

'Whatsamatter?' Harri asked drowsily. 'Is it Pepè? Damned bird . . . ' Babs placed a finger to her lips to warn her that she needed to be quiet. Harri sat up and frowned at the other girl.

Babs pointed to the towpath and whispered, 'There's someone out there, I can hear them. Someone's rattlin' chains.'

Harri frowned. 'Don't be so daft. Who on earth would be lugging chains about at this time of night? You must've been dreaming.'

Babs shook her head. 'No, definitely not. Summat woke me up and I were just about to lie down again when I heard chains clear as a bell.'

Harri moved as if to lift the curtain over the porthole, but Babs pulled at her arm. 'Don't go openin' the curtains. They'll know we're awake if you do that.'

'Who will know we're awake? And besides, what if we are? We're not the ones waking everyone up by rattling chains, are we?'

Babs swallowed hard. 'Have you ever seen *A Christmas Carol?*'

Harri swung her legs out of bed and leaned her chin on the heels of her hands. This was obviously going to be a long night. She nodded. 'Yes, I've seen *A Christmas Carol.* What of it?'

'Do you remember Jacob Marley?'

As realisation dawned, Harri pursed her lips together. 'Please don't tell me you think there's

338

some kind of ghost out there, rattling his chains?'

Babs looked hurt. 'I knew you'd laugh at me. But what other explanation is there?'

'About half a dozen, I should think. Why won't you let me lift the curtain? That way I can prove to you there's nothing to worry about.'

'Not a chance. What if you do and there's a big pair of goggly eyes staring at us through the porthole?'

Harri sighed. 'If it's a ghost, then surely it can walk through walls? A porthole's not going to stop it — ' She broke off as a distinct clinking noise came from outside.

Babs pointed a trembling finger at Harri. 'See, I told you there was summat out there! Now do you believe me?'

Harri shuffled uneasily in her bunk. 'It's probably something hitting the side of the barge. I think that's a far more likely explanation than some ghost . . . '

Babs folded her arms. 'If you're so sure, why don't you go and check? If you do, I promise to go back to sleep and not say another word about it.'

Harri's eyes widened. 'I'm *not* going out in the middle of the night in my nightie looking for ghosts. If anyone were to see me they'd think I'd gone stark raving bonkers!'

Babs raised a brow. 'Scared?'

'Scared that someone might see me and think I'd lost the plot? Yes, I suppose you could say I am, a bit.' Looking into Babs's disbelieving face she heaved a sigh. 'Pass me my coat, but I'm telling you, Babs Wilcox, after I've gone looking

339

for things that go bump in the night, such as debris in the canal, I shall expect you to keep your promise.'

Passing Harri her coat, Babs nodded. 'Are you going to take Pepè just in case?'

'In case I bump into someone, you mean? What exactly am I meant to do with Pepè? Hold him aloft and shout, 'I've got a parrot and I'm not afraid to use him'?'

Clapping a hand to her mouth Babs smothered a giggle. 'I meant you could take his blanky off and he'd kick up a right stink. It might frighten the ghost away, you never know.'

Harri grimaced. 'If I pull his blanky off and he goes off like Moaning Minnie we'll have more than ghosts to worry about. The other bargees'll wake and kick up an even bigger stink. And what am I meant to say to them? Sorry for the disturbance, but we've been doing a spot of ghost hunting, and we used Pepè as some sort of feathery exorcist?'

Babs choked again. 'All right, leave him here then. But if you need him let me know and I'll bring him out.'

Harri, wrapped in her coat, headed out of the main cabin. To her dismay a thick fog had fallen and she could barely see a couple of feet in front of her. Looking back through the main doors she saw Babs with Pepè's cage in one hand, his blanky gripped firmly in the other. Shaking her head, she stepped lightly on to the towpath. The fog made everything cold, and there was nothing to see or hear, not even the sound of ghostly chains, she thought huffily. She headed towards the engine room, just to make sure that everything was in order and nothing had come loose. The door was firmly shut, and the canvas over the cargo still strapped tightly down, and just as she turned to go back to Babs she heard a soft noise behind her, and saw a figure looming towards her out of the fog. Letting out a high-pitched scream, she bolted for the safety of the main cabin only to be brought up short when she barged into the far from ghostly figure and knocked it flying.

Hearing Harri's scream, Babs had pulled the blanky off Pepè's cage and dashed on to the deck with the squawking parrot. Within seconds, the woman from the neighbouring barge came out of her cabin, brandishing a knife. 'Where are they? They'd better not have touched my Ernie.'

'I'm looking for Harri,' Babs gasped. 'We thought we heard a ghost.'

The woman stepped on to the towpath. 'Put that bloody thing's blanket back over its cage before it sends us all deaf. And what do you mean you heard a ghost? There ain't no such thing — Gawd!' Mrs Denoven emitted a shriek. 'Ernie! Oh, Ernie, what have they done to you?'

Harri was kneeling beside Ernie Denoven. She looked up apologetically. 'Don't worry, Mrs Denoven, he's all right . . .'

Ernie Denoven groaned as he lay on the side of the towpath. 'I feel like I've been hit by a truck! What happened? The last thing I remember was someone snoopin' round the barges. The missus told me to go and check and they knocked me down. Like a bloomin' steam train they was.'

Mrs Denoven glared at Harri. 'So 'cos you two want to play silly beggars and go huntin' for ghosts in the fog, my poor Ernie's been hurt!'

Harri started to apologise, but Ernie raised a hand. 'Don't you worry your head none, love; it were a mistake, that's all. It were my fault for sneakin' up around, only I could barely see a hand in front of me face and I thought you was up to no good, you see.'

Babs leaned down beside Ernie and helped Harri pull him to his feet. 'If it was anyone's fault it was mine. I thought I heard . . . ' She glanced at Mrs Denoven, who was scowling at her. 'Well, never mind what I thought. Point is, if there was anyone snooping round the barges they'll be long gone by now.'

Ernie nodded, but his wife continued to scowl at the girls. 'I'll be 'avin' a word wi' your boss about this don't you fret!'

Back on board the *Kingfisher* Babs looked apologetically at Harri. 'I'm so sorry, Harri. I never meant for any of that to happen,' she said.

Harri was giggling so hard she had to clutch her sides. 'Don't — don't you worry, Babs. I know Mrs Denoven's quite angry about it, but she'll soon calm down and see the funny side.'

Babs chuckled. 'I bet old Ernie Denoven won't be in a hurry to tell everyone he was knocked down by a woman.'

'I should say not! He won't breathe a word about this to anyone, and I reckon he'll forbid his wife to do so either. But I'll still tell Rosie. I dare say she'll be ready for a good laugh after all she'll have been through!'

342

* ★ *

'Come on, our Rosie, rise and shine. Them cows won't milk themselves, you know.'

Rosie felt someone gently shaking her shoulder, and when she opened her eyes she saw Maggie looking at her with real affection. For a moment she thought she was still asleep, although the cold water which Maggie playfully flicked on to her face soon dispelled that notion.

Maggie smiled down at her. 'I've got the porridge on, so just you get yourself up and dressed and I'll see you down in the kitchen. Did you sleep well? I must admit I checked in on you when I came up to bed myself and you were well away.'

Rosie nodded as she knuckled her eyes. 'What time is it?' she asked, blinking blearily round the brightly lit room.

'Four o'clock, so get out of bed, sleepy head, and I'll see you — '

'Four o'clock?' Rosie squeaked. 'How long have I been asleep? You should've woken me before — ' She stopped abruptly as Maggie burst out laughing.

'Four o'clock in the morning, you goose, not the afternoon. The cows would burst if we left it that long before milking them.' She tousled Rosie's hair, and crossed the room to open the curtains. 'See? It's still dark outside, but the milking shed's well lit.'

Rosie tiptoed to the washstand, trying to keep as much of her feet off the cold linoleum as possible. She thrust both hands into the basin, and gasped. 'I — I — I thought you were bringing warm water up this morning,' she shivered as she quickly ran her hands over her face.

Maggie chuckled. 'I was going to, but when I found you still fast asleep I thought cold water would help you to wake up. I suppose I should have warned you.'

Rosie was rubbing her face with the towel, partly to get dry and partly to get the circulation back in her hands. 'I'll get dressed and I'll be right with you . . . I take it dungarees will be suitable?'

Maggie nodded. 'See you downstairs.'

When Rosie entered the kitchen a few minutes later she saw to her disappointment that Maggie was not alone. Penny, the other land girl, was also sitting at the table. 'Morning, chick. I told Maggie she should've let you lie in, but she said you were used to early risin', bein' on the canals an' that.'

Rosie sat down and pulled the proffered bowl of porridge towards her. As she took a spoonful she felt the milky goodness warm her from the inside out. She looked over to where Penny sat, also eating a bowl of porridge, and nodded. 'We work all hours at the moment, the demand's so high.' She glanced over to where Maggie stood at the Aga, pouring tea into three mugs. 'Good porridge. Just what you need after a cold wake-up call.'

Maggie pulled an apologetic face. 'Sorry about that. I s'pose I may have been a bit over-enthusiastic. Mind you, it did the trick.'

Rosie raised her brows. 'It certainly got me up and at 'em. How much time do we have before the cows have to be milked?'

Maggie smiled approvingly. 'I told Penny you was a hard little worker, but don't you fret: you've got plenty of time to get outside that porridge as well as a couple of rounds of toast. Penny's agreed to help us with the milking and then she'll do the chickens an' that while we take the cows back to their meadow. That way we can have a bit of a chat an' all, if that's okay with you?'

Rosie paused for a moment before she nodded. 'As long as you show me what to do I'm sure we'll be fine. I can't imagine it's too hard.'

The grin that spread across the other women's faces told Rosie that she might have made an error of judgement. 'There's a kind of knack to it but once you've got it you'll be all right. Best you watch me first, though, and of course Penny will help out too, so no need to worry.' As Maggie spoke she was carving a loaf of bread into thick slices. 'I'll start on the toast now, but in the meantime here's your tea, strong and sweet.'

When Rosie felt she could not take another bite, Maggie handed her a pair of wellies and an old set of overalls. 'Get these on, 'cos cows ain't fussy about where they do their business. And put these on too,' Maggie continued as she handed over a pair of large woolly socks. 'They'll keep your feet warm, and the wellies'll fit better 'n' all.'

When they got to the milking shed Rosie was surprised to see that the cows were already inside. 'Me and Penny got 'em in while you was still sleepin',' Maggie informed her. She grabbed a pail from the shelf and picked up a small three-legged stool. 'Here's what you do . . . '

When Maggie and Penny had milked half the herd, Rosie ventured a turn at the stool. At first she got more milk on herself than she did in the galvanised bucket, but after the sixth cow she seemed to be getting the hang of it. 'It's a rhythm, isn't it? Pull and squeeze, pull and squeeze . . . '

'And aim!' Maggie shrieked as she leapt out of the way of a jet of milk.

'Sorry.' Rosie giggled.

Maggie smiled, and put a hand on her shoulder. 'You're doing well, queen. It took me a lot longer to learn how to milk. Mr Plevin was right when he said I was slow to learn, although I gather Penny here was like you; a bit of a natural, you could say.'

Penny smiled reminiscently. 'Only problem I had was Mildred kicking the bucket over . . . on purpose, I might add.'

Maggie laughed. 'See the one with the black face and the white bottom, Rosie? That's Mildred. I did her today because we know that she likes to play silly beggars with people who are new to the yard.'

The next task was to transfer the big churns from the shed to the back of the milk wagon. The driver knew Maggie by name, and he clearly knew who Rosie was. 'Crikey, I cannot believe your mam got you up this early on your first day. Fair play to you, kiddo — most folk would've still been tucked up in their beds.' He nodded in Maggie's direction. 'You can tell whose daughter you are.'

Maggie smiled sheepishly. 'Get away with you, Bill. Shall we see you tomorrow?'

He nodded as he swung himself up into the driver's seat of the wagon. 'Can you shut the gate behind me?'

Maggie gave him the thumbs up and walked slowly behind the wagon until he had success-fully cleared the gateway.

She turned to Rosie. 'Come on chick, let's put these cows back in the top meadow. We don't have to go on the roads, just up a grassy track. The cows know their way, so they won't give us no trouble, and it's not far. When we get there I'll show you Cuthbert's coffin.' She chuckled as Rosie's eyes rounded in a look of horror. 'It's not a real coffin. It's a stone what's shaped like a coffin, and they calls it Cuthbert's coffin 'cos Mr Plevin's great-grandfather said it reminded him of a coffin, and his name was Cuthbert. Get it?'

Rosie nodded, watching Maggie as they herded the cows up the lane. The older woman looked as though she had been doing the job all her life. She clicked the gate shut behind the last of the cows and walked over to the brow of the meadow, indicating that Rosie should sit beside her on the coffin-shaped stone.

'I'm glad you wrote to me, our Rosie, 'cos I've been meaning to have a bit of a talk with you.'

'Snap. That's why I wrote to you too, but perhaps it's best if you say your bit first, because mine might take a while.'

Maggie looked down at her hands, and started to fiddle with her wedding ring. Looking up, Rosie noticed that the other woman looked haunted. Maggie started to speak but the words caught in her throat, so she gave a sharp cough and sat up straight. 'Before I start I just want you to know that I never intended to hurt you. It's just that I was young — younger 'n you — when . . .' She took a deep breath. 'When I met your father I was no more than sixteen and your father was twenty-five.' She looked straight into Rosie's eyes. 'And you were no more than two.'

Rosie's eyes fell as Maggie's words washed over her. She wanted to stop her, tell her that she already knew, but she couldn't: she had to hear Maggie's version of events. If she spoke out now she might never hear the truth as Maggie saw it . . .

Maggie and Jack were desperately in love, something Jack had thought he would never feel again after the loss of Rosie's mother, who had died while giving birth to their only daughter. Rosie had been born on the *Piper*, the barge on which Jack, Maggie and Rosie had travelled the Shropshire Union Canal. Her face showing no emotion save for the tears which trickled from her unblinking eyes, Rosie was aware that Maggie had stopped speaking. She looked at the older woman, her head tilted, waiting to hear the rest. Maggie sniffed loudly. 'The day your father died . . . ' Maggie continued, her voice getting higher as she went on, the words not wanting to come out and getting stuck in her throat. Jack had slipped between the lock gates as he saved his daughter from certain death.

Rosie released herself from Maggie's clasp. 'So it's true,' she said, her voice no more than a whisper. 'It's my fault my father died . . . my God, no wonder you hate me.'

Maggie clasped Rosie's hands in her own and looked earnestly into her step-daughter's face. 'It was *not* your fault that your father died! Why would you think such a thing?' She pulled back. 'I hope you didn't think that's what I meant. I don't hate you *or* blame you, my dear, darling Roseanna; if anything I blame myself . . . and your father. I should have insisted, should have kept you with me on the barge each time he took you to moor up or open the locks. I *told* him it was unsafe, I *said* it was a bad idea to take you along, but he wouldn't listen. I should have made him, should've insisted. If I'd taken control, your father would be alive today.' She released Rosie's hands and fished a handkerchief from her bra. She dabbed her eyes and blew her nose before placing the hanky in her pocket, a look of puzzlement crossing her face. 'You said 'So it's true', as if you knew . . . has someone said something to you?'

Rosie looked into Maggie's tear-wet eyes and nodded. She told the other woman all about her encounter with Ronnie, finishing with: 'She said you should have put me into an orphanage — only she called it the workhouse — but you didn't, did you? Why? You could have. You had no duty to me. I wasn't your daughter.'

Maggie looked utterly dismayed. As she spoke the tears fell freely down her cheeks, the words coming out between sobs. 'I couldn't . . . not my little Roseanna . . . my Jack's daughter. You were the last remaining tie, and I loved you like you were my own.'

Rosie lifted her chin skywards as she fought back the tears. After a moment she gathered herself together and spoke. 'But you treated me like a slave . . . as if you didn't even like me, let alone love me . . . I was more like a crew member than your daughter. You wouldn't let me go anywhere, or have any friends. That's not the behaviour of someone who loves their child.'

Maggie looked pleadingly at Rosie. 'I couldn't . . . I daren't. If I let you go off without me anything might have happened. Those kids on the canals, their parents let them do what they want, go where they want, just like Jack . . . I couldn't risk losing you, Rosie. It would have broken my heart all over again. I let you out of my control once and look what happened . . . if your father hadn't stopped you that day it would have been *you* who died in the lock . . . '

Rosie flung her arms around Maggie's neck. 'Oh, Mam, so *that's* why you were so harsh. You were protecting me.'

Maggie nodded tearfully. 'When you became Number One and Harri and Babs joined the *Kingfisher*, I knew I'd lost control over you. I became consumed with fear that something bad was going to happen. I couldn't prevent you from leaving the barge any more, not once you were in charge of those two, but I knew they wouldn't look after you the way I could. I just wanted things to go back to the way they used to be, but of course I knew they couldn't and that's why I left, before I said or did something so bad that you'd end up hating me.' Maggie looked around her. 'Coming here was the best thing I could have done. It was Ken's suggestion. He knew that the canals were getting too much, especially after we converted to an engine.' She looked at Rosie. 'The day you overheard Ken trying to persuade me that engine power beat horse power wasn't because I thought horse power was best. I knew it wasn't. It was because the *Piper* was engine powered — that was how your father was able to run it on his own — and it brought back too many memories. Jack insisted that it was me who took the barge through the locks while you and he opened them. That way you could wave to me as I went through, and anyway the locks are hard work for a woman on her own.'

Rosie cradled her mother in her arms. 'And you've been living with this secret all these years! But why?'

Maggie shook her head. 'I couldn't talk about it, not even to you. That's why I always hushed you up if you brought up the subject of your father. I thought that if I buried it all deep enough, in time things would get better, but I was wrong; they got worse. You grew up and needed more freedom — the one thing that I was terrified of giving you — and then Ken persuaded me that it was for the best.'

Rosie snapped her fingers. 'I knew there was something else. So Ken knows?'

Maggie nodded. 'He knew about the accident,

and all about you.' She looked at Rosie from beneath her lashes. 'Do you hate me?'

Rosie wiped her tear-stained cheeks with the back of her hand and shook her head. 'What, for loving my father? Or trying to keep me safe? Or keeping me out of the orphanage? Of course I don't hate you. I just wish you'd been able to tell me all this sooner; then I would have understood and we could have had a proper mother and daughter relationship.' It was Rosie's turn to clasp Maggie's hands. 'But don't they say 'better late than never'? What d'you reckon?'

Maggie hugged Rosie so tightly that she thought her mother was going to squeeze the very air out of her. 'I reckon that's the best thing I've heard for a long time.'

★   ★   ★

Fortunately the train that Rosie was to travel home on was relatively empty, and as she stood by the carriage door she slid the window down and leaned towards her mother. 'Bye, Mam. It's been so good seeing you, and I promise it won't be so long next time.'

Maggie smiled up at her step-daughter. 'I shall miss you more with every day that passes, my dear Rosie, so just you make sure you write, and tell that Tim Bradley to pull himself together.'

Rosie cast her eyes skywards and chuckled. 'I will, and I'll let you know what happens.' The whistle blew, and as the guard waved his flag a jet of steam hissed between the wheels. 'I love you, Mam. Give Mildred my best!'

Maggie was walking alongside the train. 'Will do . . . and I love you too.'

A conductor patted Rosie on the shoulder. 'Back in you come, miss. You need to take your seat and I need to shut that winder.'

Rosie obediently went into the carriage and took her seat by the window, just in time to see Maggie waving frantically from the edge of the platform. Rosie waved back until her mother was lost from view, then sank back into her seat. What a weekend it had been! She had learned more about her past in the last forty-eight hours than she had in the last twenty years; she had been taught how to milk a cow, shown how to herd pigs, and taken to find the hens' eggs in their secret laying spots.

She could see now why Maggie loved the farming life so much. For a start, the farmhands never got jealous of the amount of work you were given, and everyone was treated equally, male or female. Mrs Plevin had very kindly given her half a dozen eggs to take back to the *Kingfisher*. 'Boiled, scrambled or fried, it's a quick tea what'll fill the three of you up,' she had said as she handed over the brown paper bag.

She closed her eyes and listened to the rhythmic clickety-clack of the train. It had been the most wonderful time she had ever spent with her mother. A small smile curved Rosie's lips as she slipped into the land of dreams where she, Maggie, Ken and Tim all lived in a huge farmhouse down by the canal; Daisy was in the pasture with Merlin and the sweet aroma of freshly baked scones filled the air . . .

12

'Lime Street station . . . '

Rosie's eyes snapped open and she floundered to get off the train before it started moving once more. 'Hang on, wait for me. Don't go just yet!' she shouted as she grabbed her satchel from under her seat and cannoned out of the carriage. A porter stood on the platform, his brows raised at her hasty descent.

'You all right, luv? You look in a rare panic. 'Ave you missed your connection?' he asked, looking concerned.

Rosie gave a small chuckle. 'Sorry, no, I've not missed anything. I thought I might be stuck on the train. I fell asleep, you see . . . ' She paused as she looked wildly around her. 'You did say this is Lime Street station, in Liverpool?'

The porter laughed. 'You really were fast off, weren't you? Yes, I did say that this was Lime Street, so you've no need to panic.'

Rosie heaved a sigh of relief and smiled thankfully at the porter. As she headed for the concourse she swung her satchel on to her shoulders. Not too much longer and she would be back aboard the *Kingfisher*, and what a lot of news she would have to impart. A thought suddenly struck her. She hadn't got her friends so much as a stick of rock, and she did not feel eggs to be an appropriate gift. I'll nip to the market, she told herself; I can always get something cheap and cheerful there that the girls will love. Maybe a bag of humbugs, or some liquorice — I know they both love that.

As she neared the market, she saw a small boy standing outside the entrance. He couldn't be more than five, and Rosie could see that he had been crying. His mucky face had little clean tracks running down his cheeks.

'What's up, chuck? You lost your mam?' Rosie said kindly, bending down so that she might look into his face.

The boy nodded and wiped his nose on the back of his sleeve. 'I ha — hasn't seen her for hours and hours,' he wailed pitifully.

Rosie selected the cleaner of his hands and held it firmly in hers. 'Let's go and see if we can find her. What's your name?'

'Joey.' He sniffed. 'We was in Paddy's Market and I must've gone out the wrong entrance and I couldn't find me way back in.'

Rosie frowned. Paddy's Market was a fair distance from where they stood. 'D'you know your address?' she asked hopefully.

Joey nodded. 'Scottie Road. Don't know the number, but I know which door it is.'

Rosie gave him a triumphant smile. 'You can show me when we get there, but first I have to buy some sweets for my friends, and I'm sure I can scrape a few extra pennies' worth for little boys who've got lost . . . what do you think?'

Joey nodded eagerly, and to Rosie's relief a huge grin spread across his cheeks.

As they walked towards the Scottie — Joey wading his way through a small bag of humbugs as they went — Rosie felt that this weekend could not have gone any better. It was almost as if fate was smiling down on her for a change. I must try to ring Tim while my luck's holding, she thought.

Standing at the bottom of the Scottie, Rosie bent down and addressed little Joey. 'C'mon then, which one's yours?'

Joey's eyes blinked his incomprehension as he looked up the long road ahead of him. 'None of these,' he said matter-of-factly. 'I told you, I live on the Scottie.'

Rosie stood up, and despite herself checked the street sign on the brick building. 'But this is the Scottie Road.'

'Is it?' Joey said, his eyes rounding with astonishment. 'Oh. I don't live there then.'

Rosie gathered herself together and tried again. 'Well, where do you live? I thought you lived on the Scottie.'

Joey nodded thoughtfully. 'So did I, so I s'pose we're both wrong.'

Taking a deep breath, Rosie knew she had no choice. 'I'll have to take you to the scuffers. P'raps they can find out where you — '

Joey let out a howl of dismay. 'Not the scuffers. I don't wanna be 'rested — I's too little to go to jail! It's not my fault me mam's allus losin' me . . . '

Rosie tried to quieten Joey's wails. 'Don't worry. You won't go to jail, but they'll find your mammy for you. How about that?'

Joey sniffed and looked up at Rosie, his bottom lip jutting out. His voice wobbled when he spoke. 'Are you sure?'

Rosie nodded reassuringly. 'Positive, so you've no need to worry.'

Joey instantly brightened and clasped Rosie's hand in his, wiping his nose on the back of her sleeve as he did so. 'You're the best. Ta, queen.'

Rosie grinned back at the cheeky young cherub, then grimaced as she looked down at the mixture of mucus and dirt that now adorned her coat sleeve. Fortunately, the police station was not too far from where they stood, and the uniformed officer who stood behind the desk proved to be most helpful.

'Joey Matthews! You get lost more than any kid in Liverpool! Lemme guess, you been out shoppin' wi' your mam again?'

Rosie smiled thankfully. 'Thank goodness. I must admit, I thought we might have our work cut out. He doesn't know his address, and I did wonder how on earth — *Danny?*'

As Rosie had been speaking to the officer the small window of an office door behind him had fallen within her line of sight. There, behind a desk, sat Danny Doyle, wearing the same clothes he wore to do the stock-take.

The officer looked surprised when Rosie said Danny's name. 'Friend of yours, is he, miss? He's free if you want a word.'

Rosie shook her head, her mouth still agape. 'Is he, er, is he . . . ' she began, but stopped short as she watched him stand up from behind the desk and file some papers in a cabinet. She had been about to ask if Danny was in trouble, but it certainly did not look that way from where she was standing. 'Sorry, constable, but does Danny, erm — '

The constable cut across her. 'Work here?' He nodded. 'The inspector's been here for a couple of years now. Know him, do you?' The constable had half turned as if he were about to go and fetch Danny, so Rosie spoke quickly.

'No, not really. Not very well, at any rate.' She smoothed her coat down and smiled at Joey. 'You stay with the nice constable, Joey, and don't go wandering off again. And don't eat all those sweets at once.'

Before Joey could answer Rosie left the station, the door swinging on its hinges behind her. Her heart raced as she tried to make sense of what she had just been told. What on earth was Danny doing working both as a police officer — an inspector, no less — and as a clerk in the yard? Breaking into a trot, Rosie had decided that the sooner she got back to the *Kingfisher* the better when a hand landed heavily on her shoulder.

Squealing with fright, she turned to address her captor and found herself looking into Danny's face.

★   ★   ★

Danny pulled the chair out for her. 'Thanks for coming in here with me, Rosie. I didn't want to talk about my private business in public.'

Rosie looked around the small café. She had never been in here before. It was a workmen's café, with no waitress service, and Danny went

358

to the counter to get a pot of tea for two. When he returned he smiled sheepishly at her.

'I s'pose you were wonderin' what I've been up to in order to wind up in the nick?'

Rosie waited for him to put the tray he was carrying on the table and sit down before replying. 'Not really,' she lied. 'The scuffer behind the desk said that you've been workin' there for a couple of years, so what I really want to know is what you're doing at the boatyard and why you're pretendin' to be office staff.'

Danny looked as though she had pulled the carpet from under him. Clearly he had not been expecting such a forthright answer. She saw his Adam's apple bob nervously in his throat as he reached for the teapot. 'What did he say, exactly?'

Rosie shrugged. 'Not a great deal, just that you were an inspector and had been working at that particular station for a couple of years.' She tilted her head on one side, then leaned across the table. 'So tell me, Inspector Doyle, what the hell are you playing at?'

Danny put the teapot down and rubbed his hand thoughtfully across his chin. 'And you can stop thinking up a string of lies,' she snapped impatiently. 'I've just come back from seein' me mam, and it turns out that my whole life has been one big lie, so I'll be damned if I'm gonna sit here and listen to you spoutin' me a pile of drivel!'

Danny arched his brows. 'I wasn't going to tell you a pile of drivel. I was merely trying to work out the best way to tell you what's going on without putting you in danger.'

'Oh,' Rosie said. She had been so sure that she was about to be lied to again that she felt rather deflated. 'Sorry if I snapped; it's just that I've had rather a long weekend.'

Danny placed his hand on top of hers. 'I know it's not what you want to talk about now, but did everything work out with your — with Maggie in the end?'

Rosie was still annoyed with Danny but she had manners, good ones, which her mother had instilled in her from an early age, so she nodded politely. 'We're fine, thank you, probably better than we've ever been, but as you said, I'm not here to talk about my mam. I'm here to find out what an inspector is doing working as a stock-taker down at the canal offices.'

Nodding thoughtfully, Danny steepled his fingers and rested his chin on top of them. 'It's quite simple — the whole time I've been at the boatyard I've been working undercover because there's been a lot of smuggling and stealing going on down at the docks and we think they're using the yard to store or transfer their contraband. Pete's a good enough chap, but he could come under pressure if the thieves knew he was involved, so we've decided to keep it very hush-hush, with no one from the canal offices or the docks knowing what's going on.'

Rosie frowned. 'Well, that wasn't difficult, so why should I be in any danger?'

Danny heaved a sigh and leaned across the table, beckoning Rosie to do the same. 'If you don't say anything to anyone — not even the girls on the *Kingfisher* — then you should be fine. But knowing a secret like this can be hard to deal with. You'll find yourself watching everyone around you, and if they think you're on to them . . . let's just say they're not a nice bunch of fellers.'

Rosie was intrigued. 'You know who they are, then?'

Danny shrugged. 'Even if I did know, I can't say. It'd be as good as placing you in the firing line, not to mention the fact that you might blow my cover by accident.'

Rosie drummed her fingers on the table. 'Do I know any of them?'

Danny gave a mirthless laugh. 'I told you, I'm not at liberty to say.'

Thinking of another avenue, Rosie leaned back in her seat. 'But you said I might be in danger. Surely it'd be safer if you warned me?'

For the first time since they had entered the café, Danny looked worried and averted his eyes as he spoke to her. 'Rosie, you really are better off forgetting that we ever had this conversation.'

Rosie's heart started to thump in her chest. 'Do I know these people?'

Danny said nothing and kept his gaze firmly on the floor.

Rosie's eyes rounded as the penny dropped. 'Am I *friends* with them?'

Danny's eyes flicked up to meet hers before dropping back down. 'I really can't say, Rosie. It'd be more than my job's worth.'

Rosie looked aghast. 'And what about me? Am I more than your job's worth?'

Danny shifted uneasily in his seat. 'It's not like that, queen. You've got to understand that this is the best way of keeping you and the crew of the *Kingfisher* safe.'

Rosie's mind was racing as she sifted through her list of friends, trying to think of any who could be capable of being dangerous. She could think of none, but then another thought struck her. 'Awhile ago we came back to the *Kingfisher* after a night out and found that Pepè was soaking wet. That must mean that one of those people had been on the *Kingfisher*, so you *have* to tell me who they are.'

Danny shook his head, but Rosie was having none of it. She pushed her chair back from the table. 'If you won't help me, Danny Doyle — sorry, *Inspector* Doyle — I might as well be off.'

Danny stood up hastily and pleaded with her to sit back down. 'It was me,' he said, his tone defeated. 'I was the one who got Pepè wet.'

Rosie sank into her chair. 'You? But what were you doing on the *Kingfisher*? And what did you do to Pepè?'

Danny waved her into silence. 'I knew that you were all at the dance, and we'd had a tip-off that something was happening that evening, and that one of the barges was involved. I was checking all the boats near Tuppenny Corner and thought I'd call in on you girls just to make sure you were okay, but I bumped into Pepè's cage in the dark and must have knocked the door open somehow, because that bloomin' bird flew straight past me. He settled on the roof of the cabin, but you know what he's like. He went off like an air raid siren and in order to shut him up I chucked his blanket over him. Unfortunately, I must have thrown it a bit too hard and he and it ended up in the water. Luckily I managed to scoop him up before anything worse happened.'

Despite herself, Rosie chuckled. 'So *that's* how he got wet. We've been racking our brains trying to work out what happened. We knew the latch on his cage door was faulty, but that still didn't explain how he'd gotten so wet.' Her brow creased into a frown. 'But hang on a mo. You said you knew that we were at the dance?'

Unaware of his mistake, Danny nodded. 'Yes. What about it?'

'So why did you go into the cabin if you knew we weren't there? A second ago you said it was to check that we were all right, but you've just admitted that you knew we weren't there.'

Danny looked stunned. His voice faltered as he spoke. 'I'm not sure what you mean. I think you're getting confused. I — I — '

Rosie was having none of it.

'No more lies, Danny Doyle. Why were you on our barge? Do you think we're smuggling stuff, is that it?'

Danny looked into her angry face, his mouth gaping as he fought for an answer.

'My God, you must do! You think we're in on it!' She stood up from the table, her chair hitting the wall as it rocketed backwards. 'You can shove your pot of tea, *and* your friendship, Danny Doyle.' Reading the dismay on his face, she leaned forward. 'Oh, don't worry, your secret's safe with me. But as far as our friendship is concerned you can forget it. Anyone who could think that Harri, Babs or I would be stealing stuff, and in wartime too . . . well, they ain't no friend of mine.'

Before Danny could reply she had left the café, slamming the door behind her as she went. Hot tears coursed down her cheeks as she headed for the *Kingfisher*. How could he? I bet that's why he got friendly with me, so that he could snoop around the *Kingfisher* and see whether we had stuff hidden there. She cursed inwardly as she thought back to the Christmas and Boxing Day they had spent together, over a year before. *That's* why he wanted to be with me, so that he could have a good look round the barge. She heard running footsteps behind her and was angry to see that it was Danny.

'Rosie, please. I'd never think you capable of doing something so terrible, or Babs or Harri. I really was just checking the barges. I saw some of the lads we think are doing the smuggling coming down the towpath, so I jumped into your cabin to hide. It was on the way out, after they'd gone, that I bumped into Pepè's cage . . . and the rest you know.'

Rosie looked into his face. This time she was sure that he was telling her the truth. 'You've been here for two years, the constable said . . . tell me, did you ask me round for that first Christmas dinner just so that you could use me for information? Or did you really want to spend the day with me?'

Danny clasped her hands in his and gave her a

wry smile. 'Rosie, if the truth be known, when I followed you on to the train to Buxton it *was* to see if you had any information which I might find useful, but after I got to know you better I really did become very fond of you, and spending Christmas and Boxing Day with you was my pleasure. That's why I kissed you outside the *Kingfisher* that night.'

Rosie blushed. 'If that's the case, why didn't you try to take things further? Instead you seemed to back right off. And it still doesn't change the fact that you won't tell me who I need to be wary of.'

Danny ran a hand through his hair. 'My boss began to suspect that we were getting too close. He was worried I might let something slip, so he told me to back off.'

Rosie shook her head, a half smile on her lips. 'You really are all about your work, aren't you? Any other man would've told his boss to back off, but instead you did as he asked.'

Danny wagged a finger at her. 'None of that. He was right in what he said — I was getting too close. After all, my job is to protect the public, not put them in danger.'

Rosie opened her mouth to protest that by not telling her who to look out for he was doing exactly that, but casting a glance skywards he went on, 'And that's why I'm leaving.'

Rosie cocked an eyebrow. 'It's a bit late to worry about placing me in danger, so why are you leaving now?'

He put his hands in his pockets and sighed. 'I'm afraid my cover might be blown anyway

— and before you ask, that wasn't anything to do with you — but as a result I have to leave, for the sake of the operation, and for everyone's safety.'

Rosie shook her head. 'No — you can talk about everyone's safety, but it's the operation you're really bothered about. I've been through the mill lately, what with one thing and another, but out of all the people in my life I thought you were one of the ones I could trust. I see now that I was wrong.' Danny opened his mouth to protest, but Rosie waved him into silence. 'I'm not saying you're a bad person, Danny, you're just not the man I thought you were. When will you leave?'

'Within the next couple of days.' He jerked his head in the direction of the police station. 'Once I've explained everything my boss'll send me elsewhere.' He gave a mirthless laugh. 'Luckily for me there's stuff being transported all over this country that shouldn't be, so there's plenty of choice.'

Rosie fished around in her satchel for a fresh hanky. 'By rights, Danny Doyle, I should be glad to see the back of you and think no more about it, but I can't just switch off like that. I'd like to think that if we'd met under different circumstances . . . '

Seizing his opportunity, Danny placed a comforting arm round her shoulders. 'Who knows? Forming a relationship during wartime is hard enough, but when one of you is leading a double life . . . '

Rosie smiled up at him. 'Just make sure you keep yourself safe wherever they send you. Some of the bargees and dockers can be right nasty pieces of work, although it sounds as though you know that already.'

Danny chuckled. 'Yup, I sure do. And believe me, Rosie, if I'd thought at any point that you were in immediate danger I would have done something about it. Just trust me when I say that the less you know the better, and don't worry.' He glanced back at the police station. 'I'd best be saying goodbye. I've got an awful lot of explaining to do, and it's not going to be easy.' And before Rosie knew what was happening he had placed his hands on the sides of her face and kissed her gently on the lips. 'Goodbye, Rosie O'Leary. Take care of yourself.'

★   ★   ★

As the *Kingfisher* glided along the canal Rosie felt the hot summer sun shining down on her bare arms and legs. A few months had passed since Danny had left the warehouse and for the first time in a long while Rosie felt at ease. The workload was still high, but the other bargees on the Leeds and Liverpool seemed to have put their war with the waterway women on hold, at least for the time being. Danny's sudden departure had caused quite a stir amongst the men in the yard and Rosie could not help wondering if any of them had suspected his true identity. Babs and Simon were a thing of the past and the bubbly blonde had started to see more of Charlie.

'A girl likes to have a man pay her his full

367

attention, and not keep beggarin' off some place or other,' she had said when Harri had enquired after Simon's whereabouts one evening. 'All that Simon was interested in was keepin' me dancin' till his mates come along.'

Rosie had decided that she would grab the bull by the horns and ring Tim within the first couple of days after she had returned from Plevin's farm. She had walked to the telephone in the village and at first she had thought the instrument must be out of order as there was no queue outside it. Half of her had felt relieved as it meant she would not have to confront the situation between herself and her old friend, but when she picked up the receiver and heard the operator's voice on the other end she knew that she had to see it through.

'Is that you, Tim? It's me, Rosie. Oh, dear, I can't hear a thing, the line's ever so bad. Are you there?'

'Rosie! I can hear you, but only just. You're right — this line is awful. You're going to have to shout.'

A smile had formed on Rosie's lips. It had been a long time since she had heard his voice, and it sounded exactly the same: bright, cheery and the same old Tim.

'IS THAT BETTER?' she had bawled into the receiver.

She heard him chuckle. 'Blimey, you've still got a good set of lungs on you, I see! Perhaps I shouldn't have told you to shout.'

Despite her nerves, Rosie too had giggled. 'Sorry! How're things your end? I believe you said you wanted to talk?'

There had been a noticeable pause, and when Tim spoke again his voice had sounded uncertain. 'I do, but it's quite busy in the NAAFI tonight. I think it'd be best if I spoke to you in person.' His voice brightened. 'It's so good to hear you, Rosie. I must say I've missed you an awful lot. Would it be okay for me to come and visit you one day, on the Leeds and Liverpool I mean?'

Rosie bit her lip thoughtfully as she considered her reply. Should she mention Patsy? She could not very well say no to him without a good excuse. 'I don't see why not. I've got some news for you too — a lot of news, in fact.'

She could hear that he was grinning on the other end of the line. 'Floating nuns?' But before she could reply he had added, 'Don't mind me, I'm only pullin' your leg. I won't be able to get to you any time soon, but as soon as I can I promise you I'll be right there.' There had been an awkward pause before he spoke again, and this time his voice was more inquisitive. 'Danny won't mind, will he?'

'*Caller, your time is up. Please replace the receiver and make way for the next in line.*'

'What was that about Danny? Tim? When are you coming, do you think?' She had strained her ears, desperate to catch some sort of reply. 'Tim? Tim, are you there?'

But it was no use. The silence emanating from the earpiece informed Rosie that the operator had disconnected them. She placed the receiver carefully back, then exited the cramped red booth. As she had walked back to the *Kingfisher* her heart was singing. Tim had not sounded like a man in love with another woman, and he had said he wanted to come and see her on the *Kingfisher*.

Now Rosie smiled at the memory. She was bringing the *Kingfisher* into Liverpool, where she expected — and hoped — to find Tim waiting for her. Since that phone call they had only had one other conversation, which was to arrange a day and time to meet. The war was coming to an end — or so everyone said — and the servicemen and women were allowed very little leave, so Tim had been extremely lucky to get away at all. As she brought the *Kingfisher* round the bend she saw the familiar figure sitting on his mate's motorbike, his head craning to read the identity of the approaching barge.

'Rosie!' He was waving frantically at her. 'Well, I'll be . . . '

Babs appeared by Rosie's side and, putting her hand on the tiller, gave her Number One a nudge. 'Go on. You've been waitin' for this moment for ever such a long time.'

Taking her cue, Rosie leapt from the barge on to the towpath and ran towards her old friend, who swept her up into his arms and hugged her tightly. He set her down and planted a rather clumsy kiss on her lips, adding hastily, 'Oops, sorry. Aimed for your cheek and missed,' while giving her a large wink.

Rosie blushed and slapped his arm playfully. 'What are you like, Tim Bradley?'

He tousled the top of her hair. 'Just the same,

only more handsome, if that's possible.' He glanced shyly at her from under a thick set of lashes. 'Much like yourself, Miss O'Leary . . . I take it you are still Miss O'Leary, not Mrs something?'

Rosie's blush continued to sweep up her cheeks. 'Of course I'm Miss O'Leary, you cheeky devil. Come to that, is there a Mrs Bradley?'

Her smile froze on her face when Tim, looking surprised, said, 'Of course there is. You've met her.'

Rosie felt as if someone had squeezed all the breath from her body and stopped the hands of time. She stood staring at Tim, who was indeed still as handsome as ever, the deep tan showing off his hair, which had been bleached by the sun, and the gorgeous white teeth that gleamed when he smiled, as he did now. Before she could find her tongue, he continued, 'You've met me mam — I know you have.' He chuckled, but soon stopped when he saw that Rosie did not look amused. He pulled a face. 'Sorry, queen. I was just havin' a bit of fun.'

Rosie sniffed contemptuously. 'Doesn't bother me if you are married, Tim Bradley. While we're on the subject, how's Patsy?'

Tim grimaced. 'Now that's how you kill a conversation, by bringing that girl's name into the mix. It was because of her that I left my old station.'

As quickly as she had plunged into despair, Rosie felt her heart soar. He and Patsy were not together, and by the sound of it he didn't even like her any more. Trying to keep the delight from her face she looked enquiringly at her old friend. 'Oh, dear. Whatever happened? I thought you two were quite close.'

She listened as he repeated Patsy's confession, how she had interfered with their correspondence, and how she'd led Tim to believe that Rosie was courting one of the Gaspots. By the time he had finished Rosie felt quite dumbstruck by the enormity of his revelations.

'Blimey,' she breathed. 'I know I had reservations about her but even *I* didn't think her capable of that kind of deception.' She scowled at Tim. 'How could you have believed her? To think that I would stop writing is one thing, because obviously I thought you'd done the same, but to think that I was hanging around with thugs like the Gaspots?'

Tim grimaced awkwardly. 'I know, I know, and in my defence, I did think that if you were with one of them it was probably a mistake, before you realised who they were. But you'd stopped writing . . . '

Rosie shook her head. 'That's no excuse, Tim, and when I tell you about Maggie and Danny you'll understand why trust is such a big issue for me.'

Tim's visit was a fleeting one, and when he left later that evening the two old friends both felt as if they'd been hung out to dry.

'I've got so much more to tell you,' Rosie said as he straddled his bike, 'but I can't remember half of it. Promise you'll come and see me again?'

Tim nodded eagerly. 'Just you try and stop

me, queen.' He leaned forward and tapped his cheek with his forefinger.

'What's on it?' Rosie said, peering at the spot that he had indicated with his finger.

Tim gave her a cheeky wink. 'Your lips, if you're lucky . . . '

'Tim Bradley! You — ' But it was too late. Her voice was lost in the roar of his departing motorbike.

★ ★ ★

So far the winter of 1944 had been quite good to the bargees, with very little snow or ice. Over the summer Tim and Rosie had been in frequent contact. Tim had made his feelings for Rosie clear by asking her — in nearly every letter he wrote — whether she would be his Maid Marian. When once Rosie would have leapt at the opportunity to be Tim's girl, now she felt it better to leave things until after the war, as she told him in one of her letters.

When the war's over and things have returned to normal, we'll see how things pan out, but until then I'm just not ready to lay myself open to anyone, especially after finding out that one of my closest friends was someone completely different from who he claimed to be — a bit like Maggie, I suppose. I'm not saying no, I'm just saying not yet.

Now, sitting on one of the mooring posts, Rosie scanned the letter before her. 'I don't believe it!' she said, the misery clear in her voice. 'Me mam says Ken's been hit by friendly fire and she won't be able to come home for Christmas after all. Instead she's going to be lookin' after him at Plevin's farm — that's where they've sent him to recuperate.'

Babs pulled a face. 'Poor Ken. Is it bad?'

Rosie let out a giggle, then cleared her throat and read aloud, '*Some fool was messing by one of the ack-ack guns and the bullets just missed Ken's unmentionables — which of course is a good thing — and hit him in the top of his right thigh, so he can't walk . . .* '

Babs smothered a chuckle. 'I suppose we shouldn't laugh, but your mam's right — he has been lucky in one way, although it's a shame she won't be coming home for Christmas, especially after all the trouble you've gone to.'

Rosie sighed, and looked glumly at Babs. 'Thank goodness you and Harri decided to stay this year.'

Babs rubbed a soothing hand over her friend's arm. 'Tell you what, Charlie and Lord PeeWee suggested going for a drink in the Old Boot. Why don't you come along?'

Rosie nodded. 'That's a great idea. It'll be nice to spend some time away from work.'

Later that afternoon they all gathered on the towpath to sing carols along with the other bargees who had moored at Tuppenny Corner. As they began the chorus of 'Silent Night', Rosie looked around at her fellow carollers. Each face had a pink glow to it, and Rosie hoped that in Taddy's case it was not caused by the whisky that most of the bargees had had a small nip of before the singing began. Everyone was wrapped up in scarves and thick jumpers, underneath jackets purposely too big to allow for extra layers. There was much jigging around and stamping of feet as the singers tried to stay warm, because tonight Jack Frost had paid the Liverpool end of the canal a visit and left a sprinkling of ice that glistened in the light of the lamps some of the carollers held aloft.

When they had finished 'We Wish You A Merry Christmas' everyone had a warm mince pie, courtesy of Mrs Madison, which they ate as they headed to the Old Boot to end the day. Although Tim had told her he was unable to return to the canals for Christmas, Rosie was still hoping he might turn up to surprise her.

She turned to Babs and Harri. 'I'll join you all at the Boot, but I just want to nip up to see Daisy and Merlin, just to wish them a merry Christmas. I won't be long, so if one of you gets me a ginger beer I'll stand my round when I get back.'

When she reached the farmyard she was pleased to see that Mr Pank had got all the horses in from the fields, probably because of the lack of grass and the hardness of the ground. Hearing the familiar nicker of welcome, Rosie crossed the frosty cobbles towards Daisy. Sliding the bolts silently open, she had to push Daisy and Merlin back before she could squeeze her way into the brick stable. 'How are you, old girl?' Rosie asked, as she broke one of Mrs Madison's mince pies into two pieces. She held one out to the foal, who eagerly snuffled the tasty treat from her palm, and absent-mindedly wiped the residue of saliva on to Daisy's thick winter coat. 'Just you and me again this Christmas — family-wise, I mean,' she added quickly. 'Everyone else seems to come and go, yet you and I remain, as we always have.' Burying her face in the mare's thick mane, she let the tears trickle down her cheeks and disappear between the strands of horse-hair. 'I miss Maggie and Ken, and Tim of course, and I wish they were all here with me, but at least I still have you Daisy O'Leary, even if you aren't truly mine any more.' She stood up straight and wiped her hands across her face. 'I'm so pleased that you've settled into your new home, and that you have a family of your own now,' she said, stroking Merlin's curious muzzle as he stretched out towards her, his top lip lifting as he searched for more mince pie. Rosie giggled. 'Just like your mam, always on the hunt for food.' Before she left the warm stable she placed a gentle kiss on Daisy's soft velvety nose. 'I'll come back and see you on New Year's Day, and I'll be sure to bring something tasty with me, then you and I can celebrate the new year together.'

Walking back down the lane, Rosie took care not to slip on the frosty surface. She could see the trail of smoke puffing out of the pub chimney, and imagined the warm orange glow of the fire that would be burning in the grate. She hurried on.

When she joined her friends at one of the small round wooden tables inside, Charlie asked,

'What are you gals doin' for Christmas Eve? Me and some of the lads are goin' into town — we did that last year and it was really festive. Everyone gathers round the church and sings carols. They're doin' the same again this year. It'd be grand if you could all come along. What do you reckon?'

Babs clapped her hands together. 'I think it's a grand idea. We've not been into town for ages.' She raised a quizzical brow at Rosie and Harri.

Harri pulled a face. 'Sorry, Babs, but it's a no go for me. I promised Alby that I'd meet him in the village hall. I didn't get to see him last year.'

Babs looked hopefully at Rosie. 'I'm afraid I offered to help with the refreshments. Poor old Mrs Arkwright does it every year so I said I'd take her place.'

Babs sighed. 'I'd really like to go into town — ' she began, but Rosie interrupted before she could get any further.

'Then you must! This is yours and Charlie's first Christmas together, and by all accounts it's gonna be a grand one. I'm sure Charlie will pick you up and see you home.'

Charlie nodded hastily. 'Course I will. It's a real shame you two can't join us, but there's allus next year.'

Babs beamed with anticipation. 'Oh, go on then! It sounds so excitin'.'

Charlie twiddled his glass. 'That's settled, then. Anyone fancy another?'

* * *

377

It was mid-afternoon on the day before Christmas Eve and everyone was busy loading up ahead of the holidays. As a result, the locks had queues of barges lined up waiting to go through. Rosie and the girls had had their ticket from the canal offices. 'Rice,' Babs said, as she handed the ticket over to Charlie, who was operating the crane. 'You still on for tomorrer, chuck?'

Charlie nodded. 'You bet I am!'

'Rosie wants us to leave here and get a good spot at Tuppenny Corner. She reckons we can stop there til after Boxing Day, then take the cargo straight on to Withercoombe's.'

Charlie nodded as his workmate proceeded to loop the rope on to the crane hook. 'Sounds like what most of the bargees are doin'. You plannin' as big a meal for Boxing Day as you are for Christmas?'

Babs rolled her eyes. 'Honestly, all you ever think about is your belly! But seeing as you're askin', then yes — whatever food we don't manage to get through on Christmas Day we'll finish off on Boxing Day. Goodness knows we've enough grub to sink a ship, lerralone a barge!'

Charlie patted his stomach with one hand and looked pleadingly at Babs. 'Am I invited for Christmas dinner?'

Babs smiled and shook her head. 'You've no scruples, have you? And yes, Rosie said as how you and Lor — Alby was welcome to come and join us.'

Charlie smiled and winked at her. 'She's a good 'un, that Rosie, ain't she?'

Babs laughed. 'She sure is. You boys can finish that whisky off an' all. Ever since we opened the bottle for the carol singers it's been stinkin' the cabin out, and I'm sure Pepè's gettin' pie-eyed from the fumes. He's slurrin' his speech.'

Charlie chuckled. 'What could be more entertainin' than a drunk parrot?'

Shaking her head, Babs walked over to the *Kingfisher*, calling over her shoulder as she did so, 'See you tomorrer.'

When the *Kingfisher* was fully loaded, the girls set off. 'As soon as we get to Tuppenny Corner I'm going to go to the village and try to send me mam and Ken a telegram. You know, wishin' them all the best an' that. I thought I'd ring Tim tomorrer so's I can wish him a merry Christmas,' Rosie told the others.

Harri smiled. Ever since Rosie had returned from Plevin's farm she had not referred to her stepmother as Maggie once. 'I'll give Pepè a bit of a spruce up; you know, so that he looks good for all his guests,' she said, beaming at her crewmates. 'He loves a good party.'

Babs giggled. 'I remember the last time we had a get-together we had to stick him on the cabin roof 'cos we couldn't hear ourselves think above his squawkin'. He makes sure he's the centre of attention, I'll give him that.'

'It's such a nice crisp day, why don't you get Pepè out now and let him stretch his wings for a bit? That way you can have his cage cleaned before we moor up, and maybe after a bit of exercise he'll be less talkative,' Rosie said, crossing her fingers behind her back as she did so.

Harri smiled appreciatively. 'Good idea. If I get him all ready for Christmas now, I could come to the kiosk with you tomorrow and phone my folks.' Harri was the only person Rosie knew of whose family had their own private home telephone. Even the Plevins in their huge farmhouse had to use the village post office if they wanted to call anyone.

Rosie stood at the tiller watching Pepè flying just above the *Kingfisher;* she loved watching the colourful parrot as he glided gracefully along. His language may have been as colourful as his feathers but in the air he was truly elegant as he flew just below the tree branches, never straying far from the barge. Rosie smiled to herself as she recalled Danny's version of how Pepè got so wet.

It had been a couple of weeks after Danny had left the yard before Rosie had deemed it safe to confide his true identity to the girls. They had been halfway to Leeds when Babs had brought up the subject of Danny's sudden departure. 'I spoke to Pete in the office and he said that Danny didn't give no notice, just come in one day and packed his stuff.' She shot Rosie a meaningful glance. 'D'you reckon he got into some kinda trouble . . . or mebbe got some girl into some kinda trouble?'

Rosie's brows had shot towards her hairline. 'Babs Wilcox! How could you think such a thing? Danny's a good man. He wouldn't go runnin' off, or gettin' someone into trouble in the first place. He's not like that.'

Babs had shifted uneasily on her seat. 'Sorry. It just seems a bit odd, tekkin' off like that, and

some of the fellers down at the yard was sayin'
they reckoned — '

Rosie decided she could not listen to Danny's
name being dragged through the mud any more.
'If you must know — and I'm swearing you both
to secrecy before I say another word . . . '

Harri and Babs had leaned forward, the two of
them nodding eagerly. 'Cross me heart and hope
to die an' all that,' Babs had said, vaguely waving
the sign of the cross over her chest.

'Me too,' Harri had added when Rosie's
glance fell on her.

'This is serious, and you really must keep
shtum, but our Danny was working under cover
for the police.' Rosie had sat back triumphantly,
awaiting the anticipated ooohs and aaahs.

'Bloomin' scuffer. Might've known; 'e was far
too clean to be a regular bloke,' Babs had said,
the disappointment on her face clear for all to
see. 'I thought you were gonna say that he were
a secret millionaire, or a prince or summat, but a
scuffer? What's so hush-hush about that?'

Rosie had rolled her eyes. 'Because he was
trying to catch smugglers and thieves and stuff
like that. If the ones who were doing it had
found out who he was they could've lynched
him. Anyway, to cut a long story short he told
me his secret when I came back from seeing me
mam . . . '

Rosie had gone on to explain how she had
come across little Joey and the consequences
that unfolded as a result, finishing with the tale
of Pepè's dip in the drink.

'Goodness,' Harri had breathed. 'I'd never

have thought of that. Danny should've been more careful. He knew Pepè lived on the *Kingfisher* . . . '

Rosie had been taken aback. She had expected her friends to be amazed by her story, but instead they were either disappointed by his secret or annoyed with him for letting Pepè out. 'You're missing the point . . . ' she had begun, but Harri and Babs could clearly not have cared less so she gave up. After a month had passed, she could not help but feel that she had blown the whole thing out of proportion. Certainly the police had not found it necessary to replace him in the stockyard, so the crimes he was investigating must not have been a top priority.

Now, as they pulled up at Tuppenny Corner, Rosie jumped off the barge and set off for the village to send her telegram to Maggie, and Harri threw Babs the mooring ropes. Then looked up at the sky. 'Come on, Pepè,' she cooed, 'time for bo-bos. Mummy's done your bed and now you need to go to sleep like a good boy.'

Babs shook her head and rolled her eyes. 'For goodness sake, he's not a child, Harri.'

Harri raised her brows at Babs but continued to talk to Pepè. 'Don't you listen to the nasty lady. Of course you're Mummy's baby boy . . . '

Babs tied off the rope and threw her hands in the air. 'I give up. That bird knows an awful lot of bad language for a baby. You should wash his mouth — or should I say beak — out with soap and water.'

Harri cast Babs a hurt look and opened the

door of Pepè's cage. 'In you come darling,' she cooed, and the bird swooped straight in without a fuss. 'This door's still a bit dodgy. I'll have to get Alby to take another look at it.' She looked at Babs. 'What time are you off with Charlie tomorrow?'

Babs jumped back down on to the deck. 'He said he'd pick me up around one o'clock. Why?'

'I thought we could all give the cabin a good sort out. The hold's not entirely full, and if Rosie agrees, I thought we could store some stuff in with the cargo.'

Babs nodded approvingly. 'Sounds like a good idea to me. That way we won't have to faff around tomorrer tryin' to find space for all the food and everythin'.'

Harri nodded. 'Right. We'll ask Rosie as soon as she gets back.'

★ ★ ★

It was Christmas Eve and the girls woke later than usual. As they ate a hearty breakfast of toast followed by porridge they discussed the plans.

Standing astride the tarpaulin of the cargo Rosie gave out the orders. 'Harri and I will shift the sacks around, because they weigh a ton, and Babs, you can start getting all our things together.'

The girls were surprised to find that it took them a good hour to get the barge sorted out. 'It's like some kind of enormous puzzle,' Rosie said as they finally got themselves into some kind of order.

There was a sharp cry from the hold. 'Damn! Oh, for goodness' sake . . . ' It was Babs. 'Oh, Rosie, I'm so sorry, but when I pushed the stool back against the boards a nail must've snagged against one of the sacks on the bottom. It's split it open and some of the rice's spilt out.'

Rosie laughed. 'Don't worry, queen. It was an accident, and besides, I've got a needle and some sacking thread for just such occasions. I'll sew it up after lunch and no one'll know any different, so don't you worry.'

Babs smiled thankfully at Rosie as she climbed out from the hold. 'It was my fault, so I should be the one that fixes it.'

But Rosie shook her head. 'We work as a team here, and me and Harri haven't much to do except ring home, so there's plenty of time to fix things. Now let's get lunch or you'll be going off on your shenanigans wi'out so much as a bite inside you. No need to fasten the tarpaulin again yet — I'll tie it down properly when I've mended that sack.'

★　★　★

After lunch, Rosie and Harri helped Babs get ready for her day out with Charlie, Harri applying her rouge and mascara while Rosie brushed her blonde curls up into a bun. When they had finished they stood back to admire their work.

Harri grinned. 'Charlie won't know what hit him.'

Hearing a wolf-whistle, Babs turned and

giggled as Charlie approached, doffing his cap. 'My oh my, don't you look a picture, Miss Wilcox. I shall be right proud to take you about town and show you off as my girl.'

Babs grinned at her suitor. 'You don't scrub up so bad yerself.' Turning to Rosie and Harri, she gave each a kiss on the cheek. 'Have a good time. I'll see you later.'

Rosie chuckled. 'You too, and you, Charlie. Don't forget — although I'm sure you won't — lunch here on the *Kingfisher* at twelve sharp tomorrow!' She smiled as she watched the couple go off up the towpath arm in arm.

'That could be you and Tim if only you'd stop being so stubborn and agree to be his girl,' Harri said, an impish grin forming on her lips. 'All those years you mooned after him.'

Rosie let out a short burst of laughter. 'I did *not* moon over him, Harriet Swires, and don't you go tellin' everyone that I did.'

Harri held up her hands in a gesture of mock surrender. 'Don't shoot the observer . . . '

Shaking her head Rosie headed into the cabin. 'Come on, let's get these dishes sorted, then we can head off into the village and make those phone calls before the queues get too big.'

★ ★ ★

Standing outside the telephone kiosk, Rosie held the door open for Harri as she exited. 'Well, that's my duty done. I said I'd ring again on New Year's Day. Now you go in and ring Tim. Good luck at getting through — even though

385

there's no queue here, the operator said the lines are hellish.'

Rosie picked up the receiver and crossed her fingers. She had not arranged this phone call with Tim and had no idea whether he would be in the NAAFI or not. She waited patiently for a voice to come on the other end and was not surprised when a stranger answered.

'Hello? Is Tim Bradley there, please? It's Rosie O'Leary.'

'Strike me down, it's Tim's Rosie! Hello, Rosie, it's Jimmy here, Tim's pal. I'm afraid he's on duty at the moment, but can you ring back later on, say around three?'

Rosie felt disappointment envelop her, but she had known she was taking a risk by ringing unannounced. She ran her fingers along the telephone cord as she spoke. 'Hello, Jimmy. It's nice to finally . . . meet you. Tim talks about you all the time.'

Jimmy chuckled. 'No, he talks about *you* all the time. He'll be disappointed that he missed you. Will you be able to ring back?'

From force of habit, Rosie nodded. 'Yes, that'll be fine, I'll ring around three like you said. Happy New Year, Jimmy.'

As she left the phone box her disappointment must have been clear to see, for Harri came forward and put an arm round her shoulders. 'Never mind, queen. You thought it was a long shot.'

Rosie shrugged. 'It's not all bad. I spoke to his mate Jimmy, and he said to ring back at three.'

Harri squeezed Rosie's shoulders. 'That's

brilliant. So you'll get to speak to him before Christmas Day itself. Now all we've got to do is sew that sack up.'

'Good job you said — I'd forgotten all about that. Come to think of it, I'll have to find my needle first.'

Back at the *Kingfisher* the two girls searched every nook and cranny of the main cabin until a cry of 'Ouch' confirmed that Harri had found the sewing kit. Sucking her finger, she held the needle and twine aloft. 'C'mon, let's do this,' she said, the words muffled by the fingertip in her mouth.

Following her round to the hold, Rosie heard her cry out again, but this time it was nothing to do with a needle. When Rosie turned to see what was wrong, she found her friend cradling a small limp body in her arms. 'Oh Rosie, Pepè's dead. He must've snuck out while we were looking for the sewing kit and eaten some of the rice. I know they can't eat everything we do, and rice must be one of the things that isn't good for them.'

Rosie looked at the lifeless little form and swallowed hard. 'Maybe it's not too late. Mr Pank's good with animals — he may know what to do, and he's not too far away either.'

Without further ado, the girls raced across Scruff's field and crossed the lane into the Panks' yard. Rosie hammered her fist on the kitchen door while Harri stood, rocking from side to side, the tears trickling down her cheeks and dripping off the end of her chin to land on Pepè's scarlet tummy plumage. 'It's all my fault. I should've made sure that the cage door was properly shut. Poor, poor Pepè.'

Mrs Pank opened the kitchen door abruptly. 'What the . . . ' she began, but when she saw Harri's distress and the pathetic bundle in her arms she beckoned the two women into the house. 'Come in, my dears. I'll get my hubby.' She ran into the yard and returned a few moments later with Mr Pank, who looked deeply concerned. Gently, he lifted Pepè from Harri's arms and stroked the feathers on his neck. 'What's he ate?'

Harri gulped. 'Uncooked rice.'

Mr Pank looked up at her over the rims of his glasses. 'He's not dead, you daft mare, he's just ate too much!'

Harri and Rosie looked closely at the bird in Mr Pank's arms. As they watched, they saw his tummy rising softly.

'You great fat pig!' Harri said tremulously between tears and laughter. 'Frightened me half to death, you stupid greedy parrot.'

Rosie, on the other hand, was holding on to Mrs Pank to try to control her mirth. 'Oh, oh, Harri, Pepè really is something else. Fancy him eating so much rice that we thought he was a goner.'

Harri looked apologetically at the farmer's wife. 'I'm so sorry, Mrs Pank. You must've thought all hell'd broken loose the way we knocked on your door.'

Mrs Pank waved a sympathetic hand. 'Don't you worry, luv. Better to be safe than sorry.'

By the time they left the Panks, Pepè had begun to stir, and before they had crossed

Scruff's field he had taken his perch on Harri's shoulder. She looked across at the shelter as they walked. 'It seems ages since we were here last. I can't see Scruff anywhere. Do you reckon they've put him in for a bit?'

Rosie shrugged. 'Doubt it, but they did have a cart, if you remember. Maybe someone's taken him out for a drive.'

They carefully climbed the gate out of the field and headed for the *Kingfisher*. Rosie looked at her watch. 'Goodness, it's nearly time for me to ring Tim. We'd best get that bird of yours back in his cage and that sack sewn up.'

Placing Pepè in his cage, Harri admitted that she still couldn't shut the door properly. 'Alby tried to mend it the other day, and to be fair it's a lot better than it was, but I still wouldn't trust it. I'll ask him to take another look tomorrow, but in the meantime I'm sure if we put the blanky over and keep the main doors shut, at least we know he'll only be in the cabin, and not out stuffing his face somewhere.'

Stepping down into the hold, Harri held the torch while Rosie threaded the needle. Looking at the split sack, Rosie groaned. 'I'm afraid Pepè's made it a lot worse. Keep that light up while I try to stuff some of the rice back in. It won't be easy, but I'll do my best.'

Harri came closer and lowered the light so that it was about a foot away from the sack. Rosie began to scoop the rice back in, but unfortunately the movement made more spill out. 'Oh, heck. I'm going to have to sew this up as it is and then we'll try to find a bag to hold what's been spilt. I'll just have to explain what happened to Withercoombe's.'

Harri was peering into the sack. 'Hang on a mo. There's something in there that isn't rice . . . can you see?'

Rosie stared hard and saw the light of the torch glinting off something inside. She looked sideways at Harri, who nodded her unspoken approval, and carefully brushed some of the rice away with her finger. She turned to Harri. 'It's glass! Who on earth would put glass in a sack of rice? What if it broke? That could really hurt someone.'

Harri looked grim. 'They're probably doing it to fool the scales. You know, make it seem as though the rice is heavier than it really is.'

Rosie was frowning. 'That can't be right. The people at Withercoombe's would notice and kick up a stink . . . no, there's more goin' on here than meets the eye.' Her mind made up, she reached in and pulled out a bottle. She brushed the rice dust from the label, then held it up for Harri to see.

'Whisky! Blimey, is it full?'

Rosie nodded. 'It looks as if Danny wasn't being daft after all. The *Kingfisher's* being used to smuggle black market goods across the country.'

13

The two women sat in the main cabin of the *Kingfisher*, the bottle of whisky on the table between them.

Harri, her voice full of concern, said, 'What should we do?'

Rosie hung her head in her hands. 'Hold on. I'm trying to think.'

The pair sat in silence as Rosie picked the bottle up, then set it back down before picking it up again. 'We've sewn the sack back up and covered the cargo, so for now we're okay. We know they can't unload it until we reach Withercoombe's, so we're safe till then. I'm going to try and get in touch with Danny, although I don't know how, because we've not seen hide nor hair of him since he left the yard, and Pete told Babs they didn't even know he was going, let alone where he went.'

'But why Danny?' Harri cut in. 'Shouldn't we just go straight to the police?'

Rosie shook her head. 'He said it wasn't, but I think it's because of me that Danny had to drop the investigation, and I shouldn't imagine it went down too well with his bosses. So if we tell Danny and he solves the case he might get back in their good books, so to speak. Plus he knows us and everything that's been going on, so he'll take us seriously. The scuffers at the local station might just think that we've had one too many and we're talking nonsense. But I'll see if I can persuade them to tell me where he is, and after I've spoken to him I'll ring Tim and tell him everything.'

After a moment's contemplation Harri nodded. 'Sounds good to me, so let's get going. I don't fancy sitting here, I don't know why, it just doesn't feel right.'

'I know what you mean. It sort of makes you feel uneasy, as if they're going to suddenly spring out of nowhere, just because we've found their stash. I'll feel a lot easier when we've told Danny and Tim!'

★ ★ ★

At first no reply came from the other end of the line, but she could hear a muffled voice as the person who had picked up the phone placed their hand over the receiver and called out, 'Is there a Tim Bradley here? Tim Bradley, anyone?'

The line went quiet and then to her relief she heard Tim's voice. 'Hello, Tim Bradley here. Is that you, Rosie?'

Nodding, Rosie remembered she was on the telephone and spoke hastily into the receiver. 'Yes, it's me! How are you? I would have rung you tomorrow, but I'm guessing the lines will be even busier than today with people trying to get through.'

'I should say so. The fellers in the NAAFI reckon the phone's been ringin' off the hook all day. But that's enough of that. How's my best girl, and have you rung to say you'll be mine?'

392

'No,' Rosie said, abrupt in her desperation to get as much information across as she could before her time was up. 'You've got to listen to me carefully, Tim. Remember how I told you that my friend Danny had been investigating the stock at the yard because a lot of stuff was going missing?' Before Tim could answer she continued, 'Well, Harri and I had a bit of an adventure this afternoon. I won't go into details, but the long and short of it is that we've found hidden bottles of whisky on the *Kingfisher*. I've tried to get hold of Danny, but no one seems to know where he is. I tried to explain to the constable at his old police station what was going on, but he told me to grow up and stop wasting his time, and then he put the phone down on me. So Harri and I have decided we need to set a trap to catch the smugglers before they get a chance to move their stuff. We're bound for Withercoombe's the day after Boxing Day and we think that's where they're going to hide it. We reckon the factory owner must be in on it or — what do you think? We reckon we'll be safe enough staying on the *Kingfisher* til then, but obviously we feel a bit uneasy about it. What do you think?'

'*Caller, your time is up. Please replace the receiver . . .* ' It was the voice of the operator.

Rosie turned to Harri. 'Bloomin' operator cut us off before Tim had a chance to reply. Now what are we going to do? I suppose I could ring Scotland Road police station again and try to get them to take me seriously.'

Back in the NAAFI, Tim slammed the receiver down.

One of his comrades called out, 'Oi, steady on, Tim, it's not the phone's fault.'

But Tim wasn't listening. He was striding off in the direction of the officers' mess.

★　★　★

Sitting in the village hall, watching the dancers move across the floor, Rosie heaved a sigh. 'I can't believe that all I got was 'Thank you, we'll do our best to pass on your information'' . . .

Harri shrugged. 'You've done the best you can. You've told Tim and you've tried to get a message to Danny; all you can do now is sit and wait, and keep quiet. When we deliver the cargo, don't say a word, let them get on with it, and then when we get back to the yard we'll go to the police station in person.'

Rosie nodded dejectedly. She knew that they really didn't have a choice. They couldn't abandon the *Kingfisher*, and they couldn't apprehend the villains themselves. When the door of the hall opened Rosie saw Alby coming in. Turning to Harri, she nodded in his direction. 'Are you going to tell him?'

Harri shook her head. 'He'd want us to abandon the barge, but we both know that's something we just can't do, because if nothing else, it would arouse suspicion.'

With not long to go before midnight, Rosie had begun to give up hope of seeing Danny. She had specifically told the officer in the station where Danny might find her that evening, but she was beginning to suspect that the man on the other end of the telephone had not passed on her message.

The door to the village hall opened again and both women looked expectantly at the figure that appeared in the frame. 'What's he doing here?' Harri said, jerking her head towards Charlie. 'And where's Babs?'

Rosie pushed back her chair and stood up. 'Dunno, but I'm gonna find out.'

★ ★ ★

Tim put the stand down on the motorbike and removed his helmet and gloves. He looked at the canal office buildings, a frown creasing his brow. The yard gate was shut, as was the door to the shed, but there was a light on inside and after what Rosie had told him earlier that evening he thought it highly likely that someone was up to no good. He slipped stealthily through the gate and made his way towards the shed door. He gave an experimental turn of the handle, which opened easily under his touch, and gingerly poked his head round the frame and looked around. When he saw no sign of life, he decided to venture further inside. Taking extra care not to make a sound, he walked forward, keeping a cautious eye out for intruders as he went. He had nearly reached the back of the shed, and had started to think that maybe the light had been left on by mistake, when he heard a soft moaning coming from one of the aisles off to the side. Guardedly, he craned his neck round some crates stacked with produce and in the far corner could just make out a shape lying on the floor. Walking cautiously towards it, he said, 'Is everything all right? Do you need any help?' The figure tried to lean up on one elbow but sank back down, letting out a groan of pain as he did so.

'Blimey!' Tim had got close enough to see the man clearly. He had a black eye and a swollen lip, and blood from a head wound had formed a small pool on the floor. His clothes were torn, and he had clearly been in a fight and lost. Tim knelt down and helped the man to sit up. 'Are you okay, mate? What happened? Do you want me to call the police?'

The man held up a hand. 'I am the police. Who are you and why are you here?'

Tim stared into Danny's swollen features. 'Are you Danny Doyle?'

Danny tried to frown, then grimaced from the pain. 'I am, but you still haven't answered my question. Who are you, and what are you doing here?'

'I'm Tim Bradley. I'm a friend of Rosie's. She rang me this afternoon . . . ' Tim went on to explain how he had managed to persuade one of the officers to use his position to get word to Danny, while Tim himself was given emergency leave to make sure that Rosie was safe from harm. He had been on his way to the *Kingfisher* when he noticed a light on as he passed the canal buildings.

Danny tried to get to his feet, but his head was swimming and he fell back to his knees. He placed a hand on Tim's arm and looked up at him. 'Rosie's at the village hall near Tuppenny Corner,' he said, his voice muffled by his thick lip. 'She thinks she's safe . . . she thinks the smugglers won't try to retrieve the goods until they unload — we all did, but we were wrong. You must stop her from going back to the *Kingfisher*. If the girls turn up while the men are still there . . . '

'Who are they? I need to know just who I'm dealing with and what they're capable of.'

Danny winced as his temper rose. 'Those bloody Gaspots, that's who and the state I'm in isn't the worst they're capable of, believe me. They came back to take another shipment while the offices were empty, only of course, thanks to your message, I was here. As soon as they saw me they realised the game was up. After they'd left me for dead I heard one of them mention the *Kingfisher* and how they'd best unload it before the scuffers turned up.' He tried to stand up but once again his limbs failed him. 'I'll go and ring for back-up.'

Tim shook his head decidedly. 'You're not going anywhere. Tell me who to talk to and I'll ring the police and explain what's happened to you, and then I'll go and find Rosie. Is there still a phone in Pete's office?'

The man nodded, and handed Tim a slightly blood-stained piece of paper. 'Ask for Detective Inspector Roger — this is his office number — and tell him that Inspector Doyle's been attacked and the whisky's not in the cellar any more, it's on the *Kingfisher*. He'll know what it means, and what to do.'

Tim nodded. 'I'll tell him to send an ambulance for you, too. That's a nasty head wound you've got there.'

Danny clasped Tim's hand. 'Make sure you take care of Rosie, she deserves a man like you.' He grimaced in pain.

Tim settled Danny into a more comfortable position. 'Don't you go moving til help arrives.' And with that he turned on his heel and ran to the office.

* * *

Rosie picked her way down the narrow country lane that ran through the Panks' land, grateful to the full moon for shining brightly enough to light her path. She glanced up at the star-studded sky visible between the bare treetops. Before the war it had been known as a poacher's moon, but now it was called a bombers' moon, although thankfully bombing raids were now few and far between. In a few hours it would be Christmas Day, and the allied forces were winning the war. If you were to believe the news reports and gossip in general, it looked as though this would be the last war time Christmas. Walking on, she soon reached the path that would lead her to the *Kingfisher*. She was grateful that Charlie had walked Babs back to the barge, but even though she was sure they would not be in danger this evening she would feel more comfortable when she had told her friend what had happened in her absence.

Charlie had told Harri and Rosie that Babs

had begun to feel unwell, so he had walked her back to the barge and seen her safely inside.

'She said she didn't want anyone makin' a fuss, just to lie down quietly and get some rest. I thought I'd best come and tell you both, though, just in case she gets any worse.'

Now, as the *Kingfisher* loomed into view, even though Rosie had not expected any signs of life she still felt a wave of relief when she saw that the barge was still and dark. She was just about to step on to the deck when she heard a muffled noise coming from the back of the barge. It sounded like mewing. She craned her neck to see if a cat had climbed on board and got stuck under the canvas, but it was too dark to make anything out so she walked down to the far end, where, to her horror, she saw that the canvas had been peeled back and a lot of the sacks of rice were missing. Looking into the hold, she was thinking that at least fifteen sacks must have gone when she heard the noise again. With her heart thumping in her chest she cautiously pulled her little flashlight out of her pocket and, shielding the beam with her hand, shone it carefully in the direction of the noise.

She let out a gasp of dismay. 'Babs! Oh, Babs, what have they done to you?' Quickly dousing her torch, she stepped on to the decking and jumped down to where Babs sat, bound and gagged, in the doorway to the engine room. She pulled the gag out of her friend's mouth.

'Oh, Rosie, we've got to get out of here. There's a gang of men what've been using the *Kingfisher* to smuggle stuff across the country . . . '

Nodding, Rosie began to struggle with the bonds on her friend's wrists. 'We know, we found out this afternoon. I've tried to ring Danny, and I've told Tim, but . . . oh, Babs, you poor thing. They've tied these so tight they're cutting into your wrists!'

Babs looked confused. 'How on earth did you find out? And why didn't you tell me?'

Rosie pulled in vain at the binding. 'It's a long story, and you were out and about with Charlie when we made the discovery. We thought we'd be safe for now, and then when Charlie came to find us and said you were on the barge alone I came straight here to make sure that you were okay.'

Babs yelled out a warning. 'Rosie!'

But it was too late. Before she knew what was happening, something hard struck Rosie over the back of her head and she slumped forward, her head swimming from the blow. Darkness enveloped her as she lost consciousness.

★　★　★

When Rosie woke, there was an awful taste in her mouth and the pounding in her head was so severe she found it hard to think. The voices which filtered through the fog in her brain did not help the pain in her head. She wanted to sit up, to tell them to be quiet, but for some reason she found herself unable to move. Lying still, she was trying to gather her thoughts when she realised what the taste was. It was blood. Her brows knitted together as she tried to remember what she had done to make her mouth taste of blood. The voices proved too much of a distraction. Perhaps, if I listen to them, they might give me some clue as to what's going on, she thought hazily. She felt a tug on her wrists.

'I hope that's the last of you, only we're in a bit of a rush, see, and tyin' folk up takes time.'

Another man laughed gruffly. 'You tell 'em, Clive. They're selfish, that's what they are. We's busy men.'

'Too true,' the first man agreed, 'although I think we've enough time to have a quick look in that cabin of theirs before we leave, mebbe see if there's summat worth takin'.'

'I dunno so much. They've got that bloomin' parrot don't forget; it went off like a bloody siren last time we was havin' a look-see,' the man with the gruff voice reminded him.

'Aye, I remember. You were that frightened, you near on ended up in the drink.' The one called Clive roared with laughter. 'You should tek him; he'll be worth a fair penny.'

'I ain't havin' no stinkin' parrot, valuable or not, squawkin' its bloody head off while we're tryin' to shift bottles of whisky.' The voices faded as the men moved away.

Rosie carefully opened a bleary eye and let out a moan of despair as her gaze fell on Babs's small form beside her. 'Oh, Babs, I'm so sorry,' she whispered. 'If I'd known you were coming back to the barge earlier than planned I would've left something to warn you.' A tear trickled down her cheek. 'We didn't think they'd be coming for it til we got it to Withercoombe's, and that's

401

what I've told Tim and Danny.'

Babs gave her friend a watery smile. 'Don't worry, Rosie, it's not your fault. I'd got a real bad headache which didn't seem to be shiftin' so I come on the deck for a bit o'fresh air and I saw Scruff was standin' next to the barge, all harnessed up with his little cart. At first I thought I must be seein' things, or that he must've run off from his owners, but then the fellers spotted me and started shoutin', and before I could get back into the cabin, they had me bound and gagged before you could say knife.' She looked apologetically at Rosie. 'Honest to God, queen, it's not your fault.'

Rosie nodded thankfully. 'I know, but I can't help feelin' responsible. Is that Simon with them? The one you used to go about with?' she asked, jerking her head in the direction of the towpath and regretting the action a moment later when a feeling like a steam hammer started pounding in her skull.

Babs frowned. 'How did you know? In fact how did you know about any of this? You were beginning to tell me when one of 'em, I think it was the one called Clive, hit you on the head.'

Rosie took a deep breath and explained about Pepè's unauthorised meal and how they had found the whisky. 'Simon's one of the Gaspots, and they're notorious among the bargees for being a bunch of wrong 'uns. I'd not put anything past 'em, but everyone thought things had gotten too hot for them down on the Leeds and Liverpool, and that was why they'd moved elsewhere. Then when Tim came over that day

402

last spring, he told me Simon was one of the reasons he took up with Patsy. She must've seen you with him, but she told Tim it was me, and when he heard that he thought I'd lost my mind!' She groaned inwardly. 'I had no idea he was related to them, and to be fair he really did seem like a decent feller. Anyway, by the time Tim told me you and Simon were a thing of the past.'

'Do you think he was using me to make sure that we all cleared off so's they could move their stuff?' Babs asked, her eyes rounding.

Rosie nodded miserably. 'Afraid so. It explains why Pepè started to talk a bit funny, too. He must've heard Simon's lisp so many times that he'd started to copy him, and we just thought he sounded drunk.' She looked quizzically at her friend. 'You say they're using Scruff to move the sacks?'

Babs nodded. 'Remember the day you went snoopin' in Scruff's stable? You said you saw a couple of empty bottles, and I'm guessing those empty crates were stacked up ready for the next lot of whisky.'

Rosie hung her head in shame. 'All the clues were there in front of me. The night I heard them talking they were on about the shelter bein' in a useful place; they must've meant being able to see where the barges moored up and when the bargees had gone off for the evenin'. And they needed it to be private — I bet that's why the man said that he didn't want anyone walking across the field, and made up the story about Scruff being vicious.' Suddenly her brow creased in a worried frown. 'I've just remembered. Harri's still at the village hall . . . what if she comes looking for us?'

Babs brightened a little. 'What if she does? Surely that can only be good news for us? When she sees what's goin' on she'll go and get help.'

Rosie shook her head. 'Not if she makes the same mistake I did. Last thing we want is for Harri to get clonked on the back of the head and tied up beside us.'

'Nah, not our Harri. She's bound to work out what's goin' on. Besides, they ain't gagged us this time, so if she comes we can call out to warn her before she gets near the barge.'

* * *

Harri came out of the dance hall and stared down the lane. Out of the corner of her eye she could see the glow of a cigarette. 'Hello, Reg. Have you seen Rosie or Babs? Only I'm getting a bit worried . . .'

Reg shook his head. 'Not a sausage, but I'm sure they'll be fine. It's Christmas Eve, after all; I dare say the only thing they're in danger of is eatin' too many mince pies.' He rubbed his stomach and licked his lips. 'I'd like to be in danger from eatin' too many mince pies. My missus meks a lovely . . .'

Harri had stopped listening and was craning her neck to see if there was any sign of movement from down the lane. 'I'm just popping back to the *Kingfisher* for a bit. If Alby comes looking can you tell him where I've gone, and that I shouldn't be too long?'

Reg looked at her suspiciously. 'Everything all right down there?'

Harri nodded. 'I hope so, Reg.'

Before he could ask her what she meant Harri had disappeared down the dark lane.

★ ★ ★

It was a good ten minutes since Rosie had regained consciousness. She and Babs had decided that they would sit tight and wait for the men to leave before trying to struggle free of their bonds.

'What about Simon?' Babs asked anxiously. 'He knows I saw him. He may think I know too much and . . . and . . . '

Rosie shook her head reassuringly. 'I wouldn't worry about that. If he'd seen you as a threat you wouldn't have been bound and gagged, they'd have got rid of you straight away.'

Babs looked alarmed. 'Blimey. I suppose I should be grateful I'm here talkin' to you, then.'

Rosie pulled a face. 'Sorry — that wasn't very sensitive of me. I just didn't want you to worry unnecessarily, that's all.'

Babs frowned. 'Shh! What's that noise . . . I'm sure I heard . . . '

Now they both heard the raised voices.

'Get your ghastly thieving hands off my bird and be gone, you foul little men! I've called the police and they're on their way!'

Babs and Rosie exchanged smiles. 'Harri!' they said in unison.

There was a loud clanging sound followed by a yelp of pain. 'Get that bloody shovel off her. She nigh on took me bleedin' head off that time!'

There was another clang and this time the man with the gruff voice yelled out, 'I'll drown that bloody bird if you don't quit hittin' people with that shovel.'

A commotion followed which involved a lot of outraged cries from the men, accusing Harri of biting and kicking.

'It's like trying to rope a bull in one of them Westerns. She ain't half strong for a woman.' There was another yelp, and then Harri's substantial figure was pushed down into the hold next to Rosie and Babs. Landing hard on her knees, Harri looked up to address her aggressors. 'The police'll be here any time now,' she shouted, but the men were walking away, rubbing their various afflictions.

Rosie looked eagerly at Harri. 'Are the police really coming? Did you manage to get in touch with Danny?'

Harri looked rueful. 'I only said that to scare them. I thought it might make them leave. I didn't know they were here, so I haven't called anyone. I'm so sorry.'

Feeling deflated, Rosie gave her friends a grim little smile. 'We're safe, and that's all that matters.' She looked hopefully at Harri. 'Does Alby know where you are?'

Harri shook her head. 'Not unless Reg tells him, but I told Reg that everything was all right. Still, I don't think he believed me, so you never know your luck.'

Reg Arkwright sank his teeth into one of Mrs Bradley's mince pies and caught the falling crumbs in the palm of his hand. It had been quite an eventful night, all in all. First there was young Rosie dashing off into the night, shortly followed by Harri. Then that posh feller, Alby, had come out asking where Harri was, so Reg had told him what Harri had asked him to say should he enquire, and Alby had disappeared back into the hall. All these young folk lead such complicated lives. I wouldn't want to be twenty-one again for love nor money, not in today's world at any rate, he thought as he licked the crumbs from the palm of his hand. Frowning, he tilted his head to one side. In the distance he could hear the sound of an engine roaring along the quiet country lane. Reg tutted to himself. Some bugger's playin' silly beggars in the blackout, he thought angrily. Stepping forward, he held up a hand as he waited for the culprit to come into view. As it's Christmas I'll just give 'im a warnin' and send 'im on 'is way with 'is tail between 'is legs, speedin' round country lanes in the dark. Bet it's one of the kids. A motorbike loomed into view and skidded to a halt in front of him.

'Righty-ho! What do you think you're playin' at, racin' round in the dark? You could've killed somebody.'

'Is that you, Reg? It's me, Tim Bradley.'

A toothy smile lit Reg's cheeks. 'Tim Bradley! Well I never, I ain't seen you in a long time. How's tricks?'

Tim ignored the question. 'Is Rosie inside?'

Reg shook his head. 'None of 'em are, although Babs might be, though I don't recall seein' her goin' in . . . '

'Where are they?'

Reg pointed down the lane. 'They've gone back to the *Kingfisher*. 'Ere, what's all the fuss about? I asked Harri and she reckoned everythin' was all right, but now you're here — '

Tim shook his head impatiently. 'You must ring the police and tell them that the women on the *Kingfisher* are in danger. I've already told them but they might be busy elsewhere.'

Reg stood, his mouth gaping like a fish. 'I must tell Alby. He wanted to know where Harri was, so he can . . . ' Reg's words were lost as the sound of Tim's revving engine drowned them out.

* * *

Even though the girls were tucked out of sight, they could hear the commotion going on around the *Kingfisher*. Rosie had tried to stand up but the ropes round her wrists and ankles had forced her back down. As she started to squirm, she rolled her eyes. Whoever had trussed her up was definitely not a bargee, nor anyone from the waterways. If Rosie had executed such a poor knot Maggie would never have let her hear the end of it. She managed to slip one of her wrists free. Bringing her hands round in front of her, she soon made light work of her bonds.

'Lean forward,' she hissed to Harri, who

obeyed without question. After a moment or two, Rosie had freed her friend. She held a finger to her lips. 'I couldn't undo Babs's. Can you try?'

Harri grinned as she leaned forward and took a knife from a shelf in the engine room. 'I use it to undo some of the screws,' she explained as she began to cut through Babs's restraints.

Babs rubbed at her painful wrists and jerked her head towards the towpath, where there was a good deal of shouting, cursing and breaking of glass. 'It don't sound like they're goin' to go quietly, so even though we're the least of their worries we'd best be careful not to get caught in the crossfire.'

Rosie gingerly poked her head above the nearest sack of rice and was not surprised to see what appeared to be a whole regiment of uniformed officers battling with the Gaspot gang. Bottles were whizzing through the air as the smugglers desperately tried to make their escape. Squinting up the length of the barge, Rosie tried to focus on an object that had been placed on the roof of the main cabin. It looked vaguely familiar but at first she could not place it, until Babs, who was right beside her, whispered close to her ear, 'They'd just got Pepè's cage out of the cabin when you came round. He'll be lucky if he doesn't end up in the canal with all the ruckus goin' on.'

Harri crouched down, meaning to crawl round the water side of the barge, but Rosie shook her head. 'Stay here. I'm a lot smaller than you, so it's easier for me to get along the edge of the barge. When I reach him I'll just open the door so he can fly to somewhere safe.'

Harri gave her the thumbs up. 'Be careful. I'll keep watch.'

Rosie crept along the side of the barge in a crab-like manner, holding on to the canvas for support and keeping an eye on the fighting men. One of them was fiddling with the ropes that moored the *Kingfisher* to the bank. She groaned inwardly. If he cast them off, it would be a lot harder for the police to gain control, and goodness only knew what they would do with the girls. As she sidled along, she tried to keep one eye on Pepè's cage and the other on the man at the ropes. If I can just free Pepè first, mebbe I can tackle that feller and stop him. A familiar noise broke her concentration. Glancing in the direction of the sound she saw, to her delight, that a motorbike was bouncing wildly up the towpath.

The man who had been trying to unleash the mooring ropes gave a sharp cry. 'What the — '
He began pulling at the mooring lines in earnest.

Rosie gave an inward cheer. She knew that there was only one man who would ride a bike on the towpath at night at such high speed, and that was Tim.

As Tim drew nearer, the man started heaving frantically at the mooring lines. Tim brought the bike around in a big arc and dropped it to the ground. Sliding from underneath it he kicked the man's feet out from under him.

Without thinking, Rosie had jumped up and begun to wave at Tim when one of the smugglers made a frantic leap from the towpath on to the roof of the main cabin, knocking Pepè's cage into the water as he did so. It was the man Rosie had seen all those years ago outside the shelter. 'You!' she cried, but she got no further as the man shoved her into the canal.

Rosie fought the urge to gasp as the cold water of the canal enveloped her. Trying not to panic, she flailed around desperately as she felt for Pepè's cage.

Harri had run along the top of the cargo and was scanning the water for signs of Rosie or the bird. She had just spotted Pepè's night-time blanky, floating morosely on the canal surface, when, to her relief, Rosie erupted a few feet away from it. She could not see the cage until Rosie, struggling hard against the weight, managed to lift its ring above the surface. Lying on her stomach, Harri stretched her arms out as far as she could, and between the two of them they managed to get the cage over the side of the *Kingfisher*, giving a cry of triumph as they did so. But their joy was short-lived. When the cage was hoisted upright, the small hinged door swung freely, and there was no sign of Pepè.

Tim ran to help Rosie as she struggled to keep her chin above water. Leaning over the side of the barge, he held both hands out. 'Come on, queen, hang on to me. I'll pull you out.'

But the cold of the canal was numbing Rosie's body, and she found it hard to raise her arms. She tried to shake her head. 'I'm — I'm too heavy,' she gasped, trying to talk and tread water at the same time. 'I'll end up pulling you in.'

411

Tim leaned further forward and looked reassuringly into her eyes. 'Rosie, you have to trust me. I won't drop you and I won't let you pull me in. Now give me your hands.'

Overcome with fatigue and cold, Rosie's hands barely broke the surface before she slid beneath the water. Just in time, she felt the firm grip of Tim's hands as he grabbed the neck of her dress and pulled her, in one swift motion, straight on to the deck of the barge.

Falling into his arms, she fought for breath as she started to sob. 'Oh, Tim, I was so frightened. And poor, poor Pepè . . . '

Babs, who had been watching the last of the smugglers being cuffed and taken away, placed a comforting arm round Harri's shoulders. 'Perhaps he got free before he went in the water,' she said hopefully.

Looking up Harri spoke softly. 'There's Alby. He must've heard what's happened. He'll be so upset over Pepè. They got on really well, you know.'

Stepping from the bank of the canal on to the barge, Alby looked at the empty cage and took Harri in his arms.

Tim, who had got up to fetch Rosie a towel, heard a growl. Looking up, he saw that the large man who had shoved Rosie into the canal had broken free from his escort's grip and was heading down the towpath towards them, his eyes fixed malevolently on Rosie as he picked up one of the broken whisky bottles. 'You interferin', no good, meddlesome little bitch!' he roared.

Tim leapt from the barge and, ignoring the yells of protest from Rosie and the others, stood square in the path of Rosie's aggressor. Despite the cold numbing her body Rosie managed to stagger to her feet. Her voice hoarse, she called out feebly, 'Tim, don't, he'll kill you! Tim, please come back . . . '

But Tim wasn't listening, and the smuggler, despite being considerably larger and in possession of a lethal weapon, stopped in his tracks. Clearly, he had not expected to be attacked himself; Tim's reaction had caught him off guard, just enough for Tim to hit him square on the jaw and send him staggering backwards. 'Don't you ever lay your hands on a woman of mine again!' Tim bellowed as he brought his arm round in a clean sweep. This time, when his fist connected with the man's huge jaw it lifted him clean off his feet, and there was a satisfying thud as he landed on the floor of the engine room. Not giving his aggressor a moment to recover, Tim leapt back on board and locked the engine room door, then turned to the startled policeman who had lost his grip on the man. 'Come on. He won't get away from you this time!'

The officer leapt on to the barge and when Tim unlocked the door the two of them wrestled the man back down to the floor where the constable placed him in cuffs. 'Gerroff! That bitch deserves everything she gets,' the smuggler spat as another policeman helped to drag him out of the engine room and on to the towpath.

Tim's voice shook as he spoke. 'Why? Because

she scuppered your plans? I don't know what the punishment is for dealing in the black market during wartime, but I do know there's been a real crackdown. I shouldn't wonder if they don't make an example of you.'

The man roared his displeasure as his captors marched him towards the waiting police wagon. As Tim headed back towards Rosie and her crew, a loud cheer went up. Blushing under the attention, he turned to Rosie, who was shaking with cold. 'I'll get you a towel and some blankets . . . arggghhh!' As he opened the main cabin doors something had flown towards him, nearly knocking him to his feet in its bid for freedom, and he heard a cry of delight.

'Pepè!' Harri shouted as the bird soared past them. They watched him circle above their heads before settling on Alby's shoulder. Leaning forward, Harri stroked Pepè's plumage as she planted a big kiss on Alby's forehead. 'Thank goodness you're no good at mending cages,' she said, her eyes shining with delight. 'Pepè, my darling, have you been helping the lovely policemen arrest those nasty criminals? No, Pepè, don't do that. Alby likes you, and it's not nice to bite people who like you . . . Pepè! That's naughty!'

Despite the horror of the situation they had all been involved in, there was a small rumble of laughter, which grew steadily until they were all clutching their sides as they watched Alby trying to fend off the feathered fiend.

Regaining her composure, Rosie looked up into Tim's face. 'But how did you know where we were? I don't understand.'

Placing the warm towel around her shoulders, Tim stroked the wet hair from her face. 'After our phone call, I went off to speak to my superiors. I told them what you'd said, and they were brilliant. Even though we managed to get a message to Danny, they still allowed me to come here to make sure that you were safe. When I saw a light on at the boatyard I thought I'd ask whoever was inside whether they had seen you or the *Kingfisher*, but then I found Danny on the floor. It was clear he'd taken a good beating.' He smiled reassuringly at Rosie. 'He'll be all right, but the Gaspots had given him a fair old walloping. But that's enough about boring things like smuggling, and catching black marketeers. There's something much more important I have to ask you, and this time I hope that when I ask you to be my girl you say yes, because when the war is over I intend to make you my wife.'

Blushing, Rosie snuggled her cheek into the crook of his neck as she linked her fingers with his. 'Of course I'll be your girl. Who could refuse a man who rode halfway across the country in the middle of the night and fought off the evil villains in order to save her?' They heard a cheer go up and cries of 'Merry Christmas' filled the night air.

Looking at his wristwatch, Tim smiled. 'It's just gone midnight. You know what that means?' Without waiting for a reply, he continued, 'We're getting to celebrate our first Christmas together — the first for the rest of our lives.'

Rosie lifted her chin and looked into Tim's

eyes. 'Merry Christmas, Tim Bradley,' she whispered.

Tim leaned in and brushed his lips against hers, kissing her gently yet firmly. 'And a merry Christmas to you too, Rosie O'Leary,' he murmured, kissing her softly on the lips.

A letter to readers from Katie Flynn

Dear Readers,

There is an old adage that family should not work together, but fortunately for me, this could not be further from the truth. As many of you already know, I have suffered with M.E. for the past twenty years, and during this time I have had to rely on others for help. One of those wonderful people is my daughter, Holly, who has been working as my secretary for the past seven years — typing up sections of manuscripts, and giving me her feedback as I write. I've loved having her input on the novels.

When I was struck down with a dreadful series of infections last year, just as I was beginning to write *Christmas at Tuppenny Corner*, I found that I was too ill to even speak without coughing and it seemed that an unplanned break in our schedule was imminent. The initial infection went on for quite some time and it started to look as though there wouldn't be a book at all! Once I was back on the road to recovery, Holly and I decided this might be a good time for her to start playing a bigger part in the writing process. And we've loved working together!

Each day we discuss new ideas or characters and their progress — Katie Flynn novels have become a true team effort. At first, I was a little worried that there might be a clash of opinions, but we seem to agree on almost everything and we are united when it comes to the storyline. With all this said, this seems the perfect time to introduce to you, my daughter, Holly Flynn, of whom I am so proud.

That's all from me, thank you again for your continued support and I hope you continue to find joy in my books. Now over to you Holly . . . x

A message from my daughter, Holly Flynn

Hello Readers!

What is it like to have an author for a mother? Well, it means wonderful stories such as *Carbonel*, *Tom's Midnight Garden* and, of course, *The Chronicles of Narnia*, were part of my bedtime routine even before I could read. Mum would sit at the end of the bed and tell the stories with such heart, that the characters would come to life. This fed my imagination and created a passion for literature that remains with me to this day. Growing up in a house filled with bookshelves was like walking into a library, which I loved as there was never a shortage of reading material.

All this being said, I never dreamt for one moment that I would be involved in writing a book, let alone a saga befitting of Katie Flynn. But after working together so closely for many years, mum's influence, experience and guidance have enabled me to set off on a path full of excitement and adventure.

Looking back I am so pleased that I am now so much more involved in the writing of my mother's books. Like every child, I wanted my mother to be proud of me. Every year I have learned more from her about how to create characters, plot and storylines, and it's wonderful to now have so much more input. I love writing and am always amazed at how quickly the pages turn into chapters — before we know it, the book is there!

With *Christmas at Tuppenny Corner*, I feel so proud of what we've accomplished together, so you can imagine my delight, when mum asked if I would continue helping her to write the Katie Flynn Sagas. Of course the answer was a whoop of joy followed by a resounding 'Yes!'.

I look forward to starting a great friendship with you all, as mum has.

Holly and Katie Flynn x